WARRIOR KING

ALSO BY EVAN CURRIE

Odyssey One Series
Into the Black
The Heart of Matter
Homeworld
Out of the Black

Odyssey One: Star Rogue Series
King of Thieves

Warrior's Wings Series
On Silver Wings
Valkyrie Rising
Valkyrie Burning
The Valhalla Call
By Other Means
De Opresso Liber

Other works
Heirs of Empire
SEAL Team 13
Steam Legion
Thermals

WARRIOR KING

odyssey one

(Book5)

EVAN CURRIE

47N●RTH

Published by 47North, Seattle

www.apub.com

Amazon, the Amazon logo, and 47North are trademarks of Amazon.com, Inc., or its affiliates.

ISBN-13: 9781503935969
ISBN-10: 1503935965

Cover design by Adam Hall

Printed in the United States of America

PROLOGUE

Imperial Space, World Kraike, Capital Planet Hunter's Arm

▶ "Unbelievable."

The word was spat with such utter derision that it may well have been the vilest epithet in the Empire and, honestly, might very well become such if the contents of the meeting were ever made public.

That would *never* happen, of course.

Not if anyone in the conference hall wanted to keep their lives.

"What you're telling this council is that you authorized an expedition against the Oathers, gave said expedition access to self-replicating weapons of mass destruction . . . and they *lost* control of said weapons?"

The addressed man sighed heavily. "Essentially, yes."

"Unbelievable."

"Admiral, do reports indicate *how* your ships lost control of the Drasin?" Another man leaned forward, scowling in displeasure as he spoke. "I've seen initial reports on the development and was assured that they were under control."

"They were until this unknown species entered the scenario," the admiral said, calling up an image of the primary source of contact they had with the referenced species. "As you can see, their ship is low tech, no registrable power curve, and constructed of steel and other similar alloys."

"For a low-tech ship with no power curves, they certainly caused a lot of trouble," another council member grumbled.

"Granted. They apparently use antimatter-based weaponry, highly efficient laser weapons, and kinetic kill missiles. It is an odd mix of crude, sophisticated, and *insane* technology," the admiral admitted with a grimace.

"Antimatter? Insane indeed. How do they stabilize it?"

"We're not sure that they do."

Those who knew what the admiral was talking about exchanged incredulous looks.

"For those of us who aren't following, would someone mind filling us in?"

"Apologies, Senator," the admiral said. "Creating antimatter isn't especially difficult. We could do it ourselves easily enough, but while the power created by such a reaction is substantial, it's inherently unstable. Any stray atoms of regular matter that might infiltrate your containment structure would result in a rather explosive reaction. Eventually, storing antimatter is guaranteed to result in a critical failure, and there is no shield in existence that can contain it then. Our observations of the ship seem to indicate that it generates antimatter charges on demand, however, and then they literally sling those at their enemies with a modified electromagnetic accelerator. Crude, insane, but effective."

"They're clearly not Oathers," the first senator said finally, after everyone had taken in the admiral's words. "Nor related to the Empire in any way, otherwise they wouldn't use such a rudimentary ship design. Are those rotating habitats?"

"They are, and scanners indicate that the majority of the crew are within, using centrifugal force in the place of gravity systems."

"More than crude, then," the senator said. "Complete microgravity neophytes. An emerging world."

"Impossible!" another objected. "No emerging world could possibly have the ability to destroy Drasin squadrons."

The admiral shrugged. "We don't have enough information to be sure on that level. However, for the moment I would tend to agree with both of you. They appear to be an emerging species. Likely another seeded world, of course, and yet . . . they should *not* be at their present capabilities in that case. We're missing too much information to make a final determination. What we do know is that the Drasin *despise* them."

He looked around, his expression deadly serious. "I cannot express that enough to this council. We all know that the Drasin have a programmed hatred for life as we know it . . . It is core programming embedded in every atom of those beasts, and we've never been able to remove it. The best we could manage was to barricade it off when applied to our own ships, but even so it remained. We aimed that hatred, honed it, and loosed it on the Oathers. However, when the unknown ship entered the scenario, something changed . . ."

He hesitated, shaking his head. "Councillors, I've looked over the data telemetry from the primary first-generation Drasin that led those battles. At first, there was little reaction. The ship alone was incredibly difficult to detect, even by the Drasin . . . However, when they located the inhabited world, we lost *all* positive control. It was like the Drasin had a psychotic break, destroying our controls as they went into berserker mode. We've never seen anything like it at any point in our interactions with them."

"So what is it, exactly," the first senator asked finally, "about this world and its inhabitants that could drive the Drasin to a killing frenzy so wild as to destroy our coded leash?"

"That, Senator," the admiral said seriously, "is the very question indeed."

CHAPTER 1

Space Station Unity One, Earth Orbit

▶ Eric Stanton Weston watched the door close and waited a few seconds to be sure that the departing man was gone before turning to the admiral and speaking.

"I've heard about him," he said, referring to the man who'd just left the office. "His crew took down three of the Block's big supercarriers, the submersible ones."

"Four," Admiral Gracen said calmly. "Captain Passer's reputation in military circles almost matched yours. He would have been given the *Odyssey* command if you weren't such a hot-button topic with the press."

Eric chuckled softly. "I'm not sure how to feel about that."

"Neither is the admiralty," Gracen informed him. "Frankly, most of them wish they'd just retired you and put him in the hot seat from the start."

Eric nodded slowly, unsurprised by the fact but more than a little shocked that she was telling him about it so bluntly.

"What about you?"

"What about me?" Amanda Gracen asked with a delicate shrug of her shoulders. "I'm hardly one to cry over spilled milk, not even if it was spilled all over my home planet."

Eric grimaced. He supposed that answered that.

"In reality, I doubt he'd have done much better," she said after a moment. "Possibly he would have done far worse. You know, as I do, the Drasin were moving in our direction anyway. Maybe they'd have stopped with the Priminae; maybe they wouldn't have. If they hadn't, and if we weren't warned about their arrival ahead of time and didn't have allies to call on . . . Well, I think we got off lightly."

That wasn't something Eric would argue with. He was well aware of just what would have happened if the Drasin had landed on Earth without the entire military community standing ready to blow every last one of them back to the dust from which they came. One Drasin could become ten, and ten a hundred, in just hours. Give them *days* and they'd chew the entire world out from under your feet and leave you orbiting the Sun as a loose formation of giant spiders.

A *very* loose formation.

"Captain Passer has his orders, and now you have yours," Gracen said, handing him an electronic flimsy.

Eric accepted the clear plastic sheet, thumbing the biometric scanner automatically as he shifted the flimsy around so he could read it. The dispatch sheet was largely things he was already aware of, of course. The rumor mill was only one of the many things in human space these days that traveled faster than light, but it was still the fastest of the bunch.

"So, back to Priminae space," he said finally.

"And beyond," Gracen confirmed. "First touch base with the Priminae, assure them of our continued support, thank them for their help with the invasion and rebuilding. The new shipyard facilities they've offered to help build will be invaluable, of course."

That was no joke, Eric knew. He still had a hard time believing what he'd heard about the Priminae's Forge facility. An entire world cached deep inside the corona of a supergiant star? It wasn't the stuff of science fiction novels, it was the stuff of *fantasy*.

Alliance brass weren't planning on doing anything quite that extreme in the Sol System, but after the loss of Mars and their other space-based facilities, Earth needed the boost badly.

"Once you've managed that, take the *Odysseus* out beyond Priminae space," Gracen said. "While Passer has the *Autolycus* hunting down anomalies closer to home, I want you to backtrack the path the Drasin took when attacking the Priminae colonies and try to locate their origin point. I don't need to tell you what to do with any Drasin you happen across, I hope?"

Eric shook his head grimly.

There was no need for orders there, though he supposed they'd make it official anyway. Any Drasin ship located was to be destroyed. No quarter, no mercy. Under normal circumstances, he'd refuse any such command, but the Drasin defied "normal."

They were neither sentient, nor sapient, near as anyone could tell, but even if they were, they were simply too dangerous to leave alive. Since they were more akin to a disease than anything else, Eric considered eliminating Drasin vessels roughly on par with destroying enemy bio-weapon facilities and warheads.

A dirty job, yes. Dangerous, certainly—but without a doubt not one to be approached half-assed.

"What's the ROE for the ones holding the leash?" he asked, his tone misleadingly bland.

Gracen sat back, steepling her fingers. "That's been the subject of much debate in high circles since before the invasion."

Eric snorted. "No kidding."

She smiled thinly. "For the moment, the code is no quarter. Leave not a single ship capable of fighting if you can help it, but we're unwilling to issue the same dictate for personnel. Take prisoners if you can, but don't risk your own ship or crew in the process."

"Understood."

Eric was mildly surprised that the orders stopped there. He'd done some research into the subject and was well aware that a certain faction of military wisdom said that you didn't—no, you *couldn't*—leave an FTL or interstellar-capable enemy alive. There were just too many easy ways to commit genocide once you had that level of technology.

The Drasin were horrific, sure, but honestly, it would have been far easier and even more certain to simply buzz the solar system and nudge a few comets out of the Oort Cloud in Earth's direction. Pick the right combination of rocks and icebergs, and within a few years the human race would have gone the way of the dinosaurs.

A few might have survived on Mars along with the crews of the *Odyssey* and *Enterprise*, but the civilization of Sol would have ended with a big bang and a deep freeze.

Leaving an enemy alive who could do something like that was the height of military irresponsibility, but committing genocide yourself, that was as good as putting a gun to the very soul of your culture and pulling the trigger.

Eric didn't know what he'd decide if he were put in that position. He'd had nightmares about it since the invasion—when his dreams weren't filled with walking spiders the size of horses eating his ship from under him.

He could kill the Drasin. He could consign that whole species to the abyss without a single qualm in his soul, but he didn't know if he could do the same if . . .

Well, he'd just have to burn that bridge when he came to it.

"Understood," Eric said, standing up. "Permission to return to my ship, ma'am?"

"Granted, Captain," Gracen said, rising and extending her hand. "And do take care of her. I find myself rather fond of the *Odysseus*."

"With my soul, Admiral," Eric said, clasping her hand firmly. "I'll guard her with my soul."

"I'll hold you to that," Gracen said and smiled, some true warmth shining through in that moment.

▶▶▶

▶ Unity One was still largely under construction, but the Confederation had learned a lot in the intervening years since they'd put up their first space station. Now, with the help of the Block, they had artificial gravity pretty close to mastered, even though no one was quite willing to put a singularity reactor this close to Earth orbit just yet.

Eric made his way through the halls, heading for the docking ring. His shuttle would already be waiting to ferry him to the *Odysseus*, the beast of a ship that Gracen had brought back from Priminae space to help quash the last of the Drasin forces. The *Odysseus* was the "Warrior King," the lead ship of the new Heroic Class of starship shared between Earth and the Priminae worlds.

It was quite possibly the single most powerful vessel to exist between the stars, though Eric had his doubts. There had been too many strange new things out there recently for him to fall for the hype the media outlets were pouring out about the new ships.

Still, the Heroics measured their energy curves in *planetary masses* instead of mere terawatts, and the ships' transition drives and cannons could appear from anywhere, at any time, and lay absolute waste to anything within six light-minutes.

Frankly, Eric was *terrified* of his own ship in a way he'd never been afraid of an inanimate object before. The compressed nature of the power core meant that they were effectively living and working around a black hole of not insignificant size. Certainly, compared with the ones thought to be at the center of galaxies, the one in the *Odysseus* was effectively nothing—but it wasn't some insignificant microsingularity either.

Perhaps the core on the *Odysseus* wasn't big enough to eat star systems, but it wouldn't choke on a ship's crew by any means.

If they lost containment, the core could—and most certainly *would*—swallow up the *Odysseus* as well as anything else too close to the gravimetric shear line.

Honestly, he was rather wishing they'd just built an entire reactor around antimatter. Sure it would be at *least* as dangerous, but if that went up, it would all be over in an instant. The time compression as you closed on the event horizon would make dying by black hole a relative nightmare.

Pun painfully intended.

For all that, however, Eric had to admit that the advantages were clear. The Heroic Class of ships had near infinite power advantages over the *Odyssey* and her sister ships, and with the military tech taken from some of the best the Confederation and Block had to offer, well, they were truly monsters of the deep black.

If he had his way, then the Drasin, and whoever held their leash, would shortly be looking under their beds for any sign of the Heroics, as would the following generations for as long as they still existed in the universe.

Eric arrived at the docking ring, and he saluted the Marine guards waiting for him before walking through and across the lock seal into the shuttle.

"Captain, we're almost ready to depart. Just waiting on final clearance from Unity Control."

Eric nodded absently, grabbing a flimsy from beside his seat as he settled in. "That's fine, Lieutenant. I have some paperwork to get behind me anyway. Launch when ready."

"Aye sir."

He pursed his lips as he looked down at the flimsy, sighing at the list of mail he'd received just while speaking with the admiral.

Maybe it would have been better if they'd retired me. No more paper-work at least.

▶▶▶

AEV (Allied Earth Vessel) *Odysseus*

▶ Commander Stephen "Stephanos" Michaels scratched a phantom itch along the back of his neck, entirely displeased by the lack of hair he felt in the process. With the official disbanding of the Archangel squadron and the subsequent commissioning of the *Odysseus* into official Earth service, he'd lost the tenuous separation from the regular military that had allowed him to maintain a decidedly nonregulation haircut.

Archangel pilots were expected to be a little eccentric. Chief helm officers of the Confederation's flagship were most certainly *not* permitted the same indulgence. He was just happy that he wasn't a Marine; a buzz cut would probably have killed him.

The missing hair wasn't the source of the itch, however. Rather, he was missing the connection with the ship that his NICS allowed. All the helm officers on the Heroics had to be NICS qualified, at least for the Earth Alliance ships. He didn't think that the Priminae did the same, but then he hadn't been on their Heroics yet.

A NICS, or neural interface connection system, qualification allowed for a link between a human and a machine that went beyond most human interface systems. In his Archangel, the interface had allowed for maneuvering precision beyond belief, and on the Heroic Class *Odysseus* it did much the same.

The new system made use of Priminae computer systems, however, which were impossibly powerful.

Too bad they can't code for crap. Steph snorted softly as he walked the corridors.

The Priminae were, in so many ways, a truly bizarre people. They had access to technology that made Earth's tech base look decidedly *quaint*, yet seemed to have very little understanding of the potential within their systems. Once human coders got ahold of Priminae computers, well, the systems really started to purr.

Of course, they had to learn Priminae code first, which meant that even now there were odd bugs in the ship's core. But most of those were getting hammered out.

The end results, though, were breathtaking. Especially for a NICS pilot like himself. The *Odysseus* computer had the bandwidth to actually overwhelm the human nervous system, something his fighter computer couldn't have done in a thousand years. That meant that when he plugged into the *Odysseus*, Steph practically *became* the ship. The experience was heady, almost addictive.

That worried him sometimes, but he figured that as long as he was concerned about it, then he was probably in a decent mental space.

Steph hung a left, passing through the giant open blast doors that separated the *Odysseus'* large open gym from the rest of the ship, and paused to see who was in residence at the moment. He recognized a few of the faces instantly but had to think about many more.

The *Odysseus* wasn't quite as lucky as the *Odyssey*, taking into account a certain definition of luck. Since the official commissioning of the ship into the Confederation ranks, there had been a large influx of new faces. Certainly none of them were hopeless, but they weren't the cream of the crop that the *Odyssey* had enjoyed.

Too many Marines for that, for one. Steph smirked to himself at the thought.

He and his ofttimes mentor, Eric, had a long-standing exchange on that subject. Being a former Marine himself, Eric wasn't amused with the jarhead and leatherneck jokes Steph was likely to toss his way with regularity. Steph hadn't actually been a member of any particular military branch, having fallen between the cracks as things got desperate during the latter half of the Block War. The war had reached a point at which the hastily-tossed-together Confederation between the United States, Canada, and Mexico really didn't care about what uniform you wore, or even if you wore one, as long as you were willing to step up for the cause.

When the war ended, as a member of the Archangels, Steph had actually managed to avoid any official enlistment in any of the various military branches, because none of them wanted to let another claim the Archangel squadron.

And now here I am, wearing a Black Navy uniform. How the mighty have fallen. Steph's lips twitched at that thought.

The Black Navy uniforms were nice enough, dress whites for special occasions and space black with gold and silver trim for the rest. No hats, thank the gods. Steph had followed those proposals intently and seriously considered sending death threats to the morons who wanted them to have caps, hats, berets, or some other apparel idiocy.

We live and work in sealed habitats. Why the hell would we ever wear a hat?

He pulled off his black tunic and tossed it over a bench near a press machine. For once, some level of sanity had won out in the bureaucratic nightmare that was the chain of command. Hopefully, that would be an ongoing trend.

He doubted it though.

"Stephan?"

The light contralto voice and distinctive accent mangling his name brought Steph out of his reverie as he settled into the exercise machine. The source was approaching from over his left shoulder, but he didn't need to look around to recognize her.

"Milla," Steph said warmly as he gripped the padded arms of the press and started pushing. "Didn't know you were in here today."

"Regulations," she said as she came around in front of him, smiling slightly. "We did not have so many in the Colonies Navy."

Steph nodded, trying not to pay too much attention to the thin sheen of sweat that was making Milla's workout clothes cling to her as she moved. The Priminae *ithan*, or lieutenant, was an almost elfin-looking young lady, not much more than five feet tall, yet she'd been through a lot and come out the other side in good enough shape that he wouldn't care to underestimate her.

"Welcome to the Navy," he said a little sourly as he began a set of butterfly presses. "Travel the universe, meet new and interesting people—"

"And kill them, yes?" Milla asked, her expression a funny mix of amusement and distaste. "I have heard that joke now. Do Terrans really find such things funny?"

"Not as such," Steph said. "It's more dark humor than something you're supposed to laugh at. A commentary on the nature of things, for most people."

"Only most?"

"Some laugh; some even think it's honestly hilarious," Steph said, "but most of those are people who've lived it, and they . . . they're laughing at themselves, I find. The captain used to find it hilarious, but he was a Marine. Marines all need their heads checked. If they'd been put together right in the first place, they'd have joined the Navy or the Air Force."

Milla eyed him quizzically, recognizing that he was at least partially joking, but uncertain where exactly the humor in that statement was located. She sighed, and Stephen could see the cultural conflicts playing across her face. The Priminae were a very strange people, he reflected again. Even those who most fit in with Terran thinking were cemented so deeply in a countering cultural identity that they just didn't get Earth communication very well.

With those who were farther from the Terran mind-set, it was almost impossible to communicate at all, even when you had all the translation algorithms backing you up. You'd use the same words but never have a hope in hell of divining the meaning, and vice versa.

Just too alien.

Or maybe that was an exaggeration, Steph supposed. He'd only tried communication with a few Priminae, and the conversation had really dead-ended just a few words in. Still, none of those he had spoken to were part of their Navy.

He realized that sometimes he just got strange feelings when speaking with his alien counterparts.

Milla finally resolved whatever internal confusion she was dealing with (probably by electing to ignore it, Stephen decided) and cast a glance out of the gym. "Do you suppose we will have a mission assigned soon?"

Steph tilted his head uncertainly as he worked out. "Don't know, probably. The Heroics are good system defense, but they'd be more useful out there tracking down the remaining Drasin and whoever set them on us. I understand that there's a new class of ship coming online now too: the Rogues."

"Yes, I have seen their specifications," Milla said, crinkling her nose. "Small ships, smaller even than the *Odyssey*."

"Yeah, but with better reactors and built to fight," Steph said. "I like these floating cities we're on here, Milla, don't get me wrong . . . but you can't hide one of them from a blind man. Remember the *Odyssey*. There's power in stealth."

Milla nodded. "Truth. Still, they seem so small."

Steph couldn't help but agree. The Rogue Class destroyers would be better served as escorts than as the scout status they were likely to be relegated to. Unfortunately, for the moment there just weren't enough hulls or people to go around, and personnel were doing more jobs than they should and not always the jobs they were best at.

"Anyway, the captain will be back on board today," Steph said. "I checked the schedule. That means we're either set for more tests, or we've got a mission."

"I rather hope we have a mission," Milla admitted.

"Don't say that too loud," Steph muttered and chuckled. "Something will hear you."

She rolled her eyes. "What could possibly hear us? We are in space, Stephan."

▶▶▶

▶ The *Odysseus* had a heart.

Buried deep below the ceramic white armor that plated the outside, under the twisting composites that framed the hull, the heart of the ship didn't beat so much as hum with an intense power. The spherical core that held the heart was lined with elements that didn't occur naturally outside a high-gravity star, and even there only miniscule amounts existed.

The heart floated in the center of the chamber, always, never deviating by even a nanometer. A hundred meters across, the core was impressive in its own right, but looks can be very deceiving.

It was a very big heart.

Bigger than the physical presence it held, bigger than the ship that held it. At rest, the core massed 1.35 planetary masses, Earth standard.

Fueling the core was easy. Just dump whatever you wanted into the singularity. It wasn't picky. Rock was fine; stellar mass was more efficient, but really anything at all would do. The core would swallow up pretty much anything one cared to toss in: it was the ultimate trash compactor.

Kept just on the edge of stability, the singularity converted mass into radiation. The humans called it Hawking radiation, while the Priminae word was effectively unpronounceable by humans. But in the final analysis, the core simply consisted of high-intensity radiation.

Power aplenty to run a warship or a significantly populous planet through whatever it may have to do. That energy was raw by design, bearing no particular pattern or frequency, to increase the efficiency of the power-accumulation system.

The designers would have been shocked—and possibly disturbed—to find that was no longer *entirely* true.

Deep in the heart, so very deep in the heart of the *Odysseus*, a flower bloomed.

CHAPTER 2

AEV *Odysseus*, Earth Orbit

▶ "Captain on deck!"

"As you were," Eric said as he shifted uncomfortably in his new uniform, not having yet had the opportunity to break it in. "Ship status?"

The bridge still felt odd to him, despite his having been on it a dozen or more times since the invasion. He paused by the captain's station, let his hand drop to rest on the controls arrayed around the seat, and again noted that he rather missed the more enclosed space of the *Odyssey*. Eric felt like everything before the invasion was perhaps colored by a rosy tint, and he was now having a hard time fully trusting his judgment.

"All systems nominal, Captain," a tall blonde woman said, turning in his direction. "We're green across the board."

"Thank you, Commander Heath."

Miram Heath was his new executive officer, or XO, replacing Jason Roberts, who had been given command of the *Bellerophon*. Miram was almost six feet tall with Nordic looks, and she was a little stiffer than he'd prefer, though Roberts hadn't exactly been a smooth operator himself.

"Stand by the board for new course," Eric said.

"Aye Captain. Standing by the board," the helm duty officer replied from her position.

Miram approached Eric. "Do we have new orders, Captain?"

"We do," Eric confirmed, standing at his station and dropping an NFC, or near field communications, chip onto the surface, where it instantly connected to the ship's computer. The smooth black material lit up, showing the contents of the chip. A flick of his fingers sent the appropriate file to the helm.

"Course received. Stage one ascent to the heliopause, stage two jump to Priminae space, stage three descent to Ranquil, stage four . . ." Lieutenant Kinder frowned. "Classified and locked out. Sir?"

"I'll unlock those once we clear the heliopause, Lieutenant," Eric said. "Enter the open courses."

"Aye sir, courses accepted. All lanes report clear, and we have authorization from Unity."

"Then take us out of orbit. Port speed."

"Aye Captain. Thrusters to three-quarters . . . and we are moving," she said. "Current altitude, forty miles above sea level and climbing. Escape velocity from Earth orbit in three minutes, Captain."

"Very good. Lieutenant, have Commander Michaels report to the bridge, and let me know when we're clear to engage wave drive."

"Aye Captain."

Eric looked back to where Miram was waiting. "We're to report to the Priminae. Just a standard meet and greet—make them feel good about us being in the area."

"And the classified portions?"

"You'll find out shortly, Commander," Eric assured her before smiling. "Don't worry, I think you'll like it."

▶▶▶

▶ Steph was still arranging his uniform tunic as he crossed the threshold and stepped onto the bridge. The *Odysseus* didn't vibrate like the *Odyssey* had. The *Odysseus'* powerful wave drive had the effect of accelerating every atom within its area of influence in precisely the same direction

WARRIOR KING • 19

at precisely the same moment, unlike the old chemical propellants used by the *Odyssey*. Even so, there was a very slight sense of motion that Steph *swore* he could feel.

The engineers had told him over and over that there was no way he could feel anything, as the drive system simply didn't have any movement to feel in the classic sense. Acceleration happened in unison, with every object, every particle on the ship moving toward the forward gravity sink as one. Steph had shut the engineers up after winning enough drinks in various wagers on the subject to kill a platoon of Marines. The second they put power to the system, he knew it from wherever he was on the ship. No one had yet figured out how, not that he cared all that much.

So Steph knew as he stepped onto the bridge that the *Odysseus* was in motion. He didn't even glance at the captain's station, but instead headed straight for the helm.

"Commander," Lieutenant Kinder said as she stepped back from the secondary controls.

"I have the helm, Lieutenant," he said as he took her place.

"You have the helm, aye."

Steph stood at his station at the secondary controls, forgoing the padded and bolstered seat that housed the primaries, because it was highly unlikely that he'd need to do any precision maneuvering and he was fine standing for the moment. The course was laid in and executing by the numbers, leaving Steph with little to do but run the normal checks he always made when he took over and then scan the log to see just where they were going.

Ranquil. No surprise there.

He figured the visit was a bit overdue, though he doubted anyone on the Priminae capital planet was complaining much. Given the shake-up following the apparent end of the Drasin threat, they were probably at least as distracted as Earth's governments were, and with arguably greater reason.

While Ranquil itself hadn't been significantly touched by the Drasin, despite coming under assault at least twice, the planet was the command and control hub for over a dozen colony worlds, several of which had been entirely destroyed during the early thrust of the war. As far as he was aware, no one from Earth had a lot of contact with the civilian side of things in the Priminae worlds, but if they were anything even remotely like Earth governments . . . well, things were likely a mess there at the moment and probably would remain so for some time.

"Good check, Lieutenant," he said aloud, nodding to where she was waiting. "Dismissed."

"Aye sir."

Steph half turned, glancing back to where the captain was standing, talking quietly with the new XO. He hadn't interacted much with Miram since she'd come on board, but the scuttlebutt was that she was a bit of a hard-ass. He didn't want to know how she could be any more of one than Roberts had been. The former Army ranger hadn't *quite* had OCD, but Roberts had taken attention to detail to levels Steph had matched only while checking his Archangel.

Eric caught his eye, so Steph lifted his chin in response before turning back to his job. He'd check in with his friend later, when they both had some time.

▶▶▶

IBC (Imperial Battle Cruiser) *Piar Cohn*, Imperial Space

▶ Captain Aymes looked over the dark metal burnish that glinted from the floors of his command and nodded, satisfied.

The *Piar Cohn* was ready for service, and Aymes already had mission orders direct from Imperial Command.

Nothing could be better.

"Helm, you may bring us clear of the docks."

"Permission received, engines powering, Captain," the helmsman confirmed firmly. "Locks clear. Breaking clear of dock controls."

The big ship didn't rumble. Any vibration down to those on the nanoscale would be absorbed by the core of the *Cohn*, but Aymes felt a distant sense of movement just the same. Not everyone could, but he was one of the few who tested high enough to have a real spatial sense of movement even aboard one of the larger ships of the Imperial Fleet.

Out beyond the armored metal of the *Cohn*'s hull, the massive structure of the docks appeared to move away as the ship's engines began the laboriously slow task of launching into near space.

A few minutes later, the helmsman confirmed their launch. "Docks cleared, my captain."

"Very good. You have permission to begin ascent from the stellar well. Course to follow," Aymes said, tapping a few commands into the computer control to unlock his orders and send the course over to the navigation and helm sector.

"Permission received," the helmsman said before glancing down. "Courses received. Permission to power main drive?"

"Denied. Remain on secondaries until we clear planetary space."

Honestly, Aymes would have liked to have skipped the long, never-ending climb out of the control of the local world, but they were in the Imperial Dockyards, not some backward planet under Imperial *management*. Aymes did not want some pampered prince gunning for his head because the gravity drives dislodged a relay responsible for the socialite's favorite entertainment.

"Denied, yes, Captain. ETA to the open space . . . thirty tenth cycles."

"Very well. Go to main drives as soon as we clear planetary space."

"Permission received, only when clear of planetary space. Yes Captain."

"First," Aymes said, "you have temporary command."

▶▶▶

▶ Aymes made his way to his private office and quarters, sealed the rooms against intrusions short of emergencies from the command deck, and took a seat behind the desk that dominated the first room. His orders were straightforward enough. The *Cohn* was being dispatched as a combat scout into territory the Empire was considering for expansion.

The mission's qualifiers made the situation both confusing and more than a little disturbing. According to his orders, the area had recently repelled Imperial forays intended to pacify the region, but Aymes couldn't remember the fleet losing any ships in the recent past. Certainly not to fighting of any significant length. Now such data were rarely released to the citizenry of the Empire, of course, but generally the fleet got a heads-up somehow—even if just through rumor.

There wasn't even a hint that the Empire had been involved in fighting recently, to say nothing of having been *repelled*.

Aymes had to look up the last time the Empire had been beaten back from a region it had marked for expansion. That particular incident had occurred almost three centennials prior and involved the loss of eighty-nine heavy cruisers and over two hundred destroyers along with various support vessels.

He didn't know what was going on along this particular spiral arm of the galaxy, but it was quite clear that he wasn't being told everything.

Not that he should expect anything else, of course.

Aymes and his fellows served at the pleasure of the Imperial family and, ultimately, the empress herself. If they decreed that the information he be given be censored, it was certainly not for him to object.

Best run the crew through a few drills on the way though. They're all the best at what they do, but a little practice will save them from sucking vacuum.

▶▶▶

AEV *Odysseus*, Sol Space, Passing the Former Orbit of Mars

▶ "Number-three gun to port," Eric ordered. "Fifteen degrees up, load for effect."

"Loaded for effect, fifteen degrees up, aye."

Eric accessed the ship-wide intercom. "All hands, all hands . . . we are currently passing the orbit of Mars. I'm asking for a moment of silence and respect for what we lost here, and what we nearly lost on Earth. The *Odysseus* will fire a single salute as we pass. If you have prayers to say for the lost, now would be the time."

He keyed off the ship-wide and gestured to where Milla Chans was standing at her tactical station post. "You may fire as we pass, Lieutenant."

"Aye Capitaine," she said in her quiet voice. "Firing one in twenty seconds."

The command deck of the big ship was quiet as they passed the orbit of the former red planet, now a crumbling mass of Drasin soldier drones, most crushed by the sheer weight of their fellows. In a few million years, the Sol System would have a second asteroid belt, but for the foreseeable future, Eric supposed, Earth and its inhabitants would have to make do with a monument to the dangers of the universe and the evils that could come from the deep black.

"Salvo away," Milla reported as the number-three gun fired.

The tachyon transition cannon was the *Odysseus'* main weapon, a nuclear device capable of dispatching high megaton and gigaton explosives to any target within several light-minutes instantaneously. On the screen, just over the uneven curve that still marked the red planet's horizon, the small explosive detonated.

For a moment, a sunrise shone brightly over a portion of the ragged and fallen world, and then it was gone.

Eric let the silence hold for a moment longer, taking a breath before speaking.

"Helm, make course for the heliopause. Full power to wave drives."

"Aye Captain," Steph confirmed as he tapped in the command he'd already prepared. "Wave drives to full power. We are on course for the heliopause. ETA . . . eight hours, sir."

Eric nodded. "Thank you."

Eight hours was a fraction of the time the voyage used to take. The wave drive did away with many of the problems that used to plague the reaction drive of the *Odyssey*, including issues that arose from relativistic effects on its systems. The *Odysseus* sat securely in the middle of a warped section of space-time and simply surfed the wave while remaining in a stable state of "Earth standard" space-time.

The math made his head ache, and Eric was no slouch in mathematics, but the end result was a much faster propulsion drive that had far fewer maintenance problems than the *Odyssey*'s reaction drives had ever had. The propulsion system wasn't even an alien design, or at least it was a design that humans had come up with independently before the Priminae offered to build ships for Earth.

The Chinese scientists from the Eastern Block had built a somewhat cruder version on their own, which was one reason why many of the officers serving in even the *Odysseus*' engineering section were Chinese or other nationalities allied with the Block.

That, he hated to admit, was going to take some getting used to.

Eric had spent too many years looking at Block officers over the proverbial, and sometimes literal, rails of his guns.

I may be getting too old for this, Eric thought.

Times changed. That was a rule set in the very foundation of the universe, but men had limitations in their flexibility.

"Commander, you have command," he said as he got up from his station. "I'll be . . . on the flight deck."

"Aye sir, I have the conn," Miram confirmed, shifting stations.

▶▶▶

▶ "Marines! Left face!" the gunny bellowed as the ranks swiveled. "Forward MARCH!"

Eric stayed quietly out of sight as the Marines marched off the flight deck, having finished their own ceremony of respect for those lost on Mars. He wished he'd been on deck with them, but the captain had to be in command when nuclear weapons were to be authorized, and nothing less would have been visible over the horizon of the now-dead planet.

When the ranks were far enough away that his arrival wouldn't throw a monkey wrench into their motions, Eric stepped out onto the deck and walked across to where the colonel in charge of the *Odysseus'* Marines stood looking out over the receding curve of Mars.

"Colonel," Eric said, announcing himself. "Good ceremony?"

"Define 'good,' Captain," Deirdre Conner said, her tone a little flat.

The raw wounds of the invasion hadn't yet begun to heal for most, and Mars was and probably would remain a symbol of that pain. Eric wouldn't have had to read her file to know that the colonel had lost someone, possibly multiple someones.

"Did my Marines acquit themselves properly?" he asked.

Deirdre smiled crookedly. "Your Marines, Captain?"

"On this ship, you are all my Marines, Colonel."

"*Your* Marines performed perfectly, Captain."

"Then it was a *good* ceremony, Colonel."

He glanced over at the stocky woman in the Marine dress blue uniform. Deirdre Conner was a redhead with clear Irish roots, but somewhere along the line had picked up genes for a darker skin tone than was normally associated with Celtic blood. She'd enlisted late in the war before the Confederation Accords had been signed, crossing the border from Canada to sign up with the Corps.

That had happened frequently in those days. Canadian forces had taken a lot of hits when they'd moved to support Australian and British military in the South Pacific. Later in the war, they were willing but lacked any significant weight of metal to put men in the field.

The same dynamic happened in the south too. Mexicans, Panamanians, and various other nationalities all walked into Marine recruiting offices in such a steady stream that the phenomenon was used as evidence in support of the Confederate Charter. By the end of the war, Marines were by far the single largest service in the Confederation, and the most diverse.

"It's been a while, Deirdre," Eric said finally into the silence. "I was surprised to see your name on the candidate list."

"Oh?" She glanced archly at him. "Really now?"

Eric put up his hands in mock defense. "Claws in, hellcat. I just didn't expect that you'd put in for space duty. Last I heard, you were on the short list to take command at Parris Island. Never expected you to pass on that."

Deirdre was quiet for a short moment. "The invasion changed a lot of things. You know that better than most. Word came down that you were getting the go-ahead to track down the ones who set those things on us. That had better be true."

Eric tilted his head slightly. "Technically that's classified, at least until we leave Sol space, but that's the basic mission brief, Colonel."

"That's why I put in the transfer request."

Eric nodded slowly. "I can respect that. Just remember, Deirdre, we are professionals. Revenge is for the weak and the lost. We serve a higher calling."

"There is no higher calling than the Corps, Captain."

"Ooo rah, Colonel."

▶▶▶

▶ The *Odysseus* barreled through the solar system, hurtling at velocities that until only years earlier would have been all but unthinkable. The

Odyssey would have survived such speeds, but her forward armor plates would have needed to be pulled and replaced because of micrometeorite impacts.

Eric stepped out of the ship's transfer car onto the flight deck situated inverse to the bridge on what was considered the ship's ventral surface. Since the singularity was the source of the primary gravity impetus on the ship, many of the decks were laid out around it, making changing decks something of a challenge if you had to travel via manual access points.

The two largest orientations were above and below. While the *Odysseus*' sides did curve around the ship's singularities, the effect there was less pronounced. Basically, the lower decks were actually upside down compared with the top decks. Decks along the flanks of the ship were angled slightly as well, but Priminae gravity technology kept most of the changes controllable.

Eric walked through the open blast doors and onto the flight deck, eyes skipping past the large intra-atmospheric airframes that dominated the open space until he found what he was looking for.

The fighter had seen better days.

Her scars had been earned in honorable combat, however, and while Eric knew that his old bird was no longer deemed flightworthy by the Confederation, he was also pretty sure she had a few hours left in her.

Times change, he thought again as he stripped off his uniform tunic and pulled a large tracked tool case over beside the nose of the Archangel, snapping it open while he mentally tallied what needed to be fixed for the ship to pass inspection.

He'd handed his personal fighter over to Jennifer "Cardsharp" Samuels when pressure from the Drasin had put the squadron in a pinch for warm bodies that could qualify on NICS. When the Confederation gave her the *Bellerophon* to pilot and subsequently elected to retire the entire squadron, Eric had pulled some strings and damn well gotten his fighter *back*.

Maybe it was the last of its kind and obsolete, but if that was the case, then so was he.

"Well, let's get these plates replaced," Eric told the fighter as he grabbed a cutting torch and got ready to pop the welds that held the armor in place. "Then we'll see what kind of mess you're in under all those scrapes and dings."

"Talking to your machine, boss. Not a good sign."

Eric snorted, not even bothering to look around. "You're supposed to be on the bridge."

"Write me up," Steph said as he walked around. "The ship is tracking true, all systems green. Figured the lieutenant could use a few more hours on her book."

"Kindness of your heart, is it?" Eric asked as he used the laser torch to zap a weld.

"You know me, boss. I'm a giver."

"Of course you are." Eric rolled his eyes. "Put on a pair of goggles, would you? Last thing we need to do is blind our chief pilot."

Steph chuckled and grabbed a pair of laser-filtering glasses. "Nice to see you again too."

Eric shook his head slightly, but went back to cutting out the battle-scarred panel, talking with his friend as he worked.

It had been too long since either of them had had the opportunity to do just that.

CHAPTER 3

▶ Transitioning to Ranquil from Sol was just as disturbing as one might imagine having one's atoms split apart and tossed across space-time would be.

Oh, that wasn't *really* what the drive did, thankfully—just what it felt like.

The transition was actually more akin to being boiled than being disintegrated, which, as Eric thought about it, sounded *so* much worse. The transition drive stimulated a direct phase shift from solid matter to a tachyon state, a form of matter so unstable as to be virtually nonexistent in the universe. The change lasted only an infinitesimal period of time, by the end of which the phase shift reversed and the ship and contents returned to their normal state, dozens of light-years away from where they had started.

The process was, in a very real sense, true teleportation without any of the moral ambiguities of trying to construct an energy-conversion system. Unfortunately, transitioning didn't work reliably near significant gravity wells.

The system *would* charge and initiate a phase change, but as Eric had himself proven during a series of trials of the new Heroic Class, gravity wells could scatter the tachyons and prevent reformation.

Eric had given himself many a nightmare by *winning* that series of mock combat exercises, and probably taken a few years off the lives of some politicians who had thought the transition technology made

Earth's forces effectively invincible. Since gravity could scatter tachyons, and thus prevent proper reintegration, putting too much trust in transition technology when you were dealing with ships literally *powered* by gravity fields . . . well, it wasn't the smartest thing in the world. The things a singularity drive could do to an emerging transition would not be possible in any fair universe.

"Captain, we're being challenged," Ensign Sams announced.

Eric looked up, mildly surprised as he checked the time stamp.

"Already? Okay, I'm impressed," he admitted. "They've improved their detection net. Who is it?"

"The Priminae vessel *Posdan*, Captain."

"Is she a Heroic?" Eric asked, frowning. He didn't think so, but it was hard sometimes to keep the Priminae naming convention in his mind.

"No sir, pre-Alliance design. Similar, but no transition technology, adaptive armor, or multiclass lasers."

"Ah."

It was one of the original "giants with clubs" that both the Priminae and the Drasin had fielded and that the *Odyssey* had spent so many hours trying to avoid during their first battles.

"Well, send our bona fides," he ordered. "How close is she?"

"Eighteen light-seconds and closing, on a combat intercept course."

"Light off our colors."

"Aye aye, sir."

▶▶▶

Priminae Vessel *Posdan*

Captain Kian of the *Posdan* stepped onto the command deck of his ship, looking around at others who were already at their positions.

Not bad. Reaction times are getting better, he thought.

They should be, he knew. The crew had been drilling nearly constantly, working to improve what had once been an honestly disgraceful apathy that had infected the fleet.

"Report."

"New contact, Captain. Likely transitional signature," the instrument specialist replied. "We're waiting on challenge response."

Kian relaxed slightly, nodding. A transitional signature meant it was a returning Heroic or, most likely, one of the Terran ships. It was almost certainly *not* a Drasin vessel or squadron at any rate, so the *Posdan* was unlikely to be going into combat.

As much as he hated to admit it, that was a good thing.

His ship, as much as he loved it, could hardly go toe-to-toe with a small Drasin squadron. The most likely outcome of such a conflict was mutually assured destruction, and that was really the best he could realistically hope for. His orders in such an event were to fall back as much as he could without risking the safety of the planet, delaying the enemy until one or more of the Heroics were in position to intercept.

His *Posdan* was less than two cycles old and already obsolete, a realization that chafed Kian slightly.

"Challenge response. It's the—"

The word of who it was died in the specialist's throat as the image on the screen burst into blue, silver, and white light.

"The *Odysseus*," Kian said with a twist of his lips. "Return our colors and signal my welcome to Captain Weston and his crew."

"Shall I transmit safe passage through the defenses?"

Kian shook his head. "Confirm their challenge response with the admiral first. Procedure."

"Yes Captain."

▶▶▶

AEV *Odysseus*, Ranquil Orbit

▶ "Who's the pilot?" Eric asked as he walked the deck toward the intra-atmospheric shuttle.

"Major McQuarrie, sir," his aide, Lieutenant Lyssa Myriano, answered.

"Don't know him. Good?"

"Marine aviator, decorated. *He* was never shot down over Beijing," she replied, her tone slightly amused.

Eric shot Lyssa an arch look. "Most lieutenants would be wary of tweaking their captain so casually."

"Yes sir," she said primly.

Eric smiled a little ruefully. "Good to have you with us on this one, Lyssa. When I saw you'd re-upped, I knew I wanted you on the *Odysseus*."

"Good to be here, sir."

The first time he'd met Lyssa had been in Central Park. It hadn't really been a good time for either of them, as she had been an NYPD officer and he had been firing off a multikiloton alien weapon. Gun laws hadn't been high on either of their minds at the time, however, and he was happy to have her in the service once more.

We need every good hand we can get.

A lot of good people had died during the Drasin event, which was hard to call an invasion considering the Drasin were almost more of a force of nature than an army. After the long battle was over, though, recruitment levels went through the roof. The Alliance Black Navy had *far* more people applying now than it had ships to crew.

That was going to change, and soon. For now, the Heroics still had priority for crew selection—within reason—despite the higher demand across the fleet. Eric hadn't hesitated when it came to selecting his crew, or his new aide.

He and Lyssa stepped onto the shuttle, dropping into the heavily bolstered seats and strapping in tight.

"Admiral Tanner is unassuming," he said casually. "He comes across more like a grunt than an officer, right up until you see how his people treat him. Show respect, but don't dance around. He'll answer questions straight if you ask them straight."

"Yes sir," Lyssa answered. "And the Elders?"

"They're . . . different." Frankly, he didn't know how to describe the likes of Elder Corusc. "Think . . . realistic pacifists," he said finally. "*Very* uninterested in conflict of any type, but not to the point of cultural suicide. Not sure how they'd deal with any threat below Drasin levels, honestly."

"That's not comforting."

Eric shrugged as the turbines on the shuttle whined to life. "That's the universe in which we live, Lieutenant. Deal with it."

"Yes sir."

They shifted as the shuttle was pulled out of its lockdown position and moved into the ready one slot for launch. Clearance took only a few moments. Then the turbines' whine climbed to a roar as Eric and Lyssa were slammed to the side of their seats by acceleration as the shuttle flung itself out into the void.

▶▶▶

IBC *Piar Cohn*, Deep Black

▶ At maximum nonmilitary cruise, the *Piar Cohn* barreled through space at just over a thousand lights. That wasn't the fastest speed in the Empire, but it was respectable, and in a pinch Aymes knew his ship could pull another two hundred without overly stressing the wave-generation system. More than that and there was a fair to good chance of them blowing something irreplaceable and never seeing home again.

He was standing in the forward officers' lounge, one of the few places on the ship that offered a "view," such as it was. The thickly armored screens ahead of him were transparent, so he could look out at the visible moving stars, all blueshifted as the *Cohn* raced toward them.

Occasionally, a particularly close stellar body, ten light-years away or so, would streak past dramatically, but for the most part there was more of an ordered procession to be observed than a rampant rush into the future.

"Captain."

Aymes didn't turn around at the voice. He continued to watch the procession. "Yes First?"

"We are approaching the first checkpoint, sir. Long-range instruments detect no sign of the targets."

Aymes nodded slowly. Not really anything unexpected there.

"Proceed as scheduled. I'll make further decisions once we've got better scans."

"Yes Captain."

They wouldn't find any sign of the Drasin at their first stop, Aymes would bank on that. No useful sign, at least. The Drasin left unmistakable carnage behind them, marked into the very worlds of every system they touched, but what the *Cohn* was looking for was any information on where they had *gone*.

That wasn't going to be located so easily.

Still, he and his crew had to check by the numbers, just to be certain. The risks were too great to do otherwise.

He shuddered to think of what would have happened if the Drasin had been lost with a sufficient breeding group of first-generation drones. As it was, the havoc they would wreak was nearly incalculable, but if they had sufficient resources to propagate a new first generation . . . well, not even the Empire would be safe, he'd bet.

Frankly, Aymes thought that the Department of War was flat-out insane for unleashing such things on the universe. What good were systems that had been emptied of their most viable worlds? Certainly, the Drasin made for excellent terror weapons and a shatteringly impressive strategic threat, but from what he'd read, the orders for the last series of incursions into Oather space had been anything but strategic.

Should have cut through the small colonies immediately, gone straight to the homeworlds. Turn one or two of those into Drasin fodder and the rest would have capitulated to the Empire in days—weeks at the outside, Aymes thought, annoyed by the unprofessional nature of the action.

Someone had let their emotions and bloodlust get the best of them, he supposed. Or, perhaps more likely, they were going to use the whole exercise as an example to some of the outlying Imperial worlds. Show them what happened to those who tried to keep to old and antiquated ways.

If that was the case, however, Aymes figured that plan had backfired most spectacularly. The Drasin were loose. And the Oathers, apparently not nearly as defenseless as they should have been, now had allies.

Imperial communications corporations were working overtime to cover up any hint of the failure. If word got out, ideas would not be far behind.

And there were few things as dangerous as ideas.

▶▶▶

Priminae Capital, Ranquil

▶ "Welcome, Captain!"

Eric smiled as he walked under the looming fuselage of the shuttle, extending a hand to Rael Tanner in greeting. The admiral cut a slight figure, but Eric was well aware that judging him by his size or his subtle temper would be a mistake. He was the commander in chief of the

Priminae Navy and overall commander of their entire military, a position that held very little respect or accolades from the locals. Winning his position may not have been the challenge it would have been on Earth, but keeping his position nonetheless showed tenacious dedication to duty over all other things.

"Admiral, a pleasure as always."

"More so for me, Captain. The reports of your passing were deeply saddening."

"Well, as a once infamous personage back home said, the reports of my demise were greatly exaggerated . . ." He paused, considering his words for a moment, and then shrugged. "Okay . . . not *greatly* in my case. It was a lot closer to accurate than I'd like to admit, but still exaggerated."

"Indeed," Tanner said archly. "You will have to tell me that story, in detail, but later. I'll arrange drinks?"

"Sounds perfect, Admiral."

"In the meantime . . ." Tanner straightened and looked over the group that had disembarked from the shuttle. "I understand that you've brought more specialists?"

"As requested, yes," Eric confirmed, gesturing to a hulking Samoan officer wearing the colors of Alliance Marines. "This is Major Afano. He's a combined arms specialist and will be taking over the training program from Colonel Reed now that your forces are approaching the status of military regulars."

"Of course." Tanner nodded. "Welcome, Major. I will see you introduced to our own Commander Jehan. He oversees all nonfleet military personnel."

"I look forward to it, Admiral," Afano said in nearly flawless Priminae-speak, not using his translator at all.

Tanner pinned him with a gaze for a moment before slowly turning back to Eric. "As usual, you bring interesting people with you."

"Only the best, Admiral," Eric said. "And speaking of, this is Lieutenant Lyssa Myriano. She's my aide and will be handling the majority of my communications and such. If you need to get a message to me, send it through her and she'll see to it that it comes to my attention immediately."

"Lieutenant," Tanner said, inclining his head to her, "a pleasure."

"Likewise, Admiral," Lyssa replied. "The captain speaks highly of you."

"Captain Weston does me too much credit, I suspect," Tanner said with a self-deprecating air. "But it is very pleasant to hear."

Eric snorted loudly. "You're the supreme commander of your entire navy, and you have overarching command of the rest of your military, Admiral. Honestly, I'm continually surprised you have time to meet with me at all."

Tanner smiled at that but didn't contest the words as he gestured to his aides. "See everyone to their rooms. We'll meet later to get down to business. Captain, if you'd like, I'll show you to your room myself."

"It would be my honor, sir."

▶▶▶

▶ Later, Eric settled back into the surprisingly comfortable seat in the admiral's office and sipped lightly on the promised drink.

"That's the story, Admiral," Eric said, eyes half-lidded as he thought back to what had happened. *More or less.*

There were parts of his story that he wasn't going to share with anyone, from either world. His encounters with the entities he knew as Central and Gaia were not things he put in reports or even whispered about, as a rule. He rather liked not being in a rubber room, for one thing, and some of what he remembered as the *Odyssey* went down was Section Eight material for sure.

"It's remarkable that you survived," Tanner said. "You or your world. The Drasin didn't land in such numbers on any of our worlds."

"We were armed for bear, Admiral," Eric said. "Frankly, any invading force would be better off just bombarding us from orbit. Landing on Earth is tantamount to suicide if you've got bad intentions. I don't care how bad you are . . . nine billion pissed-off humans with just as many weapons are going to ruin your day."

"Perhaps," Tanner said lightly. "Unfortunately, however, we could not say the same."

"There are downsides," Eric said more quietly, "but in cases like this, well, I won't be complaining."

"No, I should think not." The admiral sighed. "I suppose we should move on to more serious business, however. The council wishes me to ask what your government intends now."

"Those are questions better directed through Ambassador LaFontaine, Admiral."

Tanner nodded tiredly. "This is what I said to them. They pressed despite my words."

Eric pursed his lips, not happy with the question but understanding it all the same. In fact, it wouldn't be uncommon for higher-ranking members of allied military at home to pass information through back channels.

There was a certain art to the process, however, and Tanner clearly didn't know the protocol.

"You're not supposed to just out and tell me that, you know," he said finally as he broke out chuckling.

"I'm not?"

"No, Admiral, you're supposed to inquire casually about my mission . . . nothing classified, of course," Eric said, "then maybe I drop a hint or two, and we move from there. Being so blatant is a bit of a faux pas."

Tanner looked at him quizzically. "I hadn't realized things were so involved."

"It comes from dancing through classified minefields," Eric admitted with a shrug. "Probably not needed out here, not yet anyway, but there you have it."

"I apologize then," Tanner said, seemingly getting the joke. "However, the question remains."

"Primarily, we're on a deep recon mission this time out," Eric said after a moment's deliberation. "Nothing too classified. Earth's governments want to know more about where the Drasin came from."

"Understandable," Tanner conceded.

"I'll try to keep the *Odysseus* out of the way of your forces, but we'll start by backtracking the Drasin's known contact points with Priminae worlds," Eric said. "After that, we'll be aiming to see if we can figure out a pattern. We're obviously concerned with the Drasin, but on a personal level, I'm more interested in the unidentified ships the *Odyssey* encountered on our second mission."

"Yes, I read that report. That detail was deeply troubling," Tanner said. "Have you any new information? Did you get any clear images of the ships that we can compare with our files?"

"Nothing," Eric lied without hesitating. "They stayed in the cloud. Very cagey, I'm afraid."

Tanner slumped. "Of course. Well, I wish you the best on your mission then."

Eric watched the smaller man closely, looking for any sign that the admiral either had recognized the lie or knew the truth. He saw nothing, just disappointment in the lack of intelligence. Eric still wasn't fully sure he could trust his own gut here, but he rather liked the admiral and personally hoped the man, and his people, had nothing to do with what had transpired.

He didn't believe them to be culpable, not as a whole, but those ships had been very similar to Priminae design. The materials science behind them was markedly different, but the designs were nearly identical.

There *had* to be some sort of connection.

Until he knew what that was, Eric knew better than to entirely trust anyone. Even the Priminae members of his own crew, few though there were, had to be held under some level of suspicion until they were fully cleared.

That was why Earth had, and needed, the Rogue Class destroyers. They were human ships, with human crews, tasked with digging out the truth of the galaxy.

For now, as much as it grated on him, the *Odysseus* was little more than a highly visible decoy.

"Thank you, Admiral," Eric said after a moment's contemplation. "That means a lot."

CHAPTER 4

IBC *Piar Cohn*, Outer System Approach

▶ "No signs of life or nonnatural motion in the system, Captain."

Aymes nodded tersely, unsurprised.

"Drasin signs?"

"Yes Captain. Two worlds."

Aymes suppressed a snort of derision, disgusted by the waste. Two worlds that could have supported Imperial populations, sacrificed on some altar for purposes he couldn't fathom. What was the point of all those wasted resources?

"Skirt the edge of the system, spiral course. I want scans for any sign of distorted space and time. Look for any sign of ships coming and going."

"Yes Captain."

The *Cohn* would spend days circling the system, looking for traces he knew wouldn't be there, but at this point there was little else he could do. The Drasin were too dangerous to risk any possibility of missed data.

Aymes supposed he should be happy that there was no sign that the drones had backtracked toward the Empire.

They, at least, didn't screw up that badly.

It was a cold comfort, at best.

▶▶▶

Priminae Capital, Ranquil

▶ Ambassador LaFontaine greeted Eric as he entered the embassy suite located in the immense pyramidal habitat of the Priminae.

"Captain, so pleased to see that rumors of your death were exaggerated," she told him, smiling.

"Not so pleased as I am, Ambassador," Eric said with a chuckle. "And I just had to explain that same turn of phrase to Admiral Tanner."

"Well, I'm sure he was equally pleased by the news and probably politely confused by the explanation." LaFontaine laughed. "Come in. I have, of course, received the latest from Earth, but any news you might provide beyond the orders and policy changes would be useful."

Eric nodded, taking an offered seat and relaxing a little. He rather liked the ambassador, having been her ferryman on her original trip to Ranquil as well as her primary contact with Earth, at least until the Heroics had been constructed.

"Well, rebuilding is underway, naturally," he said. "China and India took the heaviest casualties during the invasion, simply by virtue of their population size if nothing else. The Confederation was hurt badly too, of course, but I suspect we'll recover first and strongest."

"Oh? That's nice to hear, as a daughter of Canada, but why?" she asked.

"We've been using outdated infrastructure for most of the last century, and a lot of it was destroyed in the fighting," he answered. "So we're actually rebuilding with new technology rather than replacing antiquated copper lines and the like. The infrastructure damage to China and India wasn't as severe, because they've never really relied on tech to the levels we do, and what little they did rely on was already state of the art. We've been lagging behind the Block since before they became the Block, honestly. Hong Kong and Beijing had us beat in many areas since the early twenty-first century. That's about to change."

"Interesting. I hadn't considered it, but you're right," LaFontaine said as she thought about old stories. "I wonder why we allowed ourselves to lag behind?"

"Because infrastructure is a public project, and we tend to let private corporations lead the way," Eric answered easily. "That system is more flexible and tends to be more resilient overall, but corporations don't like to invest in infrastructure they don't control entirely. Since we still have antimonopoly laws in place, that slows down development in certain areas. That's why the fastest access to communications hubs have consistently been in the Block countries, while we tend to get access that's considered 'good enough.'"

"It's almost surprising we won the war, then, if that's true."

"We nearly didn't," Eric said, "though not because of that. Both systems have strengths, but while some of the best and most modern infrastructure in the world does exist in the Block, they also have large swaths of territory with effectively no infrastructure. We don't. Rich, poor, or in the middle, if you grew up in the Confederation, you had access to the world economy. More than ninety percent of Block citizens just didn't. Our system doesn't hit the peaks theirs does, as a rule, but it doesn't come anywhere close to the lows either."

"So why did we win ultimately, in your opinion?" LaFontaine asked, mildly interested in the conversation but more intent on the views of the captain of the Confederation flagship.

"We had momentum."

That answer wasn't what she expected, and for a moment she tried to puzzle it out before finally saying, "I'm not sure I understand?"

"By the time the Block War broke out, the United States of America had spent the better part of a full century stockpiling weapons. They were old, obsolete, and considered worthless . . . but they were still lethal," Eric said. "When we ran out of main battle tanks, we just opened up national guard vaults and rolled out ten thousand more. We had aircraft and tanks wrapped in plastic just rotting out in open fields, waiting for mechanics to roll in and replace all the seals and update the electronics, along with ship hulls from World War Two just waiting to be uncorked and refurbished. The war came down to what would run out first: our men, or their equipment. In the last days of the war, there were Block soldiers in the field who were issued guns they'd captured from Confederation POWs."

"I'd heard that but never made the connection."

"We didn't form the Confederation because we desperately needed minerals from Canada or factories in Mexico," Eric said, unconsciously thinking in terms of the American citizen he'd grown up as. "We needed every recruit we could pull. India and China alone had us outnumbered over ten to one."

"I always thought it was the efforts of groups like the Archangel squadron that changed the tides," LaFontaine said, thinking about the stories she'd heard about the war.

"Oh, we changed the tide of a few battles," Eric conceded. "Japan was one of the key fights, but we were more a propaganda coup than a truly effective force in the war. The war was won on the ground, like all wars are, by guys coated in mud and blood. The Archangels were more important in keeping everyone's eyes on the sky instead of buried in the mud than we ever were in terms of real impact on the war itself. We won battles, but our biggest contribution was inspiring the people who won the war."

LaFontaine sat back, surprised by that last statement. She'd never heard that before in all the reporting on the infamous Double A squadron. But then, while he'd been interviewed many times, she didn't remember anyone ever asking Eric Weston what he thought had won the war.

How strange, LaFontaine thought. Eric's response seemed at odds with conventional logic that the Confederation had beaten the Block with better innovation and more sophisticated weapons and tools.

"Well, that is very interesting, and I wish we could talk more on the subject. I find your point of view on the subject fascinating, Captain, but I suppose we should return to the present," she said, more than a little sorry to change the subject. "You spent time last night with Admiral Tanner? Did he make any . . . overtures?"

Eric smiled. "The council isn't terribly subtle, are they?"

"Not in the slightest," LaFontaine answered tiredly. "I believe that they think I am stonewalling them, but on what, I'm honestly not certain."

"They're hiding something," Eric said with certainty. "What, I'm not certain either. It may not even be something we consider important, but there's something."

"Agreed," the ambassador said, "though I'm inclined to think that it may well be important. Just *how* important remains a mystery."

"They're not an easy people to read," Eric confessed. "I've dealt with cultures all over Earth, many of whom I had far less respect for than the Priminae, but none that I had as much trouble understanding."

"I've had a very similar experience," LaFontaine said. "Since we know they're hiding something, I'm hoping that you'll use your reputation and contacts here to sound them out on just what their secrets might be."

Eric nodded firmly. "I will. Whatever they're hiding, there's a good chance it will impact my mission and Earth's security, so I'll do what I can."

"Thank you. Most aspects of the embassy run very smoothly here," LaFontaine said. "However, our intelligence gathering and analysis departments are almost literally pulling out their hair."

Grinning, Eric said, "Frankly, Madam Ambassador, that amuses me more than anything else."

"Amusing perhaps, but it isn't a joke," the ambassador said sternly. "Lives will depend on their work."

Eric held up his hands in surrender. "Message received and understood, ma'am. I'll see what I can dig up."

She pinned him with a slight glare for a moment before relaxing. "Good. Most of the bureaucracy has already been dealt with concerning your visit, so we don't have much to do here."

Eric knew a dismissal when he heard one and rose to his feet.

"I'll take my leave then, ma'am, and see what I can find."

"Good luck, Captain."

▶▶▶

▶ There was only one source on Ranquil that Eric figured would know for certain what the Priminae were hiding, but the odds of that source talking to him were fifty-fifty at best. Nonetheless, Eric decided to make the attempt.

Now, if only Central had a phone number.

The annoyingly mysterious entity, sometimes "computer," that seemed to run the day-to-day business of the Priminae on Ranquil was Eric's best bet for answers. Likely obscure, murky, and annoying answers, but answers nonetheless.

Unfortunately, just asking the Priminae for access to the chamber that they designated as Central was a nonstarter. For one, it would tip them off that he was up to something, which he really would prefer to avoid since he was . . . well, actually up to something. More to the point, however, Central himself didn't seem to have any interest in letting most people in on how he had come to exist.

Eric made his way to the shuttle pad, walking past the two Marine guards and up into the craft. He checked and found that the pilot wasn't inside at the moment, then sealed the doors and locked everyone under his rank out.

Central was, or rather *seemed* to be, far more than a computer. Eric hardly considered himself an expert on whatever it was, but the entity's own description, as well as his encounter with something very similar on Earth, told him that he wasn't dealing with a computer.

"Indeed not."

The world spun around him in a familiar manner, and Eric found himself looking around the interior of the shuttle with an irksome sense that something otherworldly had changed despite not seeing any differences.

"That's incredibly irritating," he grumbled, focusing on the nondescript human form now standing a short distance away.

Central struck him as a completely normal human except for the fact that whenever he glanced away, Eric suddenly couldn't remember him having any particular features to speak of. Eric presumed that normally the entity had some, since not having them would be even stranger than his forgetting, but frankly, he was past trying to figure out these bizarre creatures.

"Creatures? Really?" Central sounded slightly miffed. "That's hardly polite."

"Neither is mind reading," Eric groused.

"I told you once, it's not something I can help." Central waved his concern off idly. "Your thoughts *are* my thoughts, as though I thought them myself. You simply *must* convey my compliments and greetings to this *Gaia* of yours, by the way."

Eric rolled his eyes, knowing that the word "must" was a literal truth. He wouldn't have any choice in the matter as soon as he returned to Earth. His mind would simply automatically be read by Gaia without recourse.

"Not read," Central corrected. "Experienced."

"That's not any better," Eric said dryly, sighing. "Look, can we get on with this? I need a drink so I can forget as much of this as practicable."

"You Terrans are such an interesting conundrum. Violent, aggressive, and almost bestial . . . yet so easily offended in your sensibilities, as though words actually are somehow worse than physical harm."

Eric grimaced, recognizing that Central was just playing with him at this point.

"Why, yes. Yes, I am." Central smirked, somehow. Eric wasn't sure how, given the lack of features he could consciously perceive.

But Central seemed to become more serious in the next moment.

"I'm not certain what to tell you," the entity replied. "Are my people hiding information from you? Certainly, though not what you might consider *intentionally*."

"What?" Eric blurted. "That's ridiculous! How do you hide anything unintentionally?"

"Many ways," the entity said. "You can forget it, you can not realize its import, or you can simply assume the other person already knows it."

Eric locked onto the last one. "Assume we know what?"

"You've already heard that answer, Capitaine." Central laughed, his accent shifting from the normal flat tone into something familiar.

"I need to know more . . . ," Eric said, only to feel the world whirl around him again. Suddenly the mystical sensation was gone, and the walls of the shuttle were simply the walls of the shuttle.

Three loud knocks on the hatch caused him to turn his head.

"Captain? Are you alright in there?"

"Fine. I'll be out momentarily," Eric said.

Eric really didn't know what to make of the two entities he'd met, Central and Gaia. They were something *more* than human, yet they didn't seem to act much on their apparent power. Of course, for all he knew they could be constantly pulling strings, but somehow he had the feeling they didn't.

Central was analytical, logical, cool, and distant. For all his thoughts on the matter, Eric had no problem understanding how the Priminae could have mistaken the entity for a computer system. Gaia, however, was wild and fierce, more a force of nature than anything resembling a calculating machine. Eric didn't know if Gaia had taken the name of the Earth goddess, or inspired it, but either seemed likely to his mind.

Of course, the big problem with either of them was obvious and frustrating.

How the hell am I supposed to maintain any sort of operational security when there are mind-reading alien entities floating around the universe?

Not that he could really tell anyone. Even as weird as the real universe was, talking about all-seeing alien gestalts that could read minds and warp reality would basically ensure he picked up a medical discharge, mental category.

Someday I'm going to write a book. It'll have to be fantasy though, 'cause sci-fi fans will never buy this crap.

Eric sighed as he undogged the hatch and stepped out of the shuttle, nodding to the Marine who was waiting.

"Call back everyone," he ordered. "We're shipping out early."

"Yes sir!"

▶▶▶

AEV *Odysseus*

▶ Footsteps didn't echo on the *Odysseus* as they had on the *Odyssey*. Something in the acoustics of the ceramic decks and walls baffled sound, but the steady tap of a marching boot still traveled well along the length of the many long corridors, at least until a crew member encountered a corner.

Steph paused upon hearing that tapping speed up and approach, and he turned to see Milla hurrying toward him.

"Evening, Milla." He smiled at her. "I expected you to have leave?"

"Ranquil is not my home," she said with a hint of sadness that warned him not to ask any further questions.

Milla wasn't one to chat about where she'd come from, and Steph had a good idea of why that was. Too many had lost far more than soil, water, and air during the Drasin incursion, but there was something about the loss of a home that struck true no matter the scale.

"Ah," was all he said. "So what has your attentions today?"

"I was wishing to acquire . . ." Milla frowned, looking for the words. "Flight certification, yes?"

"Yes, I suppose. I thought you were checked on Priminae shuttles?" Steph asked, puzzled.

"We do not have many of those on board," she reminded him.

"Ah, good point. So are you looking for lessons or an examiner?"

Technically he was qualified to do either, but not both, by current regulations.

"Examiner," she answered. "I have been taking lessons for some time."

"Really?" Steph was surprised. He would have thought he'd have heard about that through the rumor mill. "Going well, I assume?"

"Your shuttles use very crude controls," she told him with pursed lips. "However, there is something . . . exciting about flying one."

Steph nodded. He'd flown with the Priminae a few times on their own shuttlecraft, and he knew where she was coming from. Priminae small craft relied heavily on computer-controlled systems, far more than even the most automated vessel in Terran service. Their technology allowed for extremely precise flying, but very little of it had the seat-of-the-pants thrill of putting your own hand physically on the stick.

Computer-based piloting was beyond impressive for many types of maneuvers, but it never quite matched up to the best intuitive pilots. And such systems were almost inherently predictable if your opponent had enough flight data from which to derive pattern recognitions.

"When will you be ready to test?" he asked her.

"Very nearly there," Milla answered. "I need a few more hours of stick time, yes?"

"Alright. Let me know, and I'll put aside some time and we'll get you certified."

"Thank you, Stephan," she said gratefully. "I look forward to it."

"So do I."

▶▶▶

▶ Miram Heath looked over the orbital telemetry from her station on the command deck of the *Odysseus* and permitted herself a curt nod of satisfaction.

Her specialty, pre-Drasin, had been astrometric analysis with an eye to deep spatial anomalies. After a decade of studying the most obscure pieces of data in known space, from black holes to gamma ray bursts, the nuts and bolts of navigating a starship were *almost* mundane.

Almost.

Like most people who delved into the space sciences, she'd spent her formative years dreaming about the great void. While in school, she'd desperately wanted a shot at the Mars mission, but war had broken out before she'd graduated, and by the time the dust had settled, she had been considered too valuable on the ground in Houston.

When the *Odyssey's* mission had been announced, she'd made her application, but it was a Department of Defense project, and she had been a civilian at that point. Aside from the short-term jaunts to Space Station Liberty, she had all but given up on the idea of getting into space—into the deep black.

The Drasin changed the rules.

Suddenly, the budget for deep black exploration was all but unlimited, and the new Confederation-Block Alliance was *screaming* for qualified people to man starships. She'd put her name in immediately, had her commission reactivated, and gotten her pick of the new ships.

Miram had selected the *Odysseus* without hesitation.

Eric Weston had become a symbol on Earth—many symbols, in fact. Some people saw him as a war hero, others as a war criminal. More than those labels, however, he'd become the man who had introduced them to the stars, to the Priminae—and to the Drasin.

He was perhaps the most polarizing man on the planet, or off it, she supposed.

That was one reason the Confederacy had put him back into the black as quickly as they had. Weston was off the planet where most of his detractors were focused and thus out of the public eye. Giving him the *Odysseus*, the spiritual successor of the *Odyssey*, kept his supporters happy, and he was a beloved figure in the Priminae system, which made him a boon to diplomacy.

For Miram, and her community, he was the man who had proved that humanity was not alone in the universe. He had gone out into the stars, found intelligent life, and risked his own ship, crew, and well-being to save theirs.

Eric Weston was every sci-fi captain she'd ever watched on TV and in the movies growing up. Despite her very disciplined demeanor, she was *thrilled* to serve on his ship.

Showing that was out of the question, of course. Even in the early twenty-second century, science was a shockingly male-dominated field. Not as much as it had been traditionally, particularly in the aftermath of the Block War, but enough so that she'd built a professional demeanor that had charitably been called "icy."

Now that Miram held a top post on what basically amounted to the flagship of the Confederacy and probably the most visible starship on Earth and beyond, she couldn't even imagine dropping that persona.

Maybe it's for the best.

"Inbound track, Commander. Reads as a Heroic."

Miram raised a single eyebrow. "One of ours?"

"Negative. Priminae for sure," Ensign Sams said firmly.

Now Miram turned her full attention to the instrumentation station. "How are you so sure?"

"Acceleration curve is different from Confederation procedures, ma'am. And we'd never choose violet, green, and puce as our light code."

Miram hid a wince but nodded. "Good enough, Ensign, good enough. ETA to arrival?"

"Twelve hours at current track. They're not rushing."

Miram patted the ensign on the shoulder. "Good job. Stay on them. Let me know if anything happens."

"Aye ma'am."

The space around Ranquil wasn't what Miram would call terribly busy, but there was more traffic than in Sol space. Most of it was freighters now, big and slow with power curves a tad below a quarter of a planetary mass. They affected local space-time like a reasonably sized moon when on full power and not masking their gravity.

Heroics, on the other hand, were like rogue planets blundering through a star system, impossible to miss, even if you were half-blind. When dropping into the orbit of an inhabited world, or really any world, a Heroic Class ship had to mask its gravity carefully. If they weren't careful, they could cause a tidal surge in the best case or sling a planet out of its orbit in the worst.

That last bit was more theoretical than anything else, but the point remained that Heroic Class ships were flying weapons of mass destruction, even without counting the actual weapons they packed.

CHAPTER 5

IBC *Piar Cohn*, System Approach

▶ "Drasin trace readings, Captain."

Aymes looked up from his station. "How old?"

"Two rotes, Captain. Maybe two and a half, not three."

Aymes nodded slowly. "Well, it is a beginning. Redirect our course: standard sweep around the system. Keep us in line with the planetary plane. Look for warped space and time."

"Yes Captain. Course adjusting now."

The *Piar Cohn* shifted from its entry track, moving to a planar orbit around the system primary well outside the planetary orbits. Aymes turned his focus to the long-range scanners, watching as the ship moved. Reaching out over eight light-fractals, the scanners were looking for any unexplained gradations in the local dimensional fabric.

The usual depressions and elevations were evident as they progressed around the rim of the system, and Aymes was an old hand at reading live charts. He noted the slight depressions of each of the major planets in the system as well as a nearby planetoid's incline, also taking in the corresponding elevations caused by the interplay of gravity waves.

Nothing to indicate the passage of a warp field, however.

"It's been too long," he growled. "Any trail by now is long faded."

The officer at the scanning station nodded, glad that the captain had said it first.

"Yes Captain."

"Where was the next scheduled system the Drasin were to investigate?" Aymes asked finally.

"One Three Four Nine in this sector."

"Very well. Set a new course. Least time for system One Three Four Nine," Aymes ordered.

"Course prepared, Captain. Permission to apply?"

"Permission granted."

AEV *Odysseus*

▶ Eric was down the ramp before it touched the deck of the *Odysseus*, his boots ringing on the platform a split second before those of his Marines. He curtly acknowledged the two Marines as they took up positions on either side of the ramp, but didn't slow down as he crossed the deck and headed for the lift.

"Captain."

"Commander," Eric greeted Miram without slowing or looking around.

"The course you requested has been encoded. We started warping space the moment your shuttle came to a stop," she told him. "May I ask what is going on, sir?"

"Had to get away from Ranquil for a while, Commander," Eric said simply. "We're moving on to the second phase of the mission a little ahead of schedule."

"Any reason why?"

"It got a little . . . stuffy."

Miram blinked. "On the planet, sir?"

Eric stopped in place, half turning to look at her before he pivoted back around.

"Lately, Commander, I find I prefer deep space."

She was about to ask more before he went on.

"It's . . . quieter out here."

▶▶▶

▶ The *Odysseus* warped space as soon as they cleared the orbit of Ranquil, powering up to what would be relativistic speeds with any traditional drive system. The ship was already passing a third the speed of light by the time Eric stepped onto the command deck, standing at his post as he accessed the command station.

"ETA to system heliopause?"

"Three more hours at current acceleration, sir."

"Good," Eric said, sighing nearly imperceptibly as he relaxed. He found he now really didn't feel comfortable until he was well away from planets.

Discovering Central on Ranquil was one thing. The entity hadn't shaken his worldview all that much. Ranquil was an alien planet, after all. He expected alien things.

Gaia, however, he could admit that *she*—if that was what Gaia was—*she* had shattered part of him. He hadn't realized that until he'd met Central again however. When Central isolated him in the shuttle, effortlessly slipping through his mind . . .

Eric *had* to discover what those things were. He just didn't know how.

With one eye on the vessel's telemetry, Eric accessed the ship's database and called up the files they'd copied from the Priminae computer cores. He opened the mythological database and accessed Priminae "gods."

Gaia apparently styled herself the goddess of Earth, if he were to take the name seriously, and Central had told him once that he was the source of some Priminae deity myths, long ago. Eric was more than passingly familiar with Earth mythology, but couldn't think of anything that helped him make sense of Gaia. He was hoping that something in the Priminae database would cause things to gel.

Thankfully, the admiral took the opportunity to copy the Priminae cultural database as part of the exchange deal she cut with them.

The Priminae culture was one with a long history, a history that Eric knew almost no one had even begun to scratch the surface of. The Confederacy had several analysis teams dedicated to just this sort of thing, or they had before the invasion at least. Eric wasn't sure if anyone was digging too deep into cultural nuances at the moment, considering other priorities, but for him the subject had just taken a very high place on his list.

He had to go back a *long* time to find information about deist beliefs in Priminae culture. By their standards, Earth culture was *terribly* infantile at barely four thousand years or so of reasonably contiguous written history. The first mention of anything resembling gods was over fifty thousand years before—Priminae years, actually. That worked out to almost seventy thousand, Earth standard.

The Priminae had been a spacefaring culture when humans had first begun domesticating dogs and long before anyone had started the basics of agriculture.

What bothered Eric, from all that, was that they didn't have any prehistoric records for themselves.

According to these files, the Priminae may as well have sprung fully formed from the ether. No early history, no sign of any sciences before their current level . . . and that is practically obscene.

"How the hell does that happen?" he murmured, shaking his head.

"Pardon me, sir?"

Eric looked up, noting that Miram was looking at him with intense curiosity in her eyes, though the rest of her features remained unchanged. He pursed his lips, considering her for a moment, thinking about what he'd been reading.

"Tell me, Commander, what did you do before your commission was reactivated?"

"Astrometric analysis, Captain. Why?"

"What was that, exactly?"

"Many things, especially as your mission opened up the frontier," Miram responded. "Mapping stellar anomalies, mostly, looking for signs of stellar civilizations . . ."

"SETI work?"

"Similar," she answered. "Better funded, particularly since you contacted the Priminae."

"So you know the Kardashev scale?"

"Of course. It's required reading," she said. "Some consider the measure somewhat outdated, but it is still in many ways the benchmark for stellar civilization."

"Where do you put Earth?"

"Late Type Zero, Early Type One," she answered instantly. "Depends how you calculate the power expenditures mostly. That's pre-Drasin. Post-Drasin . . . Captain, this ship alone qualifies as a Type One civilization."

Eric nodded slowly, thinking about Miram's statement. He'd actually known what she'd just conveyed, but he hadn't really parsed the information that way. The *Odysseus* had more power output than the entire Earth could produce, potentially at least.

"Alright, what about the Priminae?" he asked.

"Mid Type One," she answered, again without hesitation.

That had been the subject of many debates before she'd reactivated her commission.

"So tell me something. How does a civilization reach Mid Type One without developing fire? Without figuring out electricity?"

"What, sir?" Miram frowned. "It doesn't."

"That's not what I'm seeing here," Eric said, shifting his screen so she could see it. "I'm looking through the Priminae cultural database.

I can't find a reference to them discovering fire, not even archeological theories. No history of them figuring out electricity, magnetism, or any of the basic sciences."

"That doesn't make any sense." Miram looked down to her own screen and started entering search requests.

Eric waited.

"This makes no sense. The database can't be complete," Miram said, shaking her head. "No culture just appears out of nowhere."

"Nothing has ever added up about the Priminae," Eric said. "From the beginning I didn't know what to make of them. Genetically human, seemingly pacifists, but the weapons . . . lord, the power of their weapons . . . nothing made sense."

"They aren't, you know, sir."

"They aren't what?"

"Genetically human," Miram answered, looking nonplussed. "You didn't know?"

"I've been busy. I don't understand," he said. "Doctor Rame . . ."

"Was rushed. He looked for specific genetic markers that we associate with human," she said. "Those are all there."

"So?"

"What's missing is the extraneous DNA that Terran humans share," she responded. "Remnants from our evolutionary ancestors: reptilian, fish, avian DNA. We can track that DNA back to specific species in Earth's history. The Priminae don't share *any* of that with us. They look human, Captain, but they are not."

Eric fell silent, considering that for a long moment. That shook his view of the Priminae significantly.

"So what does that mean?" he asked. "Some kind of parallel evolution?"

"Unlikely," Miram said, shaking her head. "Though we honestly don't have enough data points to truly be certain. So far we have two known intelligent species, assuming we discount the Drasin, and they both look human. Strictly speaking, it *is* possible that the human form is the inevitable end result of evolution, but given what we know and can prove about evolution, even assuming perfect Earth-type environments, a mirror-image evolution should be next to impossible."

"So what does that leave?"

Miram shrugged. "Guided evolution?"

"Not familiar with the term. Do you mean by God?" Eric asked.

"Possible, though I have difficulty believing in the idea of an interactive God," she said with a frown. "At least if we're talking about the Christian god."

"You have something against Christians?" Eric asked mildly.

"No sir. However, the Judeo-Christian god is atypical in our cultural history," Miram said. "Most ancient gods were just . . . us, but more so. Thor, Ares, Kali: these are all people with godly powers. Even the modern incarnations of those religions share those traits. Those gods have flaws, limits. Yahweh, Jehovah, Allah: that god was different, unique really. A single deity that incorporated all the disparate gods before it, a supergod if you will."

"I'm really not following," Eric admitted.

"The supreme creator has an inherent . . . problem," she said. "By definition, such an entity *must* exist outside our frame of reference. You can't create the universe if you're *part* of the universe, so I have a problem with the idea of such a creator getting involved on a personal level."

"You don't have a problem with the other gods?" Eric asked, genuinely curious.

"Not at all," she answered. "Speaking philosophically, any of the other gods you care to name is really nothing more than a human with power. Go back four thousand years with this ship, Captain, and you could proclaim yourself king of the gods and all of us your children . . . and not a soul on the planet could argue."

"Fair enough," Eric conceded.

He wondered how that fit into the puzzle he was trying to figure out, but frankly didn't have a clue.

"So, when you say guided evolution, you're thinking something like those other gods?" he suggested.

"Yes, more or less. The theory that someone has tinkered with our evolution isn't a new one, though it's not really been one of the most respected of hypotheses. Mostly only fringe types believe it, largely because it's based entirely on little more than wishful thinking and questionable pattern recognition. People don't like the idea that they came from random chance."

Eric smiled. "So maybe they have some evidence now?"

"Maybe. However, it's still circumstantial. Right now we only have two correlating data points with no causal link as of yet," Miram said, "and in all the years since we mapped the human genome, and the genome of countless other animals on Earth, we've found no sign of any tinkering. If someone had come along a hundred thousand years ago and decided to elevate us, we'd find evidence of it, sir."

"Certain of that?"

"Yes sir," Miram said.

"That just means someone did it earlier," Eric said, "*much* earlier."

Miram considered that for a moment. "It would have to be . . . seven million years ago, or more, Captain? The half-life of DNA is a little over five hundred years . . . total obliteration is in a maximum of almost seven million years."

"So if someone wanted to elevate us, and do it without a trace, they'd have to have done it over seven million years ago," Eric said.

Miram pursed her lips. "In theory, yes, sir."

Eric shook his head. "That's a long time to wait for a plan to come to fruition."

"And it doesn't explain the Priminae not having any early history," Miram said.

"Don't I know it," Eric replied. "Which leaves me back at square one."

"Why the sudden interest, if I might ask, Captain?"

"I told you, Commander," Eric said, "something just doesn't sit right about the Priminae."

She looked at him evenly for a long time, then slowly nodded. "Aye aye, sir."

Eric turned back to his research and stared for a moment before saving the search to his personal folder and flicking the display back over to the navigation telemetry for the ship.

He'd try to figure out Central and Gaia another time. Right now, they had a real mission to work on.

Three hours later, the *Odysseus* vanished from Ranquil space in a burst of tachyon particles.

CHAPTER 6

▶ The *Odysseus*, an hour out of transition, dropped in a shallow dive through the outer gravity well of the target system. Eric was standing on the observation deck, forward of the ship. The *Odysseus* had several decks that were open to visible light from the outside, all heavily armored, of course, though the decks were triple sealed with blast doors in case of hull breach.

The view, at the moment, was pretty spectacular. The *Odysseus*, while under warp drive, gathered high-energy particles in the dip of space-time that the ship "fell" into while under drive. The artificial gravity well captured stray particles, dropping them into a sharp orbit that spun them around in front of the ship as it moved.

Normally these particles were invisible to the naked eye, plus the gravity gradient was more than steep enough to capture visible light. However, while the ship was under power, the combination of the gravity warp and the occasional glimmer of escaping light as particles slammed into one another in the makeshift accelerator made for a truly impressive view.

The computer could reverse the warping, clean up the resulting picture, and present a true space picture of the system beyond, but right now Eric just wanted to enjoy the view.

"Hey boss. Nice digs."

Eric glanced over to Steph, who was dropping into a seat at a nearby table, and nodded absently. "Yeah. I think I miss the zero-grav lounge on the *Odyssey* though."

Steph shrugged. "That was a pretty sweet view, I'll admit. I rather like being able to drink my coffee from a real cup while I enjoy this one though."

Eric tipped his head, acceding the point as Steph lifted his mug. Eric walked back and took a seat across from Steph, who slid a second mug across the table. "So what do you want?"

"Boss, I'm hurt," Steph replied with a dramatic look, "but now that you mention it . . ."

"Just get on with it."

"I've already put the request through. It's in the chain, but I figured I'd run it past you personally," Steph said. "Lieutenant Chans wants to qualify on a shuttle. She's got hours on the stick, just needs a final tagalong before she can do her solo."

Eric raised an eyebrow. "You want to do that out here?"

"Sure. Once scans clear the system, we can do a drop and cut through it. Meet up with you on the other side."

Eric thought about for a moment. "Alright, you're cleared."

"Thanks," Steph said.

"But *not* until we clear the system." Eric held up his hand. "The shuttle isn't exactly armed."

"Well, I could take her out in your Angel, boss." Steph grinned, then held up his hands when Eric shot him a dark look. "Or not."

"Even if she were spaceworthy, I don't think even you could fudge the flight record enough to give the lieutenant her quals on a shuttle." Eric paused, eyeing his junior officer with a suddenly sly look. "Not to mention that it's a single-seater . . . Unless that's what you were going for?"

"Hey, whoa, whoa, whoa . . ." Steph threw up both hands again. "Not with another officer on the same ship! I learn my lessons, boss!"

"You better," Eric said sourly. "You almost got us fragged with that lovers' spat between you and the dispatcher on the *Reagan*."

"Swear to God, boss, not happening here."

Eric looked the younger man over before nodding slowly. "Right. Well, you're still cleared. Just wait for us to finish deep system scans. If we see even a sign of active Drasin presence, or anything else . . ."

"Got it, boss. System becomes a no-go zone."

"If we see Drasin signs, the system becomes a war zone."

▶▶▶

▶ Long-range scanning across planetary distances took time, no matter what sort of systems you used. Tachyon-based detection was technically instantaneous, but it was *very* precise. That was a good thing if you knew what you were looking for and where it was, but if you didn't, it would take years to scan a system that way.

Light-speed-based systems took longer, and you didn't get real-time information, but they had a far superior range of resolution and you could scan *enormous* swaths of the sky very, very quickly.

As soon as the *Odysseus* had transitioned into the system, the crew had begun compiling light-speed images of everything around them. Priminae technology made that somewhat easier than it had been with the *Odyssey*'s reflected sensor sails. The warp field in front of the *Odysseus* bent light, thus functioning as a gathering system far larger than its actual physical size.

The crew had to adjust for interference, naturally, but since that was predictable given the drive system the *Odysseus* used, they had pretty decent resolution.

The entire system couldn't be scanned in minute detail in anything less than several years, but for the most part that wasn't needed anyway. First the astrometrics people just located all the large bodies visually and by their gravity effect. If everything worked out and there were no gravity anomalies, it was a fair bet that there were no active warp fields in the system.

While that was happening, the radio frequency systems threw their entire feed over to the computer for pattern recognition, looking for any signs of broadcasting. Similarly, the tachyon scanners started looking for interplanetary-range FTL signals, and the rapidly assembling visual images of the system were pored over for anything that looked out of the ordinary.

This was one of the Priminae's outer colony worlds, and one of the first hit by the Drasin, so the scanners quickly found minor anomalies that brought their focus to the fourth world in the system. It was now a dead and crumbling mass of former Drasin drones, but none of them were remotely active, so the teams in charge of the system evaluation tagged the world's orbit and moved on.

Other than that one world, the system was largely unimpressive. The star was a red giant, and most of the planets were barren or gas giants, though there were hints of organic chemicals in the atmosphere of the fifth world. This was tagged as an item of interest and set aside.

Hyperspectral scanners were useful for long-range analysis of such things, basically breaking down the incoming light that had passed through a planet's atmosphere, or reflected off an interesting surface, and working out what wavelengths had been absorbed. Certain compounds absorbed very specific wavelengths of light, and so from light-minutes—or even light-years—away, it was possible to very neatly identify what exactly you were looking at on a molecular level, if nothing else.

After three hours of skirting the system, nothing unexpected came back. The *Odysseus* came down from general quarters and settled in to complete the survey in a more relaxed manner.

▶▶▶

▶ Milla Chans stepped up the plank into the large shuttle, tapping on the aluminum ribbing. "Stephan? Are you in here?"

Steph appeared from the front lock. "Hey Milla. I see you got the word."

"The system has been cleared, yes?"

"That's what the official card said," Steph told her. "Captain cleared us for a test flight, so we're going to drop deeper into the system, sling around the fifth planet, and meet the *Odysseus* around the elliptic in two days. Works?"

"Yes. Works."

"Good. Preflight."

Milla nodded and moved forward, slipping past Steph and through the lock into the forward cockpit. He had signed out a Marine shuttle for the test flight, unarmed and stripped down for fast landing and even faster dustoff.

He would have preferred one of the armed versions, just as a matter of principal, but Major McAllistair had something to say about that. The Marine in charge of the *Odysseus*' contingent was as much a stickler for procedure as Eric had ever been at his worst, and while he might have to sign out a shuttle at the request of the ship's chief helmsman, giving a Navy flyboy weapons wasn't something the major was willing to do.

Steph ducked back through the lock, watching as Milla slipped into the pilot's seat with just a little trepidation. He sealed and dogged the hatch, securing the cockpit before he dropped into the copilot's seat and pulled the straps down over his shoulders.

"So, checklist?" he asked, glancing over.

"Yes sir. All systems read as green," she told him, flipping a switch. "Lifting access ramp. Seals are green, Commander."

"Good. Next?"

Milla blinked. "Call for clearance?"

Steph just stared at her.

Milla looked around, trying to figure out what she'd missed. "What?"

"Well?" Steph waved at the windows.

"I don't—oh!" Milla's hand went to her earpiece. "*Odysseus* Control, Marine lander shuttle *Eagle One* . . . *Eagle* Actual speaking."

"Go for Control, *Eagle One*."

"*Eagle One* requests clearance for departure."

"Roger *Eagle One*, you have clearance on cat nine. Confirm."

"Cat nine, confirmed. *Eagle One*, under power."

"Roger that."

Milla set three dials, then flipped a bank of switches before taking the stick and throttle. The shuttle shuddered slightly before it started to move. She steered it around, following the directions of the deck crew as they waved her to catapult nine.

Steph settled back, watching the process as the shuttle stuttered to a halt on the catapult square.

The Priminae didn't use catapult launchers. Their shuttles didn't need them, and frankly, they wouldn't have any idea of how to use one. Steph had been part of the discussion when the admiral had demanded having them installed. It had been an interesting talk.

The *Odyssey* had used an electromagnetic launcher, but the *Odysseus* worked with a gravity launcher. Once the shuttle was hooked up, a process done entirely with software, the deck crew cleared out.

"*Eagle One*, stand by."

Milla sent confirmation, opening the comm at the same time. "*Eagle One*, standing by."

Stephen checked his restraints, though he doubted he'd need them. Unlike a last-generation cat, if they felt any acceleration, the odds were it would be the last thing they'd ever feel.

Milla checked the systems again, making sure everything was still green.

"*Eagle One*, *Odysseus* Control."

"Roger, Control," Milla said. "Go for *Eagle One*."

"You are cleared to put power to your CM system, *Eagle One*."

"CM," she replied, pronouncing the letters carefully, as she flipped another bank of switches. "Activated. Powering now."

The shuttle lifted on its wheels as the counter-mass system shunted a majority of the craft's mass and inertia out of this dimension, away from normal space.

"CM fully powered, Control."

"Roger that, *Eagle One*. Stand by to launch."

An alarm went off outside and the deck crew emptied out of sight, other than a half-dozen in full vacuum suits.

"*Eagle One*, standing by."

The comm clicked off and Milla sighed, turning her head to look at Steph.

"There is so much repetition," she said wearily. "It is tiring, no?"

"That's how we make certain everyone knows precisely what everyone else is thinking," Steph said, half smiling. "It's boring, but clarity keeps people breathing."

"We have no such procedures," she admitted, "and people do not stop breathing often on a Priminae vessel, Stephan."

"How many flights does a Priminae ship launch in, say, an hour?"

"Not many," Milla said. "Likely less than one, if you wish to average them."

"A carrier on full operation can launch and trap between eighty and a hundred and twenty flights an hour at peak operation, with as many as two hundred people on the decks while they're in use," Steph said. "One mistake in that kind of a crowd can kill dozens easily."

Milla nodded slowly. "I see."

She was about to say something more, but the comm crackled before she could.

"*Eagle One*, *Odysseus* Control."

"Roger Control, *Eagle One* speaking."

"Launch is cleared at your discretion."

Milla swallowed. "Roger. Understood."

She grabbed a stick on her left side, flicking a safety switch up to clear a thumb switch. "*Eagle One*, we are go for launch."

"Roger, *Eagle One*, launch."

"Launch, launch, launch," she said as she jammed her thumb down on the button.

The deck of the *Odysseus* blurred as the shuttle was slung forward and out, the gray white of the walls replaced almost instantly by the deep black.

▶▶▶

▶ "*Eagle One* is away, Captain."

Eric nodded, eyes on the augmented imagery of the shuttle as it lanced out from the *Odysseus* and curved slightly starward.

"Keep an eye on them," he ordered, "but focus on our system scans. We have another couple days here before it's time to move on, and the research teams are going to want to make the most of it."

"Yes sir."

While their mission was now primarily military, unlike the mission of the *Odyssey*, the *Odysseus* actually had several times the lab space and civilian crew they'd carried on the previous vessel. The *Odysseus* was far more automated than the *Odyssey* and thus required fewer crew members per ton, so to speak, so they had a lot of extra room for labs and researchers. At the moment, with any information being worth more than gold, the Alliance fully intended to capitalize on that.

Every particle in the system was something the research teams were clamoring to record from as many angles as possible. In fact, Eric had shut down three requests from scientists who wanted to accompany Steph and Milla and take a closer look at the gas giant the two were going to sling around.

Under other circumstances, Eric would have likely granted the requests, but Milla wouldn't have qualified for her certification if there had been anyone else aboard besides the examiner. Academics, being what they were, didn't care about details like that. They just wanted to get as much time as they could with their instruments focused on the subject of their obsessions.

And they get touchy when you tell them they can't have what they're asking for.

He made a mental note to make it up to the researchers, if he had a chance. Normally Eric wouldn't be overly concerned about what lab rats thought about him, but he'd learned just how badly one annoying academic could disrupt his ship.

▶▶▶

Shuttle *Eagle One*

▶ "How am I doing?" Milla asked, a nervous tremor in her voice.

Steph smiled slightly, shaking his head. "You know I can't tell you that, Lieutenant. This is a flight exam."

He held up his hand, then idly tapped his finger on the microphone that was monitoring them. "But off the record, you're doing fine. Just keep on going."

Milla nodded. "Thank you."

Steph stopped tapping. "Watch our trajectory. If you waste too much Delta-V slowing on approach, we'll have to call in the *Odysseus* to pick us up. That would be a fail, by the way."

"Of course," Milla said, triple-checking the numbers. "Telemetry indicates we are on schedule for turnover in nine hours. The gravity of the large planet will do the rest for us."

Steph absently glanced over the numbers himself and was reasonably impressed. They could be a little more elegant, but he'd always been known for his theatrical flair. In terms of fuel and Delta-V, Milla's telemetry was completely serviceable. Slightly above the required numbers as prescribed by the book, in fact.

"Alright," he said. "Then we're in for a long drop."

Milla leaned forward, flipping a bank of switches to bring the autopilot fully online, then she sat back. "Automatic systems engaged. We are now on automated approach, and hands free, yes?"

"Yes, we are. Alright, now we wait." Steph pulled his belt off and let it slip back behind his seat.

He drifted loose from the seat, stretching as he floated free and turned around slightly so he could see Milla as she undid the clasps on her own belt.

"It is odd," she admitted as she floated off the seat. "Even the smallest of our vessels have gravity."

"I suppose we will soon enough as well," Steph answered, "but I'll probably miss zero g when it comes."

"I can understand," Milla admitted. "However, it is not good for the human form to be in free fall for too long. Bone density . . ."

"Yeah, we know. That's why I work out as much as I do—why we all do," Steph responded. "But even with the heaviest regime, I'd have been off space duty within two more years. Your gravity systems change that, so that's one I owe your people. The captain too. We both love our jobs too much to give them up easily."

"I wish I could take the credit, yes?" She smiled. "However, I believe that was the council's call, not my own."

"Either way, your tech is going to change a lot of lives."

"Helping us cost a lot of lives, did it not?" Milla asked softly.

Steph didn't know what to say to that at first. He was taken aback by the question but more so by the hint of guilt he could hear in her voice.

"You don't know that," he said finally. "The Drasin were sweeping in our direction. If they finished with you, we could have been next."

"You don't know that." She repeated his words with a weak smile.

"The Drasin were . . . a plague. They would have continued to spread until someone stopped them. Better it was us, now, than someone else much later," Steph said, taking a deep breath. "There's no point buying trouble anyway. We can't change the past."

"No, I suppose that we cannot," Milla admitted. "However much we wish we could."

"Anyway, enough of that," Steph said, trying to change the mood as he produced a deck of cards from his pocket. "Shall we see if you've improved your game?"

CHAPTER 7

IBC *Piar Cohn*, System Entry

▶ A soft but insistent alarm was sounding as Aymes stepped onto the forward command deck of the *Cohn* and noted with satisfaction that all the stations aside from his own were already filled.

"Report," he ordered simply, standing at his station.

"Now entering system of interest, Three Alep Nine One Du, Captain," his helm officer said. "Beginning analysis of spatial distortions, comparing to expected readings. Initial response is as expected."

"Good," Aymes said. "Time to system penetration?"

"A tenth and three," the ship's alternate commander offered from where he was working. "We're on a fast approach, no turnover."

Aymes absently checked the telemetry chart for himself. The *Cohn* was on a high-velocity approach . . . Unusual, but he remembered authorizing it for this system because there was a single gas giant exceptionally far out from the system primary that they could use as a redirect to save reactor mass.

"Very well. Any unusual signals in the band we're looking at?" he asked.

"No Captain. No active Drasin contact."

"Another wasted system," he muttered. "How deep did those abominations penetrate this arm?"

His alternate commander shrugged. "Last reported location was a rim system, thirty cycles deeper into the arm. We have extremely limited information, unfortunately."

"I know, I read the file. What little there was of it," Aymes growled. "The squadron commander who left them there should be shot."

"He likely was."

Aymes nodded wearily, knowing that was probably true enough. Abandoning assets like that would end careers at the very best. Doing so when the assets were potential threats to the Empire . . . well, he'd be surprised if any of the command crew were still to be found. Possibly some were still breathing, but he expected they'd likely been reassigned to either high-risk sectors or some other place where warm bodies mattered more than competence.

"Alright, let's get this system clear—"

A buzzer cut him off, and Aymes twisted to where the scanner chief was now working feverishly at his station.

"What is it?" the captain demanded.

"Dimensional anomaly," the chief answered instantly. "Possibly an unscanned planetoid, something from far out in the system."

"How far?" Aymes asked.

"Very far. In order to not be on our scans, it would have to be something with an extremely eccentric orbit, Captain. Thousand-cycle orbit, at least."

Aymes frowned, considering that.

It wasn't impossible. There were certainly stranger star systems in the galaxy than one with a single—or even a few—eccentric-orbit planetoids. However, this was one of the few systems the Empire had mapped out prior to launching the infiltration and assault of this arm of the galaxy.

"Could it be an enemy ship?" he asked softly, walking over to the station.

"Possibly," the chief replied. "It *is* a known Oather system, Captain."

"Well, if it's an Oather ship," the alternate commander offered, "we can easily handle them."

Aymes nodded. "True. I'm more concerned about the unknown, however."

"The anomaly wouldn't show up on dimensional warp scans," the alternate agreed.

"No, but that's the problem," Aymes said and sighed. "This anomaly is too difficult to locate for my taste."

He stared for a moment. "Continue as plotted, but lock down that anomaly."

"Yes Captain."

▶▶▶

AEV *Odysseus*

▶ "Report."

Eric strode onto the command deck, eyes swiveling to lock on the long-range scanner station.

"We have a gravity anomaly, Captain," the duty officer, Lieutenant Sierra, answered.

"Drasin?" Eric asked, standing at his station.

"No match, sir. Not on any of our databases."

"What about Priminae databases?" he asked.

"Ran those too, sir. Possible match, but too vague to be certain. We could be looking at a long-orbit planetoid, coming in from the local version of the Oort Cloud," Sierra said.

"Do the Priminae have any planetoids with that sort of orbit listed for this system?" Eric asked.

Sierra turned to look at him, eyes widening.

"It *is* one of their colony systems, Lieutenant."

"Yes sir! Sorry, sir, checking now," Sierra blurted, looking back to her console.

It took only a few seconds, then she shook her head. "No eccentric-orbit planetoids, sir."

"Sound general quarters," Eric ordered, dropping into his chair. "How far out is the anomaly?"

The general-quarters alarm sounded in the background but was muted swiftly on the bridge as systems shifted to alert status.

"Working on an orbit now, sir."

Commander Heath strode onto the bridge, pausing next to Eric as she examined the activity. "Sir?"

"Unknown contact," Eric said. "Possible enemy ship."

Miram nodded, dropping into her own seat at her station. "I see it. Not a planetoid?"

"Not according to Priminae charts," Eric answered.

"Right, of course. It's one of their former systems. They would have it properly mapped." Miram nodded again. "Still . . . it doesn't appear to be under power. I'm not seeing a change in course telemetry."

"Can you tell what course it's on?" Eric asked.

"Not quite. Just a general trajectory with a very wide margin of error," she admitted. "However, it is not slowing down. It appears to be on a ballistic course, Captain."

That *was* odd, Eric would willingly admit. A ship on system approach would have to be decelerating hard if they didn't want to shoot right through, and if they were doing that, why take the risk of entering the gravity well of the local star? Sure, there wasn't *much* more debris inside the well, but it was still a risk if you were moving at the speeds of a relativistic vessel.

If the ship was warping space, there would be no risk, but this contact wasn't warping. It was ballistic, and that made no sense.

"We're narrowing it down," Miram said. "They're aiming for a slingshot maneuver. In a little less than two hours, they're going to sling around the outer gas giant."

Eric stiffened. "Are you sure?"

"Yes sir," Miram answered, looking perplexed as she noticed his apprehension.

"Goddamn it!" Eric swore, mind racing as he started to say something, then stopped.

"What is it?" Miram asked.

"I gave Steph and Milla clearance to do a qual flight," he said, shaking his head. "They're slinging around that same damn planet."

"We can go to power and pick them up," Miram said.

"If we warp space," Eric said grimly, motioning toward the telemetry readings, "they'll *see* us."

"Sir, they must see us already. The *Odysseus* isn't like the *Odyssey*. We can't hide from their scanners," Miram said. "We mass as much as a small planet."

"Yes, but they're not Priminae, Commander," Eric said. "I'm betting they don't have full system records. Right now, at the range they're coming in from, we're just a dip in space-time. If we warp space, then they'll *know* we're not some random rock."

He stood up, walking over to the comm station.

"Get me a link to the shuttle."

▶▶▶

IBC *Piar Cohn*

▶ "Sir, we've calculated the anomaly's orbit."

Aymes looked over to his scanner chief, nodding. "And?"

"It's odd," he said. "The orbit isn't as eccentric as I would have believed."

"Oh?" Aymes took more of an interest. "How so?"

"Just that I would have expected our combat survey to have included this one," the chief said. "It's an eccentric orbit, but the opening to miss it would have been quite small."

"Hmm," Aymes grunted, turning around. "Alert status. All decks."

The alarms sounded, and people began rushing around as Aymes sat in the middle of the whirlwind of activity, glaring at the screens surrounding him.

He was probably being overly cautious, but there was no sense in following the fate of his predecessor.

He rather liked breathing.

▶▶▶

Shuttle *Eagle One*

▶ Cards were a boring way to pass the time with only two people, but Steph had always been one for tradition. After a couple rounds, however, they'd put away the game and pulled out a couple readers. Milla was working her way through some classic science fiction from Earth, while he had a soft spot for old pulp books.

They were a third of the way past turnover when the comm station chirped and the pair looked up from their books.

"Message from the *Odysseus*," Milla said, floating down to the pilot's seat and pulling the straps over her shoulders.

"Play it," Steph said, gliding over and grabbing the back of the seat to steady himself.

Milla nodded and tapped the command.

"*Eagle One*, *Odysseus* Command. Stand by for a message from *Odysseus* Actual."

Steph smirked. "Boss must want to offer some encouragement."

"Stephanos . . ." Eric Weston's voice was serious. The second Steph heard his call sign, he flexed his arms and flipped over the seat, dropping into place as the message continued. "We've picked up a gravity anomaly on course for the gas giant. Looks like you and it are planning on using the planet for the same maneuver. Great minds, I suppose. The *Odysseus* can't get to you first, even if we light off. Worst case, if it's unfriendly, you'd be caught in the cross fire."

Steph punched in a command, calling up the shuttle's scanners and overlaying them with the data packet the *Odysseus* had sent.

"We've got nothing on our scanners," he said, "but we wouldn't at this range."

"Should I change course?" Milla asked.

"Negative. We don't have the Delta-V to reverse course, and this is still our best shot at a clean return to the *Odysseus*," Steph answered. "Space—even planetary space—is a massive area. We go deep, take the plates to black hole settings."

"Roger that," Milla answered, typing in a series of commands. "Done."

"Secure scanners, comms, and all transmissions," Steph ordered. "Take us dark."

"Done. *Eagle One* is dark."

"Good work," Steph said. "Boss is going to take the *Odysseus* around and try to flank the bad guys, but that'll put us intersecting their course long before that."

"What do we do?" she asked, eyes focusing on Steph. "This is . . . above my grade, yes?"

"Reality often is, Lieutenant," Steph answered. "Don't sweat it. You'll do fine."

"This should be your bird, yes, Commander?"

Steph tilted his head, considering. "If I take it, your qual flight is over."

"It seems more important that we live through this, I believe?"

Steph waved his hand casually. "Your bird, Lieutenant. I'll take it if I need to."

"Yes sir."

▶▶▶

▶ *Eagle One* faded to near pitch black as the cam-plate armor began absorbing all frequencies of visible light and beyond. Running lights flicked off, transmissions ended. The systems on a shuttle were hardly up to the full specs of the *Odysseus*, but the small vessel didn't need to be nearly as efficient in order to hide in hundreds of millions of cubic kilometers of space.

Ahead, the gas giant loomed in the distance. To the naked eye, the world was a dim one, not having much light to reflect from the system's primary star due to distance. In fact, the local sun barely looked larger than some of the other bright stars in the black around them.

In near infrared, however, the gas giant was a beacon in the night.

▶▶▶

IBC *Piar Cohn*

▶ "Status of the unknown contact," Aymes asked as he returned to the bridge, just glancing at the screen where the gas giant was growing visibly larger.

"Still on an eccentric orbit, Captain. No change."

Aymes scowled. He almost wished there had been. At least then he'd have an idea what to do, but at the moment he was left with a bit of a quandary.

"What do we have on visible scanners?" he asked.

"Not much," the chief said, shaking his head. "It's even farther out than the gas giant, Captain. Not enough light reflecting to get much resolution with ship scanners."

He *could* go active, of course, but that would reveal his location and give any enemy a good idea of what they were up against. In exchange, he might not get much of a return signal at the current range. Whatever was out there, it wasn't on an intercept course with the *Cohn*, which could mean it hadn't spotted them yet or that it was playing dead and hoping to be missed.

That wasn't going to happen. He'd have to check it out closely before he left the system, but he'd rather not put the *Cohn* in a targeting reticule in the process.

We do not always get the things that we wish for.

"Take us to combat standing," he ordered. "Stand by to separate parasite craft, charge real-time scanners."

"Yes Captain. Systems standing by for orders. Parasite craft are being manned."

Aymes nodded slowly. "Once they're manned . . . launch the parasites and bring the light to this whole damned system."

CHAPTER 8

Shuttle *Eagle One*, Entering Orbit

▶ "I see it, Commander."

Steph leaned forward. "Where?"

Milla pointed. In the distance, a bright star moved fast against the background.

"Got it," Steph confirmed. "Get the passives on it. Try and work out its location and course through parallax."

"As you say, Stephan," she answered. "Without active systems, I am having to track manually."

"Whoa."

Milla looked up. "What is it?"

"Something just happened. Check it out," Steph said, tipping his chin toward the viewport.

She followed his gaze and spotted what he was talking about instantly. The contact she'd been following had split up. There were now at least eight or nine different spots, spreading out but moving along a similar course.

"Parasites." She whispered the word, in Priminae.

"What was that?" Steph asked, confused. "I didn't catch that."

"It is . . . an old system—parasite ships attached to a larger vessel," she answered. "We ceased using that design."

"Why?" Steph asked, trying to judge the size of the parasite craft.

They were bigger than Double A fighters, as there was no way an Archangel would be visible at this range.

"No need for them," Milla answered. "A single vessel has more than sufficient power. Parasites add very little."

"They add mobility," Steph corrected. "Options. Options are good if you're fighting a war."

Milla was about to respond, but before she could say anything, something on her screens caught her eye. She scowled for a brief moment before suddenly blurting out something that sounded *incredibly* vile to Steph, despite him not understanding a word of it.

"What? What is it?" he demanded, knowing profanity when he heard it.

"One of the parasites has altered course," Milla answered. "It is coming for us."

▶▶▶

AEV *Odysseus*

▶ The tachyon pulse set everything on its ear.

"Isolate and locate the source of that!" Miram ordered, surging to her feet.

Eric remained silent. He already knew the source. There really was only one possible place the pulse could have come from.

"Belay that," he said finally, standing up and stepping around his console. "Even armor, warp space on my command."

"Aye aye, Captain," Lieutenant Kinder confirmed. "Course?"

"Intercept, Bogey One."

"Intercept, aye."

Eric glanced over to Commander Heath. "Take us from general quarters to battle stations, Commander."

"Aye aye, sir." She stepped forward. "Battle stations! All decks report in. Secure all stations for combat operations!"

Eric watched silently as his ship rigged for war, knowing that out across the black, his counterpart was doing precisely the same thing.

▶▶▶

IBC *Piar Cohn*

▶ "Parasites launching, Captain."

"Bring light to the darkness, Chief," Aymes ordered from his station.

"Yes Captain."

The ship's FTL scanners lit off, pulsing a wide swath of the system with tachyon particles. The response hits started pouring back instantly, and the computers processed the information.

"Initial signal matches Oather designs," the chief said. "Very similar to Imperial cruiser specifications, Captain."

"Understood. Give me the overlay with our previous scans," Aymes said, looking at the screens.

"Yes sir."

The image of the unknown ship was indeed very similar to Imperial designs. Almost identical, in fact, to the *Piar Cohn* itself. There were some oddities he couldn't identify, and that bothered Aymes. Whatever was tacked on to the ship's superstructure was an unknown element.

The visual was overlaid with visible and nonvisible light data from previous and ongoing scans. Aymes frowned at the image, picking up a portable system and comparing the data from analysis of Oather ships.

"Something is off," he said a moment later. "Chief, what is this frequency spike?"

The chief walked over, checking the signal that the captain was pointing out. Finally he shook his head. "I don't know, Captain. The rest is expected materials science from an Oather design, but that spike is new."

"New?" Aymes frowned. "There are only so many materials in existence. Imperial and Oather materials science peaked long ago. When was the last time we saw an improvement in that area?"

The chief shrugged.

"Never, Chief," Aymes growled. "The Oathers took the best materials science ever developed with them when they split. That's a metal frequency spike. There isn't a metallic armor in existence that can match Oather ceramics. Lord knows, the Empire has tried. So why is an Oather ship showing a metallic frequency spike?"

"I don't know, Captain."

"Neither do I, and do *not* like things I do not know showing up in a potential combat situation."

"Uh . . . yes sir."

Aymes glared at the chief briefly, then waved him back to his station. He was turning away when another alarm went off.

"What is it?"

"New contact, Captain!" the chief cried. "Close. Very close."

"On screen! Track it!"

"Difficult, Captain. There's no visible spectrum read!"

"Instant scanners say something is out there. *Find it!*" Aymes ordered. "We may be far too close to the unknown vessel for our safety!"

"Unlikely, Captain," his alternate commander said. "The contact is too small by far. It barely registered on instant scans, and it's entering the orbit of the gas giant as we speak."

Aymes blinked, surprised. That was *close*. Far closer than anything should have been able to get to his ship without being noticed.

"Dispatch parasite *Five* to investigate the contact," he ordered. "If they resist . . . destroy them."

"Yes Captain."

▶ ▶ ▶

Shuttle *Eagle One*

▶ "Alright, that's it," Steph decided. "Sorry, Milla, my bird."

She nodded, pale with a bead of sweat on her brow. "Your bird, Commander."

Steph hit the sequence that shifted primary command to his seat, then began powering CM generators. "We're going to have to make a run for it. Talk to me—what do you know about these parasite craft?"

"Very little. I am sorry." She shook her head. "They were listed only in the history portion of my training."

"I'll take history," he told her as he worked. "Anything you remember. How fast can they warp space?"

"They do not. The point of parasite vessels is that they do not require the same power core as a full ship. They can be brought into an operational space by a starship but are much cheaper, yes?"

"Okay, no space warp." Steph flipped a bank of switches. "Good. I can work with that. Reaction drive?"

"Not like yours," she said, "but similar, yes."

"Range?"

"I am not sure." She shook her head again. "Not beyond the star system, obviously."

"I was hoping for a smaller area of operations," Steph admitted as he punched in a new course. "Alright, get ready to hang on. I'm probably going to be pushing the limit of our CM field, so we're going to be tossed around a bit. Tighten those straps."

While she was working to do that, Steph finalized the new course and brought the ship's dual reactors fully online.

"Here we go . . . ," he said as he twisted the stick and shoved the throttle all the way forward.

▶ ▶ ▶

IBC *Piar Cohn*

▶ "They're evading," the scanning chief announced.

"How can you tell?"

"I can see them when they eclipse objects behind them," the chief said. "They're diving into the gas giant. We should see them more clearly . . . now."

Aymes looked up at the screen just in time to see a black silhouette as it appeared in front of the planet. The vessel was very small, smaller by far than even one of the *Piar Cohn*'s parasite vessels. That was good news and bad news.

At least they wouldn't be in danger of combat with the unknown vessel that had plagued the initial Drasin incursion into the Oather territory. But he could tell at a glance that the target's acceleration curve was extremely high, perhaps even higher than a parasite craft's, which would make catching the ship difficult.

"Dispatch parasites *Three* and *Eight* to fence that ship in," Aymes said. "I want *Five* to continue pursuit while *Three* and *Eight* take a counter orbit and catch the craft on the other side of the planet."

"Yes Captain. Orders issued."

"Good. Keep the rest in formation," Aymes said. "We're going after their home vessel."

"On your orders, Captain."

"On my orders indeed."

▶▶▶

Shuttle *Eagle One*

▶ "Stephan, I believe they have sent others after us," Milla said, swiveling in her seat to look out to the side. "Two . . . no, wait, they are not on an intercept with us. They are going away."

"Away? Away where?" Steph asked, hitting a bank of overhead switches to shunt full military power to the reactors.

"I am not sure. However, they are moving away from us now."

"Are they closing on the planet still?"

"Yes. Why?"

"Damn. Clever bastards," Steph grumbled, a dark smile on his face. "They're gonna try a pincer."

"What is a . . . pincer?"

"One chases; the other cuts around and gets in front of the prey," Steph explained. "They're going to cut us off by countering our orbit of the planet. This is going to get tricky."

"Oh, of course. What can we do?" Milla asked, wishing suddenly that she'd spent a little more time on navigation and piloting and less on her own specialties.

Suddenly, being an expert in starship weaponry didn't feel so useful.

"I'm going to have to fly this one by ear," Steph said, "but they're clearly tracking us now . . ."

"We are dark, yes?"

"Yes, but the planet is behind us now. They can see our silhouette," he answered. "Even if we go to adaptive camo, there's no way to match the infrared output of the planet . . . not from up here anyway."

Milla shifted nervously in her seat as Stephen glowered suddenly, leaning forward as much as his straps would allow. She didn't think she liked that look, not when she was sitting across from him in a small shuttle at least.

"I am not going to enjoy this, am I?" she asked weakly.

"Depends." Steph chuckled. "Do you like carnival rides?"

"No," she answered. "I do not know *what* carnival rides are. However, I am quite sure I do not like them."

"Pity. Don't throw up," Steph said as he pushed the stick forward and dropped the shuttle into the upper atmosphere of the gas giant.

▶▶▶

IBC *Piar Cohn*

▶ "The target craft has dropped into the atmosphere. We're losing contact in the upper atmospheric clouds."

"Smart." Aymes shook his head. "Very smart. Hand off tactical command of the pursuit to the commander of parasite *Five*. Inform him I want that craft intact if possible, in pieces if not."

"Yes Captain."

Aymes shifted to look at the distant contact. "In the meantime, we have more important things to deal with."

He calculated the distance in his head, working out the numbers. Aymes figured they had another couple full cycles before the visible scanners picked up the reaction of the contact to their instant scan. However, the space dimension scanners should be showing changes very quickly.

"Alter course, plot best time intercept for the primary target," he ordered.

"Yes Captain. We have three such courses prepared. Do we assume they hold their current course, move to intercept, or average the two?" the helmsman asked.

"Average the two," Aymes said, "but lean in the direction of an intercept."

"On your orders, Captain."

"You have my orders, and my permission."

▶▶▶

Shuttle *Eagle One*

▶ "The primary vessel is altering course."

"Toward us?" Steph asked.

"No. I am getting a redshift on their signal through the passive scanners," Milla answered. "They are moving away from the planet."

Steph bit his lip, thinking about it, then shook his head.

"Must have spotted the *Odysseus*," he decided. "Well, nothing we can do for them right now. We have our own problems."

Turbulence rocked the shuttle as Steph took them into another cloud bank, heading south as *Eagle One* began circumnavigating the gas giant.

"Light off our radar," he said. "Look for turbulence behind us."

Milla nodded, killing the stealth cutouts they'd been running and bringing the shuttle's powerful radar online. She flipped the system over into Doppler mode and started running scans all around them.

"As you said," Milla noted, "strong turbulence behind us. They have entered the atmosphere in pursuit."

"Only one of them, Milla." Stephen sighed. "He's just bird-dogging us so that we can't sneak around the hunters."

"Can we get away?"

"I don't know, but we're going to have fun trying," Steph said with a grin.

Milla grimaced. "You, Stephan, enjoy the very strangest things."

He pushed the shuttle deeper down into the atmosphere, not bothering to try and mask his turbulence signature. Evading them was the ideal, but since that wasn't going to happen, Steph was more than happy to take second best—keeping them right where he could see them.

▶▶▶

PC (*Piar Cohn*) Parasite *Five*

▶ Subaltern Penae Girar glared at the scope that showed the path of the craft he was pursuing. He was tracking the ship by atmospheric disturbances, and the profile on all active scans was almost nonexistent. Penae had never seen anything like it. Even a ship as small as the one they were tracking should have a *much* larger profile.

Catching this one will be difficult, even with three parasites.

He was dealing with a small—very small—and apparently maneuverable craft. The pilot hadn't done much yet to stand out as either good or bad, but Penae had to assume that the prey was at least competent.

"Check the signal relay," Penae ordered his second.

"All scans are mirrored to *Three* and *Eight*," the second confirmed. "They see what we see."

"Good. Tighten the noose. This one can't run for long."

CHAPTER 9

AEV *Odysseus*

▶ "Something odd about that tachyon pulse, Captain." Ensign Perez frowned at his station, running pattern recognition on what they'd picked up from the pulse.

Tachyon pulses were a double-edged sword. Since they were effectively instantaneous in how fast they traveled and spacefarers would often know their source, anyone in the system could use a pulse to pick up locational data. As soon as the bogey had lit off, it had given both itself *and* the *Odysseus* a real-time peek at the situation.

"What is it, Ensign?"

"There seems to be interference around the target ship, sir."

Eric cocked his head to one side. "Interference, Ensign?"

Nothing "interfered" with tachyons, aside from perhaps gravity. They were extremely high-energy particles that generally moved too fast for any sort of interference to be visible on human scales. Gravity did affect tachyons, of course, but there was unlikely to be any source of gravity in the area remotely *chaotic* enough to be considered interference.

"I don't really know what to make of it, Captain," Perez admitted. "It looks like the ship is breaking apart."

Now *that* got Eric's attention, and he stepped away from his console to approach the signals section of the bridge.

"Show me," he ordered.

"Yes sir," Perez said, calling up the data to his main screen. "As you can see, there's something strange about the signal here."

"I see it." Eric nodded, noting that it did look like the ship was breaking up. "How long before we get light-speed signals?"

Perez glanced at the ship's clock. "A little over an hour, sir."

Eric shook his head. "That's not going to cut it. Alright, stand by for tachyon pulse. One ping only."

"Aye sir, one ping only."

"What's our current course?" Eric turned, looking over to where Kinder was working the helm.

"We are warping space for the gas giant, sir. One-third power."

"Stand by for full military power."

"Aye sir, standing by."

"Perez, sound them out."

"Aye sir, one ping," Perez answered, sending the command to loose a burst of focused tachyons.

The FTL particles appeared and vanished in the same instant, lighting up the system briefly as the command crew watched.

"We've lost sight of *Eagle One*, sir. I don't see them anywhere," Perez said, "but it looks like . . . Sir, I'm showing at least eight additional ships now in that vicinity. Mass looks like . . . pocket destroyers, sir?"

"Where the hell did they come from?" Eric muttered, shaking his head and trying not to think about what had just happened to his friend Steph.

"I don't know, sir. Light-speed scanners still show only the one ship on target, and we're over an hour away from scanning the current situation."

"Not for long," Eric said firmly. "Helm, full military power. All flank to intercept."

"Aye sir, all flank to intercept!"

▶▶▶

▶ The *Odysseus* was built around two massive gravity sinks, functionally identical to quantum singularities but held right at the edge of stability. A stable singularity would swallow the ship while an unstable one would just blow itself out while probably irradiating the *Odysseus* and everyone on board.

As the ship began tapping full power from the twin singularities, the systems began winding space-time around the *Odysseus*. A deep, sharp sink appeared ahead of the ship as a bulge began to build up behind it. As one pushed and the other pulled, the *Odysseus* began to fall through space toward the gas giant.

▶▶▶

IBC *Piar Cohn*

▶ "We have been lit, Captain," the chief signals officer said.

Aymes nodded absently but didn't reply to the man for a moment. He'd seen the burst hit their scanners, knew the signature well enough. It was unsurprising, expected even, but the signature itself was curious.

"I don't recognize that signature, Chief," Aymes said finally. "Does it match Oather signals?"

"No Captain. Close, but not a precise match."

"That is what is beginning to worry me," Aymes said.

"Captain, they've begun running their drives. Powerful signals, no course telemetry yet."

"No need to worry about that," Aymes said. "There is only one place that they could be going that would matter to us right now. They are coming for us."

Indeed, he was well aware that any other course didn't make any difference. If they were running, he'd let them run. His mission wasn't to antagonize the Oathers any more than they already had been. He and the *Cohn* were here to track the Drasin. That threat had to be secured.

The Oathers could come later.

It was more likely, however, that the target vessel and its presumed Oather crew were coming straight for the *Piar Cohn*. There was little reason to light off their reactors and twist space as urgently as they clearly were, except to come head on to try to save their little friend playing games in the gas giant.

That suited Aymes just fine.

His mission might not be to aggravate the Oathers, but he wouldn't shed any tears over them if they happened to find their end here in this forsaken system.

"It's better this way," he murmured.

"Captain?"

"I was just saying, Commander," he told his alternate, "that this may be the best of all possible outcomes."

"Our orders were not to engage the Oathers."

"True. However, I believe that they are about to engage us . . ." Aymes lifted his right hand, palm up. "And less witnesses to our mission is a good thing."

"As you say, my Captain."

"Dispatch orders to our parasite destroyers," Aymes said. "Spread them out. Give me an Alep Six formation. All weapons are to be considered available."

"Captain . . ." The alternate turned to look at him.

"*All* weapons, Altern Commander."

"Yes Captain."

The order was probably overkill, Aymes knew, but this arm of the galaxy was dark territory to the Empire right now. He wasn't going to underestimate anything here, not if he could help it.

Not even Oathers.

▶▶▶

AEV *Odysseus*

▶ "Captain, we have a real-time lock," Lieutenant Waters offered. "We can hit them with t-cannons."

Eric considered the idea for a moment, then shook his head, "No, Lieutenant. For one, we don't have eyes on Commander Michaels and Lieutenant Chans . . . and I'd rather not expose our trump card until we can be sure we've locked them all down."

"Yes sir."

"Besides, we don't know they're hostile yet," Eric said. "Our ROE allow for first strike against the Drasin, no quarter, but not against unconfirmed targets."

"Yes sir. Sorry sir."

"Don't apologize, Lieutenant. It was a good suggestion, just not one we can implement right now," Eric said. "For now, we play it straight."

"Aye sir."

Commander Heath walked over to Eric's side, speaking quietly. "Does playing it straight mean we fly right at each other and try to blast one another out of space like men? Because if it does, as the ship's ranking woman, I would like to enter an objection for the record."

Eric shot her an amused look, surprised by the humor from the normally uptight commander.

"I think we'll try hailing them once we're within a reasonable communications delay," he said. "Unfortunately, without the Priminae FTL relays, we can't talk until we're much closer."

"If we're within reasonable range to talk, we're going to be well within reasonable range to shoot each other," Miram said softly. "But you already know that, of course, sir."

"If you wanted a safe job, Commander, you picked the wrong line of work."

Miram let out a breath. "I picked the right line of work, Captain."

"Good," Eric said. "Get the damage-control teams moving, if they're not already."

"Yes sir."

Eric watched the commander move away, wondering how Miram would hold up under fire. She seemed together, but you didn't know how someone would react to combat until the chips were in the air. While the Heroics did have priority on new recruits, the demand was still such that he'd had to take several people based on how their files looked rather than how he *knew* they could perform. He was lucky to have held on to as much of his crew as he had, and at least the replacements looked good on paper.

This was the worst part of ship-to-ship combat, something he rarely had to deal with as a fighter jock.

The waiting.

It was infinitely worse in space, he'd learned on the *Odyssey*.

In the middle of *active* combat, they often had time to break for coffee and a meal while waiting for the enemies' next move. It was the very definition of insanity as far as he was concerned. Right now they could read that the enemy ship was powering hard, pulling out of the gas giant's gravity well and heading upwell of the local star, right at the *Odysseus*.

Similarly, the *Odysseus* was warping space hard *downwell*, on an intercept course.

Two immensely powerful starships, both moving as fast as anyone dared this deep inside a gravity well, heading right for one another—and he was debating whether he should take a fifteen-minute power nap so he would be refreshed when the action started.

If gods exist, they must be laughing at us right now. We are so very insignificant by every possible metric of the universe, and yet we insist on making ourselves the center of everything.

Eric stood up. "Commander."

"Yes sir?"

"You have the bridge. I'll be back in twenty minutes."

"Aye Captain," Miram said. "I have the bridge."

Eric nodded curtly and walked off the command deck of the *Odysseus*.

▶▶▶

Shuttle *Eagle One*

▶ Milla's stomach lurched as the shuttle seemed to drop out from under them, plummeting through the atmosphere of the gas giant for a thousand meters before it restabilized and started climbing again. Steph was calmly seated beside her, looking like nothing had just happened as he worked the controls.

"Keep on the Doppler," he said without looking over at her. "See if you can spot our pursuers."

"Y-yes sir," Milla blurted, refocusing on the task at hand.

The shuttle had a full scanner suite, but as deep in the atmosphere as they were currently flying, the radar systems were still the most effective.

The vessel pursuing them was, surprisingly, in Milla's opinion, not particularly stealthy. The metallic composite of the hull reflected radar quite well, something that a similar Priminae ship would not do. However, she was having almost more luck tracking the atmospheric distortion of its passing than the ship itself.

"They are still pursuing, two kilometers above us, on our six, yes?"

"Six, copy," Steph said. "Not trying to shake them yet. Don't have a lot of places to hide here."

"Then what is the plan?"

"When we make a run for it," Steph said, "we're going to need as much confusion as possible to buy us some lead time."

"But we could do that now, yes?"

"Yes, but not until I know where all our pursuers are," Steph said firmly. "If they left even one of those parasites in orbit, we'll never get clear. I need them all down here with us when I make the break, otherwise it's for nothing."

Milla wasn't sure she understood, but she nodded anyway.

"Just watch the radar," Steph said. "Need to know when the other two come into sight."

"I understand. I will inform you," Milla said. "What happens then?"

"Good," Steph said, glancing over at her and flashing a smile. "And that, my dear Miss Chans, is when the fun begins."

▶▶▶

PC Parasite *Five*

▶ "He is going deeper into the atmosphere, Subaltern."

Subaltern Penae Girar nodded. "I see the track, Saulo. What pressure are they at?"

"Three standards and increasing."

Penae hissed, annoyed.

Space-capable vessels were not particularly suited for atmospheric transit, even when they were designed to handle such conditions. The stresses on a hull were far different in the void, and thus ships had to be designed to resist vacuum rather than pressure. Certainly, they could be made strong enough to handle some significant pressure, but it seemed that either the target vessel was better suited to planetary atmospheric conditions, or the pilot was insane.

Either was annoying, but of the two he'd much prefer the ship design to be superior. Crazy people were more trouble than they were worth.

"Signal *Three* and *Eight*," Penae said. "Close the loop."

"Yes Subaltern," his subordinate said. "Orders issued."

"Helm to my command," Penae said, reaching for the controls.

"Helm is yours to command, Subaltern."

The control circuits switched over to his station, and he pushed forward, driving his craft deeper into the atmosphere.

▶▶▶

Shuttle *Eagle One*

▶ Turbulence buffeted the shuttle hard, throwing Steph and Milla around and causing the straps to bite into their shoulders and waists. Steph worked the controls hard, trying to get a feel for the state of the atmosphere but finding the task difficult through electronic controls. The Archangels had been designed with force feedback loops built into the system, not quite as responsive as the old hydraulic systems or a pure cable link, but a lot better than the video game controls he was fighting through now.

"This damn thing is a pig," he grumbled, eyes flicking to the telltales as he tried to keep track of how the shuttle was reacting to his movements.

The shuttle's lifting surfaces flexed and twisted under the stresses he was pushing it through, fighting the fast-moving atmosphere rushing around them.

"I see a new vector on the radar, Stephan," Milla offered. "Coming from ahead of us, low orbital track entering the upper atmosphere."

"That's two," Stephen said. "Come on, lucky number three . . ."

The shuttle jumped then dropped again as Steph played with the CM reactor, trying to keep a stable flight as the turbulent atmosphere tossed them around.

"There is three!" yelled Milla. "Coming in from . . . ten o'clock, very high!"

"Alright." Steph loosed a feral grin. "New game. Let's see how well you suckers fly."

CHAPTER 10

PC Parasite *Five*

▶ Penae smiled tightly at the plot he was reading.

The target was well below them, but it was rapidly running out of room to maneuver. Penae didn't care how well that little craft could handle pressures—it had to be close to its limits. With three parasites and the planet itself to pin the enemy pilot against, the capture operation should be simple enough.

"Parasite *Eight*, hold at your current altitude," he said. "Secure the outer perimeter. If they get past us, you snap them up."

The commander of parasite *Eight* acknowledged the command and leveled the ship's descent, holding altitude just inside the atmospheric envelope of the planet. The frigate would have greater speed and maneuverability at that altitude, as well as the high stance if the enemy craft managed to escape the combined maneuvering of *Three* and *Five*.

"Ensure that quantum lock systems are charged and ready," Penae ordered next, eyes still on the screens.

"All systems are blue, Commander. *Three* and *Eight* confirm as well. We are ready."

"Execute."

▶▶▶

Shuttle *Eagle One*

▸ "They are closing, Stephan," Milla warned as Steph monitored the CM levels.

"I've got 'em," he said with a nod, looking back up. "Keep an eye on the counter-mass. We're going to have to finesse that while we're this low in the atmosphere."

"I have the controls," Milla confirmed, turning her focus to the shuttle's CM systems.

"Bandit Three is holding back," Steph commented as he punched in a series of numbers, one eye on the scopes while the other checked his entries. "We're going to have to run a blockade once we're past the first two."

Milla couldn't help but smile, just a little, as she took in the quiet confidence in his voice. There was no hint of worry that the two closing frigates would pose a serious problem, despite the fact that the shuttle was hardly one of his Archangels and they were unarmed. She found herself in an unusual position for one of her people, as she was almost enjoying the anticipation of the violence that was about to happen.

Oh, they wouldn't be shooting or trying to kill anyone—lacking weapons tended to make that sort of thing difficult—but Milla had no doubt that what was to come would be violent all the same, constituting a clash of wills between the parasite frigates and Stephen Michaels.

She knew very little, if anything, about who was piloting the frigates—but regardless, Milla would place her faith in the pilot at her side.

"Punch it!" Steph ordered, causing Milla to push more power to the CM systems just as he hit the throttle and pulled hard on the stick.

Eagle One stood on its tail in the thick roiling atmosphere of the gas giant, nose pointing right at the closest frigate, and her reactors screamed in response to their commands. For a brief moment they hovered. Then the acceleration slammed Milla and Steph back into their bolstered seats with the force of a dozen Earths, and they were moving.

Like a bullet from a gun, *Eagle One* thrust vertically straight and true at the closest parasite frigate, proximity alarms screaming as the shuttle's systems warned against the impending collision.

▶▶▶

PC Parasite *Five*

▶ "Hard evasion!" screamed Penae, eyes bugging wide as every alarm in his ship seemed to come alive at once. "Get them locked! Now!"

"They're changing velocity too quickly, Subaltern!" his tactical officer called. "I am attempting to override automatic systems. I will try to catch them manually!"

Penae didn't respond. He was involuntarily gripping the edge of his seat as parasite *Five* pulled aside in an attempt to evade the oncoming craft.

Are they suicidal? he wondered. The Oathers were *anything* but suicidal, he knew, but this craft didn't fit any Oather configuration. The Empire had, on occasion, encountered other civilizations that he knew of. Mostly they were easily absorbed, but occasionally a culture with some severe social malady managed to survive the tumultuous transition from irrelevant life-form to spacefaring culture.

Those cultures generally had to be exterminated.

Penae wondered if he was looking at just such a species. But if that were the case, why did the larger contact fit traditional Imperial and Oather designs?

"I think I have them, Subaltern. Engaging lock!"

▶▶▶

Shuttle *Eagle One*

▶ A whole new set of alarms wailed into existence across the flight deck of the shuttle. Neither Milla nor Steph noticed. They were both jerked hard in their seats as *Eagle One* jolted in position, decelerating sharply for an instant before the reactors whined. Then the shuttle broke loose and continued the upward track.

"What the hell was that?" Steph cried, eyes quickly scanning his instruments.

Milla too was focused intently now, trying to find the cause of the disruption, but there were certain scanners that she was used to that the shuttle simply did not have.

"I . . . I believe it was a . . ." She scowled, thinking hard to remember the word. "A quantum lock."

"A what?" Steph glanced over briefly before refocusing on his flying.

"A quantum lock, yes?" she said. "They tried to lock the shuttle into place by linking us to the local subatomic field of space."

Steph wanted nothing more than to cross his eyes, but he thought he got the gist of it.

"Are you telling me they have a bloody *tractor* beam?"

Milla frowned. "What is a tractor? Never mind. No, it's not a beam. It's a way to cause the shuttle to link to the part of local space that is below atoms, yes? It's used to capture targets. Priminae use it often for asteroid mining."

"Yes? Are you asking me?" Steph shot her a confused look. "I'm actually pretty well educated, Milla, but I think you just left me drowning in the deep end. Okay, forget that, they have a tractor beam. Great. Okay, I can work with this . . ."

He wrenched the stick in his hand, sending the shuttle into a spiral out and around the parasite frigate and cleaving through a cloud bank that briefly cut visuals down to effectively zero. He wasn't basing his flying on what he could see, so for the moment that was the least of his concerns.

"How strong is this lock? Can we break it?" he asked as he put the shuttle through a tight corkscrew, half taking evasive action and half looking for a clean slot between the two closest parasite frigates from which to make his move.

"One?" Milla looked uncertain. "Most likely, yes. Two, however, would be very unlikely. Against three, there is no chance."

"Well, I guess we'd better not get caught, then," Steph quipped. "Give me military power on the CM field in three."

"Military power in three, aye."

Steph twisted the shuttle around, hard over, and away from the closest parasite frigate, winding up with the nose pointed right at the second bogey just as Milla threw full military power to the CM generator. The shuttle lanced forward, cutting through the storm around them and leaving contrails in its wake. The lights dimmed, however, and Steph felt his controls get a little sluggish as the energy-hungry countermass systems swallowed up everything the reactors could put out and a fair chunk of what was coming from the stored batteries.

He rolled the shuttle over, showing the heat shields of the craft's belly to the enemy ship, and hit the rockets generally used for precision maneuvers in space. Normally, those weren't remotely powerful enough to throw the big transport shuttle around, but with CM maxed out, the boost threw the duo to one side with shocking force, and hopefully with as little predictability as possible.

"Back down to full power," Steph ordered, flipping them back over and pointing the nose to the skies again.

"Full power, aye."

"Can we track their tractor beam?" he demanded.

Milla looked over at him, her expression incredulous. "What is this . . . tractor, Stephan? I do not know this word."

Steph sighed. "Later. The lock. Can we detect it?"

She scowled at him, then glared at her instruments. "None of these systems will do it, Stephan. A quantum lock molds space-time . . ."

"Like counter-mass?" he asked.

"No, different aspect of space-time," Milla answered. "Counter-mass affects mass and, thus, gravity. A quantum lock is magnetic."

"We have magnetic sensors on board . . . ," Steph said as he twisted the bird away from the second frigate. *Eagle One* was now climbing rapidly, hell-bent on flying deeper into space with both frigates turning into pursuit.

"Yes, but your electromagnetic sweep equipment is very crude for this sort of work," Milla rushed to explain, honestly shocked at how easily he was handling the flight systems while talking seriously about the situation with her. "It is designed primarily to scan large items. The lock will be *very* small, below the atomic scale."

"So you can't do anything?"

Milla grimaced. "I may be able to detect when they are trying to establish a lock. However, I certainly could not pinpoint where the lock will be focused."

"I'll take what I can get," Steph said through clenched teeth as he sent the shuttle through another spiral, trying to gain ground while the two frigates below him were still attempting not to cross one another's bows. "Get to it."

Milla stared at her instruments helplessly for a moment, then pulled up the radio intercept software, cycling through into the core settings and looking over the range she had to work with. A quantum lock was fundamentally a very focused diamagnetic point, one that could be tuned with the appropriate hardware to move through space.

Detecting the lock was relatively straightforward, though the maximum range was generally rated in meters at most. That meant that the only way they were going to detect an attempt to lock the shuttle into place was if the system had already pinpointed their position. Milla killed most of the radio intercept channels, narrowing the band to the electromagnetic frequencies a lock would affect, and then set a warning tone to go off if anything tripped the system.

"There," she said, closing the settings. "That should do it."

Steph glanced over. "That was fast. You're sure?"

"No," she answered, laughing a little nervously. "However, we will soon know."

Steph looked at her evenly for a moment, then grinned widely. "Now you're getting into the spirit of things. Let's fly."

▶ ▶ ▶

PC Parasite *Five*

▶ "That pilot is a lunatic," Penae growled as collision alarms sounded across the command deck.

Parasite *Three* was passing only a half beam away from them, almost within the margin of error for manual control and certainly too close for ships this deep in a stormy atmosphere. Still, he believed they weren't going to collide, so he turned his focus back to the craft they were chasing.

"Yes, Subaltern," Penae's own pilot agreed, his face pale and clammy.

"At least we know that the fool doesn't have any weapons." Penae forced a chuckle, trying to remain as calm as possible for his men's benefit almost as much as his own.

"How are you sure, Subaltern?" his second asked, confused.

"Because if they'd been armed, we'd likely be venting smoke by now." Penae sighed, shaking his head. "He caught us flat. That's a fast little prick."

He looked over to where the pilot was finishing up clearing their beams, noting that they were no longer at risk of slamming into parasite *Three*.

"Enter pursuit course, maximum atmospheric thrust!" he ordered.

Parasite *Five* tipped its nose up, and a shock wave erupted as the frigate began to climb hard after the fleeing ship. Under full thrust, the frigate should start to gain on the much-faster accelerating craft shortly, but there was going to be a period of time before the range could be closed again, and quantum locking was *not* a particularly long-ranged tool.

"Prime the guns," Penae said. "Solve for the fleeing craft; fire as the numbers say."

"Guns priming. Permission to clear the safeties?" Penae's weapons commander asked.

"Granted."

He'd have preferred to take the small ship intact, for the intelligence asset it presented if nothing else, but his orders from the captain left Penae more than enough room to eliminate the craft if they were at risk of letting it go.

Pity. You seem like you might have made an interesting acquaintance.

▶▶▶

Shuttle *Eagle One*

▶ A new series of alarms, ones that Steph was intimately familiar with, blared mercilessly through the flight deck of the shuttle. Milla looked around, disconcerted and concerned, clearly not recognizing them.

"We've been targeted," Steph said stiffly. "Active range-finding gear, probably a lidar variant. They're about to open fire."

"Oh." Milla's voice was soft, barely audible as she sank a bit deeper into her seat.

"Lasers are junk in the atmosphere," Steph said, talking to organize his own thoughts, "even ones as powerful as the Priminae's."

"Especially," Milla corrected. "Overly powerful laser fire will warp the atmosphere and attenuate the energy of the weapon."

"Okay, so what else will they use?"

Milla blinked. "Pardon?"

Steph looked over sharply. "You heard me."

"How am I to know?" Milla asked. "They are not known to me!"

"Bullshit." Steph's tone was flat. "You know these people. You may not know how, but you *know* them."

Milla fell silent, a mix of emotions crossing her face. Finally, she sighed. "They are using antiquated parasite frigates. Expect projectile weapons."

"Hypervelocity missiles?"

"No. Slower, but guided," Milla said, frowning. "If they are using the historical weapons from the records."

"Guided?" Steph looked a little skeptical.

Guided weapons were fine when dealing with planetary distances, a few hundred kilometers—even a few thousand. However, spacecraft had to engage weapons at millions of kilometers and speeds that made most guidance systems utterly useless. If you didn't aim them right to begin with, there was no guidance system in the universe that had the Delta-V to manage more than extremely minor corrections.

The Double A fighters had used guided missiles, but they were a knife-range platform. The frigates he was dealing with seemed like they should be solar system range at least.

If he could get into space, Steph felt he could probably get enough space between him and the enemy to negate their missiles. That really only left lasers, and at the sorts of distances you generally fought at in space, laser engagements were more of a chess game than a martial fight.

"Secure armor. Calculate cam-plate settings needed to negate their targeting frequencies," Steph ordered.

"Aye," Milla said. It was an easy order, one that the shuttle's computers were designed specifically to handle. "Done. Shall I engage?"

"Not yet. Let's hold that back for a moment. They've already got a pretty good lock on us, and they could use passives if they needed to anyway. Do the missiles use the same frequencies?"

"That I truly could not say. I know of historical weapons. I could not tell you how they were designed specifically."

"Great. Alright, hold on tight. I figure this is going to get fun in a second or two," Steph said as the alarms redoubled, signaling that more active targeting sources had locked them up. "Incoming!"

Milla unconsciously tugged on her seat's restraints, assuring herself that they were strapped and taut, though in all truth they probably wouldn't do much good. There was a relatively narrow window during which restraints were both useful and nonlethal, and she knew that without the CM generators operating to reduce the effective mass, and thus the inertia of the shuttle and its occupants, being crushed under acceleration was a real possibility.

So when Steph told her that things were about to become "fun," Milla just really wished that his definition of fun were not so removed from her own.

▶▶▶

PC Parasite *Five*

▶ "Bracket them and fire. Try to disable them, if you can," Penae ordered. "Still, I would rather have them falling through the atmosphere in shards than exiting in one piece."

"On your orders, Subaltern!"

The parasite frigate shook as its missiles were ejected out into the atmosphere of the gas giant, lancing on ahead of them. The shock waves of missiles crashing through their own sonic bubble rocked the vessel again. Penae watched as cloud trails condensed in the weapons' wake, pressure waves sucking water from the air.

Six, ten, twenty—enough missiles rocketed away to bracket the enemy craft twice over, but he wasn't certain it would be enough.

The pilot was clearly skilled and certainly reckless, a bad combination to face off against. Not a great combination to have on your own side either, in all honesty.

He and the crew of the frigate watched as the condensation trails from the missiles lanced out, arcing upward toward the target vessel. As the first three tracked in on the enemy, a burst of explosive energy caused Penae to flinch away and, for a split second, wonder if the craft had been struck ahead of his projections.

The screens equalized quickly, however, and he saw that a series of explosive bursts had been launched from the craft. Then he realized what he was seeing.

"Countermeasures." He nodded before speaking up. "Are they effective?"

"Not appreciably, Subaltern," his weapons officer answered. "We've lost some resolution on the lead missile, but the swarm is effectively immune."

That was unsurprising, but he had wanted to be certain. The missiles they had fired worked in conjunction with one another, feeding each other data and sharing information as much as possible. The lead missile would be the most susceptible to countermeasures, but the overall swarm would quickly compensate.

The missiles blew through the countermeasures, only the first one detonating prematurely as its scanners were fooled into thinking the target was closer than it was.

It was a decent try, Penae thought idly as he watched the remaining missiles home in.

At the last possible instant the vessel almost *lazily* heeled over and shifted course, diving back into the gas giant's atmosphere, causing missiles to scream past as most of the swarm tried but failed to anticipate the new course. The craft wrenched wildly, shaking the next wave of missiles that had managed to stick with them, then leveled out and waggled its wings a few times before burning hard for the upper atmosphere once more.

"Brazen bastard," Penae muttered, more amused than anything else.

"As you say, Subaltern."

▶▶▶

Shuttle *Eagle One*

▶ The skies ahead of Steph and Milla were beginning to darken from the blue green of the lower atmosphere to give way to the blue black that signified the edge of air. Steph could feel the control systems change, shifting from atmospheric resistance to extra-atmospheric reaction systems. Microthrusters and gyroresistance controls took over from ailerons and elevators, stealing some of his feedback from the controls.

Steph preferred flying in an atmosphere, though there were charms to be had in microgravity and zero-resistance flight, simply because you could *feel* the craft in atmosphere. In space, with full counter-mass powered up, it was more like flying an overhyped video game ship than the real thing.

Except for the consequences.

Those were all too real.

"Can you find me the third frigate, Milla?" he asked, tracking the missiles that were still in the air.

Those were tracking back around, clearly operating on internal guidance from what he could see, but probably also getting updated targeting data from the frigates. Stephen wasn't too worried about them. Based on their velocity, missiles that size wouldn't have enough fuel to dog *Eagle One*'s steps too far. They'd be a threat for a few passes, though, unless he did something about them.

Electronic countermeasures didn't do much, and neither did the flares. Steph wasn't too pleased about that. He hadn't expected much out of the flares, of course, not with active tracking on the inbound birds. Flares were effective mostly against passive heat seekers, but he'd held out more hope for the ECMs.

"Holding position at the edge of the atmosphere, maneuvering to maintain a CAP over our position," Milla responded.

"Good move," Steph acknowledged. Though he disliked dealing with an intelligent enemy, putting a combat air patrol over them was going to make things a lot harder on him and Milla. "They're trying to get us in a pincer. They should have more ships to pull this pincer off properly, but against this pig, three might just be enough."

He didn't know enough about their maneuvering or weapons to be certain, but Steph was fairly confident that three would, in fact, be more than enough. The two tagging them from below were going to force him to run the blockade of the third, which was waiting in the bird-dog position. As soon as *Eagle One* entered into range, the CAP frigate would simply open fire with lasers or missiles, or try to lock the shuttle in with the sort of tractor beam. At that range, and closing fast, there was no way in hell the shuttle would be able to outmaneuver incoming missiles, let alone lasers and whatever the quantum lock was.

Once he and Milla broke out into space, they needed to get as far away from their pursuers as they *possibly* could. Lasers didn't give a warning before they vaporized your hull and left you sucking vacuum.

"Okay, I've got the frigate in sight. I want you on missile track now," Steph said, tapping the throttle back a little as he lined up his course.

"Missile track, aye," Milla said automatically, shifting her instrument readings as she called up the information from the targeting beams of the still-active and lethal missiles. "On them. We appear to have lost three more. They overcompensated and went too deep into the planet's atmosphere after we turned. The rest are now tracking back on course."

"Read me the approach vectors," Steph said, eyes focused out through the screen on a light in the distance that was the frigate flying CAP overhead.

"Roger," Milla said, reflecting on how odd it was to call someone Roger when she knew his name was Steph. Terran military habits were bizarre, but she'd learned them dutifully in order to hold the role she wanted. "Main pack now approaching from Zero Nine Thirty, thirty degrees high. Impact in sixty seconds . . . mark."

Steph didn't respond as he pushed the throttle all the way forward, causing the shuttle to once again jump to full military speed as they bore down on the enemy frigate on a collision course.

If you can't evade them, try and freak them the hell out.

▶▶▶

PC Parasite *Five*

▶ "They're accelerating on a collision course with parasite *Eight*, Subaltern."

Penae could see that for himself, much as it baffled him. He quickly checked the mass estimates on the enemy craft as well as what they could scan of its composition.

There is no way they're going to cause significant damage, even if they impact. What are they doing?

"Show me my sky," he ordered.

"Yes Subaltern."

The displays shifted, showing the entire sky around them along with the plotted tracks for everything moving. Penae examined the various tracks, then relaxed slightly.

"Tricky, but this flyer clearly has no idea what he is up against," he said finally.

"I'm sorry. I do not understand, Subaltern," Penae's second said.

"He is leading the remaining active missiles toward parasite *Eight*, either hoping they'll take out the frigate or we'll take out the missiles, I suppose," Penae said.

"Why would we do that?"

"Not every species has systems as precise as ours," he explained. "Many would be forced to destruct their own missiles, or risk losing the parasite. It's not a bad gambit to play, given his situation."

"It will gain him nothing," the second-in-command of the parasite said, mystified.

"True, but he doesn't know that."

▶▶▶

Shuttle *Eagle One*

▶ Milla had a death grip on her heavily bolstered seat, eyes wide as the parasite frigate loomed ahead of them, growing larger by the second. She didn't know what Steph had in mind, but she did know that she no longer wanted to be a pilot. Not for the moment anyway.

Give her the heavy armor and, more importantly, the heavier weapons of a Heroic Class starship at her touch; now that was her place.

She hoped she would get back to her post, though at the moment that seemed less and less likely.

"Stephan . . . ," she murmured, her tone not *quite* panicked.

"Quiet now. I really need to focus for this," Steph said, actually looking away from the screen for a moment to flash a grin at her.

"Ahead! Ahead, look ahead, please!"

His rolling chuckle was an alien sound amid the thudding of her heart and the constant alarms sounding through the shuttle's flight deck, but it quickly became what she focused on. Even when the laughter passed, Milla felt she could hear the sound's ghostly echo hanging in the air, making light of everything that was happening.

She had no idea how he could be so calm about it all, but Milla realized that she very much preferred that to the alternatives.

A proximity alarm began to sound, softly at first, but with quickly growing enthusiasm as *Eagle One* closed on the enemy frigate. A nearly forgotten program on Milla's station lit up, and she jerked her head down to see what it was before letting out a surprised cry.

"Stephan! They are attempting a lock!"

The shuttle bucked and twisted as Steph killed the throttle and hit a set of retros, jerking them hard in place as *Eagle One* decelerated rapidly. Then he slammed the throttle stick forward again as he skirted around the heaviest set of signals Milla was using to try to detect any attempts to quantum lock the shuttle. The two were thrown around in their restraints as Steph used every maneuvering system at his disposal to keep them flying.

"Missiles! Vectors, now!"

Milla glanced over, automatically reading out the numbers as they were updated on the screen.

"Seven o'clock, now five degrees negative to our plane. Impact in . . ." She swallowed. "Ten seconds."

"Only need seven."

Milla had a sinking sensation that she knew what Steph was attempting. "The missiles will not target the enemy frigate, not even by mistake!"

"Of course they won't," Steph said as he tripped the shuttle's full countermeasure suite and set a program running on the cam-plate controls at the same moment. "Any second-rate IFF system would ensure that."

"Then what are you—" Milla said, but was cut off as she was physically slammed back into the seat and the shuttle jerked as the entire universe descended into chaos around her.

▶▶▶

▶ The angel silhouette of countermeasure flares exploded away from *Eagle One* as the vessel accelerated and then banked over, pulling hard along another path. Collision alarms exploded on both the Terran shuttle and the Imperial frigate as *Eagle One* skirted within mere meters of the parasite.

The pursuing missiles, in the process of calculating safe evasion courses to maintain pursuit of their target while not impacting their ally, were scrambled briefly by the blast of countermeasures released by the shuttle. They briefly lost the target, then just as they reacquired it through the confusion, the shuttle vanished entirely from their active scanners.

The lead missiles, the most affected, mistook the countermeasures and loss of positive acquisition for proximity and detonated. The explosion tore through the veil of countermeasures, intangible as they were, and gutted the ventral flank of the Imperial frigate even as the other missiles either evaded or harmlessly hit the frigate's armor without detonating.

Parasite *Eight* began smoking in the high atmosphere and started losing altitude.

▶ ▶ ▶

PC Parasite *Five*

▶ Penae was stricken silent as he stared, unbelieving, at the data.

"That should *not* have worked."

The silence, punctuated once, stretched on again for a time.

"Uh . . ." His second gulped. "Orders, Subaltern?"

Penae shook his head, trying desperately to clear it of the image of the *impossible* happening. "Status on *Eight*?"

"They can no longer maintain orbital velocities and are descending," the scanner tech responded.

"Find the enemy craft," Penae said. "Have *Three* quantum lock *Eight* and pull the parasite out to a stable orbit."

"As you command, Subaltern. And us?"

"Track the enemy craft, pursuit course," he growled. "We *will* bring them down."

CHAPTER 11

AEV *Odysseus*

▶ "Captain, we have light-speed data I think you should see."

Eric turned from his station and walked over to the scanner displays. "Show me."

"Aye sir." Perez pointed to a display. "We've intercepted light that shows where the frigates came from."

Eric watched the display, eyes widening as he saw the smaller pocket destroyers, or maybe frigates, break off from the main ship.

"Well," he murmured, "they're not Archangels, but that's a twist I didn't see coming."

"There's more, sir," Perez stated, highlighting a point on the display. "This is Commander Michaels and the lieutenant."

Eric glanced at the plot, but didn't see anything. "How can you tell?"

"Reverse telemetry. They're running black at this point, but the tachyon burst lit them up," Perez told him. "That's how the bogeys spotted them."

"Damn." Eric grimaced. "What happened?"

Perez advanced the plot, running the imagery at several times normal speed. "Three of the pocket destroyers broke off from the main group and pursued the shuttle. It appeared that *Eagle One* made for the planet, and we lost telemetry in the atmosphere. Two of the alien ships and the shuttle went in. So far, we don't have any imagery of any of them coming out."

"Lovely," Eric muttered, worried about Steph and Milla but knowing that there really wasn't a thing he could do about them just then. "Alright, good work. Keep scouring the incoming data. Let me know if you find anything."

"Yes sir."

He walked back to the command station, calling up the imagery of the ships they were currently on course to intercept. Originally, the main ship had largely appeared to be similar to Priminae design, but that was before it launched the pocket destroyers, or whatever they wanted to call those smaller craft.

There was actually a reference in the Priminae database dealing with vessels of this sort. He'd done a search, obviously. Parasite ships. Unfortunately, there were no technical specifications available—not that they'd be up to date at this point.

The distance between the *Odysseus* and the contact was now only a few light-minutes and dropping *fast*. Soon they'd be able to speak without FTL relays.

This assumed that the contact used compatible frequencies, but Eric suspected strongly that wouldn't be a problem. Whoever these people were, they were clearly linked to the Priminae somehow. And since the *Odysseus* was mostly based on Priminae construction and systems, he expected that they'd all be able to talk—assuming the contact wanted to talk, of course.

Eric watched the numbers fall until they were within two light-minutes and closing. He decided that was enough.

"Give me an open comm," he ordered. "All Priminae frequencies."

"Aye Captain. Comm open."

Eric took a brief moment to still himself before speaking.

"This is Captain Eric Stanton Weston of the AEV *Odysseus*. You have sent vessels to pursue one of my shuttles. Recall your vessels. You are in Priminae Colonial Space without clearance from Ranquil Central Command. Identify yourself. Weston out."

He chopped his hand across his chest and the signal was cut, leaving them all waiting.

"Helm, give me a one-kilometer slip to starboard," Eric said as he settled back in his seat. "Adjust forward armor for best deflection against Priminae frequencies . . . the old ones, please, not the ones we gave them."

"Aye Captain," Lieutenants Kinder and Sams responded as one.

The *Odysseus* smoothly slid to starboard as the gleaming armor shifted slightly, becoming faintly iridescent in the slight illumination of the distant star.

Eric didn't expect anyone to actually open fire at that range. Targeting was too finicky to be trustworthy over such distances without a real-time lock, but he figured it wouldn't hurt to take a few precautions.

I wish I had a couple squadrons of Double As to launch too. Those parasite pocket destroyers are going to be a problem if this turns ugly.

Eric's eyes floated to where Lieutenant Kinder was sitting in the helm's wraparound station, waiting for him to order the ship to tactical state. The young woman was one of the few people on the ship who was qualified to use NICS. The neurological link between person and machine allowed people to run aspects of the ship almost like an extension of their own bodies.

The system had originally been incorporated into his own squadron, the Double A team known on Earth as the Archangels. There had never been enough people qualified to use the system, even before they started slipping NICS into personal mechanized combat units and onto his bridge. Now, with the increased demand—and the lean toward larger capital ships—the days of the Archangels were done.

That gutted him, honestly.

Eric had spent a good many years dedicated to the Double A program, enough that it had become his life; the people in it, his family.

He'd never expected the Archangels to be considered obsolete in his own lifetime, not while he was still personally in the prime of his career—or, well, close enough at least.

Fighters were force-projection tools, however, and there was nothing in the universe that projected force quite like a Heroic Class starship.

Times changed, much as he hated it, and the universe didn't stop its motions because one man was growing old and angry at the kids on his lawn.

▶▶▶

IBC *Piar Cohn*

▶ "Captain, signal recording on Oather frequencies."

Aymes nodded, unsurprised. They were close enough now to make communications reasonable, given the lack of tachyon retransmission emitters in the system.

"Put it on."

"As you say, Captain."

The voice and image that appeared on the displays were largely unsurprising. A human male sitting at the center of a rather bright command deck delivering a short and to-the-point message. Aymes mildly approved, actually. No wasted time, no real slips to give away any information.

There was something odd, however. The voice seemed off somehow.

"Analyze the signal," he ordered. "Something seems odd about the audio."

"A moment, Captain."

It took less than that, actually, as his signals officer made a sound of uncertainty.

"Well?" Aymes asked.

"You're right, Captain. The words don't match the subject's jaw or lip motions," the signals officer offered after a moment. "The voice is artificial. The speaker isn't communicating in Imperial standard."

Aymes frowned. "That makes no sense. That ship is an Oather design, using Oather frequencies. Why would they not speak Imperial standard?"

Of course, no one answered, which was just as well because Aymes knew damn well that if he didn't know, none of his crew did, and he wasn't in any mood to put up with anyone wasting his time just then.

"Captain?"

"What?" yelled Aymes, looking sharply over at the signals tech, who flinched in return.

"Do we respond?"

Aymes scoffed. "Of course not. Weapons, lock in the target."

"As you say, Captain."

"Await my orders to fire."

"Captain, the target has shifted course slightly."

Aymes scowled. "New vector?"

"Same, just a very slight shift on gravity scanners."

Aymes shook his head, wondering what the point of that was. "Recalculate target solutions; be ready to fire."

"As you say, Captain."

▶▶▶

AEV *Odysseus*

▶ The numbers slowly fell until the time had passed for a signal to reach the alien ship and return to the *Odysseus*, ratcheting up the tension as those on the bridge waited for *something* to happen.

Eric checked the clock constantly, glancing down every few seconds as he counted down just how long it would take for the target to get the signal, listen to his message, and come to a decision.

Finally, he came to a decision of his own.

"Helm, shift course, one kilometer positive to the elliptic."

"Aye Captain, shifting course . . . one kilo positive."

Eric settled back and continued waiting.

Miram leaned in a little closer from where she was stationed. "You expect them to fire?"

"If they're the ones who leashed, and unleashed, the Drasin . . . then I expect them to be nasty sorts by definition. Nasty sorts like to fire without warning."

The commander nodded, leaning back. Considering his reasoning, there was little she could argue with.

Another minute passed. Nothing happened. Eric again leaned forward.

"Helm, shift course. Two kilometers negative to the elliptic."

"Aye, two klicks negative."

As he again settled back, Eric noticed the curiosity in Miram's eyes.

"The *Odysseus* isn't the *Odyssey*," he said, "and that ship isn't the Drasin. They seem to have Priminae technology, and that means that they have scanners that are at least our equal. They'll know we're changing course, so we need to be sure that we change course *after* they've fired."

"Ah," Miram said, understanding. *Of course.*

▶▶▶

IBC *Piar Cohn*

 "Target has shifted course again!"

Aymes was growing tired of the games his opposition was playing. Clearly, his opposite number was looking to drag this conflict down to blade range, and that concerned him greatly. The Oathers were not so bloodthirsty as that. If they had been, they likely wouldn't have fled the Empire in the first place.

So what was he looking at across the void if not Oathers?

Another species that had captured their technology, or perhaps an offshoot of the Oathers who had a tad more spine?

He supposed it didn't matter either way, of course. They were in Oather space, in an Oather ship, and they'd seen the *Piar Cohn*. They would have to go.

"Recalculate solutions," Aymes ordered, checking the range to target.

They were now close enough, he decided.

"Calculations complete."

"Fire."

▶▶▶

AEV *Odysseus*

▶ The alarms screamed to life just as Eric was about to order the fifth course change, startling him slightly but only for a split second. Even as others were calling out reports, Eric was rising to his feet.

"Evasive action!" he cried. "Tactical, what happened?"

"Laser strike, forward armor, Captain. Armor deflected eighty percent clear, but the rest burned through three ablative layers and royally screwed our adaptive armor at that point."

"Did we get a frequency?" Eric asked.

"Aye Captain."

"Adjust for full deflection," he said, "but keep an eye on those pocket destroyers. I'd wager that they're running different frequencies on their laser gear."

Or they are if they're smart.

"Aye Captain, armor adapted," Ensign Sams answered. "Damage-control teams are responding. They're bringing ablative foam to the damage location."

Eric glanced over, concerned. "Did they get through the hull?"

"No sir. The crews can inject the foam through the hull in an emergency."

Eric filed that away, kicking himself for not being fully familiar with the capabilities of the Heroic Class ships. Unfortunately, while most of the Heroic captains had been reading tech manuals, he had been leading the counterstrike against Drasin forces on Earth during the invasion.

He supposed that was a valid reason, but it was certainly no excuse.

"Weapons free," he ordered, almost snarling. "All safeties are to be considered *off*. Redesignate Bogey One to Bandit One."

What the hell is it with these people and first strikes? Not that I expect a nice formal declaration of war, but it would be nice if they'd say hi before trying to kill us for once.

"Aye Captain," Sams responded. "Weapons free. Target Bandit One redesignation completed."

Eric turned to Commander Heath. "Coordinate with the damage-control teams. Make sure you know where they are at all times. When things get hot, we could easily lose more people to them tripping over each other than to enemy fire."

"Yes sir. I'm on it."

He nodded, turning his focus back to the situation at hand. "Distance to target?"

"Eight light-seconds and closing, Captain," Sams answered instantly. "Enemy ship has initiated turnover."

"Do we do the same, Captain?" Kinder asked, half turning in his seat.

"Negative." Eric's face was cold. "This bastard isn't my first priority. We blow through."

"Aye Captain."

"Do we fire, sir?" Sams asked, sounding nervous.

Eric nodded slowly, eyes on the telemetry plot.

"Yes, Ensign, we do indeed."

▶▶▶

IBC *Piar Cohn*

▶ "Hit, Captain!"

Aymes grimaced. "Damage assessment?"

A moment passed as the numbers were crunched and the data reflected back from the laser strike were analyzed.

The silence that followed drew out until Aymes finally had to break it himself. "Well?"

His tactical officer pushed back from the station, still staring in puzzlement at the display.

"Estimates are one in eight of expectations, sir."

"What?" Aymes stepped forward, leaning over the man and staring at the details himself. "How is that possible? Even Oather ceramics aren't that durable."

"I do not know, Captain. It doesn't fit any of our projections."

Aymes could see that much, but like his officer, he couldn't see any explanations. The puzzle this ship represented was growing ever larger, and frankly, this encounter was becoming more than an irritation and was well on its way to full-fledged worry.

"Continue firing, standard spread," he ordered. "Continue as we pass. What is the deceleration rate?"

"Captain?"

"At what rate are they slowing, Altern?" Aymes asked.

"They . . . they're not."

"What?" Aymes demanded, turning to focus closely on the scanner station.

He checked the data on the scanner display himself and started cursing under his breath.

"Captain?" The man standing at the station pulled back from him.

"They're intending to bypass us and go directly to the planet." Aymes swore. "That small craft was clearly more important than I suspected."

He considered his deduction for a moment, then set his features. "Reverse power. Get me a solution to intercept the enemy vessel with a zero-point acceleration."

▶ ▶ ▶

AEV *Odysseus*

▶ "Target has flipped acceleration, Captain. They're aiming for a zero-zero intercept . . ." Sams paused, running the calculations, but Eric beat him to it.

"In the planet's orbit, right?" he said.

Sams looked down, then back at the captain with a surprised look. "Yes sir. How . . . ?"

"Not hard to work out, Ensign," Eric answered. "We'll have to adjust our course in orbit. That'll delay us enough for them to catch up."

"Yes sir. Sorry sir."

"Don't worry about it. You'll learn. Experience can usually get us close enough long before computers arrive at the exact right answer."

"Yes sir."

"Do we have a firing solution yet?" Eric asked, looking to the tactical station.

"Yes sir. Passive lock, ninety percent solid."

Eric blinked, somewhat bemused. A 90 percent solid lock meant that the enemy ship wasn't even trying to evade the *Odysseus*. He supposed that he shouldn't be surprised, given how the fighting between the Drasin and the Priminae had shaped up.

WARRIOR KING • 129

"Fire as we pass," Eric ordered. "I want maximum time on target with fully focused and adapted lasers."

"Aye aye, Captain."

As the light-seconds counted down, with the two ships barreling past one another, Eric waited until the last possible moment before issuing the order to fire.

At less than five light-seconds, he spoke. "Fire."

The powerful Class IV lasers of the AEV *Odysseus* lanced out through the black, slashing into their target a hair over four seconds later. The initial burn was significant, but it wasn't until the *Odysseus'* computers had a second to analyze the hyperspectral signature of the molecular cloud burned off the alien ship and to send that data back to weapons that things really began to heat up.

"Laser strikes on our flanks, Captain. Main battery reflected . . . The smaller beams are a different frequency. We're taking damage!"

He'd expected that, but Eric still winced at the announcement. He didn't want to spoil their own strike by dancing around too much, and frankly, at the current ranges, they wouldn't likely be able to evade much anyway. Any halfway decent prediction algorithm would nail them if the *Odysseus* implemented evasive procedures, and in exchange they'd likely lose a big chunk of their own accuracy in placing the next shot.

In the *Odyssey*, Eric would have done *anything* to keep the range open and keep moving, counting on short but fast strikes on target to end the fight in his favor. In the *Odysseus*, he was willing to engage in a toe-to-toe slugging match, betting that his armor and weapons would give him the edge.

▶ ▶ ▶

▶ The *Odysseus* and *Piar Cohn* slung past one another at closing rates that actually bettered the speed of light by a significant fraction, both throwing laser fire at one another with abandon. Alarms and claxons screamed on both ships as damage-control teams raced to answer their clarion calls, and then it was over in just a few seconds.

The ships were two ancient jousters, both still mounted and both still alive, but one had certainly been taken by surprise in the pass.

The other sailed straight and true, a flicker of light dancing in its heart.

▶▶▶

IBC *Piar Cohn*

▶ "Damage reports, decks nine through eighteen! We're venting atmosphere from all levels, critical armor failures! Captain, my board is jammed with reports!"

Aymes spun around, holding on to the edge of his station for support against the violent shudders still rocking his ship, eyes wide and expression disbelieving. "What hit us?"

His tactical officer was pale, shaking, and on the edge of shock, but Aymes didn't have time to be gentle. He grabbed the man's shoulder and jerked him around hard. "What. Hit. Us?"

"A laser, Captain."

Aymes stared in stunned disbelief. "A laser? How powerful a laser?"

"It wasn't the power, Captain. I don't know what happened, but the strike only registered the same power as one of our own."

Aymes' hand dropped to his side, and he shook his head. "That's impossible. No laser could penetrate our armor that easily, not without being massively more powerful than anything we've ever fielded."

The poor officer at tactical had nothing to say. He knew that as well as the captain did, but they both also knew that reality trumped all else.

"Begin evasive maneuvers," Aymes ordered, knowing that he was more than a little late. "Secure those decks, and get repair squadrons on location immediately."

"They're already on their way, Captain," his altern said. "Orders dispatched."

Aymes nodded tersely, glad of that. Initiative was generally frowned upon in Imperial service but was considered a required asset for command. Assuming they survived this encounter, of course. With the sheer extent of how badly they'd underestimated the unknown target, that was no longer a certainty.

"Are we still firing?" he demanded.

"Yes Captain."

"Good. Continue!" he yelled. "Link with maneuvering so you can keep ahead of our evasions."

"As you say, Captain."

Aymes took a breath, then leaned over his communications officer's shoulder. "Give me a patch to parasite *One*."

"As you say, Captain. Patch open."

"*One*, this is the captain."

"*One* here, Captain."

"We're going to need cover," Aymes said firmly.

"As you say, Captain. We live to serve."

"We all do. In the empress' name."

The altern in command of parasite *One* immediately replied in same. "In the empress' name, Captain."

Aymes straightened up, patting the comm officer on the shoulder. "Secure comms."

AEV *Odysseus*

▶ "Enemy formation is shifting, Captain."

Eric wasn't surprised. They'd just raked the flanks of the bandit vessel with fully adapted lasers, and it was clear that they'd struck home.

The analysis department was going to have a field day with the hyper-spectral readings of the bandit ship's vaporized components.

"Continue firing," he said. "We're going to be out of range quickly. I'd like to end this now if we can."

"Aye aye, Captain."

The *Odysseus* rotated, keeping her primary lasers on target as the ship continued to warp space past the bandit.

"Watch it! That pocket destroyer—"

Eric flinched as the screen briefly overloaded, the small ship diving into their beam and vanishing in a brilliant explosion. While the primaries were resetting, the display swapped over to computer-generated imagery showing a plot of the vessels as they moved against the deep black of space.

Where the pocket destroyer had been a moment earlier was nothing but a cloud of static on the generated imagery. Eric grimaced. He recognized that the static was in fact debris, dust, and expanding molecules that used to be the small ship. He wasn't overly worried about having blown apart the craft, but that static was a near-perfect laser block.

The newly formed cloud of chaff reflected and absorbed most of the energy from the *Odysseus'* lasers. If his ship hadn't been on such a fast pass, Eric could have maneuvered around to get a clear shot, but the *Odysseus* was already starting to pull away from the bandit vessel. He didn't think he was going to get that chance.

"Gutsy bastard," Eric said, mentally tipping his cap to whoever commanded the destroyer.

He supposed that the ship was possibly a drone, but he doubted it. There was no hint in Priminae records of drones being used, and the similarity of the tech between these forces and the Priminae couldn't be ignored.

Besides, they'd dispatched three of the destroyers after Steph and Milla, then headed several light-minutes away. Without FTL relays, that was a long delay with which to try to coordinate any sort of combat maneuvering.

No, some gutsy bastard had just taken one for his team.

"Good man," he said, unable to keep himself from having some admiration for his opponents despite the situation. "Helm . . . put us back head-on to the planet, all flank."

"Aye Captain. All flank."

Eric turned and walked toward the damage-control station, wondering just how badly his own ship had been ravaged.

▶▶▶

IBC *Piar Cohn*

▶ "Enemy ship has ceased fire. They are accelerating away."

Aymes considered what had just transpired as he tried to figure out what to do next.

"Analyze the data," he said. "I want to know how such an attack just happened."

"As you say, Captain." His altern nodded, already issuing orders to that effect.

Everyone looked shaken, but Aymes was pleased to see that no one seemed unable to do his or her job. The Empire usually did not receive such surprises, but it did happen. He and his crew would adapt, and, in the end, they would overcome.

CHAPTER 12

Shuttle *Eagle One*

▶ *Eagle One* twisted in space as Steph set the shuttle on an evasive path, warning alarms blaring at every station as gigawatt lasers cooked random matter around them. People thought that space was empty, but it wasn't. Space was filled with dust, debris, gasses—all things that caught and absorbed light, superheated under the glare of laser beams, and then fluoresced in all directions to warn the scanners on the *Eagle* of the passage of the beam.

"They're rather determined, aren't they?" Steph asked mildly as he set the shuttle into a tight spiral, trying to stay ahead of whatever predictive systems the other side had.

Trying to avoid a laser wasn't like dodging a bullet. Technically, you could evade a bullet from a mere few thousand meters or so. Within two hundred thousand klicks, if a laser was aimed at you, you were *hit*, not because you couldn't possibly escape before the shot hit you, but because by the time you knew you were in the crosshairs, you'd already been lit up.

So the art of dodging a laser, in space at least, was in the anticipation.

You had to figure out what the enemy was thinking, or what their computer was programmed to do, and get there *first*.

Or, rather, *not* get there.

In Steph's favor, the odds were actually stacked on his side. Space was a paradox, full of particles and gas and detritus but also emptier than anything else in the universe. That meant that he could put his shuttle anywhere he had the Delta-V to push it.

The enemy ship needed to pin him down to within a few dozen meters, and he had thousands upon thousands of square kilometers to run in.

In the other guy's favor, they only needed to get lucky *once*.

One strike and it would be game over. No reset, no extra lives. They were playing for keeps. You didn't play tag with a gigawatt laser unless you were ready to dance with demons in the afterlife.

Or had a meter or two of molecular bonded ceramic and adaptive armor between you and the laser cannon.

Neither of which were in his particular bag of tricks this time around.

"They are closing with us, Stephan . . ."

Milla's voice was surprisingly steady, Steph reflected as he rolled the shuttle around another pulse of photons. If they made it back to the *Odysseus*, he decided he was going to sponsor her for advanced piloting courses. Blood as cold as the black was a major asset in a combat pilot. He didn't know if she was going to go all the way down that route, but if she wanted it, he'd make sure she had the chance.

"I see them," he said aloud.

The frigates were hard to miss, close and getting closer, and that presented Steph with a problem. The Marine lander shuttle he was using wasn't built for speed, not even in space. The craft still used chemical drives, so it had decent impulse power, but its top end was limited by the reactors powering the CM generators, and those were sadly lacking.

Steph didn't point the nose of the shuttle toward the open black. Instead, he started looking to the gas giant's moons, hoping for a miracle.

▶▶▶

PC Parasite *Five*

▶ Subaltern Penae glowered at the stubborn symbol on his display.

The continuing existence of that symbol was rapidly becoming a personal insult. The pilot was good—*very* good. He was staying ahead of the best combat-prediction computers in the Empire with a consistency that was beyond frustrating.

"Continue closing the distance," he ordered. "Do *not* let him get away."

There seemed no particular fear of that, thankfully. The scanners indicated a relatively low technology base on the craft. Some basic space-warping ability, obviously, but that was mixed with a chemical reaction thrust. Crude beyond belief, though reasonably effective right up until the craft ran out of chemicals to burn.

He could only hope that would happen soon, otherwise Penae felt he was likely to throw something in frustration, and that would *not* look good on the field reports.

"Enemy craft is heading for the nearest moon, Subaltern."

"I see them," Penae said. "Stay in pursuit. Scanners, get me a composition of the moon, please."

"Yes Subaltern," the scanner technician answered, directing his sensors ahead of them. "Nonbreathable atmosphere, high levels of sulfur, carbon, and various oxide composites. Volcanic, likely due to the proximity to the gas giant's gravity field. Nothing out of the ordinary for a moon in this orbit, Subaltern."

Penae waved off the report. He knew there was nothing out of the ordinary about the satellite, but that didn't mean there was nothing problematic about it.

"If they get into that atmosphere, we'll have a hard time scanning through the particles thrown up by the volcanic action," he said aloud, "and if we lose them for any length of time, they'll be able to bolt for deep space. Give them enough of a head start and our speed advantage won't matter one jot."

"Subaltern, the computer can't effectively predict them. The pilot is *clearly* using an evasion protocol, and he's getting better at it after every pulse," Penae's tactical officer offered up. "They're running better software than we are."

Penae nodded slowly, then made a decision. "Take manual control. You try to predict them."

"Subaltern?" the officer asked, startled.

"You have my orders. Execute them."

"As you say, Subaltern," the anxious officer said, reaching for the console and taking the computer partially off weapons control.

At the ranges involved, there was no way he would be able to calculate and fire the beams effectively without computer aid, of course. However, he was going to pick the shots and then let the computer complete them. That meant trying to divine where in four-dimensional space the target would be at the point the laser intersected their range.

Not the simplest of tasks, but far from the most difficult the officer had ever been assigned. The difficulty lay in the lag period between when he registered the target course and speed and when the laser he fired would actually arrive on point. Within a short enough range, missing was effectively impossible. But the enemy craft had managed to carve out a significant lead, and making an accurate prediction was more an exercise in luck and frustration than true skill.

The officer took the controls with some trepidation, but firmed up his determination as he put in his first target, initiated the firing countdown, and then started entering more.

▶▶▶

Shuttle *Eagle One*

▶ "We are approaching the moon rapidly," Milla said, looking up from the radar intercept officer displays she was practically buried in.

"I see it," Steph said as he adjusted the throttle and jigged slightly down relative to the shuttle. "Give me an entry vector. I'm never going to lose these bastards in the open black."

"Adjust approach by three degrees, positive to the system plane," she said. "We are going to be coming in, as you say, *hot*."

"No choice. I'll airbrake us in the upper atmosphere."

Milla grimaced but said nothing to contradict him.

The shuttle was designed to take heavy atmospheric friction, so she had little doubt that they would be able to manage that. What worried her was the high particulate density in the moon's atmosphere and what coming in hot would do to their heat shields. If they lost the ceramic plates that protected them from heat buildup, then things would get uncomfortable rather quickly.

At the moment, however, she didn't think that Steph was likely to listen to those worries.

She could even hear his response.

You want uncomfortable heat buildup? Let's slow down and let them hit us with a beam for a few milliseconds. That would be uncomfortable heat buildup.

Worst of all, even as she heard his voice, right down to his distinctive accent, Milla knew that he would be right.

So she just sighed and started calculating the angle of attack they would need to maximize their odds of living through what Steph was planning on doing.

"You will need a steeper angle of attack," she said finally. "Atmosphere is thinner than standard and much lower to the surface. Watch for volcanic cones as we approach. The largest ones appear to reach beyond the edge of the atmosphere."

"Oh, great," Steph groused, rolling his eyes. "You've got to be kidding me."

"Partially. Depends on how you define atmosphere. In order to achieve significant braking, you may well have to drop below the height of several prominent volcanoes that I can scan from here. They *are* active, Steph. Do not fly us through their plumes."

"Right," Steph said. "Seal all exterior vents, and shield all nonessential sensors. Batten down the hatches, Milla; it looks like a doozy of a storm is coming."

Milla didn't bother trying to parse the meaning of the last bit, instead focusing on shielding all their nonessential gear. That meant that they were about to be flying half-blind, at least for a short while, since the shielding would block the scanners while protecting the ship.

"Hang on tight," Steph said as he nosed the shuttle into the moon and pushed the throttle forward again. "We're going in."

▶▶▶

▶ In space, a pursuit had the appearance of little more than two ships that happened to be leisurely flying in the same general direction. There was no exciting rush of motion, no sonic booms and engine roars filling the skies. At any scale that the action was comprehensible, the action was also nonexistent.

Lasers flashed between shooter and target, nothing but an almost festive twinkling marking their passage as the beams encountered dust particulates and vaporized them in turn.

As the moon approached, however, the action began to compress rapidly.

The shuttle nosed up as it struck the atmosphere, deploying air brakes, and the surface of the moon began to rush by. A low boom echoed across the thin atmosphere as the shuttle dug in. Plumes of smoke and fire erupted below as lasers raked the surface rather than vanishing off forever into space.

The parasite frigate's predictive computers now had an easier time of things because the shuttle's motion was less open, but atmospheric particulate made getting a lock more difficult, forcing the Imperial crew to follow their quarry down.

Sonic booms tore through the valleys and plains below, a small one trailing the shuttle and a larger one following in the wake of the frigate as it fell deeper into the atmosphere. Lasers superheated the air into plasma, causing crackling light to dance and occasionally detonating explosive pockets of gas in the atmosphere with the force of small bombs.

The action, once languid and slow, was now furious and lethally fast.

▶▶▶

PC Parasite *Five*

▶ "Do *not* lose them," Penae ordered tersely, leaning forward in his station as he glared at the screens.

The signal that marked the enemy was breaking up in the highly charged atmosphere of the volcanic moon, and the frigate was having trouble keeping the small craft in sight as the pilot threw his ship back and forth through volcanic peaks, dancing around thick plumes of smoke and dust that rendered scanners practically useless.

They *should* be right on top of the craft by this point, with their superior speed, but once again the other pilot was making them work for every *scrap* of distance they could close.

"Missiles, Subaltern?" his tactical officer asked, sounding not a little desperate.

Penae snorted. "Pointless!"

And they were. Their missiles would never track through the charged atmosphere they were flying through here, not if the parasite's own scanners were having this much trouble. Lasers were rapidly losing effectiveness as the atmosphere and its particulates thickened, which meant that shortly the parasite crew would be limited to trying to keep the target in sight and hoping to catch the shuttle when it once more left the atmosphere.

Penae was beginning to wonder if a single small craft was remotely worth this amount of hassle, but orders were orders.

"A hit!"

He snapped his attention back to the tactical station. An officer there was practically cheering. "We hit them, Subaltern!"

Though difficult to tell through the mess that was obscuring the parasite's scanners, the enemy ship did appear to be maneuvering poorly and losing altitude. Penae leaned forward, hoping that this was the end.

▶▶▶

Shuttle *Eagle One*

▶ The shuttle felt like it had been hammered by a giant fist, and Stephen's stomach was suddenly in his throat as they lost altitude in a hurry. The claxons that sounded were such that he couldn't hear himself think, but that was fine because thinking was one thing he just didn't have time for.

His hands and mouth moved on instinct, following procedures he'd trained in so many times that they'd all long since blurred into one long montage.

"Hit the fire extinguishers," he ordered. "We're losing altitude. Milla, seal up your helmet."

Milla did as she was told, first hitting the whole bank of controls that sent the signal to flood affected areas with halon gas extinguishers, then grabbing for her helmet, pulling it on over her head, and linking it to her flight suit. The seal was automatic, a Priminae design, leaving her with an additional level of protection in case the shuttle cockpit was breached.

"What about you?" she asked, her voice now acquiring a mechanical tone from the helmet communications system.

"No time," he said, eyes dead ahead. "I'll put it on if we live."

Steph supposed that he really should have already been wearing it, but honestly, the helmet seemed superfluous. Any sort of damage that might require it would almost certainly end them both before lack of oxygen could.

He opened the comm. "*Odysseus* Control, *Eagle One*. I am declaring an emergency. We are going down on the inner moon of the gas giant we were approaching. I say again, I am declaring an emergency. *Eagle One* out."

A flip of a switch and confirming squeeze of a firing stud on his control stick sent that recorded message firing out on a rocket set to play on a loop. Steph figured the rocket would have enough power to get into orbit, given the small size of the moon and low gravity, but didn't have time to be sure.

Ahead of them loomed a massive cone wall, and he was fighting the shuttle to try to maneuver around it.

"Whatever hit us must have fried the control surfaces or somehow shorted out all the relays and redundant systems," he said. "And I thought this thing was a pig *before*."

He was fighting the shuttle every inch of the way and figured that the damage had been done mainly to the control surfaces, because he was getting *some* response. If the relays were out, they'd have been a flying brick with wings.

"Brace position!" Steph called as he narrowly missed the slope of the volcano, the land falling away again for a moment as the shuttle screamed through the thin atmosphere and dropped through a low valley surrounded by smoke and fumes.

The *Eagle* hit hard, tailfirst, as Steph just managed to lift the nose a few meters at the last moment. The shuttle slammed into the alien turf with enough force to crack the fuselage in half and then entered a spin. Steph hung on to the controls as long as he could, feathering the CM generators and using the thrusters to keep them nose first while slowing the ship.

Then all went dark as the power gave out.

In the blackness, the CM field failed, and with that everything went to hell.

Stephen was jerked sideways and then snapped back into his bolster as the straps bit into his arms and body viciously. His hands were torn from the controls, and then there was a huge crunch as the light of consciousness went out just as the power had.

▶▶▶

PC Parasite *Five*

▶ Penae half rose from his station as they saw the craft slam into the surface of the moon, the thrill of finally nailing the slippery bastard surging through him.

"Bring us to station, standard overwatch position," he ordered, looking over to the scanner station. "Do we have any readings from the craft?"

The scanner tech nodded. "Two living signals, Subaltern. No weapon signatures. The craft has suffered a near-total power loss."

Penae snorted. "An impact like that? I imagine it has."

He considered the situation for a moment. "Very well. See if we can quantum lock onto the craft. It's probably not intact enough to grab in one piece, but let's try."

"As you say, Subaltern."

▶▶▶

Shuttle *Eagle One*

▶ "Wake up, Stephan."

Returning to consciousness was always a mixed blessing in Steph's experience. He was alive, that was always a good thing, but the reason he knew that he was alive was because there was no way being dead could hurt this badly in any sane or fair universe.

The thought that the universe might not *be* that sane or fair was pushed forcibly out of mind as he groaned and levered himself up. His seat restraints were undone. He assumed Milla had done that, because if they'd snapped in the crash, he would probably be paste on the walls.

"Where's my helmet?" he asked.

Milla hesitated, then shook her head slightly from side to side. "Bad news, Stephan. It was shaken loose and damaged in the crash."

Steph's eyes found the cracked polycarbonate shell, and he grimaced. "Damn."

"It is worse. There is a leak," Milla added.

"Alright, I'll make do," Steph said, grabbing a ventilator mask from an emergency overhead compartment and strapping it over his face before running the hose down to his suit's air. "It's not space. I can live without an enclosed system."

"As you say," Milla replied, though her tone didn't show much confidence in her words.

He climbed over the tilted chair and braced himself on dead consoles so he could look out the windows of the shuttle. "I don't see anything out there. How long was I out?"

"Several minutes, at least," Milla said. "However, I lost consciousness as well, so I could not say for certain."

"Right, okay. Standard capture protocol," he said.

Milla looked confused. "Capture protocol?"

Steph winced, both from the headache and her lack of knowledge. "Pull the computer core and blow it. Destroy your personal computer, everything that contains any sort of memory. We're using basic emergency gear from here on out. If they get us, that's *all* they get."

Milla nodded, and the two got to work.

▶▶▶

PC Parasite *Five*

▶ "Subaltern, we are ready to attempt a quantum lock on the target."

"Good," Penae said, annoyed that it had taken that long, though the craft was pretty badly broken up.

"Subaltern!" The scanner officer turned around. "Explosions on the craft!"

Penae grimaced, wondering if he and his forces were going to lose everything due to some crash damage. It would be a victory of sorts, but only technically. "How large?"

"Very small, focused charges."

"Charges? Not caused by crash damage?" he asked.

"Almost certainly not."

Penae grunted, lips twisting. "They're blowing their computers, then. Disciplined, structured, and with plans for all contingencies."

"Subaltern?"

"Continue with the quantum lock," he ordered. "We don't need their computers. We have them."

▶▶▶

Shuttle *Eagle One*

▶ Wisps of acrid smoke were floating through the shuttle cockpit as Steph kicked open the emergency locker and pulled out the kit he found there.

It wasn't much, unfortunately, just a small survival pack with some food, water, medical supplies, a radio, and a sidearm. Better than nothing, but only marginally.

He looked pensively to the sealed door that led back to the troop section of the shuttle.

"What is it?" Milla asked, noting his stare.

"I think that the Marines keep a ready action kit in the shuttle," he said.

Milla shook her head. "That section is likely breached. Without your helmet . . ."

"I'll be fine," Steph asserted, grabbing a pair of goggles from the emergency supplies and fitting them over his eyes. "I've got air, eye protection, and my suit is otherwise intact. It's not a vacuum out there, just very noxious. Besides, it's not like we have a choice."

"We can sit here," she urged. "You launched a beacon. The *Odysseus* is not far away . . ."

The shuttle shifted then, sending them careening into one another and then into the bulkhead behind Milla with a thud.

"What was *that*?" Steph looked around wildly.

Milla grimaced. "I believe that was an attempt to establish a quantum lock with us."

"Oh, just *perfect*," Steph groaned. "Discussion's over. Time to go."

He waited for her to steady herself, then climbed over to the door and grabbed the emergency release latch. A tug blew the door's seals, and Steph yanked it back, letting the door clang into the far wall as air hissed and streamers of fumes curled around them.

He led the way through the hatch into the troop section, whistling under his mask as he looked through the gaping splits in the fuselage out to the dark red-and-orange vista beyond.

"I think it's over here," he said, jumping over a wide split in the floor and pausing to check his ribs with a free hand before climbing, face contorting in pain, over wrecked seating to a large locker beyond.

The locker took some persuading to open, but with effort, they got in.

"Well," Steph said as he drew out an assault rifle, "I'd rather have my Archangel, but this'll do. God bless the Marines. Paranoid bastards."

Milla stared at him for a moment, but Steph couldn't make out her expression under the slightly darkened visor of her helmet. He handed her a rifle, along with a couple mags, and then reached for another.

"Carry what we can. We're going to have to abandon the ship," he said firmly. "I don't know how long it'll be before the *Odysseus* can get to us, but I'm not giving in to these bastards without a fight."

Milla felt less certain than he seemed to be, but she wasn't going to argue with him. This situation was beyond her wildest nightmares, yet strangely comforting as well. The Drasin were worse to her, but she knew just how bad they were. The enemy out beyond the hull of the shuttle were unknowns. That was both more fearsome and somehow less fearsome in ways she just didn't understand.

She took the rifle, trying to remember everything she'd learned about Terran weapons since her rescue at the hands of the *Odyssey* and crew as she awkwardly cradled the gun in her arms.

Steph was considerably more at ease, if only because he wasn't letting himself get bogged down in what might happen. He stayed focused on the next step, not what might or might not happen in the unlikely event that they lived through the next few minutes.

The shuttle shifted again, throwing them around as it began to lift off the surface of the moon. Steph pushed Milla to the back. He threw the emergency release levers on the rear hatch, blowing the portal open automatically, and waved her on.

"Jump!"

Milla hesitated only briefly before throwing herself out and landing in a sprawl on the rock-strewn slope beyond. The shuttle was a few meters up before Steph followed her, landing hard and sprawling to a stop a short distance away from her.

Beads of sweat immediately formed on his exposed skin as Steph rolled to his feet and checked his gear. The ground was smoking, tendrils rising from under rocks and through the dirt as he looked up at the pieces of the shuttle being lofted into the air above him.

Steph shouldered his rifle, seriously considering firing on the ship for a moment. But that would be a futile gesture at best. He glanced over to where Milla was getting to her feet and lowered his weapon.

"How's your suit?" he asked, concerned.

"Integrity is good," she said. "Temperature is rising."

"Yeah, it's a sauna out here," Steph said, looking around. "What's your air count?"

Milla checked her system briefly. "I have six hours, roughly."

That wasn't much, Steph knew well. He figured he had about the same, probably a little less, and he wondered if surrendering to the enemy would've been a better plan than taking their chances out on an alien moon. Surrender wasn't in his nature, however. He'd seen too many people come back from POW camps in the war and had no illusions of what his fellow man could do to him. He therefore had no desire to see what aliens could do.

"Steph?" Milla called to him.

WARRIOR KING • 149

"What?" He turned back to her, finding her looking at the bottoms of her feet one at a time.

"I do not think the suit will hold for six hours." She pointed to where her boots were smoking.

"Crap," Steph growled, checking his own boots.

The ground was hot enough that it was starting to affect the composites they were wearing. He cast a glance around, looking for an alternative, but frankly, there weren't many to pick from. Finally, he spotted a smooth plateau some distance off and pointed that way.

"Come on, let's move."

CHAPTER 13

AEV *Odysseus*

▶ The *Odysseus* was running at flank speed, putting off turnaround as long as it could as it plunged toward the gas giant. Eric was almost physically having to prevent himself from pacing the command deck, something he'd never had to worry about when he'd had a fighter strapped to his back. But making the crew nervous wouldn't do anyone any good, especially not Steph or Milla.

The alien ship was burning on a turnaround of its own, but Eric wasn't sure the opposing crew had their hearts in it. Their acceleration seemed lower than it should have been, and he realized it was possible that the enemy vessel had taken a bit more damage than he thought in the passing engagement.

It made little sense for the attackers to put off the fight if they were actually intent on a second engagement. The only thing Eric could come up with was that they were running repairs and wanted the extra time.

Certainly, the *Odysseus* itself could do with a few extra days, or weeks, and a good shipyard.

The enemy lasers had every inch the power he'd come to expect from Priminae-level beams, but they also clearly shared the same weakness the Priminae weapons had had until they'd traded tech with Earth. Overwhelming power, but single-frequency beams. Easy enough to adapt to and rarely perfectly suited to any given target. The *Odysseus* could maximize power efficiency by focusing its own beams on a narrow band that would be absorbed by the target.

That made its lasers hundreds of times more effective.

Unfortunately, the little pocket destroyers didn't use the same beam frequencies as the mother ship, so the *Odysseus* had been mauled in the passing engagement as well.

Repair crews had the situation under control, and the *Odysseus* was still combat ready, but Eric would've preferred retrieving his people and withdrawing from the fight without any further multigigawatt exchanges.

He stood looking over the massive central display as the gas giant hung ahead of them and the *Odysseus* reversed warp. There was a momentary shiver through the ship as it began to "fall" in the opposite direction, but the moment passed quickly. The vagaries of the warp drive were such that everything within the drive's field was affected equally. Every molecule, every atom, every quark. They all began to accelerate in a given direction without any sense of motion at all for the crew.

Inertia still existed, of course, but it wasn't relevant for the purposes of the drive.

"Captain." Perez called him over. "We've got an emergency call from Commander Michaels."

"Damn! How long ago?"

"Time stamp is . . . fifteen minutes," Perez replied. "He says he's going down on the inner moon."

"Alright." Eric looked around. "We've got a vector. Lay it in. I want us warping space to that moon like it already happened!"

▶▶▶

PC Parasite *Five*

▶ "Troublesome . . . .," Penae growled, eyes on the scanners.

The pair of intermittent signals that showed the two life signs they were pursuing had blinked out again, leaving them guessing blindly as to where they were going. Their scrapped vessel was trailing behind his ship, quantum locked for the duration, but the two crew members had escaped, much to Penae's ire.

"We're going to have to put men on the ground," he said. "Inform the troopers; we're dispatching them to the surface."

"As you order, Subaltern."

The moon was an inhospitable spot for any sort of stay, yet was the very thing you wanted if evading advanced scanners was your intent. Penae didn't know if the pilot had picked it for that reason or just gotten lucky, but either way, he hoped that this pursuit would turn out to be worth his time.

With the *Piar Cohn* unresponsive, again likely caused by the massive interference in the atmosphere of the volcanic moon, he was on his own for the moment. That was refreshing in some ways, but wouldn't be if he didn't have something to show when the ship returned to the *Cohn*.

"Troopers are ready to deploy, Subaltern."

Penae nodded. "Bring us in closer, and give them the countdown."

"As you say, Subaltern."

▶▶▶

Moon Surface

▶ Feet pounding into the ash, Steph and Milla ran across the volcanic grit, heading for the solid plateau ahead. They could both feel the ship above them, even without looking. A warp field reverberated through everything in its range. Even in space, approaching one left a voyager feeling like there was a deep rumble coming from somewhere nearby.

Within an atmosphere, the tremble wasn't just a feeling. The volcanic ash vibrated around them as they ran, dancing more violently as the ship dropped from its high altitude.

"I see it!" Milla called out.

"Keep your eyes on the ground ahead of us," Steph scolded. "All we can do is run. It doesn't matter what they do!"

Despite saying that, Steph risked a glance over his shoulder.

The frigate loomed large behind them, dropping fast and coming to an unnatural stop a few dozen meters over the surface the way only a warp-drive vessel could. Dust and debris were sucked up by the space warp that held the ship against the moon's gravity, smoke from the volcano curling down as the light from the distant star scattered off the hull in an iridescent rainbow.

Steph would have been more awed if not for the gleaming light shining from under the ship and the sight of figures in hard suits, likely armor, dropping to the surface.

Maybe I'll get that chance to surrender after all, he thought wryly—not that he intended to make it so easy on them.

He and Milla hit the plateau at a dead run, suddenly feeling the ash give way to stone as running got easier and their trudging, plodding steps turned into long hops in the lower gravity.

"Be careful," Milla called as she steadied herself and caught Steph as he nearly catapulted himself across the surface. "We are now pushing against a solid surface. Jumping will be dangerous, or the landing may be, at least."

"Jumping too," Steph grunted as he shuffled his steps. "We're not in a fighter here."

Milla blinked. "What? I do not understand."

"In a fighter, altitude and speed are life," he said. "You want to get high and fast if you want to live. We're on the ground here, though, and jumping only makes us easier to target. Stay low, stay slow, until I say otherwise."

Milla nodded, the motion mostly hidden under her helmet. She glanced at Steph, noting the redness of his exposed skin and the sweat beads evaporating in the low pressure of the atmosphere.

"Are you alright?" she asked softly. "Your skin . . ."

"I'll live." Steph shook his head, waving her off. "We'll run out of air before the atmosphere gets me."

"I believe that is precisely *when* the atmosphere will get you," Milla told him dryly.

He laughed, a rasping sound. Some of the chemicals in the atmosphere were slipping past the seal of the oxygen mask.

"You have a point there," he acknowledged, putting a hand on the mask to press it tighter before he took a deep draw on the oxygen and glanced back. "You can surrender to them if you want. SOP allows that long before the situation gets this bad."

Milla looked back briefly and then up into the dark sky above them. The gas giant was rising on the horizon. She thought the view of the planet would be stunning in an hour, if they were still around to see it.

"The *Odysseus* will be coming," she said, her voice not quite certain.

"Oh, you're damn right the *Odysseus* is coming," Steph assured her. "Raze don't leave people behind."

Milla looked at him as they started moving again. "Raze?"

"Raziel," he answered, shuffling along. "Secret of God. That was his call sign, back in the day."

"I do not understand."

They could feel the intense vibration of the enemy ship's drive as it hovered over the surface, but they weren't willing to look over their shoulders as they shuffled.

"Back then, the war was still cold," Steph said, coughing. "The Archangels were still known as Project Double A. Some of the tech we . . . they were using, well, it was stolen from the Block."

He grinned mirthlessly under his mask. "It was funny, in a way. They sent their best to us to be educated, we trained them in the latest technologies for decades, and they took it home. Then they invented the holy grail of transportation technology, counter-mass . . . so we stole it from them."

Milla shook her head. "That is a very strange way to be."

"Spy versus spy is old hat on Earth. We would have cheerfully bought CM technology from them, but the Block started developing Mantis fighters instead of passenger jets. Military tech was fair game to spies, especially back then. Lots of economic tension between the Block and the USA and other western nations. The Block had huge economies, but new fabrication systems were tanking the sweatshop labor a lot of their member nations depended on."

He laughed, a little painfully, but continued to speak since the talk kept Milla's mind—and his—off the situation while they moved. "It was stupid, in a funny way. Those sweatshops were the places that built the machines that in turn put them out of business. High-efficiency community fabrication units: cheap machines that built even cheaper products. The Block got desperate, watching their economy swirling down the crapper, and the one other thing they were *really* good at was building weapons."

"This way of thinking is very strange," Milla declared.

"Welcome to Earth." Steph chuckled. "Third rock from the Sun. Anyway, Project Double A was how we played catch-up. Eric was the boss man on the project, lead test pilot . . ."

Steph hesitated, glancing behind them. He could see the men on the ground now. They were moving around slowly and spreading out from the ship in a half-crescent formation, heading toward the plateau.

"And a couple other things that are still classified," Steph rasped out, laughing.

Milla didn't get the joke, but Steph wasn't going to fully explain what he meant.

"The war got very hot, very fast," he went on as they shuffled, putting a random boulder behind them. "Mantis fighters hammered us over Japan. Nothing we had back then could touch them. CM fighters were just too fast, too maneuverable. We lost eighty percent of Japan, and most of our forces were beat all the way back to Iwo Jima."

He glanced over at Milla, his eyes visible behind the goggles. "That may not mean much to you, but to the USA it was a big deal. To Eric, it was holy ground. He wasn't going to let them take Iwo Jima. Project Double A went green ahead of schedule, and the fighting over the Pacific got real hot, real fast, and real bloody. Project Double A became the Archangels, and Eric Stanton Weston became Raziel, Secret of God and patron saint of the West Pacific."

"Lofty titles," Milla acknowledged.

"Those were ugly times." Steph coughed, lifting the mask up to spit out phlegm before resealing it to take another breath. "Hope was a big thing. We became symbols, more powerful in how people perceived us than our actual effect on the battlefield."

"I . . . understand," Milla said, thinking about how people on Ranquil had reacted to the *Odyssey*.

"So that's how I know Raze is coming," Steph said. "He's a Marine to the core. Symbols mean more to him than reality sometimes."

"I . . . do *not* understand," she said.

"Semper fi," Steph told her. "Forever faithful. He's coming. Keep moving."

▶▶▶

AEV *Odysseus*

▶ "We're hitting turnaround, Captain!"

Eric nodded. "Do it."

The *Odysseus'* reactors didn't whine the way the *Odyssey's* systems would have, but the computers monitoring her telltales were *screaming* as they hit turnover. Half the systems went dead, their power being redirected entirely to the drives. Given the sheer level of power output by the *Odysseus'* reactors, the fact that they were actually *shutting down* systems to conserve power at the moment made Eric's head swim.

They'd put off turnover far longer than they should have, trying to get to the inner moon of the gas giant that much faster, but now they had to stop or the ship was going to buzz right on by.

"Reactors are spiking! We're losing reactor mass, sir. Still stable, but dropping fast," Miram announced from where she was monitoring the reports from maintenance and damage control.

"Space warp at one hundred twenty percent over flank," Lieutenant Kinder declared. "We're twisting local space into a pretzel, but it's holding steady, sir."

At that level of warping, Eric knew that the ship itself was in danger of being affected by the gravity fields they were projecting. If they lost control of the warp, it might cross the ship's hull, and if that happened, there was a major chance that the *Odysseus* would tear itself apart.

A long, low keening sound echoing through the ship's hull punctuated that thought.

Eric shook his head slowly but didn't waver from his focus. The small inner moon of the gas giant wasn't so small anymore, and the satellite was growing *very* quickly as they closed on it.

An alarm sounded, startling Eric as he twisted around. "What is it?"

"We're being actively tracked," Ensign Sams blurted. "Coming from the gas giant. I . . . I didn't see them . . ."

"Damn," Eric growled through clenched teeth, pitching his voice low enough not to carry.

Of all the things he could have done, of all the times he could have chosen, he just had to send his chief helmsman *and* his chief tactical officer off on a checkout flight right before encountering a combat situation. Eric couldn't blame Sams for missing the other pocket destroyers, not much anyway. He should have kept up on them himself.

"Light them up," he ordered. "Full power, all active scanners. I want them having FLKs after this."

FLKs, or funny-looking kids, was an old Blue Navy joke about what would happen if you ever seriously pissed off an Aegis destroyer back in the prewar days. The Aegis had a massive radar array, the AN/SPY-1, with a total power output of six megawatts. More than enough to mess up your DNA, as the joke went.

Six megawatts was insignificant compared to the power of the *Odysseus'* primary array.

"If they turn off, let them go," Eric said. "If not . . . fry them where they fly."

▶▶▶

PC Parasite *Eight*

▶ The hit was so powerful that it actually disrupted power to nonessential systems, throwing the command deck of the parasite craft into shadows briefly before backup power was rerouted from secure lines.

"We have been targeted, Subaltern."

Hora Manau snorted. "Obviously."

"They have not fired, Subaltern."

"No, *that* was a warning," Hora said into the open. "There was no need to hit us that hard just to acquire a weapon lock. They're telling us that we are too small to bother with, unless we push the issue."

The deck was filled with a long silence.

"W-what do we do, Subaltern?"

"Our duty. Signal *Three*, lock all weapons on the target, and prepare to fire. Inform *Five* that they are likely to have company very soon."

▶▶▶

AEV *Odysseus*

▶ "Live weapons in the clear, Captain!" Sams announced. "We've taken laser strikes, and there are missiles inbound."

"Weapons free. Smoke them," Eric ordered coldly.

"Aye Captain."

The command went out from tactical straight to the aft transition cannons, and they swiveled around to the rear as the *Odysseus* hurtled onward. Two of the three barreled cannons adjusted minutely before they discharged.

Quietly.

Without fanfare or a blaze of flame and smoke.

Instantly, several light-seconds away, two parasite cruisers vanished in nuclear fire.

"Targets serviced."

"Send trajectories of the missiles to point defense stations, then put scanners forward and stay on target," Eric said. "We have people in the cold."

"Aye aye, Captain."

▶▶▶

Moon Surface

▶ A small boulder exploded ahead of them, and Steph drove Milla to the ground, rolling behind another as the shrapnel rained down around them.

"Laser!" she gasped.

"Yup." Steph rolled clear of her and brought his rifle up to rest on the barrel. "High powered too. Reminds me of your people's stuff before the Drasin."

Milla shot a glance at him, mostly hidden behind her visor. "Our hand weapons were designed to be nonlethal against people. *That* was not."

Steph paused, looking at her briefly before focusing back over the sights of his rifle. "Nonlethal *lasers*? How the hell did you manage that?"

Another crack signaled the other side of their boulder popping as a laser superheated the stone and vaporized the liquid contained within.

Milla ducked. "Do we really have time to explain photon lattice theory right now?"

"No, probably not," Steph admitted as he settled a little and took a couple deep breaths. "They've got us zeroed in. Check around. See any cover we could retreat to?"

Milla did as he asked, but shook her head. "Nothing close."

"I didn't think so," Steph said. "Okay, have you been taking tactical courses?"

"Some, but not open combat. Nothing like this."

"Welcome to real-world combat 101," Steph said. "Unfortunately, we're going to have to skip the beginner stuff and move straight to the advanced course. Withdrawal under fire—definitely advanced-placement courses here."

Milla nodded, surprising herself somewhat because she wasn't shaking. "What do I do?"

"Find a boulder you can cover behind," he told her, cutting her off when she tried to repeat what she'd said earlier. "I know there aren't any close. Just do it."

Milla cast about, looking for the largest, and closest, boulder she could find. They were strewn over the plateau in haphazard fashion, like some giant had left its toys lying out after a particularly enthusiastic game night. She found one that looked large enough and was hopefully not too far away.

"Okay, I have one."

"Good," Steph said. "When I open fire, you run."

"But . . ."

"You *run*!" he snapped. "Get to cover, then you do what I tell you to do. Okay?"

Milla jerked her head up and down. "Okay."

"Get ready." Steph took a breath, settling his rifle down and dropping the fire selector over to burst mode. "Run."

The rifle barked, sending three high-velocity rounds downrange and bucking back into Steph's shoulder. He didn't bother trying to see if he'd hit anyone. That wasn't the point. Instead, he just shifted and fired another burst.

This wasn't his preferred battle rifle, but rather a lightweight, medium-caliber weapon loaded with high-velocity, low-mass rounds. Not particularly lethal, but the rifle did pack a lot of bullets in each magazine.

The first burst dug into the ash around the pursuing troops, and they reacted predictably, diving for cover as best they could even as the second burst kicked up more ash and dirt. Steph fired a third burst before Milla signaled him.

"I am behind cover."

He dropped back, leaning against the boulder. "Good. Now, listen carefully . . . Put your weapon into burst mode . . ."

"Done."

"Okay, now set up, pick a grouping of the enemy troops . . . *away* from my position," Steph said. "That part is *really* important, okay?"

"I normally handle shipboard weapon batteries, Stephan," she told him dryly. "I believe that I *am* familiar with the concept of minimizing collateral damage."

"Ah . . . right. Okay, fire when you're ready, and don't stop until I get to cover," he said.

"Roger, as your people like to say."

Steph tensed to run as the first burst roared through the thin atmosphere.

▶▶▶

▶ Moro Kav, the troop commander on the ground, huffed as he pushed dust and ash out of his faceplate and risked looking up from where he'd dived into the dirt.

"Burn them down!" he bellowed, leveling his pulse gun ahead of him and firing as best he could, half-buried in volcanic ash.

His squad responded, slowly at first, but in a few seconds the terrain was lit up with trace from the pulse discharges, most of which were not just missing wide but *far* wide as fire from their targets continued to slap into the ash around them. Moro caught a glimpse of a figure running all out, but before he could do much more, the target dived behind a large boulder and was out of sight.

"Get to cover!" he ordered his troops, crawling through the shin-deep ash toward the rocky terrain concealing their targets.

He knew that he had to get his men under cover before they could effectively start countering the target's strategy. The line of rock ahead of them should serve his needs, he figured, but there was no doubt in Moro's mind that this mission had just gotten dirty and was going to stay that way.

▶▶▶

▶ A withdrawal under fire was, perhaps, one of the most difficult tactical maneuvers to execute correctly, largely because even if you did it right, the risk was extremely high that you still weren't going to nail it. That was the problem with the enemy: sometimes they didn't cooperate by doing what you expected of them. Bastards just *live* to make life hard on you, don't you know?

So Steph was mildly surprised, yet quite pleased, not to have been boiled to a goopy smear on the rock by a stray laser as he slid around a boulder and into cover. He rolled over, got his rifle out ahead of him, and settled the stock onto his shoulder while calling Milla on the comm.

"Alright, your turn. Wait for me to open fire, then run like all hell is chasing you."

"You mean it isn't?"

Milla's voice was a little weak, but the humor told him she was still hanging in there.

Steph didn't reply. He just picked a target and took a breath. He wasn't a bad shot, but firing bursts at this range with a medium-caliber weapon took a premier marksman to reliably hit a target. Luckily, he didn't need a hit. A near miss was almost as good.

Maybe even better. A hit would put one man down, maybe scare the others. It might also piss them off, and angry troops were more apt to take risks. Steph didn't want them taking risks.

The burst ricocheted off the stone. He could imagine the whine slicing the air around the enemy, and the men went to ground just as predictably. Steph put two more bursts downrange while Milla ran. Then he let his eyes flick upward.

Of course, the real problem wasn't the guys on the ground. The true nemesis was the floating fortress following along behind them like a dutiful dog, just waiting to be let off the leash. The ship was another reason not to start chewing up their pursuers. Steph didn't want to know what would happen if the commander of that beast decided pursuit wasn't worth the cost.

"I am covered," Milla said, panting a little.

"I'm ready. Fire when ready."

▶▶▶

▶ Moro had had about as much of this mess as he was willing to endure.

His quarries were good. Not great, but good. They were calm, disciplined, and making good use of their available resources. Thankfully, they didn't have many resources to make use of. Otherwise, he suspected that they wouldn't be settling for delaying tactics.

"*Five*, Tav on call."

"We hear you. What do you need, Tav?" the communications officer on the parasite responded.

"Drop a second squad behind their position. I'm going to spread my team downslope to cut off their escape to the sides," he said.

"Understood . . . Ground command . . . ?"

"What is it?"

"What about upslope?" the comm officer asked.

"*Five* handles upslope."

There was a long silence before the comm came back.

"Subaltern confirms."

Moro didn't bother responding. He'd given orders, and he had orders.

"Alright, spread half the team downslope. Start driving them back and up. We'll wear them down before *Five* closes the lock."

CHAPTER 14

▶ "Shit."

Steph wasn't really the swearing type, but this was a situation where he was more than willing to make an exception.

"What is wrong?" Milla asked from her cover, a boulder five meters or so away.

"They're getting smarter," he said over the radio link as the frigate broke position and flew overhead. "And it looks like they want us alive."

"That is . . . good? Yes?" Milla sounded like she wished she were more certain.

"I wish I knew, but if they wanted to talk all friendly like, they could have just opened a comm link from the start." Steph sighed. "Doesn't matter. At this point, I'm going to make them sweat for their supper."

There was a long pause before Milla said anything. "You are joking, yes? You do not really think they intend to eat us?"

Steph rasped out a laugh, coughing as he tried to hold the mask tighter to his face. "No, I don't think they intend to eat us. It's possible, I suppose, but that was just a figure of speech."

"Of course."

He laughed harder at the obvious relief in her voice.

Milla was quiet for a moment, then snapped a little sulkily, "It was not that funny, Stephan!"

"Yes, it was," he gasped, still laughing.

His giggles finally petered out as he slumped against the boulder he was taking cover behind, holding the oxygen mask to his face and taking deep drags. He figured he had twenty minutes of air left at this level of activity—not that he would be able to keep up this level of activity for that long.

The adrenaline high coming off the crash was burning out, and he was pretty sure he'd bruised if not outright cracked a couple ribs. With the toxic atmosphere burning his exposed skin, and wisps of it leaking in to do the same to his lungs, Steph figured he was running on the ragged edge already. Twenty minutes would be pushing it, no question.

He risked a glance around the boulder, noting that the pursuit team was spreading down the slope and still closing on their location. The deep hum of the frigate was close, and he could see more men hitting the ground. Milla and Steph had only one direction left to go now, up the slope of the volcano. They would run out of stone and boulders in maybe a couple hundred meters and then be slogging through ash with no cover.

"Stephan? What do we do?" Milla asked him.

Steph didn't have an answer. Honestly, he'd seen enough in his life that he didn't want to be taken. POWs didn't get treated well; it didn't matter *who* took them. He didn't know who their pursuers were, but the odds seemed good that they were the ones who'd sicced the Drasin on the Priminae.

Steph had sworn a long time earlier that he wouldn't be a POW, not after the things he'd seen. Some of the stuff that happened to prisoners was . . . it was just unforgivable—and that was the stuff in Confederation camps. The Block had done worse.

He didn't know these people, but if they had anything to do with the Drasin, they weren't *nearly* as civilized as the Block.

A hail of gunfire was looking good, but he wasn't alone—and he wasn't making that call for someone else.

"I don't know," he said finally. "They've got us cornered. They're going to drive us up the slope into the ash. We could stay ahead of them for a while, but now it's really just a matter of time."

Milla was still for a moment. He couldn't see much body language through her suit from where he was crouched, but Steph imagined her thoughts easily enough. Most of the same things he was thinking, maybe with a little more optimism.

"So . . . we surrender?" she asked finally.

Or maybe she had a hell of a lot more optimism. He surely wasn't thinking that.

He'd prefer to end it on the surface of the moon, not clean perhaps, but better than the tender mercies of prison guards. He glanced over at Milla and grimaced under his oxygen mask, indecision eating at him.

Finally, he sighed. "Okay, we'll . . ."

His and Milla's radios crackled to life on the common channel.

"*Eagle One*, do you copy?"

Steph bolted almost upright, nearly exposing himself. "*Odysseus* Control? *Eagle* Actual speaking. We're under fire on the . . . um, planet-facing side of a volcano on the inner moon. Do you copy?"

"Roger, *Eagle* Actual. *Odysseus* is entering orbit of the moon. Marine landers are preparing to launch. Squawk for location fix."

"Roger, squawk out," Steph responded, thumbing the control to send a heavy signal across the band, something more easily trackable than the pulsed comm.

"Receiving. Locating. Locked. Marines inbound."

Steph slumped in place, letting out a breath he hadn't known he was holding.

"Roger that. We'll keep them occupied if we can," he said. "Glad you could join the party."

A new voice entered the conversation, one Steph knew well.

"Wouldn't miss it for the world, Stephanos."

Steph chuckled. "Welcome to my moon, Raziel. It's a bit of a fixer-upper, but the view is to die for."

"Let's hope not."

▶▶▶

PC Parasite *Five*

▶ Subaltern Penae twisted around as the alarms roared in his ears. "What is it?"

"Proximity alarms, Subaltern! Mass detection, approaching at high velocity!"

"Missiles?"

The scanner tech shook his head. "Not on intersect course. Close, but it's going to miss us."

"Give me a visual!" snapped Penae.

"Calculating speed, trajectory . . . on screen!"

Penae stared for a few seconds longer than he probably should have before he managed to comment.

"What the abyss is that thing?" he mumbled.

It was a small craft, clearly not a missile, but of no configuration he'd ever seen in his entire career in the Empire. It was also coming in incredibly hot. Frankly, the ship looked like it was going to slam into the surface.

Suicide attack that missed?

The idea seemed ludicrous, but he'd experienced odder phenomena in his years.

"Subaltern, it's decelerating hard!"

His eyes flicked to the displays again in time to see the craft hammer on a crushing deceleration, turning its descent into a curving glide path that brought the ship out over the line of troopers strewn across the slope of the volcanic cone.

"Troopers in the air! Troopers on the ground!"

Indeed there were. Men in armor were leaping from the sides of the craft, though it wasn't slowing at all, using some sort of physical air brake to reduce impact velocity, and landing hard but apparently intact right across his operations area.

"Lasers on that craft. Burn it out of the sky."

"As you say, Subaltern. Targeting . . . Holy stars of the Empire!"

Penae couldn't bring himself to chastise his subordinate for the outburst. He'd nearly done as much himself. The instant they'd achieved an active lock on the small craft, a *visible* beam of pure light struck down in front of them like the fire of the gods. Penae had to take a moment to recognize what he was seeing.

"Visible laser?" he mumbled, shocked to the core.

The power needed for that was immense. In fact, only a—

"Reverse screens! Show me the source of the beam!"

The display flickered, showing the black of space for a brief moment before a large cruiser with an almost mirrored hull appeared. The gas giant on the horizon was actually reflecting off the hull of the cruiser as it settled into low orbit over the moon. Penae couldn't see where the beam originated, as there were no molecules that high up to turn to plasma. But the subaltern didn't need to see the beam to know what he was facing.

They got past the Piar Cohn.

▶▶▶

AEV *Odysseus*

 "Comm open, Captain, broadcasting on Priminae frequencies."

"Thank you," Eric said, thumbing the comm open on his end. "This is Captain Eric Stanton Weston of the AEV *Odysseus*. Targeting my Marines is a hostile act. You have one warning. Do it again, and I will *end* your hostilities. *Odysseus* out."

He turned back to the tactical station. "If they blink, turn them to plasma."

"Aye aye, Captain," Sams acknowledged.

Eric glanced back to Miram. "Status on the Marines?"

She snorted softly. "They're Marines, sir. You know better than most, this is what they live for."

"We do indeed, Commander." Eric nodded. "We do indeed."

▶▶▶

Moon Surface

▶ Colonel Deirdre Conner tagged three targets on her heads-up display, or HUD, not pausing in her firing, and designated them to her second fire team. "Sergeant, these boys are in my way. See to that, would you?"

"Yes ma'am."

With fire team two moving to plow the road, Deirdre turned her focus to the objective.

"Commander Michaels, squawk location," she said. "We're closing on your locations."

"Squawk out." The answer came back almost instantly.

The powerful signal blast couldn't be missed by a blind man, unlike the compressed burst signals used for communications. Deirdre's systems locked onto it instantly, and she redirected her squad accordingly.

"Squawk received. We're almost there, Commander," she said, her ground-eating strides intended to keep her low to the ground.

"Watch out. These guys are packing Priminae-scale hand lasers," Steph said. "Even if your armor held up to one of those blasts, the heat would likely cook you in your suit."

"Understood. I don't think they're in any position to resist, but you never know what a cornered rat will do," Deirdre answered, then switched to squad channels. "Laser protocols, Marines! Pop smoke!"

"Yes ma'am!"

The Marines had carried diffractive smoke canisters, which were capable of spewing out dozens of cubic meters of thick smoke with suspended Mylar particles, since the Drasin invasion. The ploy wasn't perfect, but it would attenuate lasers effectively enough.

As soon as the smoke filled the battlefield, beams of lasers could be seen visibly slicing the air and lighting it up. The smoke blunted the lasers and redirected some of their energy in random directions. Colonel Conner's suit switched over to augmented reality vision as visibility went to effectively zero, highlighting her Marines using the IFF—identification, friend or foe—signals from their suits.

The networked computers also worked overtime trying to track laser telemetry using the visible beams in the smoke, giving the squad the locations of enemy forces as they fired.

Battle rifles roared in the smoke, but Deirdre remained focused as she closed on the commander's location. She vaulted a boulder and skidded to a stop on the other side. She was surprised to find the commander with nothing more than goggles and an oxygen mask to protect him from the moon's thin atmosphere.

"Are you injured?" she asked, trying unsuccessfully to link to his suit for a medical report.

"Only my pride," he smirked under the mask, and then started coughing. "And, you know, maybe my body a little."

She glanced over to where the lieutenant was taking cover nearby. "Lieutenant Chans, your status?"

"Intact." Milla waved. "Body and suit."

"Roger that," Deirdre said. "I can scan your vitals. Hold position. We're securing the area."

Milla nodded. "I am going nowhere, Colonel."

Deirdre checked the commander's air and clucked. "Almost out of air, Commander. You flyboys like to cut things close."

"What can I say, Colonel, I live on the edge."

"I can see that, Commander. Here. I've got a spare." She handed him an oxygen bottle from her rescue pack.

"Thanks," Steph said and coughed, swapping the bottles.

"Just keep your head down. I'm calling for dustoff shortly."

"No problem. I'm not going anywhere until the nice flying machine arrives."

"Flyboys," Deirdre snorted, looking over the boulder. "Those boys you ticked off are determined—I'll give them that much."

Steph risked a glance for himself, noting the sweeps of laser light refracting in the smoke. "Yeah, you noticed that too?"

She shouldered her battle rifle and swept the field with its optics. "They're firing blind for now, but this smoke won't last forever. Skipper has their air cover standing down, from the looks of it. Now we just need to figure out if we have to kill these fools."

"If they don't stop using multimegawatt lasers like flashlights," Steph grumbled, "I know what direction I'm leaning toward."

▶▶▶

IBC *Piar Cohn*

▶ "What in the abyss was that? Show me again!" Aymes leaned over the controls, glowering at the displays as the two parasite frigates opened fire on the ship called *Odysseus*, only to explode in seconds. "Where is the laser trace? Missile telemetry?"

"There is none, Captain." His tactical officer shook. "We must be too far out."

"Too far," Aymes hissed, knowing that wasn't true.

There should have been *some* trace. Not even lasers were as efficient as this. There was no sign of beam reflection against the parasite's armor, and there should have been, even if only for a fraction of an instant.

"Dump all data from the scanners to the long-term storage," he ordered. "We'll analyze it later."

The situation was rapidly becoming too anomalous for his pay grade, to say the least.

"Navigation, give me a least-time course out of this system, with a nine-point evasion route to return to Imperial territory," he said.

"As you say, Captain . . ."

"Captain . . ."

Aymes turned to his altern commander, whose hesitant tone felt profoundly irritating in that moment. "What is it, Altern?"

"What of the remaining parasite?"

Aymes sighed, considering the question.

It would hardly do to leave Imperial technology and people in the hands of unknown foes, even if said foes appeared to have access to at least part of the Oather database. Aymes returned to his station and took a seat before entering his personal access codes.

"For the Empire, we all sacrifice," he said firmly.

▶ ▶ ▶

AEV *Odysseus*

▶ "No response from the enemy ship at this time, Captain," Miram said, her voice holding a nervous edge as she observed the situation below them. "Perhaps we should signal again?"

Eric's jaw clenched as he considered the tableau arranged along the moon's surface. For the moment the ground situation was stable, but that would last only until the smoke began to thin. At that point, the Marines would have no choice but to take off the kid gloves. So far, no one appeared to have died on the ground, which meant that both sides were holding back.

He just didn't know *why* the aliens were holding back.

Eric knew that if he were still a junior officer, he wouldn't worry about motivations. Actions spoke, not intentions. Attacking his people was action enough to decide his course, even now, but he also knew that these weren't the Drasin, and part of Eric desperately wanted to know *why they'd attacked.*

Why attack Steph in the first place? Why were they even in this system?

And, of course, the big question: the genocide in the solar system, as it were. Were these the ones who held the Drasin's leash? And if so, *why?*

Why any of it?

"Signal them again," he ordered finally. "Tell them to stand down."

"Aye sir," Miram said, nodding to the communications station.

The ensign standing at the station swallowed visibly, but turned to his console and quietly began signaling on Priminae frequencies.

Eric's jaw clenched and unclenched reflexively.

Part of him wanted nothing more than to burn that pocket destroyer and its ground forces to ash for attacking his people, but if he wanted answers, then restraint was required. Additionally, he was aware that his anger wasn't entirely rational at the moment, which was a strange feeling. To *know* that you're not thinking rationally was not a comfortable thing.

Such circumstances could lead to Eric second-guessing his actions, especially if things turned out badly.

"Still no response, ma'am," the ensign said in response to Miram.

"Damn!" Miram glared at the screen. "What is wrong with them? They have to know we hold every tactical advantage."

"So did the other two," Eric said quietly, "and they still opened fire on us. There's something going on here that we're not seeing. These people, no matter what their technology seems to indicate, are *not* the Priminae."

Miram hesitated, then nodded slowly. "True enough, from what we can see."

"Captain!" yelled Sams with a jolt. His hands were frozen over the console as he was an instant from firing the ship's weapons reflexively.

Eric and Miram twisted toward the display, eyes widening in shock as the target ship vanished in a ball of fire and light.

▶▶▶

Moon Surface

 Deirdre Conner flung herself over the commander's body as the blast blew over them, shielding him with her armor and hoping that the pressure wave itself didn't kill him. The flash of light had been her only warning that something had gone wrong, but she'd seen too many explosions in her career not to recognize the signs.

The blast blew away their smoke screen, which meant that she and her Marines had other problems coming their way as they picked themselves off the ground. As she got to her feet, however, she noticed that the opposing forces were more concerned with the sudden loss of their ride home.

"Marines! Take them now, while they're distracted!" she snarled. "I want prisoners!"

She left her Marines to it, glancing down to where Commander Michaels was groaning on the ground. There was a spatter of blood inside his oxygen mask, possibly from the pressure wave. She also might have landed a little harder on him than she'd intended.

Deirdre opened comms to the lander. "Bravo Bravo Bravo. I say again, Bravo Bravo Bravo."

"Roger, Code Bravo," the pilot of the lander responded. "Dustoff in three, Colonel. Medical on standby."

The Marine lander's reactors whined in the distance, closing fast as Deirdre knelt by the commander.

"We've got dustoff inbound, Commander," she said. "You good?"

"I feel like someone dropped a couple hundred pounds of hard suit on me, Colonel." Steph chuckled from where he lay. "Guess I'm lucky that whoever was wearing it couldn't have added much more than another hundred or so."

"Flattery will get you nowhere with me, Commander. Besides, I'm one eighty and not remotely ashamed of it."

"Noted." He grinned under the spattered oxygen mask. "That would explain the pain in my kidneys."

"Are you alright, Stephan?" Milla asked, approaching cautiously while she kept an eye on where the Marines were disarming the still-stunned enemy troopers.

"I'll live," he said from the ground. "But Milla?"

"Yes, Stephan?"

"Next time, get someone else to do your check flight," he whined. "I don't think I want to be flying with you anymore. You're *way* too dangerous for this fighter jock."

The sound of the Marine lander's retros scorching the ground nearby swallowed any response Milla might have made. A medical team jumped clear of the vessel with a stretcher between them and rushed over. Deirdre had to hold Steph down as he tried to get to his feet.

"I'm not that badly hurt," he protested, his struggles ineffective against the armored gauntlet.

"Ask me if I care," the colonel said dryly. "You've got internal bleeding on some level, so you ride."

He slumped back down as the corpsmen arrived. "Fine."

Deirdre left them to it and got to her feet, looking toward Milla.

"Lieutenant Chans," she said, "you look like you can walk."

"I can."

"Good." She smirked slightly. "It is the more dignified way to get to the lander after a crash."

"Hey!" Steph struggled free of the corpsmen for an instant. "I was *shot* down!"

"Meh, whatever lets you sleep at night, Commander."

▶▶▶

AEV *Odysseus*

▶ "Was that us?" Eric asked, though he knew the answer.

"No sir," Sams swore. "I triple-checked. We did *not* engage."

Miram looked lost. "What happened then? Accident?"

Eric shook his head. "Not likely. Either they blew their own reactor, or . . ."

He fell silent, eyes drifting to the telemetry display at the scanner station. "Where's Bandit One?"

The scanner tech looked over the numbers. "Bandit One is three light-minutes out and . . . opening, sir."

Eric grimaced, his teeth gleaming in the computer lights. "Cold-blooded bastards."

"Sir? Captain?" Miram looked over, still more than a little lost.

"They"—he gestured to the Bandit One telemetry—"either ordered the ship scuttled or blew it remotely when they decided they weren't going to try and take us. Now they're running upwell as fast as that ship will carry them, which is probably faster than we can follow, since they've dropped a lot of mass and we have to wait to pick up our Marines."

"They wouldn't have . . . would they?" she asked, unbelieving.

Eric tilted his head slightly. "Yeah, I think they would. How long until the Marines are back?"

Miram shook off her shock and checked the reports on her console. "At least forty minutes, sir. They're taking prisoners."

"Good. At least we got something out of this." Eric stood up. "Get me a full damage report within the hour. We're going to have to decide if we can return to Earth or if we need a full repair bay at the Forge."

"Aye sir."

He sighed. "Probably have to be the Forge. We can comm Earth using the FTL relays at least. Commander, you have the bridge."

"Aye Captain, I have the bridge," Miram answered instantly.

CHAPTER 15

▶ Lieutenant Milla Chans sealed the seam of her uniform jacket and pushed back the still-damp flop of hair that was plastered to her forehead, feeling much better now that she'd managed to escape the tender care of Doctor Rame and gotten a proper shower. Steph was still in the medical center under an enforced stay, much to his disgust, while being treated for chemical burns to his throat, air passages, and lungs.

The Marines had rounded up the alien troopers, disarming them as much as possible, and bundled everyone onto the lander for dustoff within minutes of the destruction of the alien frigate. That flight had been about as far from comfortable as anything she'd ever experienced.

Since they couldn't exactly strip down the alien troops on the surface of the moon, and the lander was too small for those sorts of acrobatics, the Marines had crammed fourteen prisoners against the raised ramp and held no less than ten battle rifles on them at all times until landing back on the *Odysseus*. This meant that everyone else was crammed into the *other* side of the lander, just as tightly packed.

Very unpleasant, to say the least.

Milla tried not to think too hard about the Marine colonel's warning to the prisoners, reminding them that they *were* stacked against the landing ramp and if they gave any trouble . . . Well, the lander's cockpit was sealed, and explosive decompression was overrated.

It wasn't the physical discomfort that had mostly bothered her, however.

No, it was the prisoners.

They'd spoken, a little. Nothing useful in the content of their speech, not as far as she could tell, but it wasn't what they'd said that bothered her. She was discomfited because she understood their language. She had no need of the Terrans' translation process or the irascible but amusing linguistics expert Doctor Palin.

They'd spoken in clear Priminae, albeit with an accent she'd never before encountered.

Milla really didn't know what to think of that.

They *couldn't* be Priminae. They were . . . they were worse by far than the Terrans, who even Milla found occasionally distasteful in some of their actions and pastimes.

Taking a cleansing breath, she examined her reflection in the mirror briefly before deciding that she'd neatened up well enough. She made her way out of her quarters and down the corridor, heading for the bridge. She wasn't on duty, officially, but the *Odysseus* had seen combat in her absence. She wanted to determine just how well the weapons had performed in the fight and whether the enemy's arms were a significant threat to the Heroic Class cruiser.

This was all professional interest, of course. It wasn't like she was itching to find out just how badly her systems had been mauled while she was gone.

▶▶▶

▶ "Continue to track the ship when it goes to FTL," Eric ordered the scanner chief as Milla stepped onto the bridge. "Get vectors and anything you can about their drive system."

"Aye Captain."

The *Odysseus* was still close to the gas giant, deep in the system's gravity well. After the crew had recovered the Marines, shuttle duo, and prisoners, Eric had elected to remain and monitor the departure of the enemy ship from the system, using the light-speed delay to ensure nothing was missed.

He glanced in Milla's direction as she walked over to the tactical station and relieved her second.

"Welcome back, Lieutenant."

"Thank you, Capitaine." She glanced up briefly before refocusing on her instruments.

"Your systems performed admirably in your absence," Eric assured her, smiling slightly. "As did your subordinates."

"I expected no less. Both were of the finest foundation," she responded, then scowled slightly. "The enemy lasers are at least thirty percent over our own in raw power. That is . . . annoying."

"Still Class Ones, so it hardly matters."

"You have shown them your capabilities, Capitaine," she reminded him. "They are . . . not going to remain unchanged."

"Because they're Priminae?" he asked mildly.

Milla stiffened, then snapped her head around to look at him, eyes blazing. "They are *not* Priminae. I do not know what they are, but they are not my people."

"No." Eric nodded. "No, I suppose they're not. They're more ruthless, culturally, than I've known the Priminae to be, and there are enough differences in their technology to be noticeable, but you come from the same roots, Milla. You *must*."

Milla seethed, but controlled her emotions, finally nodding as well. "Yes. I can see that too. They . . . your people, and mine, are the same genetically . . . but these people, they have too much in common with mine technologically, to say nothing of the language. Someone has hidden history from us. Someone must have."

"You'll get a chance to find out who soon enough," Eric said. "We'll be returning to Ranquil for repair and minor refit."

"Thank you, Capitaine," she said, calming down steadily.

"No need for thanks. The hull repairs need attention we'll not be able to get in Sol space for at least a month, probably more, given the push for new ships taking up the slips. Ranquil is the best option, particularly given our prisoners."

"Yes . . . them," Milla hissed. "I do not know what to think of them."

"Don't," Eric said. "Not yet. When we have more facts, then you can worry . . ."

"Captain," Miram cut in, "they've gone to warp."

Eric turned back to the displays, eyes on the space-warp signature that Miram was pointing to. Technically, their attackers had gone to warp several hours earlier, of course, but with full scanners out and recording, the *Odysseus* was picking up the details just then.

"Damn. Higher velocity change than we can manage short of transition," he said. "More power in their reactors, no question."

"More control as well," Miram said. "They're playing with space-time better than we can."

"Lovely. So they've got some kind of connection to the Priminae, but they apparently haven't been stuck in the mud since the split." Eric sighed. "And they're either hostile, or just plain violent."

"There is a difference?" Milla asked, confused.

"'Hostile' generally means they have something against us," Miram filled in. "'Violent' means they might just attack at random for no particular reason."

Milla scrunched up her face even more. "That is insane, no?"

"Yes, but it also happens," Miram said. "Rarely, and not usually on a cultural level, but it does happen."

"Sometimes I find your people truly terrifying," Milla admitted.

"Join the club," Eric said, turning. "Helm, take us out of the system and put us on an arc to warp space for Ranquil."

Kinder half turned. "Warp space, sir?"

"You heard me, Lieutenant. We'll warp space for a few light-years before we transition. I don't want to leave any traces here if we can help it."

"Aye sir, course is already entered. Engaging."

▶▶▶

▶ Colonel Conner glowered through the security glass to where the enemy troops were being held. "Have they been saying anything?"

"Mostly small talk, ma'am," Lieutenant Mitchel, one of her security staff members, said. "Nothing earth shaking, but we're recording everything anyway."

She nodded absently. "I believe the Earth has been shaken enough lately, Mitchel. I'll settle for anything at all, useless or otherwise."

"Yes ma'am. Quickie DNA tests are back," he said, handing her a slate.

She glanced at the results but didn't bother reading too deeply. "Highlights?"

"They're Priminae, genetically speaking."

"The same way Priminae are human, or . . . ?" Deirdre asked, one eyebrow rising.

"Negative. We went deeper than just common human DNA markers," Mitchel said. "Their junk DNA matches the Priminae. They're of the same stock as the Colonials."

"Colonials," Deirdre grumbled. "I guess we know now why they call themselves that. Someone should have thought to ask what they were colonies of in the first place. I mean, it was right there in the word. They even introduced themselves to us as being *the Colonies*. We assumed they meant colonies from a central world within the Priminae sphere, but now I'm thinking something else."

"Yes ma'am."

Deirdre looked through the glass, eyes on the men slumped within.

"Ruthless bastards," she muttered, shaking her head. "Can't imagine serving someone who'd blow my ticket off a hostile surface just because it wasn't convenient to try and effect a rescue."

"No ma'am."

Deirdre glanced at the lieutenant but said nothing more. He was just answering with what he thought she wanted to hear, which was more or less what a good young Marine officer should do when he didn't have anything useful to add to the conversation. But it didn't help her much at the moment.

"Have we identified officers?"

"No," Mitchel said, looking a little put out by that fact. "No hints even."

Deirdre frowned, now more curious. "Really? That's odd. Body language? Reactions?"

"Nothing, ma'am. Nothing on any of our analyses in fact," Mitchel said. "They don't talk to one another any differently, they don't react to each other differently, just . . . nothing."

"We killed three on the surface," she said. "Check their gear and bodies against the living. Maybe we took out their commander."

"Yes ma'am."

▶▶▶

▶ Eric kept one eye on Milla as he worked on, filling out after-action reports that he knew the admiral was going to want—in triplicate. Milla's reaction earlier had been out of character for the normally quiet and reserved Priminae officer. Though he understood why, she had come close to the edge of proper comportment for a young officer serving on the command deck of the *Odysseus*. Whatever issues she had with the . . .

Hmm, what do we call them anyway? Eric wondered.

He was loath to start referring to them as the "enemy," even in his head. Their reaction notwithstanding, it was a very *bad* idea to start thinking of people as the enemy until you were in direct combat with them or at the very least understood why you were fighting. That sort of mental rigidity led to bad places.

They weren't really aliens either. Yet nor were they human, or even really Priminae.

Well, nothing to it I suppose but to go down there and ask some of the prisoners themselves, Eric decided, getting up.

"Commander, you have the bridge."

"Aye Captain, I have the bridge."

Eric strode off, taking the lift into Marine country, where the ship's detention cells were located.

He was only mildly surprised to find Colonel Conner there, apparently staring through the security glass at the prisoners. He suspected that she was more lost in her own thoughts than actually looking at anything.

"Have they spoken?" he asked, coming to a stop beside her.

"Nothing useful."

Eric nodded, unsurprised.

Any reasonably disciplined group wouldn't give up much in the first few hours of capture. Over time, however, it would be all but impossible to keep from slipping out *something* of value. People just couldn't maintain discipline indefinitely, not even when they *knew* they were being watched. Actually, being watched constantly was known to *erode* discipline faster than if a person believed they had some sort of privacy. The tension was just another factor eating away at them.

"I'm going to talk to them," he said as he looked in.

They wore rather grungy uniforms, though maybe he was biased. He'd always been partial to Marine dress blues, unlike most of his fellows, and the current Alliance blacks were pretty decent too. The enemy . . . troops, as he refused to call them Marines, wore dingy gray uniforms with few marking elements he could spot. Eric thought they looked like cheap coveralls.

The men themselves were sullen, but otherwise reasonably fit and solid sorts. He wouldn't care to tangle with them up close, but given the choice between them and the colonel standing across from him, Eric would take on the aliens without hesitation.

"Sir?" Deirdre's head snapped around and her eyes bored into him. "I'm not sure that's a good idea."

"You might be right," Eric replied, "but I'm not sure I really care."

With trepidation, the colonel watched the captain walk out of the room, her eyes shifting back to the security cells as the outer door cycled open.

Well, this is one way to get more data in the system.

"Conner to security stations," she said, depressing a comm link.

"Yes ma'am?"

"Have a ready response team standing by outside the prisoners' cells. The captain has decided to have a word with our guests."

▶▶▶

▶ Eric sealed the door after himself, then walked down the access corridor that ran the length of the cells, eyes scanning the cells' inhabitants as he stiffly marched by.

The *Odysseus* wasn't a prison ship. The cells primarily functioned as a brig in the event of rowdy crewmen. That didn't mean they weren't secure, but they certainly weren't what he'd normally want to use for potentially dangerous POWs.

Eric stopped roughly along the centerline, turning straight toward those prisoners who would see him directly, eyes sweeping left and right.

When he spoke, it was in Priminae, with no translator in between him and the people he was addressing.

"You lot are about as sorry looking as any I've seen," he told them in clipped tones.

That got a reaction at least, as several stirred enough to glare at him.

"We will tell you *nothing*!" one spoke up.

"You only know one thing that I care to know," Eric told them, "and you *will* tell me that."

They openly scoffed at him, but Eric was of no mind to pay them any attention.

"Technical intelligence, ship locations, tactics . . ." Eric shook his head. "You don't know any of that, and if you did, I wouldn't trust a word you told me."

"So what are you here for, then?" the speaker challenged him.

Eric focused on the only one of them brave or, likelier than not, stupid enough to speak up.

"Who are you?" he asked simply.

The group exchanged glances, confused ones that told Eric probably more than any of them intended.

They expected me to know that.

He held silent, however, knowing that there was a time to goad and a time to lie in wait. One of the first rules of any conflict was never interrupt an enemy who was in the process of making an error, but the corollary was what mattered to him just then. Once they've made a mistake, never let them recover from it.

188 • EVAN CURRIE

"You know who we are," the speaker snarled, despite glares from his fellows clearly warning him to shut up. "You and your Oathers wouldn't have forgotten . . ."

"Enough!"

Eric turned to the new speaker, hiding his satisfaction with a stern glare. "Have something to add?"

"Have *nothing* to say to you," the new man said forcefully. "No Imperial does."

"Well, that doesn't seem quite true, now does it?" Eric asked mildly. "Alright, if you won't tell me who you are . . ."

He leaned in, looking them all over. "Then who, or what, are 'Oathers'?"

▶▶▶

▶ Colonel Conner met Eric as he stepped out of the cell block, sealing the door carefully behind him.

"Have fun?" she asked dryly.

Eric glanced at the double squad of Marines standing on duty, armed and clearly disappointed they'd not had cause to breach the cell block.

"Yes, actually," he said cheerfully, starting to walk down the corridor.

Deirdre paced him precisely, the distinct taps of her steps punctuating the softer padding of his own.

"This situation just keeps getting more and more convoluted, you realize," she said as they walked.

"I'm well aware of that. The Priminae appear to be a fulcrum in this situation, don't they?"

"These new people, they're more like us than the Priminae are," Colonel Conner offered, thinking furiously.

"No," Eric said stonily. "This Empire, they're nothing like us. I would wipe out all life on Earth *personally* before I let us become like this. They *led* with the Drasin, Deirdre. You don't *ever* lead with genocide. Ever."

She sighed. "I didn't mean it that way, sir."

"You didn't think about it that way," he corrected her. "How you meant it was that they're fighters, and that must mean we have something in common."

She didn't have anything to say to that, so they walked in silence until they reached the lift and the doors closed on them.

"I've seen a lot of bad things in my career, on all sides," Eric said. "Men tortured for information, even though we both know that torture is a complete sadistic fantasy."

Deirdre sighed, but nodded. Torture was a fictional solution to real-world problems, and generally made said problems *far* worse. Some thought no one could withstand torture indefinitely. That was complete bullshit. Plenty of men and women had done just that. The easiest way was just to talk, and lie. It would take weeks or months to confirm or deny information given, and by that time you could say that things must have changed before offering up another lie.

"I've seen genocide," Eric went on. "I've even been party to it, indirectly. That's a stain on my soul that will never wash away, though I spilled enough blood trying, foolish as that sounds. I've seen my own men execute prisoners just because they felt righteous fury burning in their veins . . ."

Conner grimaced, knowing that she'd seen some of the same things in her career and been encouraged to look away.

"Through all that, however, I have never flinched from my duty," he said. "Do you know why, Colonel?"

"Semper fi, sir."

"Precisely. The Corps, and humanity, are not perfect," Eric said. "We do horrible things to one another, and all too often have no shame in the action, or remorse in the memory. But the ideals of the Corps . . . *those* are perfect."

He took a deep breath. "What I just heard in that cell block, Colonel . . . I hope and I pray that those were the words of imperfect men who have, somewhere deep down, a perfect ideal to look up to . . . but I'm very much afraid that may be a lesson we'll be forced to teach them in blood."

"If it comes to that," she said, "then so be it."

Eric's lips twisted into a parody of a smile.

"Semper fi, indeed, Colonel. Semper fi, indeed."

▼

CHAPTER 16

▲

▶ The *Odysseus* was a fast ship, even when under normal space-warp drive, but when the crew engaged the Terran transition system, there was possibly nothing in the universe, real or imagined, that could beat it.

The big ship transitioned back into real space outside the limits of Ranquil's solar wind, warping space downwell within a few minutes of reconstitution. They were met within the hour by one of the patrol ships covering the outer system.

Dropping down the gravity well of a star was, of course, the easy part, even if the competing gravity fields of the star and planets contraindicated warping past light-speed. Such a move wasn't strictly impossible, of course. Unlike the transition drive, space warps could be reliably maintained within competing fields, but the risk of catastrophic accident made it generally unwise to go much above three-quarters of light-speed. Doing so would also massively increase hull stress, leading to far fewer space hours before a complete refit was required, and not even the Priminae were so casual about those costs. So barring emergency—*real* emergencies—travel within a star system was still done the slow way.

So it took them half a day to fall to Ranquil and settle easily into orbit.

▶▶▶

Priminae Capital, Ranquil

▶ Admiral Rael Tanner examined the imagery on the large displays that were now showing the new arrival in orbit of Ranquil. The *Odysseus* was always a welcome arrival in his opinion, but from what he'd been told, it had supposedly been on a simple reconnaissance mission. So why was the big vessel streaming atmosphere?

"Analyze the damage," he ordered. "That burn pattern is . . . familiar."

"Laser damage, Admiral," the technician on duty responded. "It's difficult to calculate precisely the extent of the damages, given the new armor on the *Odysseus*, but I believe that the blast is significantly more powerful than our own shipboard weapons."

Tanner stared for a moment. "Nothing in our records has more power than one of the new Heroic Class ships."

"That damage says otherwise, Admiral."

Tanner grimaced, but didn't say anything else. He and Captain Weston were going to be engaged in a long conversation very soon.

"I expect the captain will request a repair slot," he said finally. "Reserve one for them—priority slot."

"Yes Admiral."

Tanner shook his head, getting up from his console. "I'll be up top. Contact me by mobile if anything comes up."

"Yes Admiral."

▶▶▶

▶ "Captain Weston."

Eric nodded without smiling as he descended the ramp from the shuttle. His expression was more distant than normal from Tanner's experience.

"Admiral," he said, stepping clear of the loading path and stopping to take a deep breath of fresh air.

"I saw on our monitors that you encountered some trouble," Tanner said. "Those burns did not look like Drasin beams."

"They weren't Drasin," Eric said, shaking his head.

"Then who?"

Tanner felt himself suddenly pinned by a stony stare unlike anything he'd experienced with the generally charismatic officer.

"I very much want to know that myself," Eric said steadily. "It was the same configuration vessel you were flying when the *Odyssey* first arrived in Ranquil, Admiral. So I very much want to know, who the *hell* is the Empire, and what do they have to do with the Priminae?"

Tanner frowned. "I don't know what you're speaking of, Captain. Are you *sure* they used our cruiser design?"

"No question, Admiral. Same configuration as the *Heral'c*, except for a series of what I'm told are called parasite frigates, launched as supplementary mobile firepower."

Tanner took a step back, shaking his head. "That makes no sense. Parasite craft . . . those haven't been used in . . . those are *historical* curiosities, Captain. No one uses those."

"Someone does."

"Captain Weston," Tanner said calmingly, "you're talking about someone using design specifications from well before living memory. Those files are buried deep in Central. It takes full council authority to access them . . . and the Forge itself to actually construct them."

"Admiral, you are not understanding me," Eric told him. "This . . . Empire is not some rogue Priminae nation. They're something else, something bigger, and they do *not* like you."

Tanner cast a glance around himself, checking for anyone nearby, and finding none, turned back to Weston.

"You're speaking of myths, Captain. Legends. Stories told to children to scare them at night. It cannot be real."

Eric looked at him evenly. "I think it's time you told me a bedtime story, Admiral, because while I may not be a child, I'm already scared."

▶▶▶

▶ Milla Chans looked over the curve of the planet below, eyes falling to the white clouds drifting over one of the northern seas as she settled deep into thought.

"You look serious."

She jumped, the rasping voice catching her by surprise.

"Whoa," Steph choked out, steadying her as she landed and twisted around. "Are you okay?"

"I . . . sorry, Stephan," she said, taking a deep breath. "I was thinking about . . . the prisoners."

Steph nodded. "I can see that. They're a puzzle alright."

"No." She shook her head. "It is not that. Stephan, do you remember when you and the capitaine found me?"

"Of course." Steph smiled. "Not every day you rescue a damsel in distress."

She rolled her eyes. "I know what that means now, and I find the term objectionable. However, that is not what I was referring to. Do you recall what I called you?"

Steph shook his head. "Can't say I do. Why?"

"I called you, all of you," she said, waving her hand, "the Others. Those who broke their oath."

"Right, I remember. Didn't make much sense to me then. Why, what does it mean?"

Milla shook her head. "It is an old story . . . for scaring children, yes?"

"A ghost story, sure. I've told my share," Steph said. "So what are these Others?"

"They're . . . monsters, Stephan," she said uncertainly, like she was trying to remember. "The Oath was a very old code of conduct. To uphold justice, preserve the peace . . . the wording has long been lost."

"Sounds like the code of chivalry," Steph said with a smile.

"I am not familiar," Milla said.

"Old code of honor from a few centuries back on Earth," Steph said. "Most of the actual code has been forgotten by the general public, and it's been glorified a lot. In reality it wasn't so . . . *chivalrous* as people believe, but some of the basics were there. In modern times, the code refers to treating others with respect and honoring your word, along with other similar noble qualities."

She shrugged. "Perhaps. I do not know. The Oath, as I said, it has been long forgotten. The Oath Breakers, though, they are still the source of many scary stories."

"Good monsters never die," Steph said thoughtfully. "They just get scarier with every retelling."

▶▶▶

▶ Eric appeared to be studying the sky intently, but his mind was elsewhere.

"That is a hell of a story," he said finally.

Tanner sighed. "And likely not remotely the truth."

That was an understatement, to Eric's mind. He knew that half the war stories told about his own campaign were false, yet they'd been repeated so often that sometimes he half remembered doing things that he *knew* hadn't happened in the first place. This was a legend about a myth about a campfire tale that quite possibly went back to the beginning of human civilization on Earth, maybe further depending on what you considered civilization.

"It's bloody King Arthur is what it is," Eric growled.

"I am not familiar with that," Tanner admitted.

"Terran legend," Eric supplied. "Probably started as a fairy tale about the good old days during a really bad time, got told and retold so many times that before long it was about a savior prophesized to return from the dead in the hour of his nation's greatest need."

Tanner nodded slowly. "That tale would appear to be similar, after a fashion."

"Here's the problem," Eric said, pursing his lips. "Arthur's never coming back. That's just not how the universe works. It doesn't matter how crazy things are, or how weird the universe can be—we don't get the fairy-tale ending fated to us. We have to *earn* it . . . But this Empire, *they* are already here . . . and they're pissed. Which means they've kept up their side of the story probably better than you have, and I'm pretty sure they tell it differently."

"And you believe their side may have merit?" Tanner asked cautiously.

Eric snorted, shaking his head. "Doesn't matter if it does. The past doesn't excuse the present. Even if your people were puppy-eating murderers who raped and slaughtered your way across the galaxy, that's not who you are *now* . . . and even if they were righteous knights defending the just and the innocent back then, today they're leading with the Drasin and firing on my ship without even responding to my hail."

Eric took a deep breath, his fists clenching and unclenching.

"No, Admiral, the legend isn't relevant in the reality of things," he said finally, "but I needed to hear it anyway."

Eric turned to look at Rael Tanner evenly. "And I need you to dig deeper. Find anything you can about these people, legendary or not, and get me that information."

"I will see what I can turn up."

"Good." Eric blew out a breath, feeling tired. "About my ship . . ."

"I have already secured a repair slot." Tanner smiled. "You will be fit for duty in all ways within the week."

"Good. Thank you, Admiral."

"It is a pleasure."

"Next, I need access to your FTL relay," Eric said. "I have a report to file."

"Allow me to show you to system control," Tanner said, gesturing. "I don't believe you've visited yet, despite everything."

▶▶▶

▶ The Priminae system control facility was impressive, though certainly not quite on par with their Forge shipyard complex. The central room included a large hemisphere dome that projected regions of space as needed. The dome was focused on Ranquil's orbit and the *Odysseus* when Tanner and Eric arrived.

"Holographic?" Eric asked, tilting his head slightly to change the angle of his perception.

"Not precisely," Tanner answered, "at least not as I comprehend your definition of the word."

Eric nodded absently but didn't ask for more details, as they would be, without any doubt, over his head. He didn't have time for a lecture at the moment. "Alright."

Tanner smiled thinly, as though he knew precisely what Eric was thinking, and indicated a station just off-center in the room. "You may link to your government from that station, Captain."

"Thank you," Eric said, walking over and cautiously taking a seat.

The controls for the comm station weren't much different than the *Odysseus*, thankfully. Eric activated the system and adjusted it over to the channels set aside for Terran communication before opening a signal.

A few seconds later, a young officer in Alliance dress was looking back at him through the display.

"Welcome to Alliance Command, Sol space. Where may I direct you?"

"Admiral Gracen's officer, please. Weston, Eric S. Captain, AEV *Odysseus*, calling."

The image flickered even before he finished speaking, and he very quickly found himself looking at a lieutenant commander instead.

"Captain, the admiral has been awaiting your check-in," the lieutenant commander told him. "We didn't expect you on the Priminae relay, however."

"Priority report," Eric said. "Secure records will follow. However, the *Odysseus* is in for emergency repairs at the Forge."

"One moment."

The screen flickered again, this time going black for almost a minute. When it came back, the admiral was glaring at him.

"What did you *do*?" growled Admiral Gracen. "That ship is one of the most powerful engines of destruction in the known *universe*, and it's in for repairs? You've been in command less than two weeks!"

Eric winced. "In my defense, it's not a safe galaxy out here, Admiral."

"If it were a safe galaxy, losing a Heroic wouldn't be such a big deal."

"Losing? Now hold on, the *Odysseus* was nowhere *near* lost. Hull damage, minor penetration to the outer sectors of the ship. All sealed up, no loss of life. We could have handled most of it under way, but repair at the Forge is quicker."

"What happened?"

Eric frowned pensively. "We may have found the trigger men."

Gracen leaned back, settling into her seat as she steepled her hands and fell silent for a long moment. "You have my attention, Captain."

"We encountered what appears to be the same group the *Odyssey* scanned at the Drasin hyperconstruct," he said. "Very similar design to older Priminae ships, different materials science. They seem to be markedly better in weapons technology and drive capability as well."

"That is not comforting," Gracen said. "Did you manage to talk to them, either before or after your incurred damage?"

"Not with the command structure, Admiral," Eric said. "They refused to respond to communication attempts."

"And other than the command structure?" she asked, reading between the lines.

"We've captured fourteen ground troops, no rank, no intelligence as best we can tell," he said. "However, what little we did get out of them was interesting. Secure report will follow."

"Understood," Gracen said. "I'll run it up the chain. Expect contact within a few days. We have news on our side too."

"Oh?"

"*Autolycus* hit pay dirt," Gracen said. "I advise you to redirect to their location to receive details, because they pulsed the code for major event. Maybe Drasin, but they're not calling for an all-hands strike, so I doubt it."

"Do we have time for repairs?"

Gracen seemed to consider the question, glancing off screen for a moment before turning back. "Yes. I'm sending a fast courier your way," she told him. "Maybe more. Wait for them to arrive. The *Auto* can hold on a little longer."

"Understood. Thank you, ma'am."

"Don't thank me yet, Captain," she told him with half a smirk. "There are plenty here who think you're turning into a real bad-luck charm."

"They're not alone," Eric said. "Some days, even I wonder."

The admiral laughed. "Get your ship in order."

"Aye ma'am."

"Gracen out."

Eric exhaled and leaned back in the surprisingly comfortable seat he was occupying.

"Good news?" Admiral Tanner asked, approaching now that he could see Eric was done.

Eric figured that the Priminae had recorded everything anyway—the Confederation certainly would have—but the illusion of privacy was still welcome.

"Not sure," he said. "News. Let's leave it at that for the moment."

Tanner nodded, accepting that. "As you say . . . classified?"

"No, not really," Eric lied. "Just not clear. Admiral Gracen is sending a fast courier. Hopefully that will clear things up."

"A courier? Curious. The relays are secure," Tanner said.

"Just SOP, Admiral," Eric assured him, "and it's not like we don't have time."

"This is true," Tanner conceded.

Even with the priority repairs being arranged, the *Odysseus* would have several days—either Terran or Priminae—before she was fully repaired and completely ready for deployment.

▶▶▶

AEV *Odysseus*

▶ The *Odysseus* hurtled through space, warping hard on an interception course with the bandit, lasers slashing out from the emitters even as beams crossed back and raked the flank of the speeding starship.

"Pause playback."

The imagery stopped, and Steph leaned in to carefully observe the damage as it occurred in the *Odysseus'* records.

"Frame by frame," he ordered.

"What frame rate?" the computer inquired blandly.

Steph sighed, tilting his head to the left, and considered his response. "Make it two hundred frames per second."

The image started forward again. The computer-enhanced imagery of beams lancing in from the black of space and burning into the hull of the *Odysseus* was a little cheesy as special effects went, but it still did the job he needed.

Steph made some other adjustments to the playback and set the computer working on pattern analysis. He was working on new attack programs as well as basic evasion and countermeasures for future encounters. The *Odysseus* wasn't a fly-by-wire system, not even with NICS allowing him unparalleled access to the ship's control systems. At the speeds the ship's systems would be engaging potential targets, no human could possibly keep up, not even interfaced into the computers perfectly—and NICS was far from perfect.

So Steph was coding maneuvering programs with some basic variables he could punch in on the fly, giving him the best possible mix of human intuition and computer precision. A single pass, however, wasn't a lot of data for him to extrapolate responses from.

He pushed back from the computer and glanced over to where he suspected Milla was doing much the same at the tactical stations.

"Lieutenant Chans," he called softly.

She turned and looked over. "Yes Commander?"

"These . . . Imperials, they appear to be using systems based on older Priminae designs, correct?" he asked, though he could have simply made the statement. Such an idea was patently obvious, but no one wanted to be too confrontational with the Priminae serving on the *Odysseus*. Those who knew about the encounter with the Imperials were taking it pretty personally, Milla perhaps more than the rest.

"Yes," she almost hissed out, her lips twisting slightly.

"Do your database files have tactical maneuvers and the like as well?" he asked hopefully.

Milla blinked. "Well of course, but . . ."

She fell silent for a moment, then turned and accessed the Priminae database. "One moment, Commander. I will locate the war files from the historical database. I believe I see what you hope to learn from those. You may be wrong, however . . ."

"It's more than we have to go on right now," Steph said lightly, aware that several eyes on the bridge were now focused on him and Milla.

"Very much so," Milla mumbled. "I've found the files. There is . . . less than I would have expected. Tagging them for you. I'll see if I can locate more."

Steph turned to his own screen, noting the new files showing up in his priority queue.

"These should do for the moment, Lieutenant," he said, getting to work. "Thank you."

Milla was too deep in her own work to bother replying.

▶▶▶

▶ Commander Heath listened to the conversation between her two subordinates as she worked on her own analysis of the encounter. The direction the two were taking was interesting but a little outside her specialty. She was trying to extrapolate where the Imperial ship had fled to when it left the system.

She didn't know whether the ship had attempted countermeasures, but had to assume that they had. Still, even the general direction the ship had vanished in might be a lead she could work with.

Since the invasion, the James Webb telescope had been retired in favor of new systems: the Tyson series. The network wasn't complete yet, but the stellar cartography database was already being filled with more data than Earth had ever recorded.

Along the vectors she was examining there were multiple stars with a reasonable to high probability of inhabitable planets. The problem was that most of the data they had were based off very early observations made from terrestrial observatories. The Tyson series of space-warping observations platforms were barely six months old, and while they provided nearly infinitely more data, there was one massively sized sky to explore. The vector the Imperials had departed on wasn't one of the early priorities for deep and intensive scanning.

Still, there are several interesting systems in that general direction, she noted. The Imperial ship had departed the Orion arm and headed deeper into the galaxy toward a quite crowded section along the inner galactic hub. *No radio signals or the like, and no sign of any mega- or hyperconstructs. However, it does appear to be a reasonably rich neighborhood . . . speaking in stellar terms, of course.*

Unfortunately, she didn't know what that meant as far as alien cultural interest went. There just wasn't enough historical data to draw conclusions. What Earth culture considered rich could have no particular value to another society. Hell, there weren't *any* historical data on which she could draw, and that meant she was flying blind.

Miram Heath stretched slightly and glanced at the schedule. They'd shortly be breaking orbit and heading to the Forge for repairs.

That would leave them with the better part of a week for everyone to get their pet projects whipped into a shape that might have some value in the very likely event of a rematch with the Imperials.

CHAPTER 17

IBC *Piar Cohn*

▶ The *Piar Cohn* drifted in interstellar space, not even the distant light of the galactic core giving much illumination to its hull as repairs were conducted. On board, Captain Aymes sat at his station, glowering at the black displays that were shut down while extensive sections of power relay were replaced due to combat damage.

In his mind, he was doing what he had been doing on the computers until they were shut down. He was replaying the passing engagement over and over again.

Tactically there was nothing special about their brief encounter. The enemy actions had been competent, but not spectacular or brilliant. Of course, there were limits on how brilliant you could be in open space. The enemy ship used the light-speed limit effectively, maneuvering enough to make effective targeting basically impossible but remaining on the interception course and keeping their own line of light clear.

They waited to open fire until evasion was effectively pointless, which indicated a high level of confidence in both their defenses *and* their weapons.

Confidence that Aymes had to admit appeared well placed.

The lights coming back, along with the displays, brought him from the depths of his thoughts and back to the present.

"Finally," he yelled. "Do we have access to the Imperial relay network?"

"No Captain. Signal quality is below minimum threshold for contact," his altern said.

Aymes sighed but nodded as he looked to the navigation displays. "Very well. Make for Maxim Twelve, all available power."

"As you command, Captain."

The hum of the *Piar Cohn*'s systems felt comforting to Aymes as the ship was under power once more. Imperial cruisers were equipped with point singularity reactors. When power was off-line, so were the control systems that kept those systems stable. If they tipped too far one way, the singularities would swallow the *Cohn* in a single gulp; too far the other way and he and his crew would quickly freeze to death in the interstellar void. Now that they were under way, they'd be in Imperial space in a few hours.

The Empire claimed all space enclosed within the relay network. If it existed in reach of the Imperial Information Network, it belonged to the Empire.

"Alert me when we have relay access."

▶▶▶

▶ The *Cohn* crossed into Imperial space just over three hours later, and the relay system linked up.

"Captain Aymes . . ." Supreme Fleet Lord Kaliba glared down at him from the large display. "You were sent out to locate and secure the remaining drone assets. Please tell me why you're limping your vessel back into Imperial space in defeat without having even *seen* one of your targets?"

Aymes just managed to keep from wincing at the fleet lord's tone.

"We encountered an unknown," he said by way of explanation.

Kaliba made a dismissive grunt. "I've seen the recordings from the *Cohn*'s systems, Aymes. You encountered an Oather ship . . . and *lost*. Pathetic."

Aymes stiffened. "That . . . whatever that was, it was *not* an Oather vessel."

The fleet lord scoffed. "Tell that to someone who hasn't seen the records."

"Then look *again*, My Lord," Aymes insisted. "We did not launch our assault on the Oather systems without due examination. Compare hull scans, armor, laser efficiency . . . My Lord, *none* of it matches known Oather designs. The only thing that comes close is basic hull geometry, and even that has been altered significantly, My Lord. I am telling you—"

"You are telling *me?*" Kaliba cut in coldly.

Aymes steeled himself, not flinching away. "Yes . . . My Lord. I am. We have new a player."

Kaliba was silent for a long moment. "Imperial analysts believe that the differences are merely an example of Oather technical innovation. The Drasin shook them up, Captain. Some of them are of better stock than the Oather average. My analysts indicate that the Drasin assault has simply put some of the better stock in charge."

"With all respect, My Lord, the analysts are *wrong,*" Aymes asserted. "I've reviewed all the data many times over, including the scans from my parasites . . ."

"The ones you *lost?*"

"Yes, those." Aymes just kept himself from snapping at the lord. He was all too aware that he was pushing his luck with the fleet lord, but Imperial politics were a game every line officer knew how to play. He was in too much trouble for respect to dig him out, so if defensive action wouldn't save him, Aymes would go down fighting.

"Nothing in the response matched Oather profiles. They didn't even *speak* Imperial standard, My Lord. They used translation systems."

Kaliba's expression was serious. "I had noted that. Analysts have no consensus on what that means."

"It means they have contact with the Oathers, but they are *not* Oathers, my Lord."

The fleet lord eyed him through the display. "The anomaly."

"Precisely, My Lord."

"The consensus of the senate does not match your opinion, Aymes."

Aymes took a deep breath. "The members are wrong."

Fleet Lord Kaliba smiled thinly. "Redirect orders. Put your vessel into Kraike. Await orders."

"Understood."

The display went dark, leaving Aymes to wonder if he'd won his little gambit or if there would be an inquisitor squad waiting for him and his crew when they arrived.

Ah, well, if my day is come, then so be it.

"Make our course for World Kraike," he ordered. "All available power to drives."

"As you command, Captain."

▶ ▶ ▶

AEV *Odysseus*, Forge Slip Nineteen

▶ "Signal from the Forge systems command, Captain."

Eric walked across the bridge to the communications station. "Highlights?"

"Fast courier from Earth arrived in system," the duty officer responded.

Eric nodded. "We were expecting that."

"Along with three more Heroics and an even half-dozen Rogues."

Eric froze. "What?"

The young ensign shrugged helplessly. "Those are the numbers, Captain. We've not received any updates from Command."

"This should be interesting," Eric said. "Inform me when the courier wants to deliver their message."

"Aye sir."

▶▶▶

▶ The Forge was one of the best-defended and, until very recently, most-secret facilities in the Priminae colonies. Few ships, few threats of any kind, could penetrate the corona of a star, and almost no one would think to look for a *planet* deep inside the stellar mass. Even the Priminae hadn't intended to build any such facility. The Forge's construction was a happy accident of sorts.

Only less than happy.

Just a few centuries after the Priminae arrived and settled in the Ranquil system, the local star began showing signs of instability. Such signs are easy to dismiss, however, and in the interests of complacency, the council of that era discounted them entirely.

By the time council members admitted that there was indeed a threat, the Colony Prime of Ranquil was doomed.

Or it would have been. Should have been, even.

As the star began to increase in size, its corona steadily closing on the colony world, engineers stepped in where politicians and frightened, complacent fools had failed. The energy screen hadn't begun as anything special, just a method to reflect heat away from a warming world. But as the heat intensity increased, so did the power of the screen. When the corona of the star crossed the orbit of the colony, almost three millennia later, the screen was a masterpiece of technical innovation. Necessity breeds invention.

The Forge was born in the fires of a star and would live there until the end of its time.

For those who lived in the Forge, fire was life—and death.

For those who were not born in fire, the Forge was amazing, terrifying, impossible.

▶▶▶

Forge Facility Approach, Ranquil System

▶ "I've never seen anything like this, Admiral."

"I know," Gracen said, smiling very slightly at the wonder in her companion's tone. "I remember the feeling."

They were passing through the corona of the Ranquil star and about to tunnel through the stellar mass. The view was, as one might expect, spectacular.

The captain of the fast courier was staring out at the roiling mass of flame and plasma just meters beyond his ship, both awed and terrified.

"How long will passage take?" he asked nervously.

"A few more minutes," Gracen responded. "If you think this is something, just wait . . ."

He glanced at her, confused. "More impressive than . . ."

He was cut off, his voice dying in his throat as they suddenly broke through the plasma field and into open space. Ahead of them, there was a blue-green world floating in the midst of hell itself.

"Oh my lord."

"Make for slip nineteen," she pointed. "I see my ship, and I want a word with her captain about how he's treating her."

"Aye ma'am."

▶▶▶

AEV *Odysseus*, Forge Slip Nineteen

▶ "Admiral on deck!"

Marines came to attention as the shuttle settled down on its gear, the loading ramp hitting the floor with a clang that echoed across the deck.

Admiral Gracen stepped off first, eyes sweeping the flight deck briefly before alighting on Captain Weston, who was waiting for her.

"Captain," she said, coming to a stop in front of him. "As you were."

"Thank you, ma'am," Eric said, glancing at the small courier ship and then back at her. "That couldn't have been a comfortable trip."

"It wasn't," she said simply, handing him a secure data chip. "Congratulations."

"Ma'am?" Eric blinked. "I'm not sure I follow."

"On your promotion, Commodore," she said simply.

"I . . . what?"

"Captains do not command squadrons, Commodore," Gracen told him. "And the situation is getting much more complicated out here. How long until repairs are complete?"

"Another day, ma'am."

"Good. Your new orders are your old orders," she said. "Get to Passer and the *Auto* and find out what the hell he's stumbled into. When you're done there, go get me more intelligence on this . . . Empire of yours."

Eric nodded hesitantly, his head still a couple lines back in the conversation.

"Walk with me, Commodore," she said, acknowledging the Marines as they passed.

"Yes ma'am," Eric said, subtly signaling to the Marine sergeant major that he could dismiss the honor guard.

"If those are the people who sent the Drasin our way . . . Well, we'll blow that bridge when we get to it," she said. "But it's a safe bet that the Alliance will want to express their . . . displeasure."

"I'm certain they will, ma'am," Eric said automatically.

"People want revenge," she said, "and the politicians want to give it to them. Normally the way this goes is they'll look around for the closest target they can serve up with minimal fuss, regardless of whether the accused actually had anything to do with the attack or not. I would prefer not to spend the next few decades fighting a war against the wrong people, whether they're bad guys or not."

"Been there, ma'am."

"I know you have," she said, "which is why I want you to be *sure* this Empire is the right group and, more than that, find out if we have a chance. Revenge will not keep the people we serve alive if we pick a fight with someone willing, eager, and most of all . . . capable of *stepping* on us."

"Yes ma'am."

"So recon this situation, Marine," she ordered.

"Aye ma'am."

"Listen to me, Commodore." She stopped, turning to face him. "Don't get us into a war unless it's the war we're *looking* for."

"In my defense, ma'am, they fired first."

Gracen sighed. "That would make me feel belter, Commodore, if it weren't for the fact that you appear capable of driving almost *everyone* you've ever *met* to firing on you first."

Eric shot her a dry look, but figured there wasn't much he could safely say there.

"I'm not tying your hands, Commodore. Do what you feel is necessary. Just keep in mind that we're a little strapped for resources at the moment. Political needs aside, we can't afford an extended war right now."

"I understand, Admiral," Eric said, "but if the Imperials are the ones who launched the Drasin assault . . ."

"Then we can't afford *not* to ensure they never get anywhere near our solar system again, Commodore," Gracen said firmly. "Just don't open multiple fronts in a war we haven't even really started fighting yet."

Eric nodded. "Understood, Admiral."

"Now," Gracen shifted her tone, "let's discuss what you let them do to my ship."

"Your ship, ma'am?" Eric asked, amused.

"Damn right, my ship," Gracen said. "I named her. The Warrior King is my baby, Commodore, and I'll thank you not to let random fools cut slices off her hull."

Eric laughed, shaking his head. "We're a combat ship, Admiral. Lasers happen."

"Just don't let them happen to my ship, is all I'm saying."

"Aye aye, ma'am."

Gracen grew more serious after that. "I suppose you'd best show me those prisoners now."

▶ ▶ ▶

▶ The cells were still packed. Eric hadn't been sure what to do with the men after arriving in Ranquil. Technically, they were Alliance prisoners, but his primary loyalty was to Earth and the Confederation, so he couldn't just off-load them with Admiral Tanner and hope for the best.

"DNA analysis?" Gracen asked as she looked over the stoic men in the cells beyond the two-way glass. She'd seen men just like them in times past, and rarely had cause to want to see more of them.

"Priminae, junk DNA and all," Eric confirmed. "Or perhaps the Priminae are actually Imperial, depending on how you look at it."

"Very interesting," Gracen whispered.

Her office was the first to have the odd DNA mismatch between the Priminae and Terran human stock revealed, information that still wasn't widely known in the world at large. For all intents and purposes, Terrans and Priminae were human, so there was no point clouding the issue with technical data that even the experts were at a loss to fully explain.

"There is a significant split in their genetic line, however," Eric added. "We've been mapping that over the past week."

"Split?"

"Fits with the Priminae history, as we've been told. They've been separate cultures long enough for genetic drift to become measureable. Still clearly of the same stock, unlike Terran humans, but diverging steadily."

"Ah." She nodded.

Gracen had been forced to take several advanced courses in genetics just to understand what had been coming across her desk the past couple years, and thus she more fully grasped the implications of the Priminae-Imperial link than Eric did.

"At least the Priminae aren't lying to us," she said. "That does confirm their story."

"As far as they know. I'm certain they've been honest," Eric said neutrally.

"As far as they know?" Gracen asked, one eyebrow rising.

"That's a *long* chunk of history, ma'am, and I don't think I trust their records," Eric declared. "The people today are honest, but I'm not so sure about their ancestors. I had a long talk with Admiral Tanner about just that, and even he admits that we're in mythic territory here."

Gracen considered his statement for a brief moment, deciding that it was a fair point. Whitewashing history was a relatively easy feat. Hell, a lot of the time you didn't even *need* to do so. People naturally ignored anything uncomfortable and pretended that only the good happened. Centuries had passed before anyone was willing to admit that Columbus was anything less than a heroic explorer, yet, after World War II, only a few years had gone by before the first denial of the Holocaust was uttered.

A great Machiavellian schemer wasn't necessary to whitewash history. People did that all by themselves, usually while whining incessantly about how one had to learn from history or be forced to repeat it.

"Point," she conceded aloud. "What do you want to do with the prisoners?"

"Could send them back to Earth," Eric offered.

She winced. "Not in the current political climate. Too many people, politicians and citizens alike, who want blood for blood. Can't guarantee their safety on Earth, and I'd rather not set precedent that *will* come back and bite us."

"Roger that," Eric sighed. "Well, we have a small base on Ranquil. That's probably our best option for the moment."

Grace nodded. "I'll stop by the planet and see to it, and make sure that they operate the base under the Geneva conventions. The last thing we need is another . . . well, you know."

"Agreed, ma'am. I remember."

He would, Gracen thought. "We'll run this by the books for as long as I can keep the civilians out of it. We're professionals, Captain. We don't do revenge."

"Yes ma'am."

"Good. I'll see to the situation on Ranquil," Gracen said. "You need to get my ship back out in the black and find out what Passer and the *Auto* discovered. Then take your new squadron and see if you can locate another Imperial ship and *make* them talk to you. I'm serious, Commodore. I don't care if you have to board one of their ships and chat with her commander at gunpoint. *Talk* to them."

Eric laughed, a little weakly. "I'll do my best."

"Failing that, I'll settle for rock-solid evidence that they sent the Drasin our way," she said. "If they don't want to talk then . . . we make them *scream.*"

"I believe we're on the same page, ma'am."

"Good, and good luck, Commodore," she said, extending a hand. He shook it. "Thank you, Admiral."

▶ ▶ ▶

Imperial Space, World Kraike, Orbital Command Station, Imperial Sector Capital

▶ Captain Aymes found himself standing alone in the center of a dark room, the only light focused on him. The childish psychology of it all would have made him laugh in any other situation, but he was well aware that behind the games were a man and system that honestly did not care if he lived or died. In actuality, he suspected his death would be simpler.

"Captain."

"My Lord," Aymes said, resisting the urge to shield his eyes and search the shadows for the source of the voice.

It was entirely possible that the fleet lord wasn't even in the room. No point in looking weak for no gain.

"It is the opinion of the Imperial analysts that you encountered a single Oather vessel and were *frightened* by some minor innovations on the enemy's part, causing the loss of your parasite vessels and crews."

"With respect, the Imperial analysts are fools."

Fleet Lord Kaliba laughed softly, coldly. "You are not the first to say such things, but few have lived long enough to regret their statement . . . and none of those who did were as low in rank and status as you are."

Aymes stiffened but nodded resolutely.

He really had nothing to lose at this point.

When in doubt, attack.

"Then have me killed," he said simply. "I'll be proven right in the end."

"It would do you little good, Captain, after the fact," Kaliba said idly. "However, your suggestion has merit, and the Imperial analysts have elected to follow it."

"Suggestion, My Lord?" Aymes asked, not quite able to hide his grimace.

"Having you killed, of course," the fleet lord said.

Aymes closed his eyes. "Yes, My Lord."

"The manner of your death, however, has been left to me," Kaliba said. "As such, you will return to your command and see to her repairs. When those are complete, you will join the Third Reconnaissance group and lead them to Oather space. Find these anomalies, end them if you can, return with evidence of their capabilities if you cannot. The Imperial expansion and end of the Oather sect, once and for all, will *not* be halted by some petty anomalous species. Thus I speak with the empress' voice."

"As you command, My Lord."

▼

CHAPTER 18

▲

AEV *Odysseus*, Stellar Anomaly WTF487

▶ Eric examined the smaller ship as it floated alongside the *Odysseus*, noting the rather spectacular hole blown in the side of the vessel.

"I can't believe they blew a containment bottle *inside* their own hull," he whispered to Commander Heath, shaking his head in disbelief.

Miram cringed. "I've worked with Chief Doohan in the past, Captain. I, unfortunately, have *no problem* whatsoever believing it."

"Keep him *off* my ship," Eric said. "I can accept that maybe he had to do it, since apparently Captain Passer was in accordance, but if you aren't shocked by it . . . just . . . No, he doesn't set foot on the *Odysseus*."

She laughed softly. "Oh, I'm shocked as well, Captain. I just don't have any trouble believing it. Those are two very separate emotions."

Eric rubbed his temples reflexively, eyes not leaving the image of the *Autolycus* on the primary display. Like the *Odysseus*, the *Auto* had a very basic long-range FTL transmitter, but due to power and other restrictions, the vessel was only able to broadcast very limited preset coded signals under normal circumstances. The *Auto* had been here long enough for its crew to painstakingly send out a more detailed report back to Earth, though a lot of the message's content had been a mystery to Eric until the *Odysseus* entered the system.

The *Autolycus* was one of the lead ships in Earth's search for any remnants of the Drasin menace. The Rogue Class vessel had been assigned to inspecting a series of stellar anomalies that fit the configuration the Drasin were known to construct. What they'd found out there wasn't the Drasin but could be far, *far* more important.

"Captain Passer will be coming across shortly with their find," Miram said, checking her personal pad. "And I have to say, I'm looking very much forward to seeing it."

Eric nodded, well understanding her enthusiasm.

Passer's discovery was possibly the trump card they had desperately been needing since Earth had found itself embroiled in this interstellar conflict. Hell, the anomaly itself was certainly going to be absolutely invaluable, enough so that he was going to have to cut off one of his Heroics and a couple Rogues to maintain security on the system while researchers began their jobs here.

WTF487 was a unique sort of stellar construct, smaller than most definitions of the term, barely larger than a planetary megaconstruct, but so much more powerful. The gravity lens heliobeam was a strategic superweapon, but also the single most powerful telescope ever discovered, the latter function being potentially far more valuable.

"That's the captain's shuttle, sir." Miram gestured toward the display.

Eric glanced in the direction indicated and saw the augmented icon break from the *Auto* and approach.

"Good. I can't wait to hear this story in person." Eric chuckled. "Dragons? I thought giant spiders were bad."

"I was more amused with the title of the mission report." Miram laughed softly to herself. "A bit on the nose, but funny."

"*King of Thieves.*" Eric rolled his eyes. "Captain Passer was a bubblehead in the war. The man reads too much sci-fi and fantasy if you ask me."

▶▶▶

▶ Eric looked up as the Marines admitted their visitors to the conference room, eyes settling on the man he'd met in the admiral's office only a few weeks earlier.

"Ah, Captain Passer. It's good to see you're still in one piece." Eric got to his feet and crossed the room, offering his hand.

Morgan Passer grasped it in return. "Thank you, Commodore."

"Please, Eric will do here. I have to say, you stepped in it just about as deep as I did on my first mission."

"Let's hope not," Morgan said forcefully. "We lost eighteen people on that moon. I would rather keep it at that."

Eric nodded seriously. "Yes, we can but hope. Still, you accounted well for yourselves."

"I have good people."

"I know the feeling," Eric agreed with a smile. "Well, let's be about it, then, shall we?"

Morgan agreed, taking a seat.

"I reviewed your report, of course," Eric said. "As has the admiralty. We'll get you patched up and good to return to Earth. There's a dry dock waiting for you there."

"Thank you, sir."

"Not going to take credit for that." Eric laughed softly. "As long as you haven't compromised the hull too badly, or fractured the ship's spine, they'll fix you up good as new. I have to say, intentionally popping a couple antimatter bottles? That was risky, Captain."

"No more than letting that goop eat my ship," Morgan said with feeling.

Eric frowned, knowing well enough the unpleasant feeling of seeing something actually *eat* your vessel.

"True," he said. He really didn't want to get into his thoughts on loosing antimatter on board one's *own* ship, as it would only cloud matters. "We've discussed the . . . data you retrieved. Did you bring it?"

Morgan nodded, opening a case on the table. He took the glowing gem from within and passed it to the commodore.

"Beautiful, isn't it?" Eric asked, turning the jewel over. He recognized the design from his interactions on Ranquil. "And nearly identical to Priminae long-term data storage. Our optical interface should be able to read it. Are you certain of what it contains?"

"Some of it. Doctor Palin was certain, at least."

"Palin." Eric smiled, remembering the irascible yet brilliant linguist. "You're lucky to have him."

"Some of my officers would disagree," Morgan said with the hint of a smile, "but he did pull some rather impressive tricks out of his . . . hat."

"Yes, well, he does that," Eric said, setting the gem on the reader and waiting for a response. "Interface is compatible. It's Priminae technology . . . or a precursor, I suppose. They haven't changed their technology in millennia."

"I still find that hard to believe," Morgan said.

"We all do. Huh. It's an *old* format, but readable. Here we go . . ."

A holographic image of the galaxy sprang up between them, and both men looked at it closely. A few sections were lit up, and with a swift hand movement, Eric zoomed in to see that certain stars were clearly marked.

"Precursor facilities." He breathed, recalling his discussion with Admiral Tanner about the early history of the Priminae. "This . . . confirms a lot of theories, Captain."

"Such as?"

"We've often thought that the Drasin . . ." Eric typed commands into the reader and the image shifted, showing one of the Drasin in profile next to a marked star. "We've often thought that someone was holding their leash . . . Here, a . . . prison? The Drasin were stored here."

Eric leaned back. "Someone out there accessed one of these facilities, Captain, and in it they found the Drasin. They used them as a weapon against the Priminae, and against us. We cannot ignore that."

Morgan signaled his agreement.

"Before the *Odysseus* was dispatched, the admiralty authorized a new long-term mission for the Rogue Class," Eric said. "It's contingent on what we find here, but I think I can confirm it now. You're no longer going to be hunting for Drasin facilities, Captain."

"We're looking for the people who used them?" Morgan asked eagerly.

"No, that's my job," Eric said with authority. "You're now in charge of Operation Prometheus."

"Sir?"

"You said Palin called this fire of the gods, right?" Eric asked, indicating the gem in the reader.

"Yes sir." Morgan understood the name now.

"Our enemies, whoever they are, used one of these facilities against us," Eric said. "No more. Never again. We want you to go out and steal fire from the gods, find these facilities, confirm they're intact, and secure them until a task force can arrive to take control."

"Steal fire from the gods?" Morgan laughed. "I like the sound of that."

"You accept, then?"

"Commodore, when my crew and I are done, the gods will have to bum a light from *us*."

"That is exactly what I wanted to hear, Captain," Eric said. "But first you need to get your ship repaired. Do you have damage assessments yet?"

Morgan nodded, handing over another data sheet.

Eric glanced over it, not quite able to disguise a grimace at some of the information, but overall the damages weren't nearly as bad as they could have been.

"I'm shocked, Captain, that you didn't tear irreparable chunks out of your interior framework. Those bottles had to have been placed *carefully*."

Or with more luck than anyone deserved to have, Eric added mentally.

"The chief used the magnetic containment to direct the initial discharge," Morgan said. "When the bottles blew, the antimatter discharge was focused along a predictable cone."

That stopped Eric for a moment as he lightly set the sheet down and pinched his nose. "Captain, are you telling me that your engineer devised an antimatter *shaped charge*?"

"Different mechanism, but similar result," Morgan replied, smiling a little too happily in Eric's opinion.

"I want his notes," Eric said, "though whether for future use or so I can *burn* them, I'm not sure yet."

"I believe you may have to fight my Marine commander for them, sir."

▶▶▶

▶ Repairing the *Auto* to the point where it could be certified as ready to transition back to Sol took a few days, yet was a reasonably straightforward job. The long, tedious inspections could have been handled entirely by the *Auto*'s crew but went a lot faster with help from the *Odysseus* and other Heroics in the system.

Eric had watched the *Auto* during the last few minutes of its climb out of the system and as it vanished into transitional space, mostly as a distraction from the work he and Commander Heath had on their own plates. The data files from the WTF487 anomaly were potentially game changers. Just the list of old yet potentially still-active alien sites was worth the cost of Earth's entire space program, all the way back to Apollo.

What he was interested in, however, was something that wasn't actually listed but rather was implied by the data. The location of most of the facilities fell within a section of space closer to the galactic core than Earth and Priminae space, a section that also happened to correspond with the withdrawal vector the *Odysseus* had recorded during their earlier engagement.

That was both good news and very bad news.

The good news was that the Alliance now had something akin to a confirmation concerning the location of the Empire, which gave him a search vector to work with. The bad news was that, if the other precursor facilities were *anywhere* near as valuable as this one was, a terrifying percentage of them existed in what almost *had* to be Imperial territory.

Passer had best get back in the black as soon as possible, because I believe we're officially playing catch-up when it comes to stealing this particular bit of fire from the gods. The Empire seems to have beaten us to it.

Of course, so far the only piece of the puzzle he could reasonably link to the Empire was the Drasin, but that was more than enough.

Eric looked at the ancient data crystal sitting on the reader across from him. He had the evidence the admiral wanted. He was fairly certain he could present this and the vector information from their earlier engagement and get at least a declaration of hostilities from the Alliance leadership. Combined with Bandit One opening fire first, that was enough for a state of war, he thought. That made his job all the easier, but as suggestive as the evidence was, he'd rather clinch the case if he could.

"Commander," he said, looking over to where Miram was working, "do you have any projections on likely Imperial systems?"

"A few. Why?"

"What's the closest one you think you can be reasonably sure about?" Eric asked.

Miram considered the question for a moment, then highlighted a system about fourteen hundred light-years from Earth. "This one. It's along the withdrawal vector of Bandit One, is close to one of the precursor installations on the crystal, and we already have it listed as a system of interest."

"We do?" Eric blinked. "Why?"

"Kepler 452b," Miram said. "It's been on our investigate list since the early twenty-first century as a system with a probable Earth-type planet."

"Alright, then I suppose we have a target," Eric said.

"Yes sir."

▶▶▶

▶ "The *Heracles* signals that they're ready to begin research operations," Miram said as she took her place on the bridge of the *Odysseus*. "Captain Vasquez sends her regards and wishes us luck."

"Send my thanks," Eric said, "and have the rest of the squadron ready to depart."

"*Bellerophon* and *Boudicca* both signal ready, and our Rogues are ready to travel," Miram said.

"Signal all ships," Eric ordered. "Warp space for the heliopause, ahead full."

"All ships, ahead full, aye."

"*Odysseus* ahead full, aye," Steph echoed from the helm and navigation station.

The feel of the *Odysseus* shifted just slightly as the big ship began to move, warping space-time and pulling away from the gravity of the local star and the heliobeam anomaly.

The four Rogues took point and flanking positions around the three Heroics in an escort formation based on carrier group escort SOP. Eric had taken some time to familiarize himself with the Rogue Class of ships when the admiral had assigned them to his command, and in many ways he wouldn't have minded being assigned one of them instead of the *Odysseus*.

The Rogues were very similar to the *Odyssey* in their power system, though considerably refined and several times more powerful overall. Many of the power sinks and inefficiencies of the *Odyssey's* original design had been done away with, streamlining the systems into dedicated warships. That, along with the Chinese space-warp drive, made them fast, invisible, and lethal.

By comparison, the Heroics were slow, lumbering giants in real-space encounters. Powerful beyond all sane measure, but also impossible to miss by anyone with gravity scanners.

Eric made a note to start working on tactical SOPs for using the Heroics and Rogues in combined arms operations. He was reasonably certain he could make adaptations from submarine and carrier task force operations with a few key modifications.

His Rogues would serve as fast-attack submarines, Eric decided, covering the Heroics as well as using the obvious threat of the larger ships as an opening to get in the occasional free shot.

His task force now consisted of the Heroics *Odysseus*, *Bellerophon*, and *Boudicca* in combination with the Rogues *Hood*, *Aladdin*, *Song-Jiang*, and *Kid*.

Eric just hoped the squadron would be enough. He had a bad feeling about this Empire.

▶▶▶

Imperial Space, Interstellar Meeting Point

▶ The *Piar Cohn* slowed to a halt amid the ships of the Third Reconnaissance squadron, carefully bleeding particle energy back into her singularity to avoid irradiating any allied vessels in the process of deceleration. Traveling at superluminal speeds was hazardous in almost infinite ways, but unloading high-energy particles at superluminal speeds was one of the worst dangers.

"Captain, secure comm signal from squadron commander," his subaltern told him.

"Send to my personal display," Aymes ordered, pulling his screen closer.

"Welcome to Recon Three, Captain Aymes," the woman greeted him.

Aymes inclined his head respectfully. A full salute was hardly possible in his current position. "Thank you for the welcome, Lady Navarch."

"I've been briefed on your encounter," the Lady Misrem Plotu, Navarch of the Third Reconnaissance squadron, informed him. "As well as the analyst's conclusions and your objections."

"Yes, My Lady," he said firmly. "I am here to serve."

"Yes," she told him, "you are."

There was nothing he could say to that.

"The fleet lord believes that your explanation is plausible enough to investigate," she told him, "and so that is precisely what we will do. You are more familiar with the territory than we are, Captain. What methodology would you recommend we employ in this task?"

Aymes took a breath before answering. "That depends on the ultimate goal. However, as I believe we can agree that we want to contact the anomaly species or, failing that, releash as many Drasin drones as possible, I believe the best operative method would be to sweep inward toward Oather territory, along the Drasin path as I originally did."

"I see," the navarch said noncommittally. "That will be acceptable for the moment. You will place your ship under my direct command. Do *not* interfere with the operations of Third Recon, and keep in mind . . . if I desire your input, I *will* demand it."

"I understand, My Lady."

"Good. Stand by for maneuvering orders, Captain. We will depart on my orders."

"As you command," he confirmed, barely getting in the last word before the comm channel closed.

Aymes sighed, sitting back at his station but managing to keep his temper in check. He'd known that his mission's failure would cost him, and his star in the Empire had never been particularly ascendant to begin with. Aymes had never completed any particularly impressive missions to bring himself to the attention of the higher ranks or Imperial nobility. He'd avoided failures until now, but that was merely enough to achieve the rank of captain.

Higher promotions were reserved for nobility or heroes of the Empire.

Aymes was neither, so he'd gone as far as he could expect, barring heroic action or public failure.

The second was the one that met him first.

He looked around, his crew's eyes on him. "You heard the navarch. Make ready to maneuver."

▶▶▶

IBC *Shion Thon*, Flagship, Third Reconnaissance Squadron

▶ Third Recon was one of the Empire's forward squadrons, loaded heavier than many dedicated combat units because the Third was expected to run into the unknown and unpredictable as a matter of course. Navarch Plotu had seen things in her career that had frozen even *her* blood, a task few of her peers would have thought possible.

Misrem had looked over the report from Aymes and, despite misgivings about his presence in her squadron, felt that there was a decent chance that he and the fleet lord were correct. Something was very strange about the ship he'd encountered, and those changes in design could be explained quite neatly if they assumed that the anomaly had somehow teamed up with the Oathers.

Analysts were in a state of disbelief. In order for the anomalous vessel to exist, the unknown species and the Oathers would have had to agree to a frankly preposterous level of technology sharing.

The only other possibility was that the Oathers had somehow been conquered in the short time that had passed since the last Imperial reconnaissance of their systems, and that was impossible from a tactical point of view. More likely, two entirely different species had somehow lost their abyss-emptied minds and handed highly secret military technology to one another.

The analysts didn't think either was possible, but Misrem wasn't so certain. There was one factor that they were all forgetting, a very large one that might lead to an act of desperation.

The Drasin.

She hadn't been willing to voice that theory to the fleet lord or the senate representative when she was assigned this mission, and for similar reasons she had no intention of even *hinting* that she thought Aymes might be less than insane and incompetent. Without evidence, voicing her pet theory would be akin to criticizing the senate decision to deploy the Drasin in the first place.

She was a minor noble, and Misrem was under no delusions that her status could withstand the level of response *that* move would bring down on her head.

"Hirau . . ." She walked over to her flag captain. "Does the squadron stand ready?"

"Awaiting your command, My Lady."

She nodded, having expected no less.

"Very good. Then bring us out."

"Destination, My Lady?" Hirau asked, signaling his helm controller and subaltern to issue the preparatory orders.

"We'll take Captain Aymes' advice," she said simply. "Put us on a track to approach the first Drasin target. We will repeat his original task vector."

Hirau issued the orders before turning back. "Permission to query the navarch, My Lady . . ."

"You want to know if I believe them," she said with a faint smile, "or if I'm giving the captain a charge or two in the hopes that he'll shoot himself and rid me of his presence?"

"The thought had crossed my mind, My Lady . . . and . . . more along similar lines."

"Mmmmmm," she hummed, willing to let that statement lie without clarification. She'd likely have broken anyone else who even barely intimated what her flag captain was suggesting, but they'd been together for some time and she trusted him. "Let's say, if that is what happens, I'll shed no tears."

Hirau nodded, but his eyes narrowed slightly. "If, My Lady? You believe his story?"

"I believe there's more here than the analysts have seen," she said without committing. "So we will determine just what they've missed, yes?"

"As you command, My Lady."

"As I command, indeed," Misrem said, with no room for any doubt in her tone.

CHAPTER 19

AEV *Odysseus*, Outer System, Kepler 452

▶ "Run passive scans," Eric ordered as he fought the urge to puke all over his clean command from the aftereffects of transition.

They'd dropped into the outer limits of the system, so far out that technically the task force was still in interstellar space. The system primary, Kepler 452, was a G-class yellow dwarf barely visible from their position without the use of advanced instrumentation. He hoped they were far enough out not to be detected if there were an Imperial presence in the system, but at least he was certain they could make a run for it in a pinch.

"We're deploying the squadron in a large array to maximize our scanner take," Miram told him. "So far, there's no sign of anything truly unusual."

Eric kept his face even. He was honestly a little disappointed. He'd hoped to strike pay dirt with their first shot, of course, even if that was unlikely. The take from the *Auto*'s discovery of the gravity observation construct and heliobeam had narrowed their search, but Eric was well aware that it was still a big damned galaxy.

"Have we located 452b?" he asked, genuinely interested.

Kepler 452b was the designation of the likely Earth-type exoplanet discovered in the early twenty-first century. "Earth type"

meaning that the world was likely rocky in nature and within a reasonable range of Earth's size. In this case, the planet was supposedly
60 percent larger than Earth and within the liquid-water range from
its star.

"Roger that," Miram said. "Picked it out fast on the gravity scanners, confirmed with scopes."

"We have any resolution on it yet?"

"Not yet, sir. Give us an hour," Miram replied.

Eric nodded, knowing that the job was going to be a long one no
matter how he cut it.

No matter what, at least we'll learn something.

He checked the helio database from his station, looking for the
location of the closest precursor point of interest to their coordinates.
He quickly found an installation located on a planet about forty light-
years from Kepler 452. Quite a distance, of course, but in galactic terms
right next door. That would be their next destination, should they discover nothing at 452.

▶▶▶

AEV *Bellerophon*

▶ Captain Jason Roberts of the *Bellerophon* looked over the status displays arrayed around his station with a stony expression his crew had
long since gotten used to. The former Army ranger had enjoyed something of a legendary reputation among the recruits he'd acquired both
when the *Bell* was first launched and when they picked up new crew
from Earth after the invasion had been dealt with.

The mix of Priminae and Terran crew had left him with some dif-
ficulties as he tried to establish his own command style. Adding Block
specialists to the mix also hadn't done him any favors.

That said, Jason liked to think that he'd done well. His *Bellerophon* was one of the Heroics, and he'd put his crew against any of their peers—even the flag itself.

"Imagery from 452b is coming in, sir," his first officer, Commander Michael Shriver, said, gesturing toward the secondary display over the navigation station. "Not looking like much."

"No, it isn't," Roberts agreed. "Our trip here was a long shot."

"I know, but I figured with the Weston luck at play and all . . ." Shriver shrugged with an amused chuckle.

"Luck is purely chance in my experience. In the end, fortune will always balance out," Roberts told him flatly. "So don't count on good luck helping us."

"No sir, I won't," Shriver said, eyes narrowing as he looked at the imagery again. "Huh. Well, I guess that seals that deal."

"What is it?" Roberts asked, turning his focus back to the issue at hand.

"Hyperspectral data shows the world is dead." Shriver pointed.

Roberts nodded as he read the data himself. Hyperspectral cameras read the spread of light as it passed through, or reflected off, an object—in this case, the planet's atmosphere. By analyzing the frequencies of light absorbed in the process of transmission, the cameras could determine what chemicals were present in the atmosphere, because some elements naturally absorbed more of certain wavelengths than others.

452b had no complex organic chemicals to speak of and almost no oxygen.

Dead world.

"Well, this is a bust, but we have other leads," Roberts said after a moment's reflection.

"Yes sir," Shriver agreed, but barely got the words out before an insistent alarm sounded from the computers. "Now what—well, look at that."

Roberts glanced over his shoulder, then back at the large screen. "Is that pure titanium in orbit?"

"It is. Resolution isn't high enough to pick it out visually yet, but I don't think that's natural."

"Who puts . . . It's not a station, is it?" he asked, trying to make heads or tails of the readings.

"No sir, certainly not. Too small. This looks like a debris field," Shriver said. "I'm going to have to bump this to Commander Heath on the *Odysseus*, sir. It's over my head."

"Escalate the transmission," Roberts ordered. "Something is going on in this system, even if it's not what we wanted."

"I think something *went* on in this system, Captain," Shriver said, "but whatever it was, it happened a long time ago."

"Well, at least it wasn't the Drasin," Roberts said with a carefully suppressed shudder. He *hated* those spider beasts.

"Small mercies, Captain."

▶▶▶

AEV *Odysseus*

▶ "There was a species here, once," Miram said thoughtfully as she examined the data.

Eric walked over, checking the display over her shoulder. "Native?"

"No way to tell now," Miram admitted. "Lots of space junk around the second planet, though. Could be native, an example of a prespace culture making the transition, but the debris could also be the results of a mining operation or something else I have no frame of reference for."

"How long ago?"

"That I can't say either, but it's been a while. A lot of the material is in pretty low orbit, obviously decaying. I'd say hundreds, if not thousands of years. Closer to thousands."

"Not our concern then," Eric said. "Mark the system for later study. I'm sure someone will love the job. Get the squadron ready to move out."

"Aye Captain."

Eric stepped back, looking over the stellar telemetry they were using for navigation and the data taken from the charts the *Autolycus* had recovered.

"Commander Michaels, make course for Kepler 571," he said. "We're going to check out the installation reported there and see if there's any sign of Imperial habitation."

"Yes sir," Steph said from his station, most of his chemical burns healed and his voice almost back to normal. "Insertion point?"

"Well outside the stellar influence," Eric declared.

"Interstellar space, aye Skipper."

Steph put in the course calculations, then sent the new data out to the rest of the vessels in the force. With Eric's orders countersigning them, observation duty was put aside in a few moments as the ships prepared to leave.

The task force wheeled as one, never even breaching the heliosphere of Kepler 452, and adjusted their trajectory as they prepared to transition.

Seven ships flickered for an interminable second, then vanished in a puff of reality, leaving the dead system far in their wake.

▶▶▶

IBC *Shion Thon*, Flagship, Third Reconnaissance Squadron

▶ Navarch Plotu examined the feeds from the enhanced scans they'd done of the system, noting some aberrations but nothing exceptional. The most obvious, of course, was the world that had been destroyed by the Drasin much earlier. They'd give that a wide berth, even if they had to descend into the system—which they usually didn't—just on general principle.

The odds of any drones having survived the breakup of the planet were slim, almost impossible really, but slim and almost didn't cut it when dealing with those things.

She glanced to one side, where Captain Aymes was silently waiting for her attention on one of the command displays.

He's smarter than I was led to believe, Misrem noted. Given how he'd aggressively challenged both the senate and the analysts, she'd expected a foolish hothead who got lucky. Now she was wondering if he was perhaps considerably more dangerous than that. A man with patience who both knew when the situation called for taking a risk *and* had the guts to make his bets with everything on the line—that was someone to watch.

"I see no signs of your anomaly vessel, Captain," she said coldly, casually tilting her head just enough so she could look at him without strain.

"They were never native to this system, I assure you, Navarch," he told her in a neutral tone. "Our encounter was likely pure chance."

That almost caused her to laugh at the man. He might be more than he seemed, she was willing to grant, but if he really believed that, he was still a child.

"Unlikely that, Captain Aymes," Misrem told him. "They were either here to survey the damage done by the Drasin or, more likely, backtrack the path the Drasin took when the creatures invaded. They, my dear captain, were almost certainly *looking* for you, or us, I suppose. That would preclude the very idea that the meeting was in any way pure chance."

Aymes considered her remarks, then tipped his head in acknowledgment. "Point conceded, Navarch."

The question now became, where did they withdraw to? *Or were they foolish enough to push on without repairs?* Misrem had mixed feelings about that possibility.

If they had done that, well, it was a stupid move, and more importantly, it was the sort of stupidity that would make them easy to handle in the future. On the other hand, that would also mean that a fully armed cruiser capable of taking on the *Piar Cohn* and emerging with only minor damage was now quite possibly nearing the edges of Imperial space.

Not normally a big worry. Even if they weren't Oathers, there was a limit to how much damage such a thing could do before the fleet came down on them. On the other hand, this wasn't normal times. People who'd just been hit by the Drasin were unlikely to be in a pleasant mood. She could imagine many ways to turn even the weapons of a light cruiser to the destruction of entire star systems, and so the thought of a heavy cruiser flying around unchecked in Imperial territory was worrisome.

Still, by all the data she'd seen in the *Cohn*'s reports, these people didn't appear either that aggressive or that stupid. The odds were very much in favor of them having withdrawn back to a repair station.

So, Misrem mused as she looked over the recon data they had on the Oather systems, *where would I withdraw to if I needed minor repairs in a hurry and wanted to make a report?*

The Oather capital system of Ranquil was a possibility, but it was too far away by her judgment. Certainly, it would have the best facilities *somewhere*—the failure of the recon forces to locate their chief shipyard facility was something that still greatly irked her—but the ship that had dealt with Aymes hadn't needed such extensive facilities.

The hard part was crossing out all the known Drasin-devastated systems, since some of those had been struck after the observer units were forced to pull back due to increased Oather fleet movement.

"Here," she said finally. "Make for the Oather system of Por-Que."

"As you command, Navarch."

Misrem settled in as the orders went out to the squadron. Getting all the ships moving in the same direction sometimes seemed to be the most difficult part of running such a group, but she'd learned a long time before that the secret to such a feat was simply finding people you trusted to do the hard work—but only a certain level of trust. No one trusted too easily if they were wise, as there were always up-and-coming officers looking for an open promotion slot.

The Third Reconnaissance squadron was under power a short time later, warping space and time as they left the scene of the *Piar Cohn*'s defeat. As they cleared the influence of the local star, the ships seemed to twist and stretch briefly before they vanished away into the great black ether.

▶▶▶

Odysseus Task Force, Kepler 571

▶ "Nothing."

Eric grimaced. He was running out of leads that made sense.

Oh, they had an entire database filled with what appeared to be ancient installations, thereby giving him a near endless string of "leads," but he needed one that made sense with the last known vector of the Imperial ship. He and his crew *needed* to have some concept of what Imperial territory included, but at the moment they had no real ideas at all.

Worse, Kepler 571 didn't appear to have any sort of precursor facility. *That* was a problem of a very different sort, and one that didn't bode well for Captain Passer's mission. If this lead was false, or if someone else had raided the site to the bedrock, so to speak, that might mean the others would be in a similar state.

Which would make Passer's mission a game of Whac-a-Mole without the decency of actually having a visible target.

Well, that wasn't his headache for the moment, and for that, at least, Eric thought he should be grateful.

"There should be *some* sign," Eric said as he pored over the data that was still being funneled to the *Odysseus* from the combined scanners of the entire task force. "The data crystal clearly indicated something was here."

"Yes sir, but there was no date stamp, so to speak, associated with those files . . . and we know that the heliobeam facility was mobile."

That was a point he hadn't thought too hard about, and it put a new, enormously complex spin on the information they had.

"Alright, so the facilities may or may not be mobile." Eric considered. "Can we track them?"

"Sir?"

"There were no date stamps, as such, but the system recorded data linearly, I assume? We just grabbed the latest information available and chose to work from that, right? Can we check older data on the crystal?"

"One moment," Miram said, accessing the data they'd acquired from the *Autolycus*.

She looked up again after a few minutes. "We've got something, Captain. Maybe."

"Don't sound so certain, Commander," Eric said dryly.

"Sorry, but we *are* dealing with an ancient data-storage system that we don't really understand beyond the basic physical methodology. We can read it, yes, but we don't really know *why* they stored data in the manner they did. It's like trying to decode a newspaper if you know the language, but aren't familiar with formatting."

"I'll take your word on it, Commander. What do you have?"

"The facility listed as part of this system *did* have a mobile vector," she said. "I'm putting the telemetry listed on the display, but sir . . . we don't have the time-stamp data we'd need to plot an actual course."

Eric nodded thoughtfully, looking at the information.

"Understood, Commander. I don't think we'll need it. Steph, stand by to warp space."

"Aye Skipper, standing by."

"Not transition, sir?" Miram asked.

"Not this time. Let's follow this plot and see where it takes us."

▶▶▶

▶ Ships warping space and time actually caused a detectable deformation in the very fabric of the universe, using reflected energies to set up and reinforce standing waves in gravity around their hulls. That created an effect similar to surfing a tsunami on an otherwise still ocean, where a ship in question didn't actually move so much as have the universe move around it.

The metaphor worked only to a certain extent, of course, because of the nature of space and space-time. An ocean, no matter how still, had friction, and although a wave transferred through that medium at speeds very nearly impossible under normal circumstances, a surfer trying to remain in position on the wave had to fight multiple forces, including friction from water and air.

For a wave-riding ship, however, space nicely reduced those variables to a far more manageable level, which was very good because the results of missing your cue while wave riding on a starship were spectacular in ways few humans could comprehend.

So the ships of the *Odysseus* Task Force spread out, avoiding mutual interference with their warps, and sped through space while standing still.

Each of them had limited scanner capability while using a full-powered warp. The nature of the gravity deformation ahead of them actually trapped most spectrums of light and electromagnetic energy in the same manner as a black hole, despite the event not having anywhere near the same amount of gravitational force. Instead, the path of light was distorted as it entered the gravity sink ahead of the ships. Much of it was twisted from its original path and slung outward at another angle, completely missing the ship's scanners.

While traveling at a rate many times the speed of light, having degraded scanners was a very bad thing.

Space was incalculably large, and mostly empty by human standards, thankfully. Otherwise, space travel would effectively be impossible due to a near 100 percent fatality rate, mostly because running into anything large enough to survive the gravity sink ahead of the ship was a sure way to ruin your day.

▶▶▶

▶ "We've got a contact ahead, Skipper," Steph spoke up first. "Approaching fast."

"Got it," Ensign Sams said from the scanner stations. "Large volume, limited reflectivity. It's barely showing on scanners. How did you see that?"

"Corner of my eye," Steph said. "We're coming up fast, Cap."

"Drop from warp," Eric ordered. "Let's see what we've located."

"Aye aye, sir. Dropping from warp."

The *Odysseus* dropped first, then the other ships of the squadron appeared around them in a slightly haphazard fashion that Eric took note of.

Haven't had much need to practice formation flying at high warp, he noted critically. *Going to have to change that. Our bad guys might like to fight while at warp, and that would be a hassle if we couldn't match them.*

Actually, he was well aware that it would be *far* more than a hassle. Fighting at warp had the potential to be a force majeure capability, at least if the other side didn't have *some* capacity for the same. Hitting a ship before it could even see you coming, then being gone before you knew you were hit? That was some major bad mojo to be on the wrong side of, Eric decided.

Even if they don't know how to fight at warp, we still need that capability in our quiver.

"Very little on visible wavelength passives, Captain. Not much on infrared either . . . ," Sams grumbled.

"Go active," Eric ordered.

"Sir?" Sams blinked, surprised. SOP on this mission had been to avoid active scanners like they were the Antichrist.

"Minimal risk in this case, Ensign," Eric said. "I don't think this is an Imperial installation."

"Yes sir, apologies," Sams said. "Active scanner return in three . . . two . . . one . . ."

The installation lit up ahead, quieting the crew. Or, rather, a part of the installation lit up. A *very* small part.

"Whoa," Steph muttered. "It's . . . too big to be a planet."

"Yet too small to be a star . . . system," Miram said dryly. "Frankly, Captain, I believe that I'm becoming . . . terrified of the galaxy."

"You're not alone, Commander."

The active scanners were still trying to map the surface area of the installation they were looking at, which was already registering over a light-minute across, and their computers were still being flooded with data.

"What the hell does this one do?" Eric wondered aloud.

▶▶▶

IBC *Shion Thon*, Flagship, Third Reconnaissance Squadron, Outer Limits, Priminae System, Por-Que

▶ The ships of Third Recon slowed from FTL as the gravity of the system primary began to exert enough force to make navigation a little less certain.

"Passive scanners only," Misrem said, standing as the displays began to light up as their warp drives lessened enough to allow more electromagnetic radiation through. "Look for any sign of Captain Aymes' troublemakers."

The system was a relatively small one by Imperial standards, but as previous reconnaissance indicated, there was enough of an industrial framework around the inhabited world. Several other heavily industrialized spots in the system were located around the three asteroid fields and the third gas giant, all of which she assumed were part of the Oathers' industrial infrastructure.

"One ship in orbit, My Lady Navarch," her senior scanner tech announced. "Initial analysis indicates a very close match to the contact made by the *Piar Cohn*."

Misrem smiled, satisfied.

One ship that fit the profile. She'd apparently lucked out. Still, they did have to confirm as best they could the vessel's identity before any action could be taken.

"Try to match their armor signature against the profile," she said. "That should give us our answer."

"Working. However, we're still quite far out, and the warp fields are lessening the efficiency of our scanners."

"All stop, squadron wide," Misrem ordered. "We'll coast in while we analyze the data."

"As you command, Navarch. All stop."

The ships of Third Recon continued forward on momentum as they killed the space warping that was scrambling their scanners. Then, using time and improved scanner quality, they were better able to observe the system and potential target.

▶▶▶

PW (Priminae Warship) *Heral'c*, Por-Que Orbit

 "Captain, we're detecting an anomalous gravity fluctuation from the outer system."

Captain Kierna Senthe rose from his station and walked across the command deck of the *Heral'c*. His ship had nearly been destroyed in the war with the Drasin, but it and his crew—most of them—had survived and received extensive refits. Now they were part of the colonial patrols, running through the outer systems that didn't have enough population to mount a full Heroic Class ship but still needed some significant protection.

"Inbound vessel?" he asked, leaning over the scanner station.

"That is what it appeared to be. Several in fact," his scanner tech, Ithan Kin Yorava, told him. "However, before we could confirm, the signal vanished."

That *was* odd, Senthe noted. There were few intermittent gravity sources in the universe, and almost every one of them was a constructed one. The only natural types that might qualify wouldn't have gotten within a thousand light-years of Priminae space without him knowing about it.

"Secure the *Heral'c* for maneuvering," he said thoughtfully. "Bring back any of our people on the planet."

"Yes Captain."

It was probably nothing, he supposed, maybe a scanner error or a freighter playing games. It did happen from time to time, usually when some intrepid transport captain spotted a comet or bit of space debris with valuable metals or chemical compounds.

He returned to his own station and checked the schedules. The only problem with that idea was that there weren't any arrivals scheduled, and freighters were on fairly strict run times. One might be late, but it was quite rare that any would be early, and there hadn't been any arrivals scheduled for several days before or after.

Quietly, just to be certain, Senthe ran the signals against the war database but came up with no match. He breathed a quiet sigh of relief, since his worst nightmare was another encounter with the Breaker-damned Drasin.

"Crew are reporting back, but it'll take time to get them up from the surface," his second, Commander Corva, told him, approaching quietly.

"Not a problem," Senthe told the young man. "We have time."

"Is it . . . ?"

"No, no match to Drasin profile," Senthe said with a humorless smile. "I checked."

"Of course, Captain," Corva said, trying very much to hide his relief.

"That doesn't mean it isn't trouble," Senthe said, thinking about the *Heral'c*'s last mission before the refit and the end of the Drasin war.

The Terran vessel, the *Odyssey*, had discovered and reported someone else flying with the Drasin. No Priminae ship had seen them, but Priminae vessels had mostly encountered the Drasin within Priminae systems, not far out in unclaimed territory. Senthe remembered the report, and recalled thinking it was ludicrous at the time, but the Terrans had proved worthy of at least some trust. If they were right, there was more to fear out there than the Drasin.

He would therefore treat this situation with some care.

"Adjust our armor, combat settings," he said. "And stand by to warp space as soon as everyone has returned."

"Yes Captain."

If nothing else, since the refit, they were better equipped to deal with threats than ever before.

CHAPTER 20

IBC Shion Thon, Flagship, Third Reconnaissance Squadron, Outer System, Por-Que

▶ "There, Navarch, did you see that change?" Captain Aymes said, highlighting a piece of data that had streamed across the squadron feeds.

Misrem nodded thoughtfully, tilting her head to one side as she examined the intel.

"Most curious," she admitted. "Did that vessel just alter the composition of its *hull*?"

Aymes gestured uncertainly. "I do not know, Navarch, but that is what the unknown contact did, and that modification made it nearly impervious to our primary lasers."

She idly rubbed her cheek, smiling at the screen. "Well now, this *is* getting interesting. Are you satisfied that this is your anomaly, Captain?"

Aymes frowned. "It appears to be. However, it is difficult to be certain at this resolution."

"Best guess, Captain," Misrem demanded.

"Most likely yes, Navarch."

"Excellent. Then we may begin," Misrem said, eyeing her own command staff. "Stand by all ships to warp space once more. We will proceed into the system and engage the target ship. It is the only one in the area, so we should have little issue, even given the potential Captain Aymes fears it may have. Even so, all vessels are to take the utmost care. I will *not* tolerate the loss of a ship due to incompetence or simple overconfidence."

"As you command, Navarch."

"Very well. Power the drives; take us down into the system."

▶▶▶

▶ The powerful drives of the squadron lit off nearly in unison as they began to warp space to guide their fall toward the star. Fifteen drives going to full power in close proximity were a potential risk, particularly when they were using singularity drives to create the standing waves needed to impel the ships forward. The interacting gravity waves were not always nice enough to remain where one wanted them to, and the same interactions that created drive power for one ship could easily disrupt or, far worse, enforce drive strength on another.

Having your drive accidentally enforced beyond the level your ship could take was roughly the same as accidentally having a grenade's power increased tenfold.

Very bad news for anyone in the immediate proximity.

So Imperial squadrons drilled incessantly to prevent such interactions while remaining in as close a formation as practical. Third Recon was a very well-trained squadron, and so when their drive signatures reached the *Heral'c* deep in the star system, the signal looked more like a single drive than a grouping.

▶▶▶

PW *Heral'c*, Por-Que Orbit

▶ Captain Senthe swore, eyes wide as he watched the plot. "I want Central Command on the network, *now!*"

"Yes Captain!"

Now was a relative term in space travel, as linking to Ranquil Central Command actually took a few minutes.

"Captain Senthe," Admiral Tanner addressed him from the screens, "what is happening?"

"I believe that we are about to come under assault, Admiral," Senthe said, looking over from the telemetry plot.

Tanner stiffened, leaning into the display. "Drasin?"

"I do not believe so," Senthe told him. "The signature of the drives is too tightly focused. They almost appear as one immense vessel. That is disciplined navigation, Admiral."

Tanner tipped his chin curtly. "And the Drasin are anything but disciplined. That would also rule out freighters, Captain. I will check. Perhaps the Terran's new task force is making a stop in your area."

"I believe that Captain Weston would be polite enough to call ahead by this point," Senthe said doubtfully.

"I agree. Confirm the identity of the vessels, but do not risk your ship unnecessarily, Captain. I will see what can be done to secure backup for you. However, we have no free Heroics at this time . . . and normal cruisers . . ."

Senthe nodded. He didn't need to be told.

Unlike the new Heroic Class of starship, normal cruisers were both underpowered and, far more importantly, too slow to be of help.

"Do you have imagery yet?" Tanner asked.

"No. We're still some time out before their light reaches us," Senthe said.

Tanner stared through the screen. "And they already see you. I am familiar with the peculiarities of faster-than-light tactics. Very well, Captain. You have your—"

The image of the admiral suddenly broke up into scrambled patterns as the computer tried to reconstitute the signal but failed.

"What happened?" yelled Senthe, looking around. "Get the admiral back!"

"System-wide scrambling, below the atomic level, Captain. We can no longer connect to the relay network!"

Senthe cursed. He didn't even know that it was possible to scramble the relay network, as the link was buried deep below the atomic level. There wasn't technically even a signal to scramble! The relays were linked subatomically, directly from one particle to another.

Scrambling the link to the relay, that was possible, but there was no sign of that, and the unknown ships were still too far out for such a maneuver.

"Break through the signal scrambling. I don't care how you do it," he said.

▶▶▶

IBC Shion Thon, Flagship, Third Reconnaissance Squadron, Outer System, Por-Que

▶ "Local system has been scrambled, Navarch."

"Excellent," Misrem said. "That takes care of their relays. The rest is too slow to matter."

"I believe that they did get a signal out, Navarch."

She nodded to her sub-captain. "Yes, but we know from intelligence that there are no Oather vessels within response range. We have all the time we need to deal with Captain Aymes' little anomaly."

"Yes Navarch."

She turned her attention to the imagery on her strategic displays, set up against the gravity telemetry feeds they were also watching.

"Now to deal with you, little anomaly," she said firmly. "I wonder how much trouble one ship can possibly cause?"

▶▶▶

Ranquil System Command, Priminae Capital, Ranquil

▶ "Get them back!"

"The entire system is off the grid, Admiral. We can't."

Tanner scowled. "How close are the nearest ships?"

"Days away, Admiral."

"Heroics then," he insisted. "They can transition into the system."

"We only have one in contact, and it is assigned to Ranquil system coverage," his aide responded.

Tanner winced.

Even if the council would sign off on leaving Ranquil uncovered, the ship in question was held in reserve in the Forge. It would take at least a day for the vessel to enter space, climb out of the system, and transition to Por-Que, assuming that whatever the new contact was remained in the outer system. If it didn't, adding the time needed to drop into the system . . .

Far too much time would lapse between the *Heral'c*'s call and the arrival of the Heroic.

"Connect me to Terran Command."

"Yes Admiral."

▶▶▶

Sol Command, Space Station Unity One

▶ "Admiral, contact from the Priminae. Admiral Tanner on the secure comm."

Gracen glanced over, curiosity piqued.

"I'll be there momentarily," she said.

She'd just gotten back from her little side trip to Ranquil and hadn't gotten as much time to connect with the people there as she might have hoped. Unfortunately, she doubted that this was a personal call, so she hurried to the secure room and took a seat, finding the admiral already on the display.

"Admiral," Tanner said.

"Admiral," she repeated with a smile. "I believe we spoke of this?"

"Amanda, then," he conceded, "though this is a professional issue, I'm afraid."

Gracen nodded. "I assumed as much. How serious?"

"Not Drasin. Beyond that . . . I'm not sure," Tanner admitted. "We have an incursion into one of our systems. Admiral, do you have any forces available?"

Gracen froze, thinking hard. "We just dispatched every available Heroic and most of our free Rogues with the *Odysseus* Task Force. They're out of contact, Admiral."

Tanner took a deep breath and closed his eyes. "I am very sorry to hear that."

"We have two Heroics and a small force of Rogues covering Sol," she said, "but there's no way I can shake them loose in less than a few days. The political fight alone . . ."

"I know," he assured her, "believe me, Admiral, I am aware. I suppose I must hope that the situation is not as dire as I fear it to be."

"Why are you so concerned?"

Tanner grimaced. "We've lost contact with the relay network in the system."

Gracen blinked. "I . . . didn't know that was possible?"

"It is not," he said simply, "not without having the relay be destroyed, which I am quite certain did not happen."

"Then how . . . ?"

Tanner lifted his hands helplessly. "And now, Amanda, you know why I am concerned."

"Yes," she said softly, "I suppose I do at that. I . . . I wish I could help."

"I understand. We can get a cruiser task group there within two or three of your days, and that appears to be the fastest response time we can manage." He sighed. "It will have to do."

▶▶▶

PW *Heral'c*

▶ "We've compiled visuals on the intrusion force, Captain!"

Senthe turned. "Show me."

The light-speed signals took time to reach deep into the system since the unknown ships had arrived only a few hours earlier. That meant, of course, that the enemy ships had been compiling imagery on his vessel from the moment they arrived. His *Heral'c* had been there for days, so light was streaming out for the viewing.

He blinked as the imagery appeared on the screen, his eyes widening.

"Those are Priminae cruisers, are they not, Captain?" his second asked, confused.

"We don't have that many cruisers, Corva," Senthe corrected, shaking his head. "Did you read the Terran reports from the Drasin encounters? The one with the stellar construct?"

"I did, Captain."

"Remember the unknown ship?"

Corva frowned. "Yes, but there was no description."

"Yes, there was," Senthe said. "Call for a full alert. Bring our weapons to full power now."

"Yes Captain . . ." His second sounded bewildered, but the orders were dispatched and the *Heral'c* wound up from high alert to combat alert.

"Give me a signal back to Por-Que," Senthe said. "Have all planetary defenses marshaled. They are *not* to permit those ships to close."

"As you say, Captain. I still don't understand . . . ?"

"Those ships match the configuration of the suspects *behind* the Drasin," Senthe informed him. "I do not know why they are here, but I do not believe it is for a friendly visit."

▶▶▶

IBC *Piar Cohn*

▶ Aymes found himself staring at the display as they completed their imagery refinement of the target ship. The gravity scans were a match, but the range of error on scans conducted that far away were too large for him to be sure.

When the images had first been compiled, his fears had lessened. The configuration of the ship and its armor seemed to be a match.

Even so, there was something nagging at him.

Aymes supposed that it didn't matter much at this point, as the Third Recon was committed to an engagement. The navarch had made her decision, and honestly, he didn't fault it. Either way, the system was a target of opportunity that was too good not to take, especially considering only a single ship lay in defense.

The anomaly's armor was fascinating, he had to admit, presumably an example of some sort of molecular-level transformation able to perfectly mirror laser energy. It had a flaw, however, if he was reading the situation correctly. The transformation took time, a measurably short period that was still significant. That, combined with the fact that lasers had different frequencies, meant that in a fight, two or more ships could overload the armor. One on one, the armor was impervious, but against a group—that was a very different story.

"The enemy vessel is coming out to meet us," he noted, speaking over the tactical network to Navarch Plotu. "They have to know they're outmatched."

She glanced in his direction. "Courageous, but foolish. They would be better served if they withdrew from the system and fled to somewhere they could make a stand."

Aymes nodded thoughtfully. "Agreed. Still, rushing to battle is not an Oather trait, is it?"

"Perhaps not, but then that only serves to support your anomaly story, Captain."

"There is that," Aymes conceded.

"We engage on schedule," the navarch decided. "Issue the necessary orders . . . and Captain Aymes?"

"Yes Navarch?"

"Follow my ship's lead," she ordered. "Do not get in our way."

▶▶▶

PW *Heral'c*

▶ "They've accelerated," the second announced as Kierna Senthe looked up. "Interception time has moved up."

"I see it," Senthe answered. "Hold course."

"Captain, we have no chance against that force."

Senthe turned to respond. "We had no chance against the Drasin. Miracles happen . . . And if they do not happen this time, then so be it."

He scowled at the display, trying to decide the best point to meet the intruders. Not that there *was* a "best point" in this mess.

"Stand by for course alteration," he said suddenly.

"Awaiting new orders, Captain," his navigation officer answered, half turning.

"Adjust acceleration, reverse power by two-thirds, and bring us about to interval one ninety," Senthe ordered. "Engage when plotted."

The response took only a few seconds. "Course plotted and engaged."

"That will bring them deeper into the system, to us."

His second frowned. "This is a good thing?"

"It will also put our engagement point right at the edge of the planetary defense system," Senthe said. "It will not even the game, but it should put some advantages into our hands."

Not enough, he was certain, but then there was no possible way to win this fight. He just needed to do what he could to discourage their movement toward the planet, at least until the admiral could shake a few ships loose to cover the system again.

▶▶▶

IBC Shion Thon, Flagship, Third Reconnaissance Squadron

▶ The interception moment was rapidly approaching as the target vessel shifted course on their screens, and Misrem eyed the new vector curiously for a moment as she pondered her response.

Tactics for combat within the gravity well of a star were inherently limited, but those limitations were often not as crippling as people tended to believe. However, even within those bounds, this particular maneuver was unusual.

"He's not trying to evade interception. The change only alters contact by a very short time," she whispered pensively, "so what are you up to, my poor friend?"

She shifted her focus away from the ship they were closing in on to the planet beyond and tipped her head slightly.

"You want us to waste time chasing you instead of focusing on the planet," she decided. "Very courageous, my poor friend, but unfortunately for you . . . we have no interest in the planet—not this time."

She lifted her head. "Shift course. Best-time interception. We'll play his game. Let him lead us on a merry chase."

▶▶▶

▶ As the squadron delved deeper into the gravity field of the local star, the variables stressing the drives multiplied. Planets, moons, even large asteroids became factors that required consideration by the engineers charged with maintaining the integrity of the drives. This wasn't normally an issue. Those potential variables were relatively mild and not especially difficulty to factor in. However, when combined with fifteen unstable singularity cores—more, actually, since most ships in the squadron used redundant cores—things could become touchy.

That was why, as the ships sank deeper into the system, the squadron spread out further to reduce interference while increasing weapon and scanner coverage. That had the effect of exposing their numbers, of course, but in this situation that didn't concern the navarch.

They broke into three elements of five ships apiece, two moving to flank the target ship while the third continued on a direct interception course. Approaching within a few light-minutes, they increased power to the drives as they went into terminal attack mode.

The squadron led with a brace of laser strikes, beams lancing out across the vacuum of space as an early announcement of its arrival.

▶▶▶

PW *Heral'c*

▶ "Secure armor, best available settings," Senthe ordered as he sat at his station.

The enemy were doing exactly what he wanted them to do, and that was making him more than a little nervous. They were showing no interest in the planet at all, focusing their entire weight on his ship for whatever bizarre reason they might have.

He didn't understand their reasoning. The task force coming in his direction was *far* greater than what it would realistically take to eliminate a single ship like his *Heral'c*. They could have easily detached two-thirds of their weight without risking anything.

"Why are they chasing us so intently?" he murmured.

"Captain?"

"Nothing," Senthe said, shaking his head. "Nothing."

"Yes Captain."

And now my crew is going to start thinking I'm crazy, he thought with some amusement.

It didn't matter, not anymore. The incoming squadron was clearly choosing a hostile attack vector, and unless he was mistaken, it had already opened fire.

"Best bring damage control to full alert," he said.

"They should already be on alert, Captain," his second said.

"Then make sure they are," Senthe said tersely.

"Yes Captain."

"Helm control . . ."

"Captain?"

"Evasion pattern, execute immediately," Senthe said. "I expect they've fired already. Let's not be where they expect us to be."

"Yes Captain."

The *Heral'c* shifted course, almost insignificantly by planetary standards but by several thousand kilometers from its projected position. It was the most basic of tactics, but also incredibly effective.

After that, Senthe just had to wait and see if he was right. With the alarms screaming, he got his answer just moments later.

"Report!"

"Beam trace, Captain," his weapons officer announced. "High level, over our current capacity by at least twenty percent. No variance."

Well, there's that at least, for what little it's worth.

Sadly, the fact that there was no variance in the beams didn't amount to much when there were so damn many of them. If he adapted the armor of the *Heral'c* to any one beam, the rest would turn him, his crew, and his ship to expanding vapor all the same.

"Calculate targets, return fire," he ordered.

"Which ship?"

"All of them," Senthe replied with a dry laugh.

Might as well go out in a blaze of light and darkness.

▶▶▶

IBC Shion Thon, Flagship, Third Reconnaissance Squadron

▶ "Target evaded. All beams will miss."

Misrem was unsurprised. "Continue firing. He cannot evade for much longer."

"As you command, Navarch."

She didn't reply—didn't need to. Once her orders were given, Misrem knew they would be followed. The routine confirmation mildly annoyed her, as though anyone on her crew would have the temerity not to pay attention to her every word.

The range was closing rapidly now. The target vessel wasn't even trying to keep it open any longer. She supposed that the other captain knew well enough that his number was up. It didn't matter how powerful his ship was, or how many tricks it had. Against her task force, there was no escape.

"Beam strike!"

"Who?" she twisted, eyes flashing.

"The *Cora*, the *Menaz*, the *Tiv* . . . Navarch, more reports coming in from across the squadron!"

"Damage reports. Anything significant?"

"No, Navarch. Some minor hull breaches, all sealed. Casualties are not significant. Beams were attenuated going through our gravitational warps."

Misrem nodded. "Very well."

She looked to the plot, dryly amused by the actions of her quarry. His response to her assault was immediate but amateurish at best. A professional would have struck at one or perhaps two targets, intending to inflict more significant damage.

Of course, at this range, striking at as many targets as possible *did* increase the odds of landing a strike, since even minute changes in course would result in missing by massive degrees. Still, a professional would have taken the lower odds of a hit in exchange for the higher odds of a kill.

This doesn't look particularly good for Captain Aymes' story, she thought.

It was a pity, really, as she'd almost found herself liking the rather abrasive captain. Unfortunately, he appeared to be nothing more than another fool trying to cover his incompetence.

She watched the plot carefully as the range plummeted, the slight whine of the laser discharging almost covered up by the regular sounds of the command deck.

"Navarch, we've analyzed their patterns," her tactical officer said confidently.

"Adjust fire parameters. Continue full barrage."

So now the fun part begins.

▶▶▶

PW *Heral'c*

▶ "Enemy vessels closing. They're getting closer with their fire as well, Captain."

Senthe could see that, unfortunately.

"Break contact. Maximum acceleration," he ordered. "Take us away from the planet. Lure them out; buy time."

"Yes Captain."

The *Heral'c* shifted vectors away from the inbound squadron, alarms still sounding regularly as it detected beams crossing space nearby. Senthe knew he wasn't going to buy much time, but he'd take anything he could get.

The *Heral'c* suddenly shook, a hammer blow crashing through the decks of the ship with enough force that the crew members grabbed the closest objects to steady themselves.

"Hull breach! Decks eighteen through twenty-one!"

Senthe grimaced. That had to have been a direct strike, and the hit was earlier than he had expected. He'd bought less time than he'd hoped.

"Damage control is working on it," Corva said. "Damage is extensive but—"

Another strike rumbled through the decks.

"You were about to say something?" Senthe asked wryly.

His second didn't have a response, not that anything would have mattered.

"We've sustained damage to the drives, Captain. They'll not hold stable for long now," he said finally.

"Sound the order to abandon ship. They have our range," Senthe said, gritting his teeth as a third rumble shook the deck.

"But—"

"Do it."

"Yes Captain." His second lowered his head, issuing the order.

▶▶▶

▶ The *Heral'c* was losing air across more than a dozen decks, and her acceleration was dropping fast as lifeboats began launching from the

260 • EVAN CURRIE

big ship. Strewn across several light-seconds of space, the small pods oriented themselves and attempted to connect to the local relays to signal for help. When those signals were returned with no indication of aid, the lifeboats went into backup mode and sent a short-burst call for help using limited-duration tachyon transmitters.

Third Recon ignored the calls, being quite certain that there were no ships close enough to respond in time, and continued to close on the stricken *Heral'c*.

CHAPTER 21

Odysseus Task Force

▶ Eric Weston burst onto the bridge of the *Odysseus*, still buttoning up his tunic. He'd barely managed three hours of sleep while the task force's research teams scrambled to get all the details they could on the nearby alien megastructure.

"What is it?"

"An SOS call, Capitaine," Milla responded, which was a little out of order since she was assigned to tactical operations.

Her accent was more pronounced than usual, Eric noticed. That tended to happen only when Milla was stressed.

Eric glanced at the displays. "Since there are no other ships near here, and you'd have told me if the call was from one of mine, I have to assume it's a Priminae distress call. Lifeboat model, same as we picked you up in?"

"Yes, Capitaine . . . but not one. Many."

"Many?" Eric blinked. "How many?"

Sams looked up. "Forty-three at last count. The frequency of new signals has begun to drop, but my guess, Captain, is that there will be sixty when it is all finished."

"Sixty," Eric said flatly. "That's the number of lifeboats on a Priminae cruiser."

"Yes sir."

"Location?"

"We've locked them down to a minor Priminae system called Por-Que," Sams said. "It's a short-burst distress call, so we don't have any details, but something went hot and bad there."

"Show me the system," Eric ordered, waving toward the main display.

The image on the screen flickered, replaced by a top-down view of a solar system with six planets. Eric could tell at a glance from the color coding that only one was inhabited, and the main activity in the system appeared to be mining trace materials from around the planet in question. Interesting to someone, perhaps, but not of any value to him at the moment.

"Back out. Show me the system in relation to our location," he said.

"The system is four hundred light-years away, Captain . . ."

"Back out, Ensign," Eric turned, glowering as he repeated himself, "and show me the system in relation to our location."

"Yes sir." Sams quailed under the combined glares of Captain Weston and Commander Heath.

The screen shifted again, greatly pulling back, and the two locations appeared on the screen. Eric looked at them and shook his head.

"Coincidences . . . coincidences . . . ," he murmured.

"Sir?" Miram asked, uncertain.

"The timing bothers me, Commander," he said, shaking his head, "but I don't see any connection. Ensign, show me the Priminae worlds."

"Capitaine," Milla spoke up hesitantly, "I do not understand. What are you looking for?"

He sighed. "I don't know. It *could* be a Drasin attack, perhaps . . . but we've had no contact with them since Earth."

He considered for a moment before finally coming to a decision. "If it's the Drasin, then we're too late anyway . . . but . . ."

He walked around his station and approached the main display. "Ensign, show me the systems attacked by the Drasin."

A set of systems turned red on the display in response.

"There," Eric said, pointing. "That's the system we just left, isn't it? The one we met the bandit in?"

"Aye sir," Sams responded.

"And Por-Que is the closest intact system," Eric said. "We're back-tracking the Drasin attack, right?"

"We are, Captain," Miram said, coming up beside him. "What does that matter?"

"What if someone is doing the same from the other side?" he said. "If you were tracking along the same path, from the other side, and you ran into an unknown ship . . . where would you look for them after contact?"

"Could be anywhere, Captain . . . ," Miram said.

"No, not anywhere," Eric corrected. "Not if you don't know about the transition drive."

The commander blinked, then nodded slowly. "Of course. A ship with minor damage, limited by space-warp speeds . . . they'd probably go to the closest system for a patch."

"And if you wanted to find them, then that is where you would go too," Eric said.

"You think they went looking for *us*?" Miram asked, skeptical.

"Not us specifically, but they're tracking something," Eric said, "and when we encountered them, I think that put us on their radar."

"Well, we're outside of relay range," Miram said, "but we could send a short burst with some intelligence back to Earth from here."

"No point," Eric said. "They've got the same data we do by now."

Eric looked over to the displays showing the alien megastructure just beyond their hull, then back to the star charts. He considered the odds, the mission priorities, and a thousand other things in a few seconds.

"Signal the task force," he said abruptly. "We're pulling out."

"Captain?" Miram frowned.

"Helm, start plotting transition coordinates for that system," he ordered, glancing over at Sams. "How deep in the system are the signals coming from?"

"Deep, sir, close to the fourth planet."

"Right." Eric walked over to Steph and laid a hand on his shoulder. "We're going to transition in as deep as we can . . . Steph, I need to know, how reliable is NICS on this heap?"

Steph looked up over his shoulder. "Pretty tight, Raze, but these aren't Double A fighters."

"I know that, but how tight can you maneuver this heap?"

Stephen considered the question for a moment, then gave a slight grin. "Pretty damn tight. I'll need to coordinate with the others, though."

"They're all Archangels. I don't see that as a problem."

"Right you are, sir."

Eric straightened up. "Good. Go to it."

He left his pilot to his task, then turned to Miram. "I want the Rogues online in five. I'll take it from my office."

"Yes sir."

"In the meantime, Commander, triple-check the transition coordinates," Eric said. "We're going to drop in *hot* on that AO, but I'd rather we didn't scatter ourselves across the galaxy doing it."

"Got it, sir, I'll get them locked down."

"Good." Eric looked around. "Alright, you have your orders. Get to it. Oh, and Commander? Best sound general quarters. Beat the drums, Miram, beat the drums."

"Aye aye, Skipper."

▶▶▶

▶ "Cardsharp."

"Stephanos," Jennifer "Cardsharp" Samuels said with a slightly wry look. "Nice to chat again. Been thinking you've been avoiding me."

Stephen chuckled. "Don't be like that. You know a pilot only has room for one love. How is your *Booty* anyway?"

Jennifer rolled her eyes. "The *Boudicca* is just fine, Steph. I assume this call has something to do with the general quarters call we just sounded?"

"You assume right." Steph nodded before glancing at the other screen. "Burner, you ready to fly?"

"In these tugs? Should be interesting, I suppose," Burner answered. "What bug got up the boss' butt, do you know?"

"A Primmy cruiser, one of the old class but refitted, just abandoned ship in one of the minor systems. Might not be related, but the boss thinks the cruiser's attacker might just be the bandit we tangled with a couple weeks ago."

"The ones who shot you down, Steph?" Cardsharp asked, grinning.

"I was flying a frigging *shuttle*."

"Still counts."

"It does not!"

"Burner?" she asked their colleague, chuckling openly.

"Sorry, Steph, definitely counts," Burner said, smiling tightly.

"Jerks," Steph grumbled. "*Anyway*, boss wants to check it out, so we're going in, and we're going in *hot*. So we need to talk formations and maneuvers in a hurry."

The other two pilots exchanged glances on their screens and then leaned in.

"Sounds fun," Burner said.

"Agreed," Jennifer confirmed, but looking less eager.

"What is it, Sharp?" Steph asked, reading her expression.

"I think we need to bring our engineers in on this," she told them. "Space-warp drives can interfere with one another. Any maneuvers we plan, they need to sign off on, maybe even need to be involved in during the move."

Steph groaned. "Ugh. Didn't think of that, but you're right. Okay, get your geeks in on this while I go shake down mine. Back online in an hour."

▶▶▶

▶ "Captains." Eric looked around the displays arrayed about him.

"Commodore . . . ," the one in the center, Ian Shepherd, captain of the AEV *Hood*, responded. "Since we've all gone to general quarters, I assume you plan to do something about the distress signals?"

"That would be a fair assumption," Eric said. "We're going to transition in system, as deep as we dare, and move immediately to full space-warp drives. We've got a good idea where the signals came from, and they're pretty deep inside the well, so we're going in hot."

"Excuse me, Commodore," Captain Su Lynn Jing of the *Song-Jiang* interjected, "but I do not understand the need for such speed. Reports on the Priminae lifeboats indicate that they can survive weeks without intervention."

"They can," Eric replied. "However, saving those crewmen isn't the reason for going in hot. I'm more concerned with what caused them to abandon ship in the first place."

"You think the spiders had something to do with it?" Maxine Ritter, captain of the *Kid*, asked softly.

"Unlikely, and if they did, then we'll be arriving too late anyway," Eric said. "No, I think . . . I *hope* that we're looking at an Imperial incursion."

Ian nodded. "Alright, I can see that. So what's the plan?"

"The Heroics are going to transition a few seconds before you take your Rogues through," Eric said. "We'll go to full drives as soon as we arrive, shining knight armor settings. You lot come in *dark*, behind us, and go deep."

The captain of the *Aladdin*, Benjamin Alhad, frowned as he leaned forward in the display.

"Commodore, am I to understand that you intend to use your Heroics as *bait*?"

"We can't hide, so we may as well attract some real attention," Eric said. "We can also take a beating. You can't. So we'll keep them focused while you flank them. Stay dark until you get a shot, then change course and speed after every one."

"This goes against pretty much every SOP for carrier escort, you realize?" Ian asked dryly.

"The Heroics are not carriers—we're battleships," Eric told him. "We can cover our own flanks. Do you each understand your orders?"

The captains of his Rogues acknowledged his command, some less eagerly than others, but Eric wasn't concerned with that.

"Relax. I have no intention of sacrificing another ship." Eric smiled darkly. "This is probably an unnecessary maneuver anyway. The Imperial ship we tangled with was not maneuvered by what I'd call a tactical genius. And while their weapons were more powerful than expected, like the Priminae and the Drasin they seem to rely primarily on brute force. You're all giant killers, ladies and gentlemen. Have no fear of Goliath."

"And if Goliath brought friends?" Ritter asked with a very slight Southern drawl.

"That's why we have Heroics, Max." Eric smiled. "Let us live up to our name."

▶▶▶

▶ "The difficulty isn't just in precision flying," Chief Siing Khava insisted as he spoke to the others present around the table. "As close as you want to fly, Commander, we'll need to worry about resonance between our drives."

The chief could see the others were somewhat mixed in their understanding. However, with the engineers of the other Heroics nodding along, he was gratified that the pilots seemed to have some idea of what he was saying.

"Our drives can cancel each other out, then?" Lieutenant Commander Samuels asked.

"That," he said, "or worse, they might enforce one another."

"That would be a problem in precision flying," Steph conceded.

"More than that, I'm afraid," Siing offered, sighing. "If you reinforce the drives beyond the safety limit, you risk creating an artificial singularity large enough to swallow the ship."

"Hang on," Samuels interjected. "I thought the systems were designed to keep the singularities ahead of the ship?"

"They are. However, if a singularity becomes too large, then the prow of the vessel might cross the event horizon anyway."

"I'm assuming that would be as bad as it sounds," Steph said. "Alright. If we want to get close, what sort of numbers are we talking?"

"That would depend on whether you wanted to avoid a mandatory refit after the maneuver," Siing said. "Even if we managed to maintain drive stability, at that proximity, the stresses on the hulls will be significant."

"Okay, so I need numbers from you for maximum 'safe' distance," Steph said, "and numbers for military maneuvering."

Siing paused for a moment. "I will have those compiled as quickly as possible and sent to your station. Please, Commander, do not try these sorts of maneuvers without close communication with engineering. We will have to compensate *very* quickly for any fluctuations."

"Wilco, Chief," Steph said as the other two pilots nodded in agreement.

They were pilots. Crazy was part and parcel of their résumé; stupid wasn't.

▶▶▶

▶ "The way I read the situation, Commodore," Captain Roberts, commanding the *Bellerophon*, said in his wooden way, "is that time is against us, no matter how you slice this. Unless the distress calls are after an accident, we're going to be riding in late."

"Agreed," Eric said. "I'm hoping that we'll at least be able to track any ships leaving the system if we're that late, but we might get lucky too."

Roberts didn't look happy about that last bit. Luck wasn't something he wanted to be counting on, but he'd been in the service long enough to know that sometimes that was precisely what things came down to.

Fortune favors the bold.

Not his personal motto, but it did have some merit. You couldn't get lucky if you didn't take any chances.

Of course, the reverse is also true. Nothing wards off bad luck like good, solid preparation. This thought was far closer to Roberts' personal beliefs.

Unfortunately, he knew his former captain well enough to know that given the option, he was going to take the long shot and do his utmost to make it pay off. For whatever problems Roberts had with Weston, he did respect that in the man. He may be willing to take a chance, but that didn't mean he wouldn't do everything possible to hedge his bet at the same time.

"Understood, sir," Roberts said. "The *Bellerophon* stands ready."

"As does the *Boudicca*, Commodore," Captain Alexander Dogavich said firmly. "I am concerned about this deep transition you have planned, however."

"The Por-Que system is relatively barren: few planets, only a single gas giant, and it's been heavily mined for quite some time," Eric said. "That's going to reduce the gravitational variables we have to calculate. We can do this, captains."

"It is not a question of whether we can, Commodore," Dogavich replied. "It is a question of whether we *should*. However, that is your call. After this mission, all three of our ships and the Rogues will require fairly extensive refits, you are aware?"

"I am."

"Very well. Then I have no objections. We do our duty."

▶▶▶

▶ Though the crews on every ship in the task force worked feverishly, immersing themselves in tech and crunching numbers as quickly as possible, the small group still took considerable time before they were ready to move. Thankfully, the squadron wouldn't have to waste any of that time escaping the well of a solar system, though they had taken the opportunity to put significant distance between themselves and the ancient megastructure.

Even given its massive size, the structure didn't produce anything close to the gravitational field of a star, something future researchers would spend much time on, Eric had little doubt.

Within the hour, however, they were in formation and preparing for transition out of the deep black and back to Priminae space.

"All ships report ready, Captain," Sams said from his station.

"Very well. Signal transition alert," Eric said as he tried to settle his stomach.

He honestly wasn't sure if it was the upcoming transition that was causing his gut to roil violently like a ship at sea or if it was the fear of what they would find on the other side of the jump. He didn't think they were going to encounter the Drasin again, but even the barest possibility of finding another destroyed world . . .

There were limits to what any man could take, and Eric had no desire to find his. How many times could one look into the face of genocide and walk away with sanity and morality intact? He'd had to physically hold himself while looking at the main Imperial vessel, doing anything he could to keep from calling no quarter and burning the ship down to the quantum level—and he'd only *suspected* what the so-called Empire had done.

He was a Marine, a warrior, and a citizen of a civil nation, and he would *not* fall to their level of depravity.

I will find you, he thought grimly. *I will prove what you've done, and I will see you shot by the numbers . . . but I will not become you.*

"All systems stand ready to transition," Miram announced from her station.

Eric nodded sharply. "Initiate transition on my mark . . ."

He waited a heartbeat, taking a deep breath to settle his stomach. "Mark."

The *Odysseus* Task Force vanished in a whirling, roiling mass of subatomic particles that leapt across the black in a single instant of chaotic motion.

CHAPTER 22

AEV *Odysseus*

▶ *Don't throw up. Don't throw up.*

Eric *despised* transition. For all that it was the fastest and most effi-cient method of FTL travel he knew of, it—for lack of a better word—*sucked*. Pushing his stomach back down where it belonged through force of will and little else, he kept his eyes open and on the telltale displays lighting up around him.

"Space-warp drive coming online—"

"—watch out for the *Boudicca*, she's drifting our way."

"—comm center is swamped with distress calls! We've got them on every Priminae frequency!"

Eric shook his head clear, focusing on the reports flying around the bridge as many of the people receiving and dispatching said reports were doing the same.

The lifeboat locations were on the screens, a trail strewn across almost a full light-minute of space but slowly drifting together under their own power. The planet beyond still seemed to be intact, which was a good sign even if the light-speed delay meant that the signal was well over an hour old.

Most interesting was the group of gravity signals that matched the Imperial drive specifications they had on file. The cluster of signals was at rest near the red-lit icon of the Priminae cruiser *Heral'c*.

"Fifteen of them," Eric whispered as he finished the count. "Well, this might just be interesting after all."

"Rogues transitioning in!"

He glanced at the display that showed the four Rogue Class destroyers appearing behind the screening wall of the three larger Heroic Class cruisers. The smaller ships immediately went dark as their armor shifted to black hole settings, with only their encrypted transponders indicating their locations.

Those quickly blinked out as well, much to Eric's satisfaction, leaving the Heroics alone in their charge downwell.

"Capitaine, should I establish a real-time lock?" Milla asked from her weapons and tactical station.

"Not yet, Lieutenant," Eric said. "They'll know something just happened out here, but it'll be over an hour before they get imagery to confirm, and I'd rather they were kept guessing just a little longer."

"Aye Capitaine."

He noted that the *Odysseus* was being flanked rather closely by the *Boudicca* and the *Bellerophon*, close enough to make him just a little nervous.

"Steph?" he spoke up softly.

"Aye Skipper?" Steph didn't turn around, as he was already plugged into the NICS controls.

"Are we good at this range to the others?"

"No worries, Skipper. I've got this."

Eric nodded, though his friend couldn't see it. "Very well, carry on."

He shot a glance at Miram, who leaned over in his direction.

"We're going to appear as a single contact at this range, flying this tight," she said. "Not sure if that's what you want, sir."

"I'll take it." Eric grinned wryly. "It's not a huge advantage, but I'm not giving anything up if I can help it."

"Why aren't we locking them in with the t-cannons, sir? They've clearly fired on an ally . . ."

"I know, but I want the Rogues to have time to flank them before we light them up."

"Ah, understood, sir."

▶▶▶

IBC Shion Thon, Flagship, Third Reconnaissance Squadron

▶ "Navarch, we have a contact in the outer system. Powerful gravity source."

Misrem half turned, looking over at her scanner tech with undisguised curiosity. "Where in the outer system?"

"On display, My Lady."

She examined the screen, her eyes widening as she saw the intensity and location of the contact.

"Abyssal twilight," she swore. "Why didn't the scanners pick that up earlier?"

"Unknown." The tech cringed, not that she blamed him.

Misrem would have the records scoured once they returned to Imperial space, and if the oversight was a failure on the part of the tech, he would be lucky to escape with merely the destruction of his career. For now, however, she didn't have time for such scrutiny. The game was about to begin anew.

"No scout reported Oather vessels within days of here, so who is this?" She had a sudden suspicion and flipped open the squadron comm, linking to the *Piar Cohn*. "Captain Aymes, is this new contact your anomaly?"

"It does not appear to be, based on gravity analysis, Navarch," he confessed, seemingly displeased. Again, she didn't blame him either. If it was not his anomaly, then it was a new one. "Far more powerful gravity field than we detected before . . . impossible to be certain until we get light-speed imagery, of course."

"Of course," she whispered, mostly to herself as she cut the link.

"Reorient the squadron," Misrem ordered. "Stand by for maneuvering orders. It seems we have a new target."

"As you command, Navarch."

▶▶▶

▶ The ships of Third Recon abandoned their waning interest in the stricken and slowly dying Priminae cruiser, pausing only to cut its weapons ports out with carefully placed shots to prevent any last-moment miracle strikes at their back. They left the hull largely intact, however, since their mission *was* to identify and secure any technical advantages the anomaly ship might have had, and the vessel's armor was interesting.

That would wait for later, however, as they brought their space-warp drives to full power, orienting themselves around the newly arrived contact that shone in the distance like a miniature star to their gravity scanners.

Within moments, Third Recon vessels were accelerating hard and away from the destroyed ship and its helpless crew, warping space and climbing fast out of the stellar gravity well.

▶▶▶

AEV *Odysseus*

▶ "Targets have lit off their drives," Sams announced, his voice not quite cracking from nerves.

"Thank you, Ensign," Eric responded. "We'll give the Rogues another half hour to get into position before we kick off this little party. In the meantime, primary crew . . . stand down, get a cup, grab a bite. We're going to be at this for a while, and I want you all fresh."

The replacement shift started taking positions, but Steph waved his alternate off. "I'm good here. Just bring me a cup, will you? Black."

Eric sighed, walking over. "Are you sure, Steph? It's going to be a while."

"Coordinating with engineering and the other ships is tricky. If you want to spell us out, we'll have to break formation," Steph said. "We have this, sir."

"Alright," Eric said, nodding to the replacement pilot. "Get him the cup, okay?"

"Yes sir."

He glanced at the plot. The contact time was still about an hour away. First reasonable time for conventional engagement was almost that long away as well, but he had a surprise for the targets that would hopefully set them back on their heels.

Taking his own advice, Eric went down a couple decks and got himself a cup of coffee and a light meal. He'd initiated this personal habit quite some time before, showing himself to his crew when they knew there was a fight brewing. The captain calmly munching on a snack in the cafeteria went a long way to establishing the mood for everyone else.

In his thoughts, though, he was far from calm.

Oh, Eric certainly wasn't panicking or anything of the sort, but there were issues to consider. The situation they were dealing with was becoming clearer, to be sure, but so much information was still murky as hell.

They now had enough intel to link these Imperial types to the Drasin. Between the scans from the Drasin megastructure and the swarm from Earth's last encounter, he was pretty sure he could sell that idea to an international court. Now that the Empire had fired first on the *Odysseus* and on the Priminae, who were allies, it didn't even matter if they had anything to do with the Drasin.

They'd fired the first shots of a war in which he intended to fire the *last* shots.

What was making this complicated was the fact that Eric knew Earth wasn't ready for a prolonged fight. He'd rather have played shadow games a bit longer while more Heroics and Rogues were put into space and their crews brought up to spec.

Ask me for anything but time, he mused as he considered the problem.

His personal computer beeped, reminding him of the hour and pulling Eric from his reverie. He finished the last few bites of his snack, drained the coffee down to the grounds, then got to his feet and headed for a refill.

Either way, he had a bad feeling about what he was going to do.

It just wasn't going to stop him from doing it.

▶ ▶ ▶

▶ Steph couldn't help but think of himself in terms of his call sign when flying. He felt an itch somewhere along the back of his neck, as though someone were watching him, while he made a minute course adjustment and did his periodic checks. He resisted the urge to look over his shoulder, knowing that while there were people behind him, any such motion would be pointless. He'd already checked several times, and no one was staring at him.

He was almost beginning to feel downright paranoid about the sensation by this point, however, and it was starting to show in his flying. Steph purposely took a few deep breaths, pushing the paranoia away, and saw the rough edges fade from the *Odysseus'* flight profile.

There was no excuse for unprofessional flying.

He put the feeling down to precombat jitters, though that was a problem he'd not really had in a long time.

Guess I'm still a little unsure about flying this beast. Steph figured he could admit that much to himself without injuring his pride. He'd never, until the heat death of the universe itself, admit it to anyone else.

Idly, he patted the side of the station he was seated within, whispering to the ship as he had to his fighter many times in the past.

"Don't you worry—we'll get through this," Steph said softly. "Those bastards out there, they've got nothing on us."

He relaxed a little more and noted that his flight profile had smoothed out considerably in response. Steph had rarely felt so deep in the moment, even with NICS connected, as he did just then.

The itch on the back of his neck faded, replaced by an odd feeling of camaraderie, like someone was flying his wings. That feeling was the norm for Steph, and both Burner and Cardsharp *were* flying his wings.

All was right in the universe, for a little while at least.

▶▶▶

▶ The bridge was a beehive of activity as Eric returned, acknowledging Commander Heath, who'd beat him back.

"Report," he said simply as he took his station.

"No change," Miram told him. "We're still accelerating at one another at impossibly insane velocities. So far they don't appear ready to blink."

"Range to contact?" Eric set his fresh coffee down on a magnetic circle that would hold it in place against any of the mild turbulence they were likely to experience either from their close formation flying or a fight.

If they hit anything heavier, the odds were highly in favor of him not caring what happened to his coffee.

"Just under thirty light-minutes," Miram said. "Contact is t-minus forty and counting. They'll be compiling visual confirmation from our light anytime now, sir."

Outwardly, Eric just nodded, but inside he was honestly *shocked* by the bogey's closing velocities, mostly because of how quickly both sides had become intent on accelerating into one another.

"Well, if they're that impatient, let's kick this pig, shall we? Steph, our secret is about to be let out of the box. The first one, at least."

"Aye sir," Stephen said from the pilot's station. His hands were steady on the controls, where'd they'd been since before the task force had transitioned into the system. "We're ready."

"Transition cannons, stand by to fire," Eric said, moving on.

"T-cannons, standing by, aye sir," Milla said from her station, not looking up from her console.

"Active scanners, stand ready."

"Scanners are charged and standing by, Captain," Sams said.

Eric smiled. "Well, then, you two . . . light them up."

▶▶▶

IBC Shion Thon, Flagship, Third Reconnaissance Squadron

▶ Navarch Plotu found herself intrigued by the new contact that was closing in on them confidently. Oh, the previous target they'd eliminated had certainly been courageous enough, but its tactics had plainly been intended to draw them out and away from the local planet. If not for that, she had no doubt that they would have tried to avoid contact.

Such was a natural and, more importantly, *sane* state of mind for an outnumbered vessel.

This new contact, however intense its gravity signature was, seemed all too eager for an engagement. That concerned her deeply, but she'd

280 •   EVAN CURRIE

seen enough in her career to put her trust in her squadron, even over the unknown.

The imagery was still coming together, but in another few moments she'd have her first view of this new foe. From there she would be able to properly analyze the situation.

"Active scanner pulse," her scanner tech called.

Or I will be able to see them right now.

"Signature separation, Captain—it's three ships!"

Misrem leaned forward, lips pressing together as she smiled thinly and watched the image on the displays turn from one intense gravity signature to three still quite-powerful ships spreading out slowly from one another.

Oh, very impressive. Timing was perfect, and the flying skill . . . She took a moment to admire the precision involved, both on the part of the pilots and the drive crews that had to keep those ships from interacting negatively with one another.

"Pity," she said aloud, shaking her head.

"Excuse me, ma'am?" her second asked, glancing over.

"I just said that it is a pity," she repeated. "All that marvelous precision in timing and maneuvering, and what did it really gain them? There are still only three ships, and they are about to run dead into Third Recon. 'Dead' being the operative word, yes?"

"Yes, My Lady."

She was still smiling right up to the point that explosions rocked three of her vessels, crippling two outright and sending a third entirely into the next universe in the blink of an eye. Alarms—most of which she didn't even recognize—screamed across every deck of her ship.

Misrem was in a state of disbelief.

"What the abyss was that?" she swore, right before issuing orders without fully understanding what was happening. "Evasion pattern, execute!"

▶▶▶

AEV *Odysseus*

▶ "Fire out," Milla said from her station.

"Repeat," Eric said sharply.

The *Odysseus* and her sister ships went to continuous fire with the transition cannons, sending barrage after barrage of nuclear devices instantly downrange. The FTL nature of the transition cannons made them a terrifying first-strike weapon, but it also meant that Eric couldn't see the precise results of each shot without again painting the system with FTL scanners.

The task force had the power for that, but generating tachyons was fiddly work at best, so for the moment there was no way to maintain full real-time scans of the area—and even if they could, that would just provide his enemy with the same advantage.

"Fire out," Milla called again. "Reloading."

"Check fire," Eric ordered. "Ensign Sams, paint the targets."

"Check fire, aye," Milla confirmed.

"Pulse out," Sams answered. "Return . . . on screen."

Eric looked up at the main display and instantly frowned. "Confirm scans."

Sams bent closer to his station, frowning. "Pulse out. Return . . . scans confirmed, Captain."

Eric shook his head. Something was very wrong.

"Lieutenant Chans," he said softly, "confirm target priorities, please."

"Aye Captain," she said, sounding almost as perplexed as he was. "We fired five full barrages, spread across all lead elements of the enemy formation."

"Then why am I seeing only one ship down . . . three others damaged, maybe?"

"Unknown, Captain. The cannons were on target, I am certain."

Eric leaned back unhappily.

The transition cannons were finicky things, he knew. Ideally, they were the ultimate trump card. The ability to materialize a nuclear device *within* your enemy's hull from light-minutes away, instantly no less, should be unbeatable. However, they'd just fired five full barrages from three Heroics and barely dented the enemy numbers.

Something had clearly gone wrong with the system.

"Systems check?" He looked over.

"All clear. *Boudicca* and *Bellerophon* confirm, all systems green," Milla stated.

If it's not on our side, then it's on theirs . . . Eric thought about how one could defeat the transition cannons, something he had already proven to the brass back home could be done. Then he instantly grimaced. "Damn it."

"Sir?" Miram asked.

"We never tested the system against a Heroic directly," he said. "We should have."

"Sir, why?"

"The singularity cores, Commander." He shook his head. "The Drasin use a different power system, so the issue never showed up with them, but we're trying to transition those shells right beside a rather intense gravity well. They're not reforming, is my guess."

Miram paled. "Sir . . . without the t-cannons . . ."

"We're outnumbered, and one of our key trump cards isn't quite the powerhouse we thought it was." Eric exhaled deeply. "I know."

▶▶▶

IBC Shion Thon, Flagship, Third Reconnaissance Squadron

▶ "You will tell me just *what in the abyss* hit my squadron, and you will tell me *now!*" Misrem was very nearly in a fury, held in check only by the fact that they were facing combat and only a fool lost her temper before a real fight.

"We don't know, My Lady. Something detonated within the hulls of the stricken vessels," the analyst said shakily. "Scan data shows that the source of the explosions were most likely simple atomic devices. Small ones, but . . . inside a hull . . ."

She let him trail off. There really was no need to finish that statement. Even simple atomics were more than enough to cause severe damage to her vessels if they somehow got *inside* the hull.

That didn't explain how the *abyss* they'd gotten there, however, and that was a question she needed the answer to *immediately*.

"No one has been on, or off, the ships since Imperial space," she growled. "Are we dealing with sabotage?"

"We do not know," the analyst insisted.

"Then *find out!*" she screamed. "If there are more of these devices in my squadron, I need them found and disabled—*now!*"

The analyst scrambled off, hurrying to pass on her orders and, no doubt, at least some of the responsibility. Misrem didn't have time to worry about him as she turned her focus back to the scanners.

"Timing," she murmured.

"My Lady?" her second asked tentatively.

"The timing: it's too much," she said. "Sabotage . . . How could they? But . . . what else?"

None of it made *any* sense. In fact, it made so very *little* sense that she was considering pulling her squadron back from combat and withdrawing from the system until they could get all the data from the incident analyzed properly. But she refrained from voicing such a command, because her forces were already effectively committed to at least a passing engagement, and there were only three enemy ships.

"How long until contact?" she snarled. At the very least, she wanted to deliver her displeasure directly to the enemy.

284 • EVAN CURRIE

▶▶▶

IBC *Piar Cohn*

▶ Captain Aymes found himself studying the scanner records over and over as they hurtled through the black expanse, heading into the teeth of the enemy. The situation felt like one he'd experienced all too recently, and he had no doubt now.

These new contacts, *they* were the anomalies.

Three of them this time, so they weren't dealing with a singular ship, some advanced prototype. No, this was an organized force that was putting real weight of metal into the black. They were a real threat, not like the Oathers.

He didn't know who they were besides their likely connection to the anomaly recorded at the Drasin structure, but it was clear to him that the Empire had just contacted a potentially serious threat.

We need more information, damn it to the abyss. Where did these people come from?

He opened the squadron comm. "Navarch . . ."

"Not *now!*" the navarch barked, glowering at him through the screen.

"These are the anomalies, Navarch," he said softly. "I am sure."

She rolled her eyes. "And you believe I haven't worked that out for myself? The only other possibility is that someone sabotaged my squadron back in Imperial space, Captain. Not an impossibility, perhaps. I have made enemies in the houses, but the timing reeks."

Aymes tipped his head slightly, acknowledging that much to be true.

Sabotaging an Imperial squadron wasn't mere military treason but was considered high treason against the crown. Nonetheless, the act had occurred in the past. Offhand, he couldn't recall anything as

WARRIOR KING • 285

simple as atomics being used, but there was always a first time, he supposed.

The timing issue, however, could not be easily surmounted.

"Saboteurs may have set their devices to detonate upon being scanned by FTL systems," he offered as a possibility.

Her face darkened. "If so, I'll personally end their lives. For now, however, we are committed to this engagement. Stand your station, Captain."

"As you command, Navarch."

CHAPTER 23

AEV *Hood*

▶ Ian Shepherd stretched as much as his restraints would allow as he watched the telemetry feeds they were receiving from the *Odysseus*. The implications were disturbing, to say the least, and he was working to figure out how best to use his *Hood* given the new information.

"Adjust our course," he ordered. "Increase thrusters to full military power, and bring us to bearing One Thirty-Eight Mark Nine, negative to the system plane."

"One Three Eight Mark Nine. Negative, aye sir."

His first officer looked over at him. "That's going to bring us close, Captain."

"I know, but pounding them with t-cannons now seems pointless," Ian admitted. "We don't have near the magazine capacity of a Heroic, and they barely scratched the enemy."

"Yes sir. What's the plan?"

Ian looked over the scans and telemetry. "Let's get a passing engagement, get in close, and hammer them with torpedoes instead. See how they like a face full of antimatter."

▶▶▶

▶ The *Hood* was maneuvering primarily on thrusters and counter-mass, which meant that it couldn't reach the same acceleration potential as its larger brethren, but that didn't make the smaller ship slow by any means. With CM to full power, and burning reaction mass at military levels, the Rogue Class destroyer shifted course from the planned flanking maneuver and put itself on an interception tangent.

Ian's reasoning was simple enough: his pulse torpedoes didn't have *near* the overtake needed to intercept the enemy from a flank shot, to say nothing of trying to get them from the rear. When your target could accelerate at speeds that made *light* look over its shoulder, conventional weapons had certain limitations that had to be considered.

He laughed slightly, drawing looks from his crew, but he didn't bother to explain. He didn't think it was the time to reveal to them just how ridiculous it seemed to him to consider *antimatter*, of all things, to be a conventional weapon.

"We are on interception vector, as ordered, Captain."

"Get me a firing solution, Weps," he said. "Passive lock only."

"Aye Skipper, passive lock only."

Ian leaned over to his first officer. "Break the news to the magazines. I want the munitions out of containment and ready to fire."

"Aye sir," the young officer confirmed, not looking the least bit happy about it.

Not that Ian blamed him. Anything to do with antimatter was *not* something to be happy about. That stuff was proof that hell existed and could be brought into the universe by humans in all their foolhardy hubris.

IBC Shion Thon, Flagship, Third Reconnaissance Squadron

▶ "Contact in ten."

Misrem waved the announcement off. She could read the numbers as well as anyone and better than most. The navarch already had the targets divided up and assigned, planning to hit all three ships at once with multiple beams. The scanners indicated that the armor on these contacts was similar, if not the same, as the shifting armor on the previous target they'd eliminated.

Given Aymes' earlier encounter, she was confident that she understood the nature and inherent weakness Imperial technology simply could *not* overcome. Lasers were, individually, very specific by their nature. If you could scan a laser quickly enough, and adjust your armor's reflection quotient to match, then defeating any given laser was simplicity itself.

She was honestly surprised that the Empire didn't have this technology in their archives. The concept was obvious, and she was certainly looking at evidence that proved it was far from physically impossible.

However, the weakness was significant once you recognized it. Multiple lasers with different specific frequencies would ensure that all but one beam would have the intended effect. That would force the enemy to use much less effective general armor settings. Good armor then, certainly, but not the impenetrable sort it held the potential to be.

But no matter how this one was cut, they were going to be taking a massive amount of data scans back to the Empire. That alone might be worth the cost of mounting this particular expedition, she supposed. Might.

They had work to do.

"Establish targets," she ordered. "Lead them with bracketing estimates, and fire when ready."

"Yes, Navarch. Firing."

▶▶▶

▶ The remaining fully functional vessels of Third Recon fired as one, still several light-minutes out from their targets. They had slight odds of striking their targets, of course, but lasers would hold lethal power easily enough at that range, and a lucky hit was still a hit.

Eleven groups of beams sliced space, moving at a pedestrian three hundred million meters per second, barely outpacing the ships that fired them by some measures. The ships didn't even slow their fire as they maintained the beams and swept them across space in a pattern intended to catch their targets no matter their maneuvers.

▶▶▶

AEV *Hood*

▶ "Lasers detected! Initiating evasive action!"

Ian's stomach flipped a little as the *Hood* lifted its nose and climbed relative to the system plane, letting a terrifyingly powerful beam sweep under its position.

Detecting a laser was normally difficult in the extreme, but with the power put out by the bandit contacts, a blind man could have done it.

As the beam passed through particulates in space, it transferred a small degree of energy, normally vaporizing whatever it contacted. The light from that event would then shine out in all directions, giving scanners like those on the *Hood* a data point. Even two such data points, since a laser really couldn't change course, were enough for the computers on the *Hood* to extrapolate the beam and then use augmented reality displays to draw it in for the crew to see.

The image looked very movielike to Ian as the beam swept across space like a giant sword lancing out of the black and vanishing back into it. All the scene needed was the requisite *pew pew pew* noises to complete the effect.

"Was that aimed at us?" he asked tersely, not looking up from the feed sent directly to his station.

"I don't think so, Captain," Weps said from the weapons and tactics station. "Judging from the beam's angle, and other beams we're scanning, that's heading for the Heroics, sir."

Great.

On the plus side, they'd only almost been killed by *accident*, which would have sucked royally on his epitaph. On the negative side, they now knew that there were multiterawatts of laser energy heading right for the task force. Even if the *Hood* were to break silence and signal a warning, the lasers would arrive *well* ahead of such a message.

"Stay on target," Ian murmured to himself.

"Pardon, Captain?" his first officer asked.

"Nothing," he shook his head. "Proceed as planned. How long to firing range?"

"Thirty seconds, Captain."

"Good. Signal the torpedo controls," he said. "I want them to fire as we bear. Don't wait for orders. Helm!"

"Sir!"

"As soon as we've purged our tubes, go to full thrust and get us out from in front of these maniacs," Ian said before continuing to speak in a lower voice. "Firing full beams from this far out . . . crazy sons of . . ."

▶▶▶

IBC *Shion Thon*, Flagship, Third Reconnaissance Squadron

▶ Waiting was the worst part of combat.

She'd despised it as a junior officer and she despised it as a navarch, but it was the quintessential defining factor of fighting in the void. Each side made moves based not on what their opponent had done but rather on what they *believed* their opponent had done. Since finding out if you were right or not often took significant amounts of time, you spent those moments plotting rather than reacting.

The beams they were even then firing wouldn't react with the targets for a few more moments, and once they did, Misrem knew some time would pass before results were transmitted back. That delay was closing fast, however, and in short order the waiting would give way to the second-worst thing about combat.

The dying.

That mad scramble when each instantaneous slice of time turned into an eternity, and yet, somehow, with all those terrifying eternities strung together, there still wouldn't be enough time to go around.

Misrem laughed.

A good fight made her so philosophical.

"Navarch, we're scanning something . . . odd," the scanner tech said.

That was not what she wanted to hear right before a fight with an already decidedly odd enemy.

"Define 'odd.'"

"I am not sure," he admitted. "Perhaps nothing, but there is something occasionally eclipsing the starfield."

"Where?"

"I don't know. We cannot get a parallax vector . . . It may be a very small object, quite close, or a very large one outside the system . . . I think it is close, however."

Misrem strode over. "Show me. And why do you think it's close?"

"It is blocking different stars too quickly," he said. "If it is very far, it must be moving *very* fast."

She watched the scanners as a star blinked out, then another, and the first came back as this . . . *shadow* and moved across the field.

"There's something out there. Very well," she said. "Go to active scans and find it."

"As you command. Active scans engaging."

▶ ▶ ▶

AEV *Hood*

▶ The alarms from the sudden scanner hit would have startled Ian right out of his seat if he hadn't been solidly strapped into place.

"We've been spotted!"

"Flush the tubes!" he ordered. "Evasive action! Warp space, all flank!"

"Torpedoes away!" Weps called.

"Drive warp coming up; thirty seconds to full warp!"

"All thrusters! Get us moving *now*!" Ian snapped as the *Hood* started coming to life around him, systems all lighting up as they were brought from low power settings to full combat levels. "Lasers and HVMs *free*! Fire as we bear, all weapons!"

"Aye aye, Skipper," Weps called. "All systems live, targeting solution locked. HVMs away!"

The *Hood* shuddered as the high-velocity missile banks were flushed, and Ian could more feel than hear the whine-click of laser capacitors discharging furiously.

The forces at his command didn't have the power needed to sweep space wildly the way the enemy ships did, but they could put some serious wattage downrange. If they could just get a good bounce off the enemy armor with their hyperspectral systems, they'd be able to make the most of what they had.

"Even armor," he said, eyes on the clock and the range. They had only seconds left now before a laser strike could reach them. "Go to white knight."

▶▶▶

IBC *Shion Thon*, Flagship, Third Reconnaissance Squadron

▶ The profile of the small ship in her sights was so far from what she'd expected that Misrem uncharacteristically hesitated from sheer surprise. That instant of indecision allowed the enemy captain to act before she did.

"They've fired on us . . . I think?" Her scanner tech didn't sound convinced.

"What do you mean, you *think*?" Misrem demanded, but before she could get an answer, another alarm went off.

This one was a proximity warning calling her attention to her squadron, where one of the ships was breaking formation. Misrem forgot about the odd weapons fire for the moment and flipped to the squadron channel. "Aymes, get back in formation!"

"Break formation!" Captain Aymes was yelling over her transmission. "Break formation!"

"Captain, I'll have you *shot* for . . ."

"Impact in three!"

Misrem twisted, eyes on the screens as the brilliant pulses of energy filled her displays.

"Navarch, they use *antimatter*!" yelled Aymes from the comm link.

She barely had time to remember the briefing on the original anomaly and how it had fought the Drasin before the incoming pulses spiraled erratically and slammed into her squadron with a fury unmatched by anything else in the universe.

Where the pulses struck, the armor they encountered didn't simply fail but actively turned into explosive material that tore huge gaping holes out of the sides of ships. Misrem's own ship bucked so hard under her that she was thrown to the deck, something that practically *never* happened to anyone. Under most circumstances, if your vessel moved enough to counter the effect of gravity stabilization, you were going to be paste on the deck—not merely lose your balance.

She struggled to her feet. "Report!"

"We're losing atmosphere across fifteen decks, Navarch! Sealing affected areas," the damage-control officer reported.

"Lock that ship in and return fire," she roared.

A glance at the display showed the vessel no longer hiding as it turned away and began forming a warp singularity. The damnable thing looked positively cocky in gleaming white, screaming to the universe its defiance.

I'll make you eat that defiance. She spat through gritted teeth as she held on to her seat against the continuing shudders of pain from her ship.

"As you command, Navarch . . ."

Beams lanced out even as another set of warning sounds filled the air.

"Weapon sign, Navarch . . . Brace! Brace! Brace!"

She grabbed for her station, but this time the impacts were barely felt as slight shudders through the deck. "What was that?"

"Physical strikes, Navarch. Hull breaches on four more decks, easily containable. We have laser strikes on ship three, Division Two . . . minor damage evident."

"Minor damage," she muttered. "Track and destroy that ship! Dispatch Division Two to finish it."

"As you command!"

This is getting messy. The enemy had brought reinforcements, and they had effective stealth.

Her eyes widened and she muttered a vile epithet. "Scanners! All ships, look for any other hidden vessels!"

▶▶▶

AEV *Odysseus*

▶ "They're pouring on the power, Captain. Looking hard!"

Eric snorted. "After the *Hood* just dropped that bomb in their faces, I'm not surprised."

That particular maneuver wasn't exactly to plan, but he didn't blame Ian for thinking outside the box. The original plan wasn't going to be

WARRIOR KING • 295

nearly as effective as they'd intended, not if singularity cores were reducing t-cannon effectiveness.

The *Odysseus* was feeding telemetry to its smaller sister ships, but other than the *Hood*, the flagship had no return feed from the Rogues, as that would potentially reveal their existence and location to any particularly savvy opponent.

"Prepare to fire," Eric ordered. "Sweep the range between the targets and the *Hood*. Try to cover their withdrawal."

"Aye Captain," Milla confirmed. "Laser telemetry updating. Firing in twenty seconds."

Eric nodded, almost tempted to hurry her along, but the telemetry update was important. They didn't have IFF locations on three Rogues out there, and while those ships *should* be clear of the beam lanes, it was better to wait a few extra seconds to give them time to maneuver than to accidentally smoke one of the squadron's own.

"Increase speed to flank," he said. "Signal the others that we're taking this fight up close."

▶▶▶

▶ The *Odysseus* surged ahead of her two fellows for an instant before they matched her speed, and then the trio plummeted faster through the void toward the bandit formation. Ahead, the light from the *Hood* caught up to them, showing the Rogue Class destroyer as it shifted to gleaming white armor and began to pull away from the fight.

The *Hood*'s reserves of pulse torpedoes were now gone, but it was clear that Captain Shepherd wasn't entirely willing to give up the fight, because its t-cannons were swiveling onto target.

Faint tachyon surges puffed and vanished as the *Hood* fired into the ether, her space warp firming up as she began to accelerate.

Beams lanced out from the Imperial squadron, cutting through the space the *Hood* had just vacated as beams from the *Odysseus* cut back across the void and burned into hull matter, ejecting tons of vaporized material into the black as the fighting stepped up to a new level.

If the big ship sometimes seemed to flinch away from the blasts of its own accord, it was put down to mere jet thrusting from the explosive reaction.

▶ ▶ ▶

IBC *Shion Thon*, Flagship, Third Reconnaissance Squadron

▶ Misrem seethed as new damage reports flooded her central command. Beams from the large battle cruisers were cutting deep into the armor of the ships under her command.

They've had this fight entirely too much in their favor to this point.

She continued to grit her teeth, eyes on the plot as the enemy cruisers entered into the optimal engagement range.

"All ships," Misrem called, "reverse thrust, all available power! Weapons free! Fire at will! Launch parasites!"

There was no sensation of movement as the ships began decelerating at maximum thrust, the gravity shift taking care of any inertia that might otherwise have splattered them across the decks. Still, Misrem was well aware that she was straining the drive systems immensely.

Lasers cut through space as her squadron opened fire with no restrictions and the combat parasites detached.

The *Shion* shuddered again as another laser burned through the armor and opened up three decks to vacuum, but she ignored it. The outer decks were nonvital areas and few, if any, crewmen were there now aside from damage-control personnel. They could burn through all that outer armor and vent thousands of tons of atmosphere to the deep void without significantly crippling her ships.

A yell went out from someone across the bridge. She didn't know who and didn't care as she spotted the cause. A beam from the squadron had reached out and sliced the enemy destroyer damn near in half, its reflective armor be damned.

"Good! Do that again!" she shouted. "And keep scanning for others!"

Beams were crossing one another as the three battle cruisers hammered toward them, the exchange of fire growing more accurate and intense with each passing instant. Enemy fire was still opening up the hulls of her ships to space, but it was no longer a one-sided exchange.

Trace reports were showing strikes on the enemy battle cruisers now, though their armor was significantly more capable than that of the smaller destroyer. Misrem was certain her squadron could open them up to vacuum sure as the void was cold.

"Make for the lead cruiser," she said harshly as another shudder shook the deck under her feet. "Let's make this personal."

▶▶▶

AEV *Odysseus*

▶ "The *Hood* is out of the fight!" Sams said. "They're cut in half and drifting, Captain. Distress calls coming in now."

"They'll have to hold on," Eric growled. "We've got problems of our own. Steph, it looks like the Imperials want to turn this into an old-fashioned furball. Oblige them."

"Aye aye, boss man! Engineering, I'm going to need fast adjustment from you on the fly. We're about to tangle with an enemy cruiser, up close and personal."

"Roger, Commander," the chief's voice came back. "We're ready. Manual controls to your station."

"Roger, Chief. I have the conn," Steph said as he brought up the augmented reality display over his primary readouts. "You ever see a ship this size do this?"

He pushed the engine power to full, swapping to reverse drives on the fly, then rolled the *Odysseus* to port as a laser swept in from starboard. The big ship responded on cue, twisting under the beam as the *Bellerophon* and *Boudicca* peeled away in opposite directions. A glancing beam reflected off the *Odysseus'* armor, burning away half a meter before Steph hit thrusters and dropped the ship more fully.

The *Odysseus* retrothrusted suddenly, surprising Steph because he didn't remember issuing the command. Almost at the same instant, he noted the beam they'd just ducked slash through the space they had been about to occupy and shrugged it off. If wouldn't be the first time he'd done something without actually thinking about it, and far from the first time he'd done something he couldn't remember.

Usually a lot of drinking is involved with the second option though, Steph thought just a little ruefully as he kept himself focused and resolved to check the command log after the fight. Anything odd had to be checked out, after all, even if it was a good thing.

Sometimes especially if it's a good thing.

"How close do you want this, boss?" Steph asked without looking away from his viewer.

"Why don't we let *them* decide, Stephanos?" Eric asked with a feral tone.

"Right you are, boss."

On their displays, they could see the lead element of the enemy formation breaking away, heading directly for them. Steph matched course, more or less, while still evading the incoming laser fire as best he could.

They could really only see the beams after they'd passed, but since the enemy ships were sweeping lasers across the battlefield rather than firing in pulses, the augmented reality systems could detect and overlay beam vectors on heads-up displays with little trouble. The *Odysseus* twisted and turned in space, reacting more like a small fighter than any multigigaton warship had any right to. The maneuvering systems of the big ship were entirely gravity based, so Steph had no trouble making the *Odysseus* dance.

"Captain," Sams interjected, gripping his console with white knuckles, "we're on an interception course."

"I know that, Ensign."

"No Captain, we're—Captain, we're going to *collide* with them!"

Eric grinned. "Only if they've got more balls than I give them credit for."

"I ain't flinching—that's for damn sure," Steph said from his enclosed station.

Stricken, vaguely sick looks were exchanged around the command deck, but only Miram had the courage—or temerity—to say anything.

"I feel this is probably why you shouldn't give helm control of a warship to a *fighter* pilot," she muttered under her breath, but didn't quite manage to pitch her voice low enough to keep it from traveling.

The laughter started behind him. Eric didn't know who giggled first, but it proved infectious as high-tension laughter often did. Soon around two-thirds of the bridge crew were laughing, with Steph grinning like a loon as he continued on his current course.

Eric waited for the laughter to die down before he added his two cents.

"They probably shouldn't have put one in the captain's chair either, then."

He really hoped that the crew could see through their tears as he casually opened a screen on his multifunction display, dipped into the communications control, and issued an override order as he opened a hailing line to the enemy.

I wonder what they'll think of this?

▶▶▶

IBC *Shion Thon*, Flagship, Third Reconnaissance Squadron

▶ Misrem blinked as she eyed the course telemetry that was playing out across the feeds, not quite believing what she was seeing.

"I believe, Navarch," her second spoke softly, "that they have accepted your challenge."

"These people are *not* Oathers," Misrem said, shaking her head firmly. "Where did they *come* from?"

"Respectfully, My Lady," her second said, "at this moment, let us be more concerned with where they are *going*."

He had a point. The collision course was a clear challenge, but it was also a very large threat. If the two ships passed too closely, such proximity might destabilize their drives, which would leave both of them out of the fight—at best. At worst . . . she couldn't think of many worse ways to die than being swallowed eternally into a singularity drive as gravity slowly tore you apart.

"Course change, My Lady?"

"Hold course," she ordered, leaning in.

The fighting around them faded into the background for Misrem as she glared at the screens, watching the lead enemy cruiser head straight for them. The vessel was decelerating easily as powerfully as her own ships were, which would prolong the engagement, but if her calculations were correct, they still wouldn't be able to come to a stop relative to one another.

Now, she was no longer sure she *wanted* to.

"As you command, My Lady." The helm officer's voice was fearful, but he didn't disobey.

▶▶▶

AEV *Bellerophon*

▶ Captain Roberts refrained from commenting on the insane maneuvers of his former captain, instead choosing to focus on the enemy element that was still closing on the now-crippled and drifting *Hood*.

"Cut them down," he ordered.

The *Bell*'s lasers lanced out, burning into the lead ship in the element. The Heroic Class cruiser held steady on target long enough to get a return for hyperspectral analysis to start computing the optimum frequency with which to strike. The *Bell*'s computers soon adjusted the laser frequency and tripled beam strength.

"We're taking hits along our flanks!"

"Hold to target!" cried Roberts. "Cut them in half!"

The *Bellerophon* bore down through the center of the enemy formation, lasers adapted and fully powered. The beams vaporized armor and superstructure with ease, continuing on through the inner decks as the *Bell* shrugged off fire from all sides.

When the beam cored through to the enemy ship's singularity drive, it struck one of the magnetic stabilizers and that was the end.

The vessel shuddered at first, acceleration dying while it hurtled along its previous course. Then suddenly the hull collapsed in on itself.

"Hard to port! Their core just destabilized!" shouted Roberts instantly. He wasn't his former commander. He had no intention of playing chicken with a black hole.

The *Bell* pivoted in space, pulling hard to port as ordered while the enemy ship continued on its previous course as it was slowly eaten by its own core.

A triple blast of lasers bore through the *Bell*'s hull in passing, serving notice that the fight wasn't over by a long shot.

"Damage control to decks three, four, and five!" Roberts' first officer, Sarah O'Neill, called out over the noise on the bridge. "Sir, we've got incoming, starboard side."

"I see them. Evasion pattern Delta Niner!"

The *Bellerophon* and enemy vessels swerved around the drifting wreck of the *Hood*, exchanging fire as air and crew streamed from the massive rents in the hull.

For now, Roberts didn't wish to know the butcher's bill on this fight, let alone what it would be when they were done.

▶▶▶

IBC *Shion Thon*, Flagship, Third Reconnaissance Squadron

▶ "Navarch . . . we're receiving communication from the enemy ship."

"Now?" Misrem asked, somewhat bemused. Talking was normally done before or after the fight, not during. "Put it through."

"As you command."

There was nothing for a moment, then a sound she didn't recognize at first. It took her longer than she would later admit to before she did, in fact, recognize the sound. She felt a chill run down her spine as clearly insane laughter echoed in her ears.

"They're out of their minds," she said, wonder actually entering her voice. "Are we sure that's coming from the ship we're targeting?"

"Confirmed, My Lady," her communications officer said, his tone sickly. "They're the source."

She shook her head. "That's insane . . . *They're* insane."

"My Lady," her second broke in, "if they're insane . . . they won't change course."

Misrem's eyes fell to the numbers, showing that they were almost at the point of no return, where they no longer would have the impulse to pull away on their own. She swallowed, hating what she was about to do, but finally slashed the air with her hand.

"Evasive action! Turn aside!"

▶▶▶

AEV *Odysseus*

▶ "You lose." Steph grinned as the big ship turned aside, showing her flank.

He turned his own controls and leaned the *Odysseus* into the evading ship's course, not enough to put the vessels back on a collision course but hopefully close enough to execute the next move.

"Chief, it's all you," he said as he flew, flinching as the *Odysseus* took a raking blast he chose not to evade in order to get position on the target.

"Roger, Commander. Hold on tight, we're matching their resonance . . ."

The drives of the *Odysseus* flared, surging the vessel beyond flank speed for a moment, actually causing the space warp to reach out and interfere with the passing starship. Eric looked around, alarmed as the power on his secure command deck flickered and dimmed.

"What the hell—?"

An explosion tore through the enemy ship, and her acceleration suddenly died.

"We blew her drive emitters, Cap," Steph said. "Chief, we good?"

"Just don't ask me to do that again," the chief's voice came back, "but yeah, we're good."

"Stephan!" Milla called out. "Watch for the parasites! There are too many!"

Steph redirected his focus beyond his target, and his eyes widened as he realized just how many of the parasite ships had been launched by the enemy task group. "Oh, *crap*!"

Dozens of them were swarming on course to intercept the *Odysseus*, and still more were heading for the *Boudicca* and the *Bell*, lasers glaring hotly from each and every frigate.

A web of laser trace beams tightened around the *Odysseus*, forcing Steph to wrench the big ship in ways he was sure no one had planned for during the design phase. Even so, there was no way he could avoid them all, and alarms began to sound as patches of armor were vaporized where the beams came into contact.

"Hold on," Steph mumbled, more for his benefit than anyone else's.

He put the *Odysseus* into a flat spin, using the gravity wells generated by the ship's drives to deflect and attenuate some of the beams as he searched for a way out.

Eric linked into the command channel behind Steph and accessed the squadron battle network. "Rogues . . . engage parasites at will."

▶▶▶

AEV *Song-Jiang*

▶ "Target the parasites and go to autofire on t-cannons," Captain Su Lynn Jing ordered from her position as she quickly confirmed the targeting solutions before her ship broke from the dark.

The *Song-Jiang's* cannons pivoted to targets, and the silent puffs of subatomic particles erupted from the waveguides, sending their packages onward.

Su Lynn caught sight of the *Aladdin* and the *Kid* as the other two ships entered the fray, their own cannons tearing into the parasites with ease. The transition cannons might not have been as effective as desired against the larger vessels with their singularity cores, but the parasites had no such power source.

Without gravity cores to twist and disrupt the transition, the atomic warheads reintegrated perfectly and blew instants later, turning one parasite ship after another into expanding debris and plasma.

"Fire the magazines dry," she said. "If there's anything left when we finish the parasites, retarget to the cruisers. Maybe we'll get lucky."

"Aye aye, ma'am."

Professional eyes swept the battle. Su Lynn forced down the revulsion she felt as she surveyed the damage. Death was reigning on this field, as it did on every other one she had seen in her career, but the scale here was horrifying. Even forgetting the enemy dead, the *Song-Jiang*'s computers were reporting dozens, if not hundreds, of bodies drifting around the *Hood* and the Heroics.

Men and women had been pulled into the void through hull breaches. Some of them had their suits intact with transponders that still showed life signs. But most either hadn't had on protective gear or saw their gear's life-saving properties destroyed in the event that blew them out into space.

The *Odysseus* had taken frightful levels of damage, but was still fighting, as had the *Bellerophon*. It was only then that she noticed that the *Boudicca* had gotten mixed up with a small element of enemy cruisers and didn't seem to be faring too well.

"Commander," she said, "look to the *Boudicca*."

"Damn," her first officer, Commander Kiran Hiro, swore. "They're going to need some help."

"New priority target," Su Lynn announced.

"New target, aye!"

"Let's try to give the *Boudicca* some cover," she said to Kiran. "I think we have enough left in our magazines for that."

"Aye aye, ma'am. We have firing solutions at the ready, but they're not going to be as clean as taking on parasites."

"Clean or not, we're going in."

▶▶▶

AEV *Odysseus*

▶ Steph turned and jerked the *Odysseus* through the debris field left by the transition-cannon assault from the Rogues while Milla burned anything too fast to dodge and too large to ignore.

Eric tried to focus on the battle as a whole, noting that while the weight of metal turned scrap was certainly on their side of the fight, they were still outmassed and outnumbered by the Imperial ships. The momentum of battle was turning against them.

We need to end this, and end it now, or we're going to lose this fight.

Damage reports were pouring in. The *Odysseus* had been hit by so many lasers that he honestly figured that if he were still commanding the *Odyssey*, they'd have been turned to plasma a dozen times over. Of course, if he were commanding the *Odyssey*, he'd have been able to sneak up on the enemy and likely get away clean.

"Lieutenant Chans," he said, "bring our transition cannons back into the game, fire the magazines dry. I'll take a lucky hit right about now."

"Aye Capitaine," Milla murmured, hastily calling up firing solutions for the ships around them. "Firing t-cannons and lasers."

Eric turned to Miram. "Have the *Kid* try to clear out the edges of the fight with torpedoes. Just do *not* let them fire anywhere near us or the other Heroics."

"Understood, Capitaine." Miram smirked at him as he glanced sharply at her pronunciation of his title.

"Just do it," he growled.

There were downsides to having a first officer with a newly discovered sense of humor, he decided.

CHAPTER 24

▲

AEV *Boudicca*

▸ Cardsharp grunted through gritted teeth as she whipped her ship through the raking enemy fire, trying to simultaneously avoid as much of it as possible while keeping the *Boudicca*'s main guns lined up for return fire. The good news was that they were pretty much surrounded, so giving her gunner decent shots at the enemy was easy, but the flip side was that evading enemy beams became close to impossible.

Warning alarms had long since been filtered out of her conscious thoughts, along with everything else. She was focused so deeply on what she was doing that the captain had been alerted five times that her brain waves appeared oddly low.

After the second alert, he stopped bothering her about it.

"Point defense stations," he called somewhere deep in the background. The words weren't for her, so she didn't bother listening to what else he had to say. But part of her noted that the point defense stations redirected their fire to one of the ships on their port side and a hole had opened up in the enemy formation.

Cardsharp didn't think about it. She hit thrusters and spun the *Boudicca* on its axis before throwing all military power to the drive, accelerating the ship through the opening. Three of the smaller parasites closed in on the *Boudicca*'s port flank, which had lost half of its laser emitters some time earlier.

You shouldn't harass a fine lady like the Bo, Cardsharp thought savagely as she again hit the thrusters and put the ship into a flat spin that turned into a spiral, slamming the rear gravity bulge of the *Boudicca* into the closest of the three ships.

The bulge acted like a moving hill slamming into a car that had its transmission in neutral. The parasite ship slid off uncontrollably, rammed into one of its fellows, then ricocheted off in another direction as the *Bo* continued through the spin and slipped the rest of the way out through the hole, bringing her main guns to point back the way she'd come.

Cardsharp threw the drive into reverse then, backing the *Boudicca* out of the furball as its lasers savaged anything and everything that followed.

Dimly, she noted some of the enemy ships blowing up for no reason she could spot. While she would probably be extremely curious about that later, for the moment Cardsharp was just pleased to be free from the dog pile.

▶▶▶

▶ Captain Alexander Dogavich of the AEV *Boudicca* hid a grimace as his chief helmsman, or woman as the case was, used the ship's drives as a weapon with all the brute force and subtlety of some of the less reputable members of his old nation's Spetsnaz.

He couldn't decide if he was going to put her up for a commendation, given the sheer miraculous nature of some of the maneuvers she was executing, or have her charged with blatant recklessness. All he knew was that he wasn't going to distract her with either option until the fighting was done, and as long as she still paid attention to his orders, the computers could go burn for all he cared.

"Captain, the *Song-Jiang* has engaged with transition cannons," his communications officer said. "We're being advised to stay clear of several fire lanes. Torpedoes inbound!"

"Send those to Lieutenant Commander Samuels!" he said, paling. "Mark no-fly zones on her MFD!"

"Roger that!"

Alexander checked the pilot's multifunction display on his own repeater display as the new data appeared and highlighted several areas that the *Boudicca* would most *certainly* want to avoid in the coming moments. Luckily, they were all extremely thick with enemy activity, naturally, and he was fairly certain that Samuels wasn't going to be tempted to get into another close quarters fight like that one anytime soon.

"Damage report," he asked, leaning over to his first officer.

"We're streaming atmosphere from practically every deck," the commander said in clipped tones. "Without the Priminae generators, we'd have been dead a dozen times over by now."

"I can see that," Alexander replied. "Unfortunately, it appears clear that the enemy also has similar technology, and they still have us outnumbered. This is turning into a good old-fashioned Russian boxing match. It will come down to who bleeds out first, and while we may be cutting deeper, they're cutting more. Try to get as many of those leaks plugged as possible. We need the power for lasers right now more than we need air."

"We've got teams working on it, sir. We need time without being shot at to get it done though."

"I will forward your request to the enemy, Commander."

▶ ▶ ▶

IBC *Piar Cohn*

▶ Aymes had almost no words for the sheer level of fighting that had erupted around him and his ship. The *Cohn* hadn't escaped the carnage unscathed either. Though bleeding atmosphere from a dozen deep burns in its hull, the ship had managed to evade the initial barrage of charged antimatter. That maneuver had put the *Cohn* on the edge of the fighting.

He was now quite certain these were the same species who had been encountered at the Drasin megastructure. The smaller frigates made that clear. They were much closer in configuration and capabilities to the ship that had been scanned there.

That still demanded the answer of where, exactly, they had come from. They were certainly not Oathers either in technical skill or fighting prowess. He'd have been tempted to compare them to Imperials in their fighting, but Imperial crews weren't remotely as insane as these people.

Most Imperial crews.

Aymes still couldn't believe that the navarch had ordered her ships into a toe-to-toe match with the enemy, though he understood the tactic and it was starting to work in her favor. The numbers Third Recon brought to the fight would certainly have won the day against the three battle cruisers they'd originally tracked, and he rather believed that even the four destroyers and their antimatter weapons would not be quite enough to turn the tides, but the cost . . . by the endless abyss, the cost!

"Track the navarch's ship," he ordered his scanner tech. "Are they intact?"

"Streaming air, Captain, but no signs of breaking up. No drive power, however."

Aymes grimaced. The *last* thing he wanted to do was bring his ship *anywhere* near a stricken ship that might have an unstable core, but he wasn't certain he had much choice. "Give me a least-time intercept course."

"As you order, Captain."

If his subordinate's tone was a little shaky, Aymes was inclined to ignore it. He wasn't entirely confident his own was all that steady either.

▶▶▶

AEV *Odysseus*

▶ It was hard to tell who was winning, Eric decided as he looked across the black field of battle and stared at the long list of transponders calling for help in the darkness. The enemy was tenacious, doggedly holding to the fight with courage enough for anyone, but he was in no particular mood to be impressed.

He was still angry. He could feel the emotions deep down in his gut, and Eric was now certain that he blamed the Empire. That anger would have worried him—would worry him later, he had little doubt—but for now he was inclined to let it bubble under the surface, where it was effectively keeping him from becoming sick at the destruction surrounding him.

Pulse torpedoes had effectively cleaned up whatever parasite ships the barrage of transition-cannon fire had missed and torn a few more of the cruisers to gutted hulks in the process. That lifted some of the weight off the *Odysseus* and the *Bell*, but they were still making their way through the backside of one of the heaviest bits of fighting he'd ever seen.

Even the Drasin hadn't been like this, not even when they'd come in by the hundreds at the tail end of the invasion.

"We're breaking through, Captain," Miram told him.

Eric nodded.

The two forces had flung themselves at one another at relativistic speeds. Even decelerating massively just before contact hadn't slowed them nearly enough to come to a stop relative to one another. The passing engagement was about to be over, and there would be a brief time to calculate their next option before they were again committed.

"I need damage reports for every ship we've still got," he said. "Continue deceleration at maximum rates, and bring our guns around to maintain fire."

"Aye Captain."

▶▶▶

▶ The field of ships cleared as the Alliance task force broke through the fighting, now plunging through the scattered debris of death and destruction they had wrought.

The *Odysseus*, *Bellerophon*, and *Boudicca* turned on command, accelerating toward the enemy ships, but it shortly became clear that not all of the enemy were intent on doing the same. Some did, while others continued to accelerate away. Most seemed uncertain.

Amid the confusion, the *Odysseus'* scanners tracked one ship maneuvering in close to one of the disabled vessels and apparently docking.

▶▶▶

IBC *Piar Cohn*

▶ "Connections secured, Captain."

"Good," Aymes said. "Get as many people over to the *Cohn* as possible, and *find* the navarch. Alive or dead, I want her on this ship!"

He didn't listen for a confirmation, instead intently watching the mess unfolding around him. The enemy were still organized—that was clear by their uniform maneuvering despite damage—but the Imperial forces appeared uncertain about what to do. When the navarch's ship lost contact, they'd been cut off from the command structure.

This wasn't normally a problem, but in the chaos of battle it seemed that at least two other key members of the squadron's command had been killed. In the midst of the fighting, everyone knew their jobs well enough, so the absence in command wasn't felt. But now that they were out of the immediate threat, the breakdown that resulted would be fatal if Aymes didn't find someone who could command enough respect, or fear, to get everyone pointing in the same direction.

They'd left more men and material strewn across several light-seconds of space than he'd have ever believed possible, and he was the captain who'd given warnings about just how dangerous this new culture really was. They were the anomaly culture, there was no question about that, and that meant that they had survived the Drasin's berserker attack.

So they were tough, smart, and most likely extremely angry.

Aymes didn't know for certain if the anomalies knew the Empire had held the Drasin's leash, but they had to at least have *some* idea of it. They must have acquired scans from the megastructure the same as he had, and there was no hiding Imperial design.

This is going to be a costly expansion, he thought with deadly certainty.

No one had calculated that there would be a fighting culture in the path of the Empire's movement into Oather territory, and now there was no going back. The Empire was going to pay for every system in this galactic arm in blood and metal.

He was very glad he wouldn't be in the place of those analysts once the realities of Imperial expansion became as clear to everyone else as they were to him.

For now, however, he just hoped to get his ship and the rest of the squadron out of this situation as intact as possible.

For that he desperately needed the navarch, or at least her second.

▶ ▶ ▶

IBC *Shion Thon,* Flagship, Third Reconnaissance Squadron

▶ Rescue teams braved evacuated compartments in the navarch's ship, throwing hot patches over what holes they could find just so they could

push people through and to the *Cohn* as quickly as possible. No one
knew what had happened to cripple the ship, but everyone was terrified
that it was something that would destabilize the core.
The command deck was buried deep in the superstructure of the
ship, and that was their primary goal as they worked inward. Anyone
rescued along the way was strictly a bonus, though there were other
teams spreading out to clear as much of the ship as they could.

push people through and to the *Cohn* as quickly as possible. No one knew what had happened to cripple the ship, but everyone was terrified that it was something that would destabilize the core.

The command deck was buried deep in the superstructure of the ship, and that was their primary goal as they worked inward. Anyone rescued along the way was strictly a bonus, though there were other teams spreading out to clear as much of the ship as they could.

Portable lights were necessary. Whatever had taken the ship out of play had effectively cut the power more cleanly than most had known possible without collapsing the core itself. By the time rescuers reached the command deck, smoke and powerful flood lamps turned every step into a nightmarish ordeal.

They forced the portal to the command deck open. Thankfully, the security doors hadn't been closed or entry would have been impossible in the time they had. The rescue team broke into the large open area that served as the nerve center of the squadron.

"Navarch!" called the team leader.

Without a response, the team leader waved everyone in. "Check for anyone living, give them air, and get them out of here. I've got the navarch's station."

He found her slumped over her console, fingers bloody, the displays where she'd been working smeared. A check found her alive, which was a relief, and he slapped an oxygen mask over her face.

"Navarch! You must awake!" He grimaced, then smacked her sharply, living out the fantasy of more than a few of his fellow lower-deck comrades. "She's coming out of it, but I need a healer here!"

The closest healer called out and stumbled his way through the smoke and darkness, immediately getting to work.

"I don't recommend it, but I can wake her with a stimulant," he said finally.

"Do it," the team leader said. "We need her awake. Captain's orders."

"Right. Very well. I'll stay with her then, in case," the healer said as he administered the dose.

The navarch's eyes opened wide as she gasped in a deep breath through the mask, limbs flailing as the stimulant hit her nervous system. The men held her down until they felt her calm a bit, then the team leader waved them off and helped her to her feet.

"Navarch, you must evacuate the vessel," he said. "The healer will see you back to the *Piar Cohn*."

She nodded, trying to speak, but nothing came out.

"Your voice will return shortly," the healer said. "Come with me."

The team lead watched them go and keyed his comm. "Navarch coming out. Rescue One will clear the command deck."

▶▶▶

IBC *Piar Cohn*

▶ Aymes slumped in relief when he heard that they'd found the navarch alive.

We might be able to pull this one out, one way or another, after all.

"Get the navarch to the command deck as fast as you can," he ordered one of his runners. "I want her here immediately."

"Yes Captain!"

The *Piar Cohn* and the majority of the squadron were effectively on a ballistic course, grouped around the stricken flagship. Those who'd reversed their course and were decelerating toward the enemy were still within the firing range of said enemy. Without the available support of the rest of the Third Recon, things were *not* going well for them.

Those who'd broken and run . . . They'd be dealt with later.

Once she was on board, the bewildered navarch was quickly rushed through the *Piar Cohn* and half carried onto the command deck.

"Captain Aymes?"

316 • EVAN CURRIE

"Navarch," Aymes said roughly, "good to see you in person. The situation needs your command."

She shook her head, presumably trying to clear it. "What is the situation?"

"We've broken through the passing engagement and, for now, are outside the enemy range of fire."

That wasn't strictly true, of course. They were on a ballistic course, and that made them a sitting duck for long-range beams and other weapons. But for the moment the enemy had other things to occupy their time.

"Show me," she croaked, eyes turning to the tactical display.

He waved it back, showing the overall situation. "The squadron lost other commanders in the engagement and lost some cohesion, My Lady. Few, if any, ships are undamaged . . . but we can say much the same for the enemy as far as that goes. They still have their three battle cruisers, however badly we struck at them, so I would not care to estimate how powerful they remain."

"All that, and we only destroyed one small ship?" Misrem asked angrily.

"The other three small vessels remained at a distance and fired from stealth positions," he said, "and the battle cruisers have similar toughness to our own ships, but with significantly better armor and very efficient lasers. We lost four ships outright. Three others were effectively crippled, including your own. Judging by our own ships, I believe if we re-engage, we can eliminate the cruisers. However, the smaller ships have gone back to stealth, and they utilize antimatter, My Lady."

She nodded weakly.

Antimatter weapons were something that was effectively impossible to defend against conventionally. Having them fired from very nearly invisible enemy ships was a nightmare she didn't care to think too hard about.

It chafed, however, to call a retreat.

Yet they'd certainly accomplished the first brief of their assigned task. There was no *way* these were Oather vessels, and thus they had confirmed that the Oathers had allies—ones who were ready, willing, and even *eager* to fight.

"Our mission is accomplished," she said finally. "We've confirmed your report, Captain. This is no longer a task for Third Recon; it is for the fleet."

"I agree, My Lady."

She turned to the console. "Give me squadron-wide communications."

▶▶▶

AEV *Odysseus*

▶ "They're leaving, Captain!" Sams called as the enemy ships began to redshift on the screens.

Eric nodded slowly, almost surprised. Given the ferocity of the engagement, he'd been expecting the fight to run a lot longer. He was fairly certain that the enemy ships could have turned the tide. There were limits to how much even a Heroic could take, but the Imperials had apparently lost their taste for the battle.

Why doesn't that make me feel good?

As long as they were withdrawing, he wasn't in the mood to chase them. Well, honestly, he was, but he didn't have the Delta-V to catch up, and he knew it.

"Continue engagement with the stragglers, unless they kill their drives. I want them burned out of my sky," he ordered, "but I want combat rescue in the black in two minutes."

"Aye Skipper," Miram said. "Combat rescue is launching now."

He slumped a little, oblivious now to the insanity running around him.

Why withdraw? They're not cowards, not most of them at least. This fight could have been turned around. They had to know that.

He figured from the way the fight deteriorated that they'd gotten lucky and taken out a fair chunk of the command structure. After the engagement had passed, the enemy obviously didn't know what to do.

That was the sort of thing he expected to see from a second-rate military, not from an advanced culture. Yet that sort of rigid command structure did fit the mold of an empire.

Eric was certain this wouldn't be the last time the Alliance had the opportunity to test the Empire's prowess and flexibility in battle.

▶ ▶ ▶

▶ Amid the debris and horror of the battle, shuttles launched rapidly from the *Odysseus*, *Bellerophon*, and *Boudicca* as well as the three remaining Rogues.

The battle had taken mere minutes, a passing engagement that could easily have been counted in seconds, in fact. But the cleanup would take *days* to complete.

In the deep black, death was never far away.

CHAPTER 25

Priminae System Por-Que

▶ Admirals Gracen and Tanner stood at the viewport as their fast courier ship slowed its descent into the Por-Que system, each observing the wreckage strewn across a light-hour of space and more. Nearly intact ships still drifted in space nearby, and the hulk of a Terran Rogue Class ship was first among them.

"Once again, I find myself in your debt," Tanner said tiredly.

"Once again, I find myself wondering if I should commend Weston or kick his arse."

Tanner shot her an odd look, but she assumed the humor had parsed well enough, because he didn't have any questions.

"I hope you'll pardon me for siding with the commendation idea?" he asked, surprisingly mildly.

That tone caused her to do a slight double take and laugh quietly. "I don't think I'll blame you for that, Admiral." Gracen sighed deeply. "We need more intelligence on these people, these Imperials."

"On that we agree wholeheartedly," he said.

Ahead of them, the three Heroics were on station as repair ships from Por-Que and Ranquil swarmed around them. She could see that they were still running flight operations amid all the work and assumed that it was probably for research and recovery of alien tech.

The squadron should have found all the survivors by now and any of the bodies they were going to find.

The lost crew would likely reach into the thousands once the Priminae deaths from the *Heral'c* were added in, though most of those who reached lifeboats had been rescued. The losses in battle had been high, but could have been far worse.

"I've seen the report you gave to Weston," she said, "about the old legends. He seems to think that they're involved, but I need to know your thoughts."

Tanner looked troubled—not that she blamed him—as he considered her words.

"I will be honest, Admiral. I do not know. Legends are . . . legends," he said. "They are not supposed to show up one day and announce themselves with lasers and monsters."

"No argument there."

"However, whether these be legends or not, they have announced themselves with lasers and monsters, and my people are at a loss for how to handle that," he admitted. "We have been at peace for . . . ever."

"Not forever, Admiral," she said. "No one designs the ships you had in your archives without having an enemy to goad them on. You may not remember it, but you were fighters once. All survivors are."

"Perhaps, but are we that now? Can we be so again?" Tanner asked helplessly. "I do not know."

"Imitate the action of the tiger, Admiral," she told him. "Summon up the blood. It will remember."

AEV *Odysseus*

▶ Eric watched as the alien lander barreled into the flight deck faster than he would have preferred, but he knew that the Priminae trusted automated systems more than he did. The craft slowed to a halt just meters away from him. He stiffened to attention as the Marines behind him followed suit.

The short and slim Rael Tanner stepped off first, followed by Amanda Gracen, both in their respective uniforms.

"Admirals on deck!"

Eric and the row of Marines all saluted in unison as the admirals surveyed them.

"As you were." Gracen spoke softly but with enough volume to carry as she walked toward Eric.

"Commodore," she continued as he relaxed marginally, "you can't seem to help but step in it, can you?"

"In my defense, Admiral, I believe that my mission brief this time actually specified that I should 'step in it,'" he said.

"So it did. Well, then, good work," she responded dryly before motioning toward the far side of the deck where the lifts were.

Eric nodded. "This way, Admiral."

▶▶▶

▶ "What're your thoughts on the Imperials, Commodore?" Gracen asked once they were in the *Odysseus'* conference room. "Alliance Command wants everything you've got, yesterday."

"I'll have a record of everything we scanned during the fight arranged for you to take back," Eric said. "As to my personal impression, they're rigid fighters. Skilled but dependent on a distinct chain of command. Very little flexibility, if this fight is typical of their deployments."

"How so?" Tanner asked, curious.

"We think we took out their command structure in the fight," Eric said. "The effect wasn't noticeable at first. They fight well, and with a crisis on the table they held it together, but once the engagement passed . . . they lost cohesion very quickly."

"Huh, that's not something I'd expect out of a technologically superior, more ancient culture," Gracen mused. "Command should have devolved to the next in line automatically. A decent network should have assured that."

"And I'm certain they *have* a very good network," Eric said, "but I think we're looking at an Empire in more than just name. We've gotten bits and bobs out of the prisoners we rescued, nothing actionable, but I think they have a nobility structure, not only in their government, but also in their military."

Gracen blinked. "That's . . . I don't even know what that is."

"I know." Eric nodded. "If they're running nobles as their top officers, then the underclass may not be *able* to respond to new situations effectively in their absence."

"That's going to throw our cultural analysts into a tizzy," Gracen said.

"The Priminae have never had a system like this," Tanner said, perplexed. "I am not certain I understand the implications."

"It means that they're going to react very differently than a Terran, or even Priminae, group would," Gracen said. "In many ways, we have more in common with you than with them. An imperial system, if the captain is right about our foes, can be *very* effective when properly managed. However, they're only going to be as good as their commanders."

Eric nodded. "We, on the other hand, build from the ground up. Our lower-ranking people are often at least as good as their commanders and can do the job if they have to. If I'm being honest, the imperial system . . . When it's good, it's potentially better than we can field. However, we won't be crippled by an idiot getting into our command structure. They'll take a heavy hit in effectiveness in the same situation, and nobility systems are notorious for breeding fools in the high ranks."

"I see," Tanner said. "This is very interesting, but I believe that what most concerns me isn't their culture, I am afraid."

"No, that's true," Gracen said. "This could be vital information, but we are getting ahead of ourselves."

Eric had to agree.

Of all the information they'd recovered so far, the one thing they all wanted—no, *needed* to know—was the one thing that none of their prisoners had been willing to speak on.

The elephant in the room, the question none of the three wanted to voice, still remained.

How big of an Empire were they really dealing with?

▶ ▶ ▶

Impear Coron, Imperial Capital System

▶ Captain Aymes walked stiffly alongside Lady Misrem Plotu, marching through the gates of the Imperial fortress and onto the smooth black metal where their shoes clicked loudly with each step.

"Be silent until spoken to," Misrem told him. "I will handle this discussion."

"Yes, My Lady," Aymes said quietly.

They continued in toward the courts where their mission statement would be given, walking under the holographic representation of the 148 stars of the Imperial constellation.

ABOUT THE AUTHOR

Evan Currie is the bestselling author of the Odyssey One series, the Warrior's Wings series, and more. Although his postsecondary education was in computer science, and he has worked in the local lobster industry on the Magdalen Islands steadily over the last decade, writing has always been his true passion. Currie himself says it best: "It's what I do for fun and to relax. There's not much I can imagine better than being a storyteller."